"Ford keeps the reader turning pages at a rapid pace, trying to separate event from illusion as three kids with an absent father and a mother whose heart is permanently out to lunch come to grips with the enemy. Better yet, he finishes off *The Shadow Year* with a surprise you won't likely see coming. And to make a good book even better, the real drama is seeing how kids whose parents are too preoccupied to notice can survive—and triumph." —*Chicago Sun-Times*

"*The Shadow Year* captures the totality of a lived period, its actualities and its dreams, its mundane essentials and its odd subjective imperatives; it is a work of episodic beauty and mercurial significance." —Nick Gevers, *Locus*

"Surreal, unsettling, and more than a little weird. Ford has a rare gift for evoking mood with just a few well-chosen words and for creating living, breathing characters with only a few lines of dialogue." —*Booklist*

"Spooky and hypnotic. . . . Recommended for all public libraries." —*Library Journal*

"Put Jeffrey Ford's latest novel, a Long Island bildungsroman replete with marvels and monsters, on the shelf with Harper Lee, Lynda Barry, Ray Bradbury, Tobias Wolff. *The Shadow Year* is the kind of magic trick writers dream of being able to pull off—Ford evokes the mysteries, the inhabitants, the landscape of childhood briskly, unsentimentally, and with such power that you come away feeling as if someone has opened up a door to another world."

—Kelly Link, author of
Stranger Things Happen
and *Magic for Beginners*

"Properly creepy, but from time to time deliciously funny and heart-breakingly poignant, too. For those of you—and you know who you are—who think the indispensable element for good genre fiction is good writing, this is not to be missed."

—*Kirkus Reviews* (starred review)

"Ford travels deep into the wild country that is childhood in this novel . . . the observations and adventures of these sharp, wayward children provide more than enough depth to be satisfying."
—*New York Times*

"Children are the original magic realists. The effects that novelists of a postmodern bent must strive for come naturally to the young, a truth given inventive realization in this wonderful quasi-mystery tale by Jeffrey Ford."
—*Boston Globe*

"[T]he setup is perfect for the bleached-out nostalgia [Ford] does best: suburban malaise hiding unspeakable darkness. . . . Setting has always played a central role in Ford's work, and he clearly knows this yellowed glimpse of Long Island very well—the streets, the trees, the frozen lakes all bear the imprimatur of reality. That's what keeps you turning pages."
—*Los Angeles Times*

Praise for
THE DROWNED LIFE

"*The Drowned Life* raises a banner to salute the power of the imagination. . . . As wildly different as these stories are, they show us one thing: The imagination should be nurtured, allowed to run into its darkest corners and up to its brightest peaks. Or maybe, it just needs to stretch for a spell, under a tree in the backyard."
—*Los Angeles Times Book Review*

CRACKPOT PALACE

CRACKPOT PALACE

stories

JEFFREY FORD

wm

WILLIAM MORROW
An Imprint of HarperCollins*Publishers*

FIRST EDITION

Designed by Diahann Sturge

Library of Congress Cataloging-in-Publication Data has been applied for.

ISBN 978-0-06-212259-9

12 13 14 15 16   OV/RRD   10 9 8 7 6 5 4 3 2 1

For Bill Watkins, who told me, "Irony is the engine of the world."

Contents

Introduction

Crackpot Palace

Midway upon the journey of my life, I had been passing alone along a singularly dreary stretch of shoreline, and at length found myself, as the shades of evening drew on, within view of Crackpot Palace. To my right was the angry surf, all iron gray and foam. Above, brown clouds filled the sky like shoveled dirt, as if the setting sun were being buried alive. To my left, rising above the tops of the tallest dunes that surrounded it was a most bizarre structure, a cockeyed monolith of a dwelling made of planks, crafted in the shape of a human head. Its physiognomy was evident in the large, eyelike windows, in the gable ears, in the white seabirds that sat upon its sloping roof like the close-cropped hair of an old man. The poorly joined wooden flesh of its architecture sagged, and the entire building listed forward as if deep in thought or nodding off to sleep.

It came to me that I'd completely forgotten what it was I was doing there, how I'd gotten there. And in that same instant a frigid wind blew in off the sea, pushing ahead of it a squall of large, luminous flakes. The snow seemed to have its own light but did nothing to melt my loneliness or quell my shivering. I climbed up and over the closest dune and made my way toward the strange head. As I approached its entrance I, of course, found that the doorway looked much like a gaping mouth, and a tattered awning above that portal served as a nose. Climbing the steps to its porch, I heard the splintered behemoth above me creaking in the wind.

I looked up to try to determine if the structure was safe, and in that instant noticed candles suddenly spark to life in the large, oval windows upstairs; a sleeper waking. Before me, the door slowly swung open, and from within the palace there issued the sounds of laughter, weeping, mumbled conversation, desperate sighs. I stepped through the entrance and called out, "Hello?" The moment I spoke, all the noises ceased and I heard nothing but the howling of the wind and the distant crashing of the surf. I shut the door behind me and left the foyer in search of the caretaker or owner.

I met no one on my expedition through the place—"expedition" being the correct term, as there were so many twists and turns to the journey that a mental picture of the floor plan was impossible. Irregular rooms with slanted walls led on to yet more distorted rooms, to rickety spiral stairways, to curving hallways and cramped passages with angled ceilings. Books spilled from shelves in static cataracts, and odd curios were displayed under glass—in the kitchen, an owl egg (as attested to by a small handwritten card beside it); in a bathroom, a desiccated, severed foot; in a small parlor, a vial of green liquid.

Throughout it all, I never saw a soul, but the voices returned, whispering, snickering, occasionally shouting my name, at which I'd turn my head suddenly, only to sense the noise was really the banging of some loose shingle or shutter. Always, from a distant room I could never find, there issued the sound of a Victrola playing. At times I was certain the record was Jane Russell, singing "Two Sleepy People"; at other instances I knew it was merely the wind in the eaves.

Eventually I sat down at a desk, exhausted, and watched as a mist coalesced and drifted around the room. As it floated by it transformed quickly, like faces in the clouds—a man on horseback, wielding a sword; then a long-legged spider wearing a hat; then something else again. I shut my eyes for a moment and when I opened them there was an old computer before me, turned on, screen glowing. I put my fingers on the keys and started typing.

Somewhere in the long night, my wife's voice called out, "Come to bed," and startled me from my infernal work. "How could she be here?" I wondered. Then the palace began to tremble at its foundation, and the shifting mists lifted from before my eyes. I felt the snow and wind in my face, and looked up to see that I'd left my study window open. A thin ridge of snow lined the sill. As I stood, the images of dreams and scraps of story that had buried me to the neck sloughed away like so much sand dispersed by the wind blowing through the window. I closed it and turned out the light. Shuffling through the dark toward the bedroom, I finally remembered where I was and what I was doing.

Polka Dots and Moonbeams

He came for her at seven in the Belvedere convertible, top down, emerald green, with those fins in the back, jutting up like goalposts. From her third-floor apartment window, she saw him pull to the curb out front.

"Hey, Dex," she called, "where'd you get the submarine?"

He tilted back his homburg and looked up. "All hands on deck, baby," he said, patting the white leather seat.

"Give me a minute," she said, laughed, and then blew him a kiss. She walked across the braided rug of the parlor and into the small bathroom with its water-stained ceiling and cracked plaster. Standing before the mirror, she leaned in close to check her makeup—enough rouge and powder to repair the walls. Her eye shadow was peacock blue, her mascara indigo. She gave her girdle a quick adjustment through her dress, then smoothed the material and stepped back to take it all in. Wrapped in strapless black, with a design of small white polka dots like stars in a perfect universe, she turned profile and inhaled. "Good Christ," she said and exhaled. Passing through the kitchenette, she lifted a silver flask from the scarred tabletop and shoved it into her handbag.

Her heels made a racket on the wooden steps, and she wobbled for balance just after the first landing. Pushing through the front door, she stepped out into the evening light and the first cool breeze in what seemed an eternity. Dex was waiting for her at the curb, holding the passenger door open. As she approached, he tipped his hat and bent slightly at the waist.

"Looking fine there, madam," he said.

She stopped to kiss his cheek.

The streets were empty, not a soul on the sidewalk, and save for the fact that here and there in a few of the windows of the tall, crumbling buildings they passed a dim yellow light could be seen, the entire city seemed empty as well. Dex turned left on Kraft and headed out of town.

"It's been too long, Adeline," he said.

"Hush now, sugar," she told him. "Let's not think about that. I want you to tell me where you're taking me tonight."

"I'll take you where I can get you," he said.

She slapped his shoulder.

"I want a few cocktails," she said.

"Of course, baby, of course. I thought we'd head over to the Ice Garden, cut a rug, have a few, and then head out into the desert after midnight to watch the stars fall."

"You're an ace," she said and leaned forward to turn on the radio. A smoldering sax rendition of "Every Time We Say Goodbye," like a ball of waxed string unwinding, looped once around their necks and then blew away on the rushing wind.

She lit them each a cigarette as the car sailed on through the rising night. An armadillo scuttled through the beams of the headlights fifty yards ahead, and the aroma of sage vied with Adeline's orchid scent. Clamping his cigarette between his lips, Dex put his free hand on her knee. She took it into her own, twining fingers with him. Then it was dark, the asphalt turning to dirt, and the moon rose slow as a bubble in honey above the distant silhouette of hills, a cosmic cream pie of a face, eyeing Adeline's décolletage.

She leaned back into the seat, smiling, and closed her eyes. Only a moment passed before she opened them, but they were already there, passing down the long avenue lined with monkey-puzzle trees toward the circular drive of the glimmering Ice Garden. Dex pulled up and parked at the entrance. As he was getting out, a kid with red hair and freckles, dressed in a valet uniform, stepped forward.

"Mr. Dex," he said, "we haven't seen you for a while."

"Take a picture, Jim-Jim," said Dex and flipped a silver dollar in the air. The kid caught it and dropped it into his vest pocket before opening the door for Adeline.

"How's tricks, Jim?" she asked as he delivered her to the curb.

"They just got better," he said and patted his vest.

Dex came around the back of the car, took his date by the arm, and together they headed past the huge potted palms and down a brief tunnel toward a large rectangular patio open to the desert sky and bounded by a lush garden of the most magnificent crystal flora, emitting a blizzard of reflection. At the edge of the high, arching portico, Dex and Adeline stood for a moment, scanning the hubbub of revelers and, at the other end of the expanse of tables and chairs and dance floor, the onstage antics of that night's musical act, Nabob and His Ne'er-do-wells. Above the sea of heads, chrome trombone in one hand, mic in the other, Nabob belted out a jazzed-up version of "Weak Knees and Wet Privates."

A fellow in a white tux and red fez approached the couple. He was a plump little man with a pencil-thin mustache, a fifty-year-old baby playing dress-up. Dex removed his homburg and reached a hand out. "Mondrian," he said.

The maître d' bowed slightly and, raising his voice above the din of merriment, said, "Always a pleasure to have you both back."

Adeline also shook hands.

"You're looking particularly lovely tonight," he said.

"Table for two," said Dex and flashed a crisp twenty under the nose of Mondrian. "Something close to the dance floor."

The plump man bowed again and in his ascent snatched the bill from Dex's hand. "Follow me, my friends," he said, and then turned and made his way slowly in amid the maze of tables and the milling crowd. As they moved through the packed house Adeline waved hello to those who called her name, and when someone shouted to Dex, he winked, sighted them with his thumb, and pulled an invisible trigger. Mondrian found them a spot at the very front, just to the left of the stage. He pulled out and held Adeline's chair, and once she was seated, he bowed.

"Two gin wrinkles," said Dex, and in an instant the maître d' vanished back into the crowd.

Adeline retrieved two cigarettes from her purse and lit them on the small candle at the center of the table. Dex leaned over and she put one between his lips. She drew on the other.

"How does it feel to be back in action?" he asked her.

She smiled broadly, blew a stream of smoke, and nodded. "It always feels right, the first couple of hours on the loose. I'm not thinking about anything else at this moment," she said.

"Good," he said and removed his hat, setting it on the empty chair next to him.

The music stopped then and was replaced by the chatter and laughter of the crowd, the clink of glasses and silverware.

Nabob jumped down from the band platform, hit the ground, and rolled forward to spring upright next to Dex.

"Dexter," he said.

"Still sweating out the hits," said Dex and laughed as he shook hands with the bandleader.

"Bobby, aren't you gonna give me a kiss?" said Adeline.

"I'm just savoring the prospect," he said and swept down to plant one on her lips. The kiss lasted for a while before Dex reached his leg around the table and kicked the performer in the ass. They all laughed as Nabob moved around the table and took a seat.

Folding his willowy arms in front of him, the bandleader leaned forward and shook his thin head. "You two out for the stars tonight?" he asked.

"And then some," said Adeline.

"So fill me in," said Dex.

"Well, same old, same old as usual, you know. And Killheffer's been waiting for you to return."

A waitress appeared with two gin wrinkles—liquid pink ice and the Garden's own bathtub blend of gin. The glasses caught the light and revealed tiny bubbles rising from a fat red cherry. Dex slipped the young woman a five. She smiled at him before leaving the table.

"Fuck Killheffer," said Dex, lifting his drink to touch glasses with Adeline.

"He's been in here almost every night, sitting back in the corner, slapping beads on that abacus of his and jotting numbers in a book," said Nabob.

"Killheffer's solid fruitcake," said Adeline.

"A strange fellow," said Nabob, nodding. "One slow night a while back, and most nights are slow when you fine folks aren't here, he bought me a drink and explained to me how the world is made of numbers. He said that when the stars fall it means everything is being divided by itself. Then he blew a smoke ring off one of his cigars. 'Like that,' he said and pointed at the center."

"Did you get it?" asked Adeline.

Nabob laughed and shook his head. "Jim-Jim makes more sense."

"If he shows that shit-eatin' grin in here tonight, I'll fluff his cheeks," said Dex.

Adeline took a drag of her cigarette and smiled. "Sounds like boy fun. I thought you were here to dance and drink."

"I am," said Dex and finished the rest of his wrinkle, grabbing the cherry stem between his teeth. When he took the glass away, the fruit hung down in front of his mouth. Adeline leaned over, put one arm around his shoulder and her lips around the cherry. She ate it slowly, chewing with only her tongue before it all became a long kiss.

When they finished, Nabob said, "You're an artist, Miss Adeline."

Dex ordered another round of wrinkles. They talked for a few minutes about the old days; distant memories of bright sun and blue skies.

"Break's over," said Nabob, quickly killing the rest of his drink. "You two be good."

"Do 'Name and Number,'" called Adeline as the bandleader bounded toward the stage. With a running start, he leaped into the air, did a somersault and landed, kneeling next to his mic stand. He stood slowly, like a vine twining up a trellis.

Dex and Adeline applauded, as did the rest of the house when they saw the performer back onstage. The willowy singer danced

with himself for a moment before grabbing the mic. The Ne'er-
do-wells took their places and lifted their instruments.

"Mondrian, my good man. Turn that gas wheel and lower
the lights," said Nabob, his voice echoing through the Garden
and out into the desert.

A moment later the flames of the candles in the center of
each table went dimmer by half. "Ooooh," said Nabob and the
crowd applauded.

"Lower," he called to the maître d'.

Mondrian complied. Whistles and catcalls rose out of the dull
amber glow of the Garden. The baritone sax hit a note so low
it was like a tumbleweed blowing in off the desert. Then the
strings came up, there was a flourish of piccolo and three sliding notes from Nabob's chrome T-bone. He brought the mouthpiece away, snapped his fingers to the music and sang:

My dear, you tear my heart asunder
When I look up your name and number
Right there in that open book
My flesh begins to cook
It's all sweetness mixed with dread
And then you close your legs around my head
As I look up your name and number . . .

As Nabob dipped into the second verse, Dex rose and held his
hand out to Adeline. He guided her through the darkness to the
sea of swaying couples. They clutched each other desperately,
legs between legs, lips locked, slowly turning through the dark.
Within the deep pool of dancers there were currents of movement that could not be denied. They let themselves be drawn by
the inevitable flow as the music played on.

When the song ended, Adeline said, "I have to hit the powder room."

They left the dance floor as the lights came up and walked toward the huge structure that held the casino, the gaming rooms, the pleasure parlors of the Ice Garden. Three stories tall, in the style of a Venetian palace, it was a monster of shadows with moonlight in its eyes. At the portico that led inside, Dex handed her a twenty and said, "I'll see you back at the table."

"I know," she barely managed and kissed him on the cheek.

"You okay?" he asked.

"Same old, same old," she said and sighed.

He was supposed to laugh but only managed a smile. They turned away from each other. As he skirted the dance floor on the return journey, Dex looked up at Nabob and saw the performer, midsong, flash a glance at him and then nod toward the table. There was Killheffer, sporting a tux and his so-called smile of a hundred teeth, smoking a Wrath Majestic and staring into the sky.

Arriving at the table, Dex took his seat across from Killheffer, who, still peering upward, said, "Gin wrinkles, I presumed."

Dex noticed the fresh round of drinks and reached for his.

"The stars are excited tonight," said Killheffer, lowering his gaze.

"Too bad I'm not," said Dex. "What's it gonna be this time, Professor? Russian roulette? One card drawn from the bottom of a deck cut three ways? The blindfolded knife thrower?"

"You love to recall my miscalculations," said Killheffer. "Time breaks down, though, only through repetition."

"I'm fed up with your cockeyed bullshit."

"Well, don't be, because I tell you I've got it. I've done the math. How badly do you want out?"

"Want out?" said Dex. "I don't even know how I got in. Tell me again you're not the devil."

"I'm a simple professor of circumstance and fate. An academic with too strong an imagination."

"Then why that crazy smile? All your antics? That cigar of yours smells like what I vaguely remember of the ocean."

"I've always been a gregarious fellow and prized a good cigar. The hundred-tooth thing is a parlor trick of multiplication."

"I'm so fucking tired," Dex said.

Killheffer reached into his jacket pocket and brought forth a hypodermic needle. He laid it on the table. "That's the solution," he said.

The large hypo's glass syringe contained a jade-green liquid.

Dex stared at it and shook his head. Tears appeared in the corners of his eyes. "Are you kidding? That's it? That's the saddest fucking thing I've ever seen."

"You have to trust me," said Killheffer, still smiling.

"If you haven't noticed, we're here again. What is it? Poison? Cough syrup? Junk?"

"My own special mixture of oblivion; a distillation of equations for free will. I call it 'Laughter in the Dark,'" said the professor, proudly smoothing back his slick black hair.

Dex couldn't help but smile. "You're a malicious crackpot, but okay, let's get on with it. What's the deal this time?"

"Mondrian is, right at this moment, upstairs, on the third floor, in Sizzle Parlor number four, awaiting a female associate of mine who has promised him exotic favors, but unfortunately will never deliver. Instead, you will arrive. I want him dead." Killheffer hurriedly tamped out his cigar and snapped his fingers to the passing cigarette girl. She stopped next to Dex and opened the case that hung by a strap around her shoulders.

There were no cigarettes, just something covered by a handkerchief.

"You think of everything," said Dex and reached in to grab the gun. He stood and slipped it into the waist of his pants. "How do I collect?"

"The cure will be delivered before the night is through," said the professor. "Hurry, Mondrian can only forgo his beloved tips for so long."

"What do you have against him?" Dex asked as he lifted his hat off the chair beside him.

"He's a computational loop," said Killheffer. "A real zero-sum game."

At the head of the long dark hallway on the third floor of the pavilion, Dex was stopped by the night man, an imposing fellow with a bald head and a sawed-off shotgun in his left hand.

"What's news, Jeminy?" said Dex.

"Obviously you are, Dex. Looking for a room?"

He nodded.

"Ten dollars. But for you, for old times' sake, ten dollars," said Jeminy and laughed.

"You're too good to me," said Dex, a ten spot appearing in his hand. "The lady'll be along any minute."

"Sizzle Parlor number five," the big man said, his voice echoing down the hall. "Grease that griddle, my friend."

"Will do," said Dex, and before long slowed his pace and looked over his shoulder to check that Jeminy had again taken his seat facing away, toward the stairwell. He passed door after door, and after every six a weak gas lamp glowed on either wall. As he neared parlor number 4, he noticed the door was open a sliver, but it was dark inside. Brandishing the gun, he held it straight up in front of him. He hesitated a moment, held back

by an odd feeling, either a rare shred of excitement or a pang
of conscience. "Poor Mondrian," he thought, remembering in
an instant how the mustached homunculus had rendered his
maître d' services with the most steadfast dedication.

Opening the door, he slipped inside, and shut it quietly behind
him. Moonlight shone in through one tall arched window, but
Dex could only make out shadows. He scanned the room, and
slowly the forms of chairs, a coffee table, a vanity, and, off to the
side of the room, a bed became evident to him. Sitting up on
the edge of that bed was a lumpen silhouette, atop it the telltale
shape of the fez.

"Is it you, my desert flower?" came the voice of Mondrian.

Dex swiftly crossed the room. When he was next to the
figure, and had surmised where his victim's left temple might
be, he cocked the gun's hammer with his thumb and wrapped
his index finger around the trigger. Before he could squeeze off
the shot, though, the slouched bag of shadow that was Mondrian lunged into him with terrific force. Dex, utterly surprised
that the meek little fellow would have the gumption to attack,
fell backward, tripping on the rug, the gun flying off into the
dark. He tried to get to his feet, but the maître d' landed on him
like three sacks of concrete, one hand grabbing his throat. No
matter how many times Dex managed a punch to Mondrian's
face, the shadow of the fez never toppled away. They rolled over
and over and then into the moonlight. Dex saw the flash of a
curved blade above him, but his arms were now pinned by his
assailant's knees. Unable to halt the knife's descent, he held his
breath in preparation for pain. Then the lights went on, there
was a gunshot, and his attacker fell off him.

Dex scrabbled to his feet and turned to find Adeline, standing next to the open door, the barrel of the gun she held still

smoking. From down the hall, he heard Jeminy blow his whistle, an alert to the Ice Garden's force of leg breakers.

"Nice shot, baby," he said. "Kill the lights and close the door."

She closed the door behind her, but didn't flip the switch. "Look," she said to Dex, pointing with the gun at the floor behind him. He turned and saw the hundred-tooth smile of Killheffer. The fez was secured around the professor's chin by a rubber band. A bullet had left a gaping third eye in his forehead.

"The rat fuck," said Dex. He leaned over, grabbed his hat where it had fallen, and then felt through Killheffer's jacket pockets. All he came up with was a cigar tube, holding a single Wrath Majestic. He slipped it into his inside jacket pocket.

"They're coming," said Adeline. She hit the lights. There was the sound of running feet and voices in the hallway. "They're going door-to-door."

"We'll shoot our way out," said Dex.

Adeline was next to him. She whispered in his ear, "Don't be a jackass; we'll take the fire escape."

Dex moved toward the window. Adeline slipped off her heels.

Somehow Mondrian had known to call the car up, because when Dex and Adeline arrived in front of the Ice Garden, breathless, scuff marks on their clothes, the Belvedere was there, top down and running, Jim-Jim holding Adeline's door.

"I like your shoes," said the boy, pointing to her bare feet.

"My new fashion, Jim," said Adeline.

Dex moved quickly around the car. Mondrian was there to open the door for him. As Dex slid in behind the wheel, he said, "No hard feelings about tonight," and flashed a tip to cover the intended homicide. Mondrian bowed slightly and snatched the bill.

"Ever at your service," said the maître d'. "Safe journey." He shut the car door.

Dex took a silver dollar out of his pocket, hit the gas, and flipped the coin back over the car. Jim-Jim caught it and before he could stash it in his vest pocket, the Belvedere was no more than two red dots halfway down the avenue of monkey-puzzle trees.

"My feet are killing me," said Adeline as they screeched out of the entrance to the Ice Garden and onto the desert highway.

"You are one hell of a shot," he said.

"Lucky," she said, her voice rising above the wind.

"I'll cherish the moment."

"All well and good," said Adeline, "but what's his game this time?"

"Laughter in the dark," said Dex and cut the wheel hard to the right. Adeline slid toward him and he wrapped his arm around her shoulders. The car left the road and raced along an avenue of moonlight, plowing through tumbleweeds, trailing a plume of dust across the desert. Adeline switched on the radio and found Dete Walader, crooning "I Remember You."

They lay on a blanket beneath shimmering stars. A light breeze blew over them. Here and there, the dark form of a cactus stood sentry. Ten yards away, the radio in the Belvedere played something with strings. Adeline took a sip from her silver flask and handed it to Dex. He flicked the butt of the Majestic off into the sand, and took a drink.

"What is this stuff?" he asked, squinting.

"My own special mixture of oblivion," she said.

"That's Killheffer's line," he said. "Did you see him tonight?"

She nodded and laid her cheek against his chest. "In the

ladies' room, he was in the stall next to the one I chose, waiting for me."

"He gets around," said Dex, " 'cause he was at our table when I got back to it."

"He whispered from the other stall that he wanted me to kill Mondrian. I said I wouldn't, but then he said he had the solution and was willing to trade me for the murder. I told him I wanted to see it. The next thing, the door to my stall flew open and he was standing there. I almost screamed. I didn't know what to do. I was on the toilet, for criminy's sake. He had that stupid smile on his face, and he pulled down his zipper."

Dex rose to one elbow. "I'll kill him," he said.

"Too late," said Adeline. "He reached into his pants and pulled out this big hypodermic needle with green juice in it. He said, 'You see the tip at the end of that needle? Think of that as the period at the end of your interminable story. Do you want out?' I just wanted to get rid of him, so I nodded. He handed me a gun and told me Mondrian was in Sizzle Parlor number four."

A long time passed in silence.

"But, in the end, you decided to off Mondrian?" said Dex.

"I guess so," said Adeline. "What else is there to do when we go to the Ice Garden but fall in with Killheffer's scheme? Mondrian might as well be made of papier-mâché and that's the long and short of it. He's polite, but, sure, I'd clip him for the possibility of a ticket out."

"I'd miss you," said Dex.

"I wouldn't leave you here alone," she said. "I was getting the needle for you."

"You didn't think of using it yourself? Baby, I'm touched."

"Well, maybe once, when I realized that if it worked, you wouldn't come for me anymore and I'd spend each go-round in that crappy apartment building back in Dragsville watching the plaster crack."

"I was ready to blow Mondrian's brains out for you too," he said. "I can see how stale it's getting for you."

"You never thought of yourself?" she asked.

Dex sat up and pointed into the distance at a pair of headlights. "Let's get the guns," he said. He stood and helped her up. She found her underwear a few feet away and slipped them back on.

"Who do you think it is?" she asked, joining him at the car.

He handed her a pistol. "Ice Garden thugs," he said.

When the approaching car came to a halt a few feet from the blanket, Dex reached over the side of the Belvedere and hit the lights to reveal a very old black car, more like a covered carriage with a steering wheel and no horse. The door opened and out stepped Mondrian. He carried an open umbrella and a small box. Taking three furtive steps forward, he called out, "Mr. Dexter."

"Expecting rain, Mondrian?" said Dex.

"Stars, sir. Stars."

Adeline laughed from where she was crouched behind the Belvedere.

"A package for the lady and gentleman," said Mondrian.

"Set it down at your feet, right there, and then you can go," said Dex.

Mondrian set the package on the sand, but remained standing at attention over it.

"What are you waiting for?" asked Dex.

Mondrian was silent, but Adeline whispered, "He wants a tip."

Dex fired two shots into the umbrella. "Keep the change," he called.

Mondrian bowed, said, "Most generous, sir," and then got back in the car. As the maître d' pulled away, Adeline retrieved the package. Dex met her back on the blanket where she sat with the box, an eight-inch cube wrapped in silver paper and a red bow, like a birthday present, on her lap.

"It could be a bomb," he said.

She hesitated for an instant, and said, "Oh, well," and tore the wrapping off. Digging her nails into the seam between the cardboard flaps, she pulled back on both sides, ripping the top away. She reached in and pulled out Killheffer's hypodermic needle. She put her hand back into the box and felt around.

"There's only one," she said.

"Now you know what his game is," said Dex.

She held it up in the moonlight, and the green liquid inside its glass syringe glowed. "It's beautiful," she said with a sigh.

"Do it," said Dex.

"No, you," she said, and handed it toward him.

He reached for it, but then stopped, his fingers grazing the metal plunger. "No," he said and shook his head. "It was your shot."

"It probably won't even work," she said and laid it carefully on the blanket between them, petting it twice before withdrawing her hand.

"We'll shoot dice," said Dex, running his pinkie finger the length of the needle. "The winner takes it."

Adeline said nothing for a time, and then she nodded in agreement. "But first a last dance in case it works."

Dex got up and went to the car to turn up the radio. "We're in luck," he said, and the first notes of "Polka Dots and Moonbeams," drifted out into the desert. He slowly swayed his way back to her. She smoothed her dress, adjusted her girdle, and put her arms around him, resting her chin on his shoulder. He held her around the waist and they turned slowly, wearily, to the music.

"So, we'll shoot craps?" she whispered.

"That's right," he said.

Three slow turns later, Adeline said, "Don't think I don't remember you've got that set of loaded dice."

Dex put his head back and laughed, and, as if in response, at that very moment, the stars began to fall, streaking down through the night, trailing bright streamers. First a handful and then a hundred and then more let go their hold on the firmament and leaped. Way off to the west, the first ones hit with a distant rumble and firework geysers of flame. More followed, far and near, and Dex and Adeline kissed amid the conflagration.

"Pick me up at seven," she said, her bottom lip on his earlobe, and held him more tightly.

"I'll be there, baby," he said, "I'll be there."

With the accuracy of a bullet between the eyes, one of the million heavenly messengers screeched down upon them, a fireball the size of the Ice Garden. The explosion flipped the Belvedere into the air like a silver dollar and turned everything to dust.

A Note About "Polka Dots and Moonbeams"

The project that this story was part of was a blast from start to finish. When Al Sarrantonio and Neil Gaiman contact you and say they want you to write a story, then give you very few rules to follow beyond just basically to tell the kind of story that makes the reader want to know at each turn what happens next, and offer you some great pay for it, there's no downside. I've known Al for a long time, and perhaps it was our shared interest in jazz that made me land on a story title borrowed from one of the standards done to perfection by the incomparable Lester Young, perhaps my favorite musician of all time. I started with that title and, listening to the tune, just let my mind go and spin out the story you've just read. The result of this project was, of course, the anthology *Stories: All-New Tales,* a book packed with great short fiction by heavy hitters like Peter Straub, Michael Moorcock, Chuck Palahniuk, Joyce Carol Oates, Jodi Picoult, and more. After the book came out, Neil Gaiman kindly invited me to participate in a panel discussion about it at Columbia University in New York along with himself, Walter Mosley, Lawrence Block, Joe Hill, Kurt Andersen, and Kat Howard. A fun time. The anthology and Neil's story, "The Truth Is a Cave in the Black Mountains," both went on to win Shirley Jackson Awards (2010). Also from *Stories,* Elizabeth Hand's novella "The Maiden Flight of McCauley's *Bellerophon*" and Joyce Carol Oates's "Fossil-Figures" both won World Fantasy Awards in their respective categories for 2011.

Down Atsion Road

I live along the edge of the Pine Barrens in South Jersey, 1.1 million acres of dense, ancient forest, cedar lakes, cranberry bogs, orchids, and sugar sand. Black bear, fox, bobcat, coyote, and some say cougar. There are ghost towns from the Revolution, dilapidated shacks and crumbling shot towers that can only be reached by canoe. I've hiked through much of it in my years, and still I get a feeling that some uneasy sentience pervades its enormity. If I'm quite a distance from the trailhead where my car is parked and twilight drops suddenly, as it does out there, I feel a twist of panic at the thought of meeting night in those woods. You will, of course, have heard of the Jersey Devil. He's for the tourists. The place is thick with legends far more bizarre and profound. If you learn how to look and you're lucky, you might even witness one being born.

Sixteen years ago, when my wife and I and our two sons—one in second grade, one not yet in kindergarten—first moved to Medford Lakes, I noticed, every once in a while, this strange old guy stomping around town. He was thin and bald and had a big gray beard with hawk feathers tied into it. His head was long, with droopy eyes and a persistent smile. He pumped his arms vigorously, almost marching. Rain or shine, summer or winter, he wore a ratty tan raincoat, an old pair of Bermuda shorts, black sneakers, and a red sweatshirt that bore the logo of the '70s soft-rock band Bread. Every time I passed him in the car, it looked like he was talking to himself.

Then one day I was picking up a pizza in town, and he was in the shop, sitting alone at a table, a paper plate with pizza crusts in front of him. He studied me warily, whispering under his breath, as I passed on the way to the counter. Behind me, a woman and her little girl came in. When he saw the little girl, the old guy pulled a brown velour sack from somewhere in his coat. He opened it and took something out. I was watching all this from the counter and wondered if something crazy was about to go down, but the mother let go of the girl's hand. The old guy slipped out of his seat onto one knee. The kid walked over to him, and he gave her what looked like a small, hand-carved wooden deer. The mother said, "What do you say, Helen?" The kid said, "Thank you." The old guy laughed and slapped the tabletop.

About a week later, Lynn and I were at the lake down the street from our house one evening. We'd taken a thermos of coffee and sat on a blanket, watching the sun go down behind the trees while the kids messed around at the water's edge. A neighbor of ours, Dave, who we'd met a few weeks earlier, was out walking his dog, so he came over and joined us, sitting on the sand. We talked for a while about the school board, about the plan to dredge lower Aetna Lake, he gave us his usual religious rap, and then I asked him, "Hey, who's that crazy old guy in the raincoat I see around town?"

He smiled. "That's Crackpop," he said.

"Crackpop?" said Lynn and we broke up.

"His name's Sherman Gretts, but the kids call him Crackpop."

"He's on crack?" I asked.

"He just seems like he's on crack," said Dave. "A few years ago this kid who lives about two blocks over from where your house is, Duane Geppi, he's in my older son's class, overheard his father, who works down at the gas station, call the old guy a 'crackpot.' Duane thought he said 'Crackpop,' and called him that ever since. Now all the kids call him that. I think it's perfect."

"What else do you know about him?" I asked.

"Nothing, really. He's an artist or something. Lives all the way down Atsion Road, by the lake."

"That's a long walk," said Lynn.

"Eight miles," said Dave.

"He seems deranged," I said.

"He probably is," said Dave, "but from what I hear, he's not a bad guy."

As time went on, and we settled into our life in Medford Lakes, I'd see Crackpop now and then trudging along under a good head of steam, jabbering away, the raincoat flapping. I always wondered how old the guy was. He looked to me to be in his sixties, but with all that walking he did, keeping him in shape, he could have been a lot older. Lynn also started bringing me reports of him. On her way to work and back, she'd take Atsion Road to get to Route 206, and every couple of days she'd spot him going east or west or sitting somewhere in among the trees.

For our first Christmas in town, Lynn and I were invited to a party. The couple whose house it was at had a son in our older son's class. I met a lot of people from town and beyond, and we drank and shot the breeze. When the living room got too crowded and hot, I stepped out into the backyard to have a cigarette. It was lightly snowing, but it wasn't all that cold. I was only out there for a minute before the door opened and this older woman, a little heavyset but tall, with white hair, came out and lit up. I introduced myself, and she told me her name was Ginny Sanger.

I talked to her for quite a while. Eventually she said she was an amateur historian. The origins of the area had always interested me, so I asked her when it had been settled.

"Well, the first people were, of course, the Lenape, the grandfather tribe of all the Algonquin nation," she said. "They go way back here. The first Europeans, you're talking early 1600s, Swedish trappers. Stuyvesant came in 1655 and shooed the Swedes out. The English eventually kicked the Dutch out."

"What got you into the history?" I asked.

"After my husband died ten years ago, I really had nothing to do. He left me with plenty of money, so I didn't have to work. One summer day, about seven years ago, I went over to Atsion Lake for a swim. Do you know where I mean?" she asked, pointing east.

I nodded.

"I was out in the lake swimming around, and I stepped on something sharp. I knew I had to find whatever it was; there were a lot of kids in the water that day. I reached down to the bottom and felt this big piece of metal. Bringing it up, I saw it was a flat, rusted figure of an Indian in a big headdress, shooting a bow and arrow. He was attached at the feet to about a four-inch shaft. It was pretty corroded, but you could definitely make out the form."

"So that got you started?' I said.

"No, what got me started was my neighbor, who told me to take the thing over to Sherman, who lived just a little way up Atsion Road from us."

"Sherman?" I said, and the name rang a bell but I didn't place it.

"You've seen him. The old guy with the raincoat."

"You know him?" I said.

"Everybody up that way knows him. I took the Indian to him, and he told me that it was an ornament for a weather vane and had been forged in the iron works at Atsion Village, probably in the mid-1800s. He started telling me stories about the early settlers and the Lenape. We sat all afternoon on the screened back porch of that crazy house of his, sipping iced tea from blue tin cups, and he told me about a place called Hanover Furnace, a story from the time of the settlers that involved a description of how iron was made, an evil spirit of the woods, and the last Lenape sachem."

"From seeing him around town, I got the impression he's kind of out of it."

"Well . . ." she said.

Lynn came out looking for me then, ready to split. I introduced her to Ginny and we quickly said good-bye and left through the back gate. On our way home, in the snow, we walked around the lake and I told her what the old woman had said about Sherman Gretts.

Months went by, and I was deep into writing a book, so I didn't go out much. Crackpop was about the last thing on my mind until one Friday evening in February. Lynn came home and told me that in the morning on her way to work she saw the old man going into a house down by the end of Atsion Road. "I never noticed the place before," she said. "And I can't believe I didn't because it's bright yellow."

The thought of Crackpop in a yellow house made me smile.

"You've got to see it, though," she said. "I always thought, when I passed, that there were trees, like tall dogwood, growing around it, but today, when I saw him and knew it was his place, it became clear to me that they're not trees but sculptures made of limbs and pieces of trees. He's got like an army of tree-beings in his yard."

Saturday we drove out Atsion and Lynn slowed down as we passed the sagging yellow house. The sculptures were primitive, writhing forms like Munch's *Scream*, made of twisted magnolia wood. "Jeez," I said and made her turn around and pass it twice again.

Crackpop appeared in and disappeared from my life well into the spring. I didn't see him as frequently as I had at other times, and when I did spot him, I thought of his sculptures, and studied him closely. During the summer's first thunderstorm, I caught him tromping along Lenape Trail toward the pizza shop. The rain was beating down, and he was drenched. The two cars in front of me, one right after the other, hit the puddle along the edge of the road, sending a sheet of water up over him. He never slowed down or even acknowledged what had happened, but stayed on parade, jabbering away. A few weeks passed then where I didn't see him, and out of the blue at dinner I asked Lynn if she had. She said she saw him coming out of the woods down by 206 one night on her way home.

That first summer, we spent a lot of time at the lake with the kids. On the weekends we cooked out, and then, as the sun was setting, we'd walk the twisting trails of town. The dark brought a certain coolness and the breezes would ripple through the oak leaves, carrying scents of wisteria and pine. The kids ran after toads, and every now and then someone would appear out of the dark.

Late one night in the middle of July, we crossed the dirt bridge that spans a section of Upper Aetna Lake. I had my younger son on my shoulders and Lynn had his older brother by the hand. We approached a bench that faced the water, and just as we drew up to it, I was startled by the sudden bright orange glow of a cigarette. The spot was cast in deeper shadow by a stand of oaks, and the figure was invisible until the ash glowed and momentarily lit up a face. I did a double take when I saw that it was Ginny Sanger.

I said hello to her and reminded Lynn that we'd met her at the Christmas party. The old woman said that she was visiting the couple who'd had the party, and while they were getting the kids ready for bed, she decided to duck out for a walk. "I like this spot," she said.

"We're trying to get these two guys home before they both fall asleep on us," I said.

"We're losing the race," said Lynn.

"I see you have to go," said Ginny as she stamped out her cigarette. Now it was perfectly dark under the oaks. "But I never got a chance to finish telling you how I got into the local history."

"Yeah, you told me it was that guy Sherman," I said.

"That's true," she told me. "I started reading books and going to lectures on the area after talking to him. This is the part I wanted to tell you, though. From my own study and from having related some of Sherman's stories to a Lenni-Lenape storyteller I met at a conference, it became clear to me that Mr. Gretts was making everything up. The place names were right, and some of the details, but in all the texts I've scoured I've never seen any of the things he's spoken to me about." There was a moment of silence and then she laughed.

"That's pretty interesting," I said, and an image of Crackpop marched through my thoughts.

Ginny nodded. "Sherman spends a lot of time in the woods," she said. "One of his big things is, and he always whispers this one to me, like someone he doesn't want to might be listening, that there is still a band of Lenape roaming the Pine Barrens, living in the old way, like it was before the Europeans. They've always been there, he says."

I would have liked to hear more, but we had to get back home. As we trudged along, now each holding a sleeping kid, passing beneath tall pines on a carpet of needles, Lynn said, "I bet Ginny tried to corroborate Crackpop's story about the band of Indians hiding in the Barrens with that Lenape storyteller."

"So?" I said.

"Say the storyteller was in on it, and he told her he'd never heard of it in order to keep people from searching for his ancestors."

"Don't you think Crackpop's just nuts?" I said.

"Of course," she said.

It was early November and Atsion Road was littered with yellow leaves the same color as Crackpop's house. I drove to the end of the road, looked both ways, crossed over Route 206, and entered a dirt driveway with a steep incline. The car dipped down and then ascended a little hill. On the other side of that hill I could see a grass parking area and beyond that the steeple of a church from behind the trees. There were two other cars there but no one in sight. I parked, got out, and put my jacket on. It was cool and there was a strong breeze.

I was only twenty yards from the trailhead. I'd done some research of my own and knew that if I'd had the time and fortitude that trail would've taken me through the heart of the Pine Barrens and ended fifty miles later, at Batsto, another early iron settlement where they'd made shot for the Revolution. I started into the woods. About a hundred yards later, off to my left, there was a large clearing, and sitting in the middle of it was a white church. I'd read up on it. The Samuel Richards Church, a Quaker establishment built in 1828. Richards had owned the foundry at Atsion Village. His mansion still stood over by the lake.

There was a graveyard next to the building, the stones planted in concentric circles. At the far end of it was the most enormous oak I'd ever seen. The tree was ancient, and the way it stood there, barren of leaves against the blue sky, made me feel as if it could be thinking. I walked into the graveyard and looked at the markers. They were thin, with an arch at the top, and were made of some white stone that could have been marble or limestone. I read some of the names and dates that were still legible, the oldest being 1809. Some disaster took four of the Andrews family in one day. As I walked back to the trail, I looked quickly over my shoulder at the oak.

I walked a mile or more that first time in the Barrens and saw no one. Finally, at a place where a stream ran alongside the trail, I stopped, surrounded by endless pine and oak. Red and yellow leaves covered the underbrush. It was so quiet that when the wind blew, I could hear the pines creaking as they swayed. Off at a distance, a crow cawed. Right then I felt something curl in my chest, and I turned around and started back. I saw deer watching me from deeper in among the trees.

Back in my car, I went up the dirt hill and crossed Route

206. On my way up Atsion toward home, I spotted a large, hand-painted sign on the side of the road. In bright green on an orange background it read ART SHOW TODAY! ALL WELCOME! Then I saw it was at Crackpop's house, and I was pulling over. There were a number of cars parked along Atsion and more pulled up into the lot next to the house. When I got out of my car, I saw people in the backyard and smelled a barbecue.

I passed beneath the writhing tree giants in front and went around back. There were more of the crazy sculptures in the big backyard and from their twisted hands hung paintings and mobiles made from animal bones. Some people sat under them smoking pot, and pretty much everybody there had an open beer. People just nodded to me and smiled. Kids and teenagers and old people, black, white, and a woman made up like an Arab sheikh in white robes. When I passed the grill a young guy with a goatee and tattoos all over his arms, holding a spatula, offered me a hot dog. I accepted and moved on, strolling around from painting to painting.

Crackpop was no Picasso, but the images were sort of charming in their neo-kindergarten style. They were all depictions of events in the Barrens—Indians and deer and settlers hunting wild turkey. There was one of a burial beneath a giant oak, and a whole series of what looked like demons. I felt self-conscious there, so I lit a cigarette and strolled closer to the house. When the music, Faron Young's "Hello Walls" scratching away on an old Victrola, ended, I heard a woman call my name. I looked around.

"In here," I heard her say, and I turned and looked into the shadow of a screened porch I was standing near.

"Who is that?" I said, shading my eyes to try to see.

"Ginny Sanger," came the voice.

I walked over to the concrete block that stood where steps should have, hoisted myself up, and opened the screen door. My eyes adjusted, and I saw Ginny sitting in a redwood lawn chair next to Crackpop, who wore some kind of animal pelt over his shoulders; a red, white, and blue headband; and his usual getup. He had a joint between his fingers that was as thick as a cigar.

Ginny introduced me and said, "This is Sherman Gretts, the artist." I stepped over and shook the old man's hand.

"Seen you at the pizza place," he said.

I nodded. "I was looking at your paintings," I said.

"Want to buy one?" he asked and laughed.

"How much?" I said.

He motioned for me to sit down in the empty chair next to his. I did. He passed me the joint and I took a hit. Ginny took it from me. Gretts leaned close and said, "She tells me that you're a writer."

"I am," I said.

"Why do you write?" he asked.

"Because I like to," I told him and he laughed.

He stubbed the joint out and said, "Okay, you want to witness something?"

"What do you mean?"

"I'll give you a painting if you bear witness to me. Ginny'll be my other witness."

"To what?" I asked.

"I'll show you," he said. He reached down beside his chair and lifted into his lap a rolled-up pink bath towel. He laid it on the coffee table in front of us. "First thing, you gotta listen to me," he said.

I nodded.

"Back in 1863, a book titled *The American Nations*, written by this gent Constantine Samuel Rafinesque-Schmaltz, was published. In it Rafinesque, as he was known here, claimed to have had revealed to him by the Lenape a copy of the Wallum Olam, a book written on tree bark in ancient pictographs, telling the narrative of how the Lenape had arrived in the area from far away due to a great flood." The old man took a beer off the table, snapped it open, and handed it to me.

"Rafinesque even hinted that some of the scenes had shown the early Lenape beginnings in Siberia. By the time the book came out, though, he said the actual Wallum Olam had been destroyed in a fire, but assured the reading public that the reprinted pictographs in his book were authentic. But of course they weren't. Of course they weren't." Here Crackpop went silent for a moment and leaned back in his seat.

I glanced over at Ginny and she winked at me.

"His was a fraud," the old man began again. "But like so many things labeled false, it holds some pieces of truth. I'm telling you the Wallum Olam is a real thing. Let's just say that I have contact with a certain sect of the Lenape who guard the real Wallum Olam at the dark heart of the forest. What I'm going to show you is a page of it." Sherman put his yellow-nailed hand out and unrolled the towel. Within it was a roll of the thinnest piece of birch bark, so supple it appeared to have the texture of cloth. It was off white, and in the center was a black drawing of a giant turtle with a man straddling its back.

"You didn't make that, Sherman?" asked Ginny with a stoned smile.

"Oh, it's real," he said. "If they find out I took it, they'll send a mahtantu after me."

"What's that?" I asked.

"A kind of demon," said Ginny.

"You didn't notice this when you came in I bet, but my house is surrounded by a small concrete gutter full of water. I keep a pump running twenty-four/seven in it so the demons can't get in. I was taught that evil spirits can't cross running water."

"What happens when you leave the house?" I asked.

"I have to be really careful, perform rituals and such before I go out. I can't mess up."

"What are the chances of that?" I asked.

"I can do it," he said, "but the question is, can you two? Remember, you're my witnesses. If you tell anyone outside of this protected area, even in a whisper, about what I've shown you, they'll know I took it and it won't matter how careful I am. So you've got to promise not to tell anyone."

"Okay," I said. "It's a deal." I stood up and shook his hand. I said a quick good-bye to Ginny, thanked the old man, and split, almost missing the concrete block on the way down. Crackpop said I could take a painting, and as much as I wanted to just get out of there, I had to stop and consider it. The old man was truly insane, and his slow revelation of it on the porch gave me the creeps, not to mention old Ginny smoking a joint and secretly mocking him to me. On the other hand, I knew that years later, if I didn't have something tangible to attach to this story, when I told it, no one would believe me. I grabbed the rendering of the oak tree burial from the hand of a tree-being. As I relieved it of the picture's weight, the wooden giant moved, as if stretching. All the way home, with that painting in the backseat, I kept checking the rearview mirror.

Lynn took one look at the painting and said, "No," so I hung it in my office. Later that night, in bed, she asked me about my walk. I told her about the church and the art show. I really wanted to tell her about the bizarre episode of my bearing witness, but I swear I didn't. And the fact that I didn't followed me into sleep.

Time passed, a couple of years, and both kids were in school and Lynn and I were both working. The Curse of Crackpop wasn't the worst that could happen, and so the whole thing faded pretty quickly from my thoughts. Occasionally, I'd see him on the move, and I'd wonder what rituals he'd performed in order to walk so far from home. At other times, I'd notice the painting hanging in my office, and that would make me think of him as well. All this was fleeting, though, in the onrush of our lives. Through all of it, even drunk at the holidays or stoned with old friends, I kept the old man's secret.

More time passed, and the whole thing was as prevalent in my thoughts as my third birthday party, when one night Lynn came home from work pretty upset. She was trembling slightly.

"Crackpop," she said. "I almost hit him. He's drunk or something, stumbling around in the middle of Atsion Road."

"Uh-oh," I said.

"Fuck him. I almost hit a tree trying to avoid him."

"What should we do?"

"What are you going to do?" she said. "Stay out of it."

"Somebody's gonna hit him," I said.

"He's popped his last crack," said Lynn. She picked up the phone and called the local cops.

Maybe a month after that, I heard, in a matter of two weeks from different neighbors and the guy at the 7-Eleven, that Crackpop had a meltdown at the pizza place, engaging in some unwelcome bellowing, then he was spotted weaving along Atsion one afternoon, literally frothing at the mouth; after that a car did hit a tree, trying to avoid him, though no one was injured. This chain of events ended in his being hit and killed one night by a semi. Our neighbor, Dave, told us about it at the beach. He knew one of the cops who was called to the scene. "Gretts was completely obliterated," he said.

I waited a few months out of some strange sense of respect, and then I told Lynn at the end of summer. We sat out back on the screened porch, having coffee by candlelight. The crickets were strong and the night was cool. When I finished telling her about my bearing witness to Crackpop, the first thing she said was, "Does that mean Ginny told someone and the old man was possessed by a demon?"

I laughed. "I didn't think of that," I said.

Soon after, there was another fatal accident down on Atsion. Four high school kids in a white Windstar, drunk and high, veered off the road into a large oak tree. The driver was killed instantly, the two in the back died later, and only the front passenger, having been thrown from the vehicle, lived. That person was Duane Geppi, and when he finally came to, he swore to the cops that it was Crackpop, back from the dead, who had come lunging out of the shadows at the van. That story made the rounds. I heard it from a number of different people and told it to more. Hence a legend was born. Weird old guy, hit by a truck on Atsion, comes back from the dead to walk the road, seeking revenge against the world that shunned him. Reports of his ill-intentioned specter showed up frequently in the local paper around Halloween, and I heard from my older son that kids sometimes drove out that way toward the lake, hoping for an encounter. Eventually, Crackpop's house burned down in a fire of "mysterious origins," as it was reported. They didn't know the half of it.

What really scared me was something else entirely. That question Lynn had asked me about whether Ginny might have given away the old man's secret came back to me every time I'd see the oak tree painting in my office. I knew the only way I could find out whether she had or not was to meet her face-to-face. I believed that even if she lied to me when I asked her, I'd be able to detect the truth in her expression. I called the couple who'd had us to our first Christmas party in town, where I'd met Ginny, and spoke to the wife. I told her I wanted to get Ginny Sanger's phone number. She said she didn't know who I was talking about. I described the stately older woman with white hair, and she said, "I can tell you for sure, we don't know anyone like that."

"She doesn't visit you sometimes? She lives down Atsion."

"You must be thinking about one of your books," she said, laughed, and hung up.

I scoured the phone book, paid for an Internet trace, stopped and talked to old people when I'd see them out in their yards along Atsion Road. Nobody had ever heard of Ginny Sanger. I took some solace in the fact that Lynn attested to having met her. There wasn't a Sanger in the county, though. It took me years to figure it out, my kids are in college now, but I had the answer hanging in front of me the whole time.

I found her yesterday, in the circular cemetery next to the white church. The giant oak looking on, I scraped some moss off one of the stones and there she was: VIRGINIA SANGER, BORN 1770—DIED 1828. Like I said to Lynn, don't ask me to explain. I don't understand my own part in what happened, let alone Ginny's. What I was fairly certain of, though, was that, if I went into that church and went through their archive, I'd find some thread of a story about her, a sketch, a letter, and then there'd be no end to it—legend giving way to legend, like a hydra. That's the way it is here. The mind of the place manifesting in human legends that intersect and interbreed into a vast invisible wilderness all their own. We really only live along the edge of the Pine Barrens, but, still, for whatever reason, that spirit reached out and gathered us in.

A Note About "Down Atsion Road"

The Jersey Devil isn't the weirdest thing in New Jersey by a long shot. As a matter of fact, when I lived there, I had neighbors who make him look like a patsy. That creature has gotten the most publicity, though, which is a shame because there are literally hundreds of legends that exist in and around the Pine Barrens. There's the White Stag, the Black Doctor, the Atco Phantom, Captain Kidd at Reed's Bay, the Rabbit Woman, Jerry Munyhon (a kind of Barrens wizard who, when turned down for a job at Hanover Furnace, cast a spell and filled it with black and white crows), more ghosts from every era than you can shake a stick at, and that's not mentioning any of the Lenape legends. If you live there for a while and keep your eyes and ears open to these tales, as I did, being a writer of the fantastic, it soon became evident that there was something about the place that engendered legend. Part of this has to do with the enormity of the wilderness, its loneliness and mazelike quality, but I think the main reason is that there is some kind of sentient energy at its heart, as if it is aware and scheming, imbuing the lives of those who live in it or near it with some kelson of its primordial consciousness. The feeling is palpable. I've only felt this from a landscape in one other place I've been, the Scottish Highlands. I spent ten days there once in a cottage near the Isle of Skye. The place was remarkably beautiful, but haunted. There was a pervasive feeling of melancholy and loneliness mixed into the spectacular views of the mountains and lochs. I definitely felt as if the place was alive, like some sleeping giant dreaming. "Down Atsion Road" is my attempt to chronicle the supernatural influence of the Barrens. Believe me when I tell you that most of this story is true, and the parts that aren't are the incidentals. The strange wilderness has been shaping legends since humanity first set foot there. They crisscross and interconnect like a web. Through them, it communicates with us. Consider this, a vast piece of real estate in the Northeast, within commuting distance of New York City, that remains virtually untouched. Think of the money it would be worth to developers, think of the towns and malls and roads that could be cut into it. As other landscapes fall to the onslaught of "progress," the Barrens has retained itself. Pretty damn cunning, if you ask me.

Sit the Dead

Luke was in his room at his computer, looking at used cars. His cell phone rang. He answered with it on speaker.

"Darene," he said.

"Gracie died," she said.

He pictured the deceased, hairdo like a helmet, overweight, in flowered stretch slacks. Her earrings were disco balls; her face a half inch of powder and pale green lipstick. He'd met her at a barbecue in Darene's backyard. "You're in for it, kid. God bless ya," she'd said to Luke and kissed his cheek green.

"That sucks," he said.

"Is that all you have to say?" asked Darene.

"I only met her once," he said. "I'm sorry you feel bad, though."

"My father's inviting you to sit the dead."

"Sit the dead . . ." said Luke.

"It's a family ritual."

"I don't have to touch her, do I?"

"Don't be a tool," she said. "You just have to go and sit with the body in the church for a few hours."

"Like a wake," he said.

"Yeah, but nobody else but you and one other person will be there."

"You just sit there?" he asked.

"Two members from our family have to sit with Gracie till they take her to her grave. It's a family tradition going all the way back."

"Sounds weak."

"Your shift starts at midnight."

"Me and you?"

"No, you and Uncle Sfortunado."

Luke closed his eyes and shook his head.

"This means my family is officially accepting you," said Darene. "My father says it's a test of your manhood."

Luke laughed.

"I can see you're not mature enough," she said.

Two nights earlier they'd been at the lake on the picnic bench. She sat on his lap facing him, her legs on either side of his. There was a cool autumn breeze, but she glowed with warmth as they kissed.

"Okay, sign me up," he said, "but my parents are gone for the weekend with the car. I'm stranded."

"I'll pick you up at eleven thirty," she said.

He turned the computer off and went to take a shower.

Luke always got stuck sitting next to Uncle Sfortunado at the Cabadula family parties. After a while the reason for it became clear to him—no one in the family wanted to. The ancient patriarch often spoke in some foreign tongue, and when he did talk in English, he mumbled cryptic sayings involving animals—"The moon in the lake is for the fish" or "A spider in the mouth will empty your pockets." When Luke stared back in puzzlement, the old man would spit out the word *"gaduche,"* which Luke was sure meant "stupid" or worse. Once he'd asked Sfortunado what country the Cabadula were originally from. He guessed Greece, Italy, Romania, Turkey, Russia.

The old man squinted and shook his head to each.

"Are you gypsies?" asked Luke.

"I wish," said Sfortunado.

"I give up. Where then?"

"Another country."

"Which one?"

"The old country, up in the hills," he yelled and shook his head in annoyance.

As the shower water fell and the steam rose, Luke closed his eyes. "I'm gonna have to get blazed for this," he thought.

Darene pulled up in her old Jeep Cherokee at exactly eleven thirty. Luke had never known her to be on time. He got in. She was dressed all in black—T-shirt, jacket, jeans, and he knew, even though he couldn't see her feet, that she'd be wearing black socks and sneakers. She gave him a quick kiss before he could slide across the seat and put his arms around her. Just as he reached, she turned, started the car, and pulled away from the curb.

"Put your seat belt on," she said.

"Where are we going?" he asked and lightly touched a ringlet of her hair.

"The church over on Gebble Street."

"That's a crappy area."

"That's our church," she said and made a stern face.

"How about we make a detour to the lake and you can test my manhood?" he said and laughed.

"Are you high?" she asked.

"No," he said. "I'm tired. I was asleep when you called."

She sighed, and from that point on it was silence until they pulled into the church parking lot.

"I can't go in with you," she said. She opened her door. He also got out and met her at the front of the car. She put her arms around his waist and he leaned back against the hood.

"I know this is beat," she said, "but it means a lot to me." She looked up and he smiled. She put the side of her face against his chest.

"You've got nothing to worry about," he said. "I'll sit the dead like my father sits the bowl."

"Seriously," she said.

"I'm all about it."

The next thing he knew, she was closing the front door of the church behind him. He stepped into a dark alcove and a sudden smell of incense and old wood made his spine twitch. Luke looked through the open doors and down the aisle before him, past the rows of darkened pews, to the altar—white marble, crowded with statues, and holding the candlelit coffin of Gracie. He took a deep breath and moved toward the light.

Between the first pew and the altar, there was an empty folding chair set up next to Uncle Sfortunado's.

"Hello," Luke said too loud, sending echoes everywhere.

The old man turned and stared through thick glasses. He wore a gray cardigan dotted with cigarette burns. His beard was a week old and white as snow, his hair crazy. "*Gaduche*," he said, raised a trembling hand, and farted.

"Good to see you again," said Luke.

"This is who I get to sit the dead?" said Sfortunado, shouting into the dark. He grimaced. "The cat makes the owl bleed . . ."

"Darene's father told me to come."

"Yeah, yeah." The old man waved a trembling hand in front of his face.

"My condolences about Gracie," said Luke.

Sfortunado laughed and pointed at the altar. "Go tell her you're sorry," he said.

Luke got up and slowly ascended the three steps to the coffin. Gracie came into view, a deflated balloon made of dough. She wore a white dress, a giant version of a little girl's party rig, pale green lipstick, and her blond hair helmet was slightly askew. A hand grabbed the side of the coffin. Luke started and then saw it belonged to Uncle Sfortunado, who stood beside him.

"Looks like shit," said the old man. "What do you think?"

Luke stalled by rubbing the back of his neck. Finally he said, "Well . . . she's dead."

Sfortunado shrugged and nodded. "This is true."

"What happened to her?"

"Something bad."

Luke went back to his chair. Sfortunado mumbled a few words to Gracie and then announced, "She smells like flowers." He threw his head back and laughed loud. The echoes rained down and Luke considered splitting. The old man hobbled back to his chair, and less than five minutes later was asleep.

Luke studied the statuary on the altar, elongated marble figures in the throes of agony gathered in a semicircle at the center of which hung a large golden sun made of gleaming metal. He took out his cell phone and texted Darene, WT RELIGN R U? Uncle Sfortunado was swaying slightly from side to side, snoring, his arms folded across his sunken chest. Darene's reply came back. NO TXTING. C U @ DAWN.

Time stood still in the candlelight, and Luke listened to the church quietly creak. The rapid scuttling of some tiny creature echoed like a whisper from the shadows. Somewhere something was dripping. It didn't take long before the creepiness gave way to boredom. "They should have a TV set up here," he thought. Eventually his mind turned to Darene.

They'd been together since the previous autumn, junior year. Whatever her culture was, it demanded an old-fashioned formality between kids their age. They went to all the parties together, movies, some concerts, but she insisted he meet her family and attend the holiday and birthday gatherings at her house.

Both his male and female friends told him he was pussy-whipped, but he didn't care. Darene's hair, ringlets of black springs that seemed alive, her smooth dark complexion, her green eyes and unabashed laugh, canceled out all of their scorn. She definitely knew her mind, and yet he wasn't particularly good at school, or good-looking by anyone's standards. The whole thing was a mystery he enjoyed pondering.

Luke's memory returned to that night at the picnic table by the lake for quite a while and then he checked his phone for the time, sure that at least a couple of hours had passed. He discovered that not even a half hour had gone by since Sfortunado had fallen asleep. Taking a cue from the old man, he put his phone in his pocket, folded his arms across his chest, and closed his eyes. As he began to doze, a putrid stench, the first stirrings of which he attributed to Uncle Sfortunado, slowly overcame the aroma of old incense and pervaded the place. "Gracie's not embalmed," was his last thought before sleep and then he dreamed of going naked, late, to the SATs.

"Gracie's not embalmed," was the first thought he had upon

waking suddenly at the touch of someone's hand upon his shoulder. The church was freezing and that death stench was now thick as perfume. He looked over and caught a burst of adrenaline upon seeing a gun in the old man's wobbling hand. Luke made a move to bolt, but Sfortunado's eyes got big behind his glasses, and he brought his finger to his lips. He waved with the gun toward the altar. "The squirrel claws my heart," he whispered.

Luke tried to get away, but the old man grabbed his wrist. *"Fashtulina,"* he said and touched the gun to his chest. He released his grip on Luke's wrist and turned to face the altar.

"Okay," said Luke, reluctantly sitting back in his chair.

"She's got it in her blood," whispered Sfortunado.

"What's in whose blood?" asked Luke.

"Gracie," said the old man. "Every fifty years or so one of us Cabadula is born with the *gritchino* in the blood. You can't tell till they die. But this one," he said, pointing at the coffin, "I always had a feeling."

"Gritchino," said Luke.

At the sound of the word, Sfortunado touched his yellowed left thumbnail to each lens of his glasses and then kissed his middle finger. "The breeze. Do you feel it?" said Sfortunado.

Luke could feel a cold wind in his face. The candle flames danced wildly. "It's freezing," he said, teeth chattering, and noticed his breath was now mist.

"The wind of eternity," said the old man. He pointed with the gun again toward the altar.

Luke looked up to see the lid of the coffin slowly closing. "What the hell," he said. He wanted to run but was paralyzed with fear. The wind increased, whipping around the church and screeching above in the darkened dome. Luke was shivering. Uncle Sfortunado was shivering too, but when the coffin lifted slowly off its platform, the old man stood and brought the gun up in front of him.

The coffin, as if lifted with invisible strings, rose six feet off its platform. Then it began to move through the air like a slow, wooden torpedo. As it swept by above and out over the pews, Uncle Sfortunado aimed and fired at it. He pulled the trigger three times and the echoes from the shots and splintering wood careered everywhere. As Gracie passed into the dark toward the front of the church, he said, *"Fasheel,"* and tapped his forehead with the barrel of the gun.

"Let's get out of here," said Luke, trembling. He stood and saw the coffin cruising back out of the shadows, returning toward the altar. He ducked. Sfortunado again took aim and fired two more shots in rapid succession as she passed overhead. Splinters fell in Luke's hair, and he noticed the coffin begin to wobble in its flight. It gained speed and then took a nosedive at the altar, crashing into the metal sun and smashing the head off one of the sculptures.

As Uncle Sfortunado moved toward the altar steps, the lid of the coffin swung open on its hinges and what was left of Gracie levitated slowly into a standing position. Her blond wig was crooked and her face drooped in lumpy folds. She was pale as milk, even her long tongue was white, and her eyes had lost their pupils. Her lopsided green smile revealed sharp incisors.

"She's a fuckin' vampire," said Luke.

"Fly like the wren," said Sfortunado over his shoulder, and Luke didn't need a translation. He bolted down the aisle toward the front door of the church. He heard the gun go off again, and he stopped and turned to see the old man hobbling after him, waving at him to move. On the altar, Gracie was screaming like a wounded cat.

Luke made the door, burst out into the night, and then held it for Sfortunado, who was little more than halfway, limping and scuttling with all he had. Behind him, Gracie was floating up off the altar.

"Come on," yelled Luke, and just as the old man reached him, he saw Gracie swoop through the air toward them. He grabbed Uncle Sfortunado by the arm, pulled him outside, and slammed the door. There was a thud against it from inside.

"She's coming," yelled Luke.

The old man leaned back against the door and bent over to catch his breath. In between heaves, he held up a trembling index finger and said, "She's trapped in the church . . . till dawn." Then he laughed and again couldn't catch his breath. "I knew she was *gritchino*," he said. "I told them all and they said, 'Oh, Sfortunado, he's losing his marbles.' "

"She can't get out?" said Luke.

"I already told you. Call Darene, tell her *gritchino*. Tell her to bring guns."

Luke took out his phone and did as he was told. He still wanted to run and keep on running till he was back at his house, in his room, earphones on, sitting at his computer. Darene finally answered.

"What are you doing to me, here?" said Luke.

"Quit complaining," she said, "you're already more than halfway through the night."

"*Gritchino*," he said. "Gracie's gone wild."

Darene didn't answer, but he heard her running from her

room. From a distance he heard her scream, "Dad, Gracie's *gritchino*."

Two minutes passed, and while Luke waited for Darene to pick up again, Uncle Sfortunado limped over to a stone bench to the right of the church doors and sat down with a sigh.

"Stay there," Darene finally said into the phone. "We're coming."

"Your uncle says to bring guns. Darene, what the hell?"

She hung up. Luke walked over to the bench and sat next to the old man. "This is all wrong," he said.

Sfortunado smiled. "Only wrong if we don't kill her."

"Forget we," said Luke. "I'm done."

The old man waved a hand as if to dismiss him. "Cowards get no treasure," he said.

"What treasure?"

"You kill the *gritchino*, cut off the left leg, and there's a diamond, right here," he said, leaning forward and pointing to the back of his leg. "Inside the calf muscle, a gift from the great spirit for killing the creature."

"Get out of here," said Luke.

"This big," said Sfortunado and made a fist. "You help kill it, you get a share."

"How hard is it to kill the *gritchino*?" asked Luke.

"Ehh." The old man rocked back and forth. "Sometimes not so hard. First you shoot it, shoot it, shoot it, and then you gotta nail the head."

"What do you nail it with?"

"Brass. This long," he said and stretched his thumb and forefinger apart six inches. "Right here." He touched his finger to the middle of his forehead. "With a hammer." He pantomimed a mighty hammer blow. "Pfft, finished."

"What if she gets me before I get her?"

"*Gritchino* likes the organ meat—liver, kidney, heart, you know. Likes the blood."

"What is it?"

"It's in the blood. People say it's a demon, evil spirit, goblin, but this is the twenty-first century. It's a hereditary germ. It makes *gritchino* every fifty years or so."

"If it's a hereditary germ, how does the diamond get in her leg?" said Luke.

Uncle Sfortunado shrugged. "You ask too many questions. Just shut up and kill the *gritchino*."

"Was that a twenty-first-century flying coffin?" asked Luke.

"*Gaduche*," said the old man and shook his head.

Five minutes later, Mr. Cabadula's black Mercedes pulled into the parking lot. As soon as it stopped, Darene got out of the passenger side and came running toward the bench. Luke stood up to meet her, but she passed him and went to Uncle Sfortunado. "Are you okay?" she asked, leaning down and putting her arms around him.

"Yeah, yeah, I had *gaduche* to protect me," he said, staring at Luke over her shoulder.

Mr. Cabadula walked up and began talking in another language to Sfortunado. Darene went to Luke, took him by the arm, and moved him away from the men, to the other side of the church doors.

"I'm sorry," she whispered.

"Are you kidding? She's some kind of vampire," he said.

"Once in fifty years out of all the Cabadula. Why Gracie?"

"So, when do we call the cops and leave?" asked Luke.

"We have to kill it," said Darene. "It's our family duty."

"That's crazy."

"You can go home if you want," said Darene. "I'll call you a cab."

"Listen, I've seen Gracie and she's nasty. Come back with me."

"I can't," she said.

"So, are we ready?" asked Mr. Cabadula, now standing behind his daughter. He had a wave of graying hair and a mustache. His arms were folded across his chest.

"Luke's going home," she said to him.

"Going home," said her father in a flat voice.

"No . . . I'll help," said Luke.

"Ever shoot a gun?" said Mr. Cabadula.

"Sure," he said, though he'd never even touched one.

"Come to my car," said Darene's father.

As they followed him, she put her arm around Luke and kissed his ear.

"If I get killed, my parents are gonna be pissed," he said to her.

Sfortunado was already at the trunk of the Mercedes. Mr. Cabadula opened it and stepped aside. "Take one," he said. Luke looked in and saw a row of six pistols lying on a beige woolen blanket. The guns didn't look like anything he'd seen in the movies. They were old, with rounded wooden stocks and silver filigree work on the barrels.

"Three shots," said Darene's father as Luke reached in and took one in his hand.

"What gun has only three shots?" asked Luke, backing out of the car and lifting the piece to inspect it.

"Three shots," Mr. Cabadula repeated. "The bullets are made with shards of witch bone."

Luke held the gun straight down at his side, afraid it might go off from either age or magic. Darene's father then handed both her and Luke flashlights.

Sfortunado left the revolver he'd used in the church and took two pistols, as did his nephew. Darene slid hers into the waist of her jeans.

They stood by the church door and Mr. Cabadula gave instructions. All Luke heard was the first point, that Gracie could be lurking right inside the front door, and after that he was too scared to concentrate. Darene looked over at him and touched his shoulder. "Do you know what you're doing?" she asked. He nodded, and then Uncle Sfortunado, one gun in the pocket of his baggy pants, wrapped his fingers around the handle of the church door. Mr. Cabadula crouched slightly and took aim with his pistols. Darene drew the gun from her waist and nudged Luke back a few steps. "Now," said her father, and the door swung open.

"Flashlights," yelled Mr. Cabadula. Luke and Darene aimed their beams into the darkened foyer. "All right," he said. "Let's go in." The next thing Luke knew, he was standing in the dark with the old man, and Darene and her father were halfway down the center aisle to the altar. The place stank of death, and the temperature hadn't risen a degree.

"*Gaduche*," said Sfortunado, "sometime before dawn."

Luke came to his senses and started toward the altar, the flashlight trained ahead. He thought of Gracie floating up by the ceiling or crouched in one of the pews, licking her green lips. He realized his index finger was near to squeezing the trigger of his pistol and tried to relax. The candles on the altar had gone out. The mysterious wind had died.

Sfortunado whispered, "Remember the diamond."

The skin on the back of Luke's neck tingled. He spun around and shone the flashlight behind them and then into the pews, up at the ceiling, at Sfortunado, who looked like he'd just crawled out of a coffin himself.

The old man laughed and pointed forward with his guns. On their way toward the front row of pews, Luke kept an eye on Darene's flashlight beam. She and her father had moved off to the left of the altar. Sfortunado said, "Go right," when they reached the front row of pews, Luke passed the beam of his flashlight over the altar, the fallen coffin, and the rubble around it. They moved on into a more profound darkness at the side of the church where thick wooden beams arched toward the dome, like the rib cage of a monster.

At the opposite end of the church, Mr. Cabadula yelled, "There." Luke turned to see Darene's beam aimed upward. Something flitted through it. There was a sudden flash of orange light and then a bang. Luke called, "Darene," and started back along the front row of pews.

When he reached the center aisle, before the altar, he heard Sfortunado yell, "Down." Luke fell to the floor and felt the sweeping breeze of Gracie pass overhead. Two shots went off and he winced and covered his ears. The next thing he knew, Darene was lifting him to his feet. He turned and saw Mr. Cabadula on the altar, setting the candles back up and lighting them. A glow grew around them, and even that meager light was a relief.

Out of the shadows shuffled Sfortunado, grumbling. They gathered on the altar with their backs to the wall, their pistols out. Luke said to Sfortunado, "How did you see her? I had the flashlight."

"I knew in my head that you were screwing up."

"You're psychic?"

"Did you duck?" asked the old man.

"I have to go into the back of the church and find the switch for the lights," said Mr. Cabadula. "It's stupid to challenge her in the dark. If I get the lights on, we'll finish this up in a half hour."

No one said a word. They listened, trying to hear Gracie move out beyond the candlelight. Luke was standing in front of the crashed coffin, trembling. Darene stood close to him.

"This place stinks," she said.

"The wind of eternity," said Sfortunado.

Mr. Cabadula put one of his pistols in his belt, removed the flashlight from Luke's hand, and descended the altar steps. "I'll be back in a minute," he said over his shoulder. When he passed into the dark, they followed him by the white beam searching above and below. Then he disappeared behind the altar.

Luke could hear Gracie purring, moving among the distant pews near the front door. Then, in the next minute, she seemed to be just out of sight beyond the glow of the candles.

"Stand back," said Sfortunado as he took a step forward. "I'll call her in."

"What do you want to do that for?" asked Luke.

"Darene, explain," said the old man in a whisper over his shoulder.

"Uncle Sfortunado is going to use the *Lamentalata* to draw Gracie to us so we can shoot her," said Darene. "Stand on that side of him, two feet behind, and have your gun ready. I'll cover this side."

Luke took his position and lifted his pistol, his hand trembling.

Sfortunado half-turned to look at him. "When you pull the trigger, bullets come out," he said and laughed. A moment later, the old man called out to Gracie in a high-pitched wavering voice. The sound of it startled Luke, and he turned to look at Darene, who smiled.

Sfortunado paused after calling her name five times, and then he made what sounded like bird calls—whistling, gibbering, cawing, singing in an even higher tone than before. Even though the threat of Gracie lunging out of the dark had him sweating, Luke couldn't keep a straight face. His nervous laughter lasted only a second before he saw a white form slowly passing into the grainy light, halfway up the center aisle. The pale blob wavered with the candle flame and then became clearer—Gracie on all fours, crawling obediently toward the altar.

Spit was flying from Sfortunado's lips as he trilled and whooped. He swung his arms for more power and lifted up on his toes. His head darted back and forth, up and down, like a bird's. Luke thought the old man was going to keel over from his efforts. Gracie inched ever closer, purring in such a way that the sound echoed everywhere.

When she reached the foot of the altar, she grunted and slowly rose to her feet. Her wig had come off; she was completely bald. Her white tongue lolled down over her chin and her eyes were closed. She began snoring. Sfortunado quit his bird impersonations, stumbled backward, and fell onto the altar.

"Now," said Darene and stepped forward with her gun out. Luke froze for a heartbeat, and in that brief space, the lights of the church went on. He blinked and brought his free hand up to block out the sudden glare. From between his fingers, he saw Gracie's eyelids slide open. Then he saw the fangs. She pounced like a flying leopard, arcing upward through the air. A shot rang out and then another, and the next thing Luke knew, Gracie had landed at Sfortunado's feet and sunk her fangs into his left calf muscle. Blood sprayed over the altar and the old man screamed in agony.

Sfortunado's cry brought Luke to his senses. He aimed at

Gracie's back and pulled the trigger. The pistol kicked in his hand and the slug went wide and dug into the altar floor. Darene took aim, fired, and hit Gracie in the side, tumbling her off Sfortunado and right at Luke's feet. He jumped back a step and the gun went off, splintering the boards. At the sound of the shot, Gracie sprang up and away from him. She bounded once and in an instant had her hands wrapped around Darene's throat. Darene's arms were between Gracie's and she struggled to hold back that pale, gaping mouth.

Luke sprang into action, but thought, "What am I doing?" as he managed to sling an arm, hand holding the stock of the pistol, around Gracie's neck. With his free hand, he grabbed the end of the barrel of the gun and pulled back, forcing it against her windpipe. Rearing away from Darene, Gracie tried to break his grip with her hands. She bucked and whipped from side to side, turned in circles. He barely held on. Her flesh was the consistency of wet clay, and she stank like rotting meat. She dug her nails into his forearms, and he head-butted her as hard as he could at the base of her skull. She growled and tipped backward, losing her balance at the edge of the altar.

Luke caught a glimpse of Darene, aiming her gun at them as they fell. He didn't know whether to let go or hold on tighter. If Gracie landed on him he was sure he'd lose her, but, though he cringed in anticipation, he never slammed against the church floor. Instead, he opened his eyes as she lifted off the edge of the altar and ascended. Luke looked down and screamed.

"Let go," Darene yelled.

He held on tighter as they circled upward. In seconds, they'd reached the height of the dome, and Gracie leveled out, now placidly flying, like Superman, with her arms out in front of her. They orbited the inside of the dome, and, amid his panic,

Luke noticed the images painted on the curved ceiling—scenes of people with bird heads feasting on platters of insects, a grasshopper with a halo on a throne, trees and mountains, all amid a sky-blue background with white clouds.

Gracie was babbling in the language of the bald dead, and Luke eased up on his grip, resting upon her back. She swept so smoothly through the air, it felt like a dream.

"Luke," came a voice from below. He roused and looked down over his shoulder from the dizzying height. Mr. Cabadula and Darene now appeared to be the size of grasshoppers. Behind them Sfortunado was writhing in pain on the floor.

"Choke her down," called Darene's father. He lifted his gun, holding it in two hands like Luke was, and pulled it in tightly toward his throat.

"Choke her down," whispered Luke. He gathered his strength and pulled back hard on the gun barrel. Gracie wheezed with the pressure and bucked her hips, trying to shake him off her back. They descended in a slow spiral.

"Keep the pressure on no matter what," said Mr. Cabadula. Luke looked down and saw Darene's father handing her a mallet and a long brass nail. She then turned and walked to the edge of the altar. Mr. Cabadula walked to the opposite edge and crouched down.

Gracie reached a certain altitude and no matter how much Luke put into choking her, she'd not go an inch lower. They went into a wide orbit fifteen feet above the altar, moving in an arc out over the pews and back.

"I gotta let go," Luke yelled.

"One more minute," said Darene.

He looked down to find her on the altar as they circled toward it. He heard her father say, "Now, Darene." At this, she took off, sprinting toward him, her arms pumping, her hair flying. Luke watched her dash across the altar to her father, who had his hands cupped, fingers laced, in front of him. She placed her left foot into his hands and at that instant, he pushed upward with his legs, lifting Darene, pitching her high into the air.

Luke saw everything, but it seemed at a distance. Once Darene was in flight, though, he noticed how closely they'd circled in toward her. He pulled back hard on Gracie, afraid that Darene would collide with them. She rose in an arc, flipping in midair, so that as she passed just in front of them, she was completely upside down, her face toward them. At the perfect moment, she reached out, set the nail to Gracie's forehead, and, with one deft blow, slammed it through her skull. Luke heard the sickening crunch of bone, felt Gracie go slack, and then realized that Darene was next to him. She shoved him hard. He lost his grip and fell, screaming, into the arms of Mr. Cabadula, who set him carefully on the altar. They both immediately looked up. Darene had removed her belt and had it around Gracie's throat. She'd turned the belt tight, like a tourniquet, and had the ends wrapped around her wrist. She sat straight up on the back of the vanquished *gritchino,* her legs hanging down, and seemed able to direct the course of their slow descent by tugging in one direction or another.

Darene steered the remains of Gracie in a slow, meandering descent that ended in the open coffin. Luke shivered at the fantastic precision of Darene's delivery. She hopped off the *gritchino* as it fell, like an avalanche, into the box. The lid eased down of its own accord and latched with a distinct click. Then the whole casket turned to steam and evaporated.

"Forget it," said Luke and covered his face with his left hand.

Darene and her father were on either side of Sfortunado, who was whimpering. Luke inched closer, but really didn't want to see either the old man's chewed-up leg or, worse, his face. Mr. Cabadula took Darene by the arm and led her away from Sfortunado to where Luke was standing.

"Here're my keys," he said, putting the ring of them in her hand. "You go on ahead. I'll clean this up."

There were tears in Darene's eyes when she nodded.

"What's gonna happen with Sfortunado?" asked Luke. "Is he *gritchino*, like vampires make other vampires?"

"Don't worry," said Mr. Cabadula and cocked the hammer of one of the pistols. "You watch too many movies."

"Come on," said Darene. She put her arm around Luke's back and pulled him down the altar steps and up the aisle toward the door.

Out in the parking lot the air was so fresh. There was a ribbon of light at the horizon. A bird sang. They got into the black Mercedes. Darene started it and pulled out of the parking lot. Neither of them spoke, and Luke dozed briefly before the car eventually came to a halt. He opened his eyes and saw that she had driven them to the lake.

They sat on a bench beneath the pines, facing the water and the dawn. He had his arm around her and she leaned against him.

"That was sick," he said. "What's with your family?"

"Do you still love me?" she said.

"I loved it when you spiked Gracie. You and your dad are like a circus act or something."

"They teach you that when you're a kid," she said.

"So what's with Sfortunado? He's not *gritchino*?" asked Luke. "I thought your father was going to ice him."

"Relax," she said and brought her hand up to lightly trace,

with the nail of her index finger, an invisible design on his forehead. Luke felt the tension leave his muscles. His eyes closed and a moment later he was asleep. When he woke with the sunlight in his face, Darene was gone, as was the Mercedes.

Luke played sick on Monday and Tuesday and stayed home from school. He spent those days on the computer going randomly from one site to another or playing Need for Speed. The implications of the *gritchino* made him dizzy. He wanted to call Darene, or at least text her, but when he reached for his phone, the memory of her flying upside down and striking that nail into Gracie's skull made her even more a mystery to him than the wind of eternity.

When he did return to school Wednesday, he found out that Darene hadn't been to class that week, either. He looked for her at all the times and places they'd usually meet on a school day, and asked around for her. By fifth period he knew she wasn't there. He cut his seventh-period class and slipped out the side door of the gym. On the path through the woods, he smoked a joint. A half hour later, he stood in front of Darene's house.

The windows had been stripped of their curtains and the whole place was sunk in that eerie stillness of the vacant. There was a FOR SALE sign in the ground next to the driveway. "She's gone," he said aloud, realizing he wasn't sure if it was for the best or the worst.

Two nights later, Luke was awakened from a nightmare of the church by a light nudging at his shoulder. "Shhhh," whispered a voice. At first he thought it was his mother who'd heard him crying out from his dream. He turned to see her, but instead saw a ghastly visage illuminated from beneath and appearing to be floating in the dark. Luke gasped, then groaned, backing up against the headboard.

"Fashtulina," said the voice. The figure moved and the glow that had lit the face revealed itself to be a flashlight.

"Uncle Sfortunado?" said Luke.

"Who else?"

"What do you want?" asked Luke, turning on the lamp next to his bed.

The old man came into view, wearing a long black coat and a beret. "Surprised to see me, *gaduche*?" he said, turning off the flashlight and putting it in his coat pocket.

"How's your leg?" asked Luke, trying to swallow.

"The wasp makes the eye cry out," said the old man with a sigh. "That Gracie, she could bite."

"What are you doing here? Where's Darene?"

"I'm here to give you this . . ." Sfortunado reached his gloved hand into the breast pocket of the coat and brought out a thick roll of cash circled by a red rubber band. "Three thousand," he said and dropped the money onto the top of the nearby dresser.

"You're giving me three thousand dollars?" said Luke.

"Your cut of the diamond."

"That was real?"

"What I say?" He smiled.

"And Darene?"

"They were called back to the old country for their shame."

"Shame for what?"

"They didn't do it. I told them they should, but my nephew loves his uncle."

"You've got the *gritchino* in you now, don't you? After Gracie bit you, you got it in you," said Luke.

Sfortunado shambled over and sat on the edge of the bed.

"Are you going to eat my kidney?" asked Luke, pulling his legs away from the old man.

"Not tonight," said Sfortunado. "I came to ask you to please, now, put a brass nail into my head." He put his thumb to the spot above the bridge of his nose. "Darene and her father could not, and now they have been banished from here. I couldn't go back with them because I have the *gritchino* in me. Until I die I'm almost the same old Sfortunado, but after that I will be as Gracie was."

Luke listened and shook his head. "Forget it," he said.

Sfortunado reached into the pockets of the coat and brought out a mallet and a long brass nail. "You see," said the old man, "there are no Cabadula here anymore. When I come from the coffin, there will be no one to stop me. I will feast on many. This will happen."

"No way," said Luke.

"When vanquished by the nail, like *gritchino*, I will evaporate. And then I am gone and Darene and her family can return. You miss the girl, *gaduche*, I know," he said and reached the mallet and nail toward Luke.

"No," yelled Luke.

Sfortunado stood up. "Do it," he growled. When his lip trembled, the sharp tips of his incisors were visible. He took a step toward Luke, but from down the hallway outside the bedroom door there came the sound of footsteps on the stairs. The old man's head turned, like a bird's, listening.

"My parents are coming," said Luke.

"Turn off the light," said Sfortunado.

The instant the dark came on, Luke knew he shouldn't have followed the order.

"Think about it, *gaduche*. When you are ready, turn on your phone and whisper my name three times. I will come with the mallet and nail."

The doorknob turned.

Sfortunado stepped back and his silhouette melted into the dark. Then the door opened, the lights came on, and Luke's parents were there, but the old man had vanished.

"We heard voices and then you yelling, 'No,'" said his father.

"Where'd this money come from?" asked his mother.

Luke couldn't answer. He turned on his side, curled up in a ball, and pulled the blanket over his head.

A Note About "Sit the Dead"

In recent years I've written quite a few stories for themed anthologies, especially for editors Ellen Datlow and Terri Windling. I enjoy doing them for two reasons. The first is that in working with Ellen or Ellen and Terri, it's understood that they want you to do something different, idiosyncratic. They want to be surprised and delighted by the story you send them. I've always thrived as a writer with editors like that. On the other hand, many of the themes of these themed anthologies could very easily be described at first glance as played out or used up. What I like about doing them, though, is the challenge of being given a very traditional theme and set to the task of doing something unusual with it. When Ellen and Terri sent me the write-up for the anthology *Teeth*, and I saw it was to be a YA vampire anthology, I very nearly passed on it. I mean, it's one thing to try to breathe new life into a flayed theme, but vampires? That's almost a trope too far. With the exception of zombies, I can't think of any other horror theme more worked over than vampires. Then I remembered a Swedish film I'd seen only a couple of years before, *Let the Right One In*, and how I was so impressed with the way the story reenvisioned the vampire theme. This was an impetus to take on the challenge and give it a go. My story, "Sit the Dead," was influenced somewhat by two things. The great Nikolai Gogol's crazy story "Viy," from which I lifted the flying coffin, and the eternal cultural horror story of trying to fit into your girlfriend's or boyfriend's family when you're a young adult. As to whether I was successful in this challenge, that, of course, is up to you.

The Seventh Expression of the Robot General

In his later years, when he spoke, a faint whirring came from his lower jaw. His mouth opened and closed rhythmically, accurately, displaying a full set of human teeth gleaned from fallen comrades and the stitched tube of plush leather that was his tongue. The metal mustache and eyebrows were ridiculously fake, but the eyes were the most beautiful glass facsimiles, creamy white with irises like dark blue flowers. Instead of hair, his scalp was sandpaper.

He wore his uniform still, even the peaked cap with the old emblem of the Galaxy Corps embroidered in gold. He creaked when he walked, piston compressions and the click of a warped flywheel whispering within his trousers. Alternating current droned from a faulty fuse in his solar plexus, and occasionally, mostly on wet days, sparks wreathed his head like a halo of bright gnats. He smoked a pipe, and before turning each page of a newspaper, he'd bring his chrome index finger to his dry rubber slit of a mouth as if he were moistening its tip.

His countenance, made of an astounding pliable, nonflammable, blast-beam-resistant, self-healing rubber alloy, was supposedly sculpted in homage to the dashing looks of Rendel

Sassoon, star of the acclaimed film epic *For God and Country.* Not everyone saw the likeness, and Sassoon himself, a devout pacifist who was well along in years when the general took his first steps out of the laboratory, sued for defamation of character. But once the video started coming back from the front, visions of slaughter more powerful than any celluloid fantasy, mutilated Harvang corpses stacked to the sky, the old actor donned a flag pin on his lapel and did a series of war bond television commercials of which the most prominent feature was his nervous smile.

It's a sad fact that currently most young people aren't aware of the historic incidents that led to our war with the Harvang and the necessity of the robot general. They couldn't tell you a thing about our early discoveries of atmosphere and biological life on our planet's sizable satellite, or about the initial fleet that went to lay claim to it. Our discovery of the existence of the Harvang was perhaps the most astonishing news in the history of humanity. They protested our explorations as an invasion, even though we offered technological and moral advancements. A confluence of intersecting events led to an unavoidable massacre of an entire village of the brutes, which in turn led to a massacre of our expeditionary force. They used our ships to invade us, landing here in Snow Country and in the swamps south of Central City.

It was said about his time on the battlefield that if the general was human he'd have been labeled "merciless," but as it was, his robot nature mitigated this assessment instead to simply "without mercy." At the edge of a pitched battle he'd set up a folding chair and sit down to watch the action, pipe in hand and a thermos of thick black oil nearby. He'd yell through a bullhorn, strategic orders interspersed with exhortations of "Onward, you

sacks of blood!" Should his troops lose the upper hand in the
mêlée, the general would stand, set his pipe and drink on the
ground next to his chair, remove his leather jacket, hand it to
his assistant, roll up his sleeves, cock his hat back, and dash onto
the battlefield, running at top robot speed.

Historians, engineers, and AI researchers of more recent years
have been nonplussed as to why the general's creators gave him
such limited and primitive battle enhancements. There were
rays and particle beams at that point in history and they could
have outfitted him like a tank, but their art required subtlety.
Barbed, spinning drill bits whirled out from the center of his
knuckles on each hand. At the first hint of danger, razor blades
protruded from the toes of his boots. He also belched poisoned,
feathered darts from his open mouth, but his most spectacular
device was a rocket built into his hindquarters that when acti-
vated shot a blast of fire that made him airborne for ten seconds.

It was supposedly a sight the Harvang dreaded, to see him
land behind their lines, knuckle spikes whirling, belching
death, trousers smoldering. They had a name for him in Harvang, Kokulafugok, which roughly translated as "Fire in the
Hole." He'd leave a trail of carnage through their ranks, only
stopping briefly to remove the hair tangling his drill bits.

His movements were graceful and precise. He could calcu-
late ahead of his opponent, dodge blast beams, bend backward,
touch his head upon the ground to avoid a spray of shrapnel and
then spring back up into a razor-toed kick, lopping off a Harvang's sex and drilling him through the throat. Never tiring,
always perfectly balanced and accurate, his intuition was dic-
tated by a random-number generator.

He killed like a force of nature, an extension of the universe.
Hacked by axe blades or shot with arrows to his head, when

his business was done, he'd retire to his tent and send for one of the Harvang females. The screams of his prisoner echoed through the camp and were more frightening to his troops than combat. On the following morning he would emerge, his dents completely healed, and give orders to have the carcass removed from his quarters.

During the war, he was popular with the people back home. They admired his hand-to-hand combat, his antique nature, his unwillingness to care about the reasons for war. He was voted the celebrity most men would want to have a beer with and most women would desire for a brief sexual liaison. When informed as to the results of this poll, his only response was, "But are they ready to die for me?"

Everywhere, in the schools, the post offices, the public libraries, there were posters of him in battle-action poses amid a pile of dead or dying Harvang that read: LET'S DRILL OUT A VICTORY! The Corps was constantly transporting him from the front lines of Snow Country or the moon back to Central City in order to make appearances supporting the war. His speeches invariably contained this line: "The Harvang are a filthy species." At the end of his talks, his face would turn the colors of the flag and there were few who refused to salute. Occasionally, he'd blast off the podium and dive headlong into the crowd, which would catch his falling body and, hand over hand, return him to the stage.

In his final campaign, he was blown to pieces by a blast from a beam cannon the Harvang had stolen from his arsenal. An entire regiment of ours was ambushed in Snow Country between the steep walls of an enormous glacier—the Battle of the Ice Chute. His strategies were impossibly complex but all inexorably led to a frontal assault, a stirring charge straight into the mouth of Death. It was a common belief among his troops that who'd ever initially programmed him had never been to war. Only after his defeat did the experts claim his tactics were daft, riddled with hubris spawned by faulty AI. His case became, for a time, a thread of the damning argument that artificial intelligence, merely the human impression of intelligence, was, in reality, artificial ignorance. It was then that robot production moved decidedly toward the organic.

After the Harvang had been routed by reinforcements, and the Corps eventually began burying the remains of those who'd perished in the battle for Snow Country, the general's head was discovered amid the frozen carnage. When the soldier who found it lifted it up from beneath the stiffened trunk of a human body, the eyes opened, the jaw moved, and the weak, crackling command of "Kill them all!" sputtered forth.

The Corps decided to rebuild him as a museum piece for public relations purposes, but the budget was limited. Most of his parts, discovered strewn across the battlefield, could be salvaged, and a few new ones were fashioned from cheaper materials to replace what was missing. Still, those who rebuilt the general were not the craftsmen his creators had been— techniques had been lost to time. There was no longer the patience in robot design for aping the human. A few sectors of his artificial brain had been damaged, but there wasn't a technician alive who could repair his intelligence node, a ball of wiring so complex its design had been dubbed "the Knot."

The Corps used him for fund-raising events and rode him around in an open car at veterans' parades. The only group that ever paid attention to him, though, was the parents of the sons and daughters who'd died under his command. As it turned out, there were thousands of them. Along a parade route they'd pelt him with old fruit and dog shit, to which he'd calmly respond, "Incoming."

It didn't take the Corps long to realize he was a liability, but since he possessed consciousness, though it was man-made, the law disallowed his being simply turned off. Instead, he was retired and set up in a nice apartment at the center of a small town where he drew his sizable pension and history-of-combat bonus.

An inauspicious ending to a historic career, but in the beginning, at the general's creation, when the Harvang had invaded in the south and were only miles outside of Central City, he was a promising savior. His artificial intelligence was considered a miracle of science, his construction the greatest engineering feat of the human race. And the standard by which all of this was judged was the fact that his face could make seven different expressions. Everyone agreed it was proof of the robot builder's exemplary art. Before the general, the most that had ever been attempted was three.

The first six of these expressions were slight variations on the theme of "determination." *Righteousness, Willfulness, Obstinacy, Eagerness,* and *Grimness 1* and *2* were the terms his makers had given them. The facial formation of the six had a lot to do with the area around the mouth, subtly different clenchings of the jaw, a straightness in the lips. The eyes were widened for all six, the nostrils flared. For *Grimness 2,* steam shot from his ears.

When he wasn't at war, he switched between *Righteousness* and *Obstinacy.* He'd lost *Eagerness* to a Harvang blade. It was at the Battle of Boolang Crater that the general was cut across the cheek, all the way through to his internal mechanism. After two days of leaking oil through the side of his face, the outer wound healed, but the wiring that caused the fourth expression had been irreparably severed.

There is speculation, based primarily on hearsay, that there was also an eighth expression, one that had not been built into him but that had manifested of its own accord through the self-advancement of the AI. Scientists claimed it highly unlikely, but Ms. Jeranda Blesh claimed she'd seen it. During a three-month leave, his only respite in the entire war, she'd lived with him in a chalet in the Grintun Mountains. A few years before she died of a Harvang venereal disease, she appeared on a late-night television talk show. She was pale and bloated, giddy with alcohol, but she divulged the secrets of her sex life with the general.

She mentioned the smooth chrome member with fins, the spicy oil, the relentless precision of his pistons. "Sometimes, right when things were about to explode," she said, "he'd make a face I'd never seen any other times. It wasn't a smile, but more like calm, a moment of peace. It wouldn't last long, though, 'cause then he'd lose control of everything, shoot a rocket blast out his backside and fly off me into the wall." The host of the show straightened his tie and said, "That's what I call 'drilling out a victory.'"

It was the seventh expression that was the general's secret, though. That certain configuration of his face reserved for combat. It was the reason he was not tricked out with guns or rockets. The general was an excellent killing machine, but how many could he kill alone? Only when he had armies ready to move at his will could he defeat the Harvang. The seventh expression was a look that enchanted his young troops and made them savage extensions of his determination. Outmanned, outgunned, outmaneuvered, outflanked, it didn't matter. One glance from him and they'd charge, beam rifles blazing, to their inevitable deaths. They'd line up in ranks before a battle and he'd review the troops, focusing that imposing stare on each soldier. It was rare that a young recruit would be unaffected by the seventh expression's powerful suggestion, understand that the mission at hand was sheer madness, and protest. The general had no time for deserters. With lightning quickness, he'd draw his beam pistol and burn a sudden hole in the complainant's forehead.

In an old government document, "A Report to the Committee on Oblique Renderings Z-333-678AR," released since the Harvang war, there was testimony from the general's creators to the fact that the seventh expression was a blend of the look of a hungry child, the gaze of an angry bull, and the stern countenance of God. The report records that the creators were questioned as to how they came up with the countenance of God, and their famous response was, "We used a mirror."

There was a single instance when the general employed the seventh expression after the war. It was only a few years ago, the day after it was announced that we would negotiate a treaty with the Harvang and attempt to live in peace and prosperity. He left his apartment and hobbled across the street to the coffee shop on the corner. Once there, he ordered a twenty-four-ounce Magjypt black, and sat in the corner pretending to read the newspaper. Eventually, a girl of sixteen approached him and asked if he was the robot general.

He saluted and said, "Yes, ma'am."

"We're reading about you in school," she said.

"Sit down, I'll tell you anything you need to know."

She pulled out a chair and sat at his table. Pushing her long brown hair behind her ears, she said, "What about all the killing?"

"Everybody wants to know about the killing," he said. "They should ask themselves."

"On the Steppes of Patience, how many Harvang did you, yourself, kill?"

"My internal calculator couldn't keep up with the slaughter. I'll just say 'Many.'"

"What was your favorite weapon?" she asked.

"I'm going to show it to you right now," he said, and his face began changing. He reached into his inside jacket pocket and brought forth a small-caliber ray gun wrapped in a white handkerchief. He laid the weapon on the table, the cloth draped over it. "Pick it up," he said.

He stared at her and she stared back, and after it was all over, she'd told friends that his blue pupils had begun to spin like pinwheels and his lips rippled. She lifted the gun.

"Put your finger on the trigger," he said.

She did.

"I want you to aim it right between my eyes and pull the trigger."

She took aim with both hands, stretching her arms out across the table.

"Now!" he yelled, and it startled her.

She set the gun down, pushed back her chair, and walked away.

It took the general two weeks before he could find someone he could convince to shoot him, and this was only after he offered payment. The seventh expression meant nothing to the man who'd promised to do the job. What he was after, he said, were the three shrunken Harvang heads the general had kept as souvenirs of certain battles. They'd sell for a fortune on the black market. After the deal was struck, the general asked the man, "Did you see that face I had on a little while ago?"

"I think I know what you mean," said the man.

"How would you describe it?" asked the general.

The man laughed. "I don't know. That face? You looked like you might have just crapped your pants. Look, your famous expressions, the pride of an era, no one cares about that stuff anymore. Bring me the heads."

The next night, the general hid the illegal shrunken heads beneath an old overcoat and arrived at the appointed hour at an abandoned pier on the south side of town. The wind was high and the water lapped at the edges of the planks. The man soon appeared. The general removed the string of heads from beneath his coat and threw them at the man's feet.

"I've brought a ray gun for you to use," said the general, and reached for the weapon in his jacket pocket.

"I brought my own," said the man and drew out a magnum-class beam pistol. He took careful aim, and the general noticed that the long barrel of the gun was centered on his own throat and not his forehead.

In the instant before the man pulled the trigger, the general's strategy centers realized that the plot was to sever his head and harvest his intelligence node—the Knot. He lunged, drill bits whirring. The man fired the weapon and the blast beam disintegrated three-quarters of the general's neck. The internal command had already been given, though, so with head flopping to the side, the robot general charged forward—one drill bit skewered the heart and the other plunged in at the left ear. The man screamed and dropped the gun, and then the general drilled until he himself dropped. When he hit the dock, what was left of his neck snapped and his head came free of his body. It rolled across the planks, perched at the edge for a moment, and then a gust of wind pushed it into the sea.

The general's body was salvaged and dismantled, its mechanical wizardry deconstructed. From the electric information stored in the ganglia of the robotic wiring system it was discovered that the general's initial directive was—To Serve the People. As for his head, it should be operational for another thousand years, its pupils spinning, its lips rippling without a moment of peace in the cold darkness beneath the waves. There, the Knot, no doubt out of a programmed impulse for self-preservation, is elaborating intricate dreams of victory.

A Note About "The Seventh Expression of the Robot General"

I'm still not exactly sure why the U.S. became embroiled in a war in Iraq. When I ask people what they think, most can't figure it out either (some of these friends were even there) and those who have an answer aren't very convincing. The mission was, at best, murky, and yet thousands of our soldiers were killed, wounded, and traumatized. Billions of dollars were squandered. And the citizens of our country who didn't have loved ones in harm's way basically slept through it. I wondered what it was that made the U.S. leap so readily and so blindly into the Grand Guignol of that affair. I know that something about the mystery of mindless war making for its own sake is at the mechanical heart of "The Robot General." Vigorous flag waving and statements like "If you're not for us, you're against us" led us down the garden path into a futile morass. As an American who has some knowledge of the history of America, I like to keep in mind a quote from William Samuel Johnson: "Patriotism is the last refuge of scoundrels."

86 Deathdick Road

I had on my good pants, the uncomfortable ones, and was in the car with Lynn. I knew we were going somewhere I didn't have any interest in going, because I was wearing a tie and jacket. She had on the lemon perfume I'd bought her two Christmases back.

"When was the last time we were out on a date?" she said. She wore a brightly colored shawl, paisley in gold and orange. It came to me that her hair, when I wasn't noticing, had gotten longer, the way she'd worn it back in college.

"Long time," I said, and made the turn on 206, heading south. Twilight was giving way to a cool spring night, and we drove with the windows open. "Who told you about this guy?" I asked.

"I saw Theda in the market Wednesday. She and Joe went to see him. She said the guy's amazing."

"The Man Who Knew Too Much?" I asked.

"No, he's the Smartest Man in the World."

"But, come on, fifty bucks to behold his brilliance . . ." I said and sighed through my nose.

"Don't be insipid," she said. "You can ask him anything and he knows the answer."

"I could stay home and get that on the Internet for free," I said.

Her smile went to a straight line. Before things could get rotten, I said, "How many questions do you get to ask?" It was all I could think of.

"Everybody gets one question," she said, staring through the windshield.

"What are you going to ask him?"

"Why you're such a turd," she said.

"What did Theda ask him? Two plus two?"

"She asked him if she was ever going to have a kid."

"It doesn't take the smartest man in the world to answer that one," I said. "She's fifty if she's a day."

"He told her, 'No,' but after he gave his answer, she said, he got up from his throne and walked over to her table. He shook hands with Joe, and then leaning over Theda, the smartest man in the world cupped her left breast with his right hand and whispered, 'Know this.' She said she felt a spark inside her that went straight to her brain and exploded—that's what she said. She started crying, the audience clapped, the guy returned to his throne and took the next question."

"*Know what?*" I asked.

"I don't know," said Lynn and laughed.

We drove on, listening to the radio, neither of us saying much except for me wondering aloud if there was going to be any booze involved.

Lynn gave a curt "No," and then said, "Okay, you have to slow down here. We have to look for a dirt road, going into the trees up on the left."

"What's the address?" I asked, easing down on the brake.

She lifted a piece of paper off her lap and unfolded it quickly. Turning on the overhead light, she read, "Eighty-six Deathdick Road."

Suddenly I was almost past the entrance in the trees. I slammed on the brakes. There was no other traffic behind us, so I backed up a little and made the turn.

"Okay, look for Deathdick," she said.

"Are you kidding? Deathdick?" I said. I didn't see any streets, just the dirt road ahead, winding through the woods, lit by my headlights.

"The place is called Mullions," she said.

I looked over at Lynn, and her hair was glowing. When I looked back at the road, we were driving on asphalt through a posh suburban neighborhood of McMansions and landscaped lawns. Up ahead, I saw a lot of cars parked along the street on both sides.

"I guess that's it," I said.

"But which house?" asked Lynn.

I slowed way down and crept to the end of the car line on the right-hand curb. We got out and I joined her on the sidewalk. Lynn pointed to the front lawn two doors down, at a bright tube of violet neon twisted into the name MULLIONS.

"Is this place legal?" I asked.

"I guess so," she said.

We were met at the front door by a thin woman on the down side of sixty. She wasn't fooling anyone with the surgical cinching of her face. "Millions to Mullions," she said. "I'm Jenny. I hope you're ready for some answers tonight." She flashed us a smile of giant teeth and held out her hand, palm up.

Lynn dug through her purse and retrieved our fifty. Once

Jenny had it in her hand, she said, "Ask well," and then stepped aside as we passed into the living room.

Once we were out of earshot, Lynn said, "What was up with her face?"

"It's better to ask well than look well," I said.

The living room was packed, people milling around, talking, sitting on the gold-upholstered furniture. A huge bad painting of a garden with a waterfall and a McMansion in the background hung in an ornate frame in the center of the wall, above the couch. The carpet was also gold, and there was a small chandelier above. I looked around, and right off the bat, I spotted some of my neighbors from town.

I pointed out Dornsberry to Lynn and she rolled her eyes and whispered, "Not that douche bag." I'd never seen this guy at a party in town when he wasn't lecturing some poor bastard on the finer points of golf. A holy-rolling, cigar-smoking runt. His presence was bad enough, but off to the left of us was Mrs. Krull, laying out for some old guy on the verge of either sleep or death one of her long bummer stories. When her one-legged aunt had succumbed to cancer of the vagina, she'd called and kept me on the phone for an hour with the excruciating details. I'd heard she had a pair of gray parrots on perches in her dining room that crapped willy-nilly and constantly repeated the phrase "Just kill me" in her husband's voice.

Lynn saw I'd noticed Krull, and she said, "Sorry."

"This smartest man better be really smart," I said. Then a woman walked by carrying a small plate with hors d'oeuvres on it. I thought I caught a glimpse of pigs in a blanket. "Eats," I said.

"If they have anything to drink besides soda, bring me a glass," said Lynn, and I was off, wending my way through the

crowd, happy to have a purpose. On the way, not really knowing where I was going, I spotted a good-looking young woman
with a pile of blond hair, holding a plate with water chestnuts
wrapped in bacon. "Not bad," I thought, and hoped there'd be
spareribs or maybe shrimp. I got jostled by the crowd, excus-
ing myself a dozen times for every few feet traveled. It was the
sight of someone holding a beer that gave me the fortitude to
continue.

Within that sea of bodies it got really hot and I started to
sweat. The deep rumble of conversation washed over me from
all directions, snatches of dialogue differentiating themselves
for a moment and then melting back into the general hubbub.
"I told her, don't try it, bitch." "Peter did so well on the SATs
they had to invent a new score for him." "The dog is old, it craps
on the rug every day now." "It's supposed to snow later." When
it felt as if I'd been on my pigs-in-a-blanket search for a half
hour, I finally went up to a woman I vaguely recognized from
the grocery store in town where she was a cashier.

"Hi, do you know where the food is?" I asked.

She shook her head, and when she did, right on the spot, she
turned into Dornsberry. He gave me a look of contempt. "We're
all Christians here," he said and took a long swig of his beer.
"What religion are you?"

"Where'd you get the beer?" I asked.

"You've been asked a question," he said and pushed his
glasses up the bridge of his nose with the back of his beer hand.

"I'm a product of the age of reason," I said. "Where's the food?"

He shook his head as if in disgust and pointed behind me.
I turned around, the crowd parted, and there was a long table
with bowls and plastic cups and a crystal punch bowl half
filled with a yellow liquid. As I walked away from him, I heard

Dornsberry hurl the insult, "Clown," at me. Any other time I might have pounded his face in, but instead I just laughed it off.

The food table, in the state I found it, held a bowl with three pretzels in it and five other bowls of a tan dip that had crusted dark brown at the edges. A live fly buzzed in the middle of one bowl, unable to free itself.

"That'll be a fossil someday," said a voice behind me.

I turned to see a thin man in a black tuxedo. He had a wave of slick dark hair in front; big, clunky, black-framed glasses; and a thinly trimmed mustache.

"Pretty appetizing, huh?" I said to him.

"Allow me to introduce myself," he said. "I'm the smartest man in the world."

I shook his hand and told him my name. "If you're the smartest man in the world," I said, "how'd you wind up here?"

He gave a wry smile and told me, "I only answer questions for money."

I felt in my pants pockets for a crumpled bill. Taking it out and flattening it for him, I said, "Five bucks if you can tell me where I can get a beer."

"Five won't do it," he said. Now he had on a top hat and a cape and looked like Mandrake the Magician with glasses. "But five will get you half an answer."

I handed him the bill. "I'll take it," I said.

"You've got to go through the kitchen, that way," he said and pointed. "Once you're there, go out the side door onto the patio. That's all I can afford to tell you."

"A steep price for some pretty thin shit," I said to him and couldn't believe I was getting belligerent with the smartest man in the world. There was something exhilarating about it.

"When your wife asks her question later," he said, "after I

answer it, I'm going to kiss her and slip her the tongue so deeply I'll taste her panties. She'll see God, my friend." He tipped back his top hat and laughed arrogantly.

I picked up a crusted bowl of dip. "Touch my wife and you'll be the deadest man in the world," I said. Then I threw the bowl at him. He ducked at the last second, and the bowl flew into the face of a heavyset older woman in a sequined gown. Tan goo dripped from her jowls and the bowl hit the wooden floor and shattered. For a moment, I wondered where the carpet had gone. The woman I'd hit had been standing with an aged gentleman wearing a military uniform and sporting ridiculously thick muttonchop sideburns. "Preposterous," he shouted and his monocle fell from his eye. He reached for the sword he had in a scabbard at his side. Meanwhile the smartest man in the world had lived up to his name for once and had split. I didn't see him anywhere. I followed his lead and merged into the crowd, moving fast, sweating profusely.

In the kitchen, there was a fire-eater. He was performing in the corner by the range. People had gathered around to watch and it was impossible to get through to the patio door, which I could glimpse occasionally between heads in the crowd. I had to wait for him to finish his act and hope the logjam broke up.

I watched him. He had two little torches that he held with the middle finger of his right hand. He'd pour lighter fluid on them and then turn on the range and light them off the burner. He had a small blond ponytail and a beat-up face, broken nose, and scar tissue around the eyes. He was a lackluster showman. His approach was to say, "I'm gonna eat fire now," in a low, placid voice, and then he ate it.

After you've seen someone eat fire once, there's not much else to it. I watched him eat fire five times, and by the fourth time, even though nobody left, nobody was clapping, either. I had cold beer on my mind, so, after the fifth time, I said in a loud voice, "All right, let's get on with it." To my surprise, people started leaving the kitchen. The fire-eater tried to see who'd said it, but I kept my gaze down and pushed gently forward.

I found the cooler of beer out on the patio. It was filled with ice and Rolling Rock. I took one and sat down at a glass-topped table, on a wrought-iron chair with arms my fat ass barely fit between. I was alone out there in the dark. The night was cool but pleasant, and I could feel the sweat drying. Someone had left behind a pack of cigarettes, Lucky Strikes (I didn't know they still made them), and a lighter. That beer tasted like heaven, and the cig wasn't far behind. I took out my cell phone and dialed Lynn.

It rang and rang, and then she answered. "Where are you?" she said.

I told her, "I'm out on the patio, having a beer."

"The show's going to start any minute," she said. "I got us a table."

"You can't believe how big the place is," I said. "How many people are here. It took me forever to get to the food table."

"Bring me a beer," she said.

"Will do. And listen, if I don't get back in time and the smartest man in the world answers your question, don't let him touch you." There was silence from the other end of the line. I said her name a couple of times, but it was clear that either we'd been cut off or she'd thought we were through and hung up.

I put the cigarettes and lighter in one jacket pocket, and then took another beer and put that in my other jacket pocket. I put my smoke out in a planter at the edge of the patio and then turned to head back in. As I moved toward the house, I saw the smartest man in the world's face at the window of the door. He smiled at me and waved before looking down, as if he was going to open it and come out. An instant later he was gone. I tried the doorknob and realized that what he'd done was lock it. When I knocked on the door, I looked inside and saw the kitchen was completely empty.

I heard a window opening above me on the second floor. I backed onto the patio and looked up. The smartest man in the world poked his head out. He was again wearing his top hat. "Perhaps like in Chaucer's 'Miller's Tale' you can climb up here and kiss my hairy ass," he said.

"Let me in," I said.

"There's a reason they call me the smartest man in the world," he said. "The show starts in ten minutes."

"I'm going to call the cops," I told him.

"Dornsberry says you're a pussy," said the smartest man.

"I'll kill you both," I shouted.

"No you won't. Now hurry around front and pay again to be let in. You might catch me answering your wife's question." I heard Dornsberry's laughter in the background. The window shut with a bang.

I took out my cell phone, but when I flipped it open it was dead. "Shit," I said, and headed for the edge of the patio. Only then did I notice that the side of the house butted up against the edge of a forest. In the moonlight I could make out tall pine trees in both directions. There was a path that went either around the back of the place through the trees or, in the other direction, to the front of the house. I was just about to head for the front when I realized that had been the smartest man's advice. What were the chances he was going to tell me the best way to go? I stepped onto the path and headed toward the back.

There were stretches of perfect night where the pines blocked the moon completely.

I walked fast for a ways, but soon I was out of breath and my Achilles tendon was aching, so I slowed down. Just then I noticed something like a lectern, on the side of the path. I stepped over to it. It was a chest-high stand with a plaque on top situated at an angle. There was something written on it. I took out the lighter, flicked it, and quickly read the plaque. It said: BEWARE OF OWLS! MULLIONS IS NOT RESPONSIBLE FOR ANY DAMAGES OR DEATHS CAUSED BY OWLS.

I flicked the lighter again, and this time noticed that beneath the writing there was an etching of a large owl in midflight, grasping in its talons the severed head of Jenny, the Mullions hostess. "Killer owls?" I said aloud. A stiff breeze blew the flame out and it felt more like autumn than spring. I noticed the path was strewn with fallen leaves. "That's ridiculous," I said, and started walking again. Two minutes later, I wrapped my hand around the neck of the beer bottle in my pocket and took it out to use as a club.

"Fuck those owls," I told myself, "I have to get back to Lynn." I put on as much steam as I could manage, and with almost every step, the tendon in my left heel got worse. "She'll never let him touch her," I said to myself. "If he tries, she'll punch him in the face and break his glasses." I hobbled a few more yards, and then thought, "Or will she?"

That's when I happened to look up and notice the pairs of yellow eyes trimming the trees like dull Christmas lights. They were everywhere. My knees went weak and my heart began to pound so hard I could hear it in my right ear. I desperately wanted to run but knew I wouldn't get far. Instead, I crept forward, trembling, praying they hadn't noticed me and wouldn't.

In whispers, like a novena, I recited the theme song to the afternoon television cartoon of my youth, "The Eighth Man."

I got only as far as, "The F.B.I. is helpless. It's twenty stories tall," when a shrill screech tore through the dark. An owl's flight is silent, but I heard the beating of their wings in my mind as they swooped after me. The breeze picked up and I pushed against it, trying to run, waving the beer bottle over my head and ducking. It was like running through water. I felt their talons at my back and what hair I have. Feathers whipped my cheeks. I tried to scream, but it came forth a long, breathy fart.

Just when I thought I was finished, I collided with another person on the path, and for some reason the owls miraculously retreated. I lit the lighter to see who it was, and only when I saw it was Mrs. Krull did I realize she'd been talking the whole time. There was a glassy, vacant stare to her froggy eyes. Her lips were moving and she was in the midst of the story of her one-legged aunt. I gathered my wits, walking alongside her, and said, "Mrs. Krull, what are you doing out here?" She moved steadily forward, staring straight ahead, as if in a trance. All the time the words spilled out of her.

It came to me not as a thought but as a feeling that it was precisely her grim tale that kept the owls at bay. They were above us and to the sides everywhere, but they didn't stir from their perches. Occasionally one would hoot in the distance, a feather would fall, but they wouldn't attack. When she was finishing up the story of her aunt's demise, for the first time in my life, I hoped she had another one ready.

There was a mere half-a-breath pause before the next pathetic tale was born. She spoke about a couple she knew from her old neighborhood. Nice people. They had three kids. They all went on a vacation in upstate New York. They drove all day and into the night. Here, she went into the details of the family, and time seemed to pass in a whirl before I again picked up the thread of the story with the father pulling over on the side of the road to take a piss. They were on the interstate. He got out, told his wife he'd be right back, and then, mounting a small hill, disappeared over the top.

"Some time passed," said Mrs. Krull. "The wife started wondering, how long will my husband piss for? Finally, after almost twenty minutes, she told the kids she'd be right back and to stay in the car. She went to look for her husband. Up the hill she went in the dark. The kids were alone in the car and probably eventually got scared when their mother didn't return."

I noticed that all around us, as Mrs. Krull ground out her story with relentless persistence, the owls were keeling off their branches and falling to the forest floor. I knew in my heart that it was my neighbor's tragic droning that rendered them insensate. "Right over the rise of that small hill, unbeknownst to him and her, was the edge of a cliff. Both hadn't seen the edge in the dark and had fallen two hundred feet to their deaths," she said.

The owls fell like pillows, hit the ground with muffled thuds. Every now and then there was a weak squawk. "Then the kids," said Mrs. Krull, "one after the other. First the oldest, a boy, Kenneth, who was in my Robert's grade (he was a mean-spirited kid), and then the middle one, the sister, she was adorable. They each went looking in their turn and each fell to their death. They probably screamed in terror but no one heard them. Maybe they landed on their parents, but it still killed them."

Mrs. Krull's story was making even me dizzy. It appeared that she had subdued the owls, so I worked up the courage to escape her. "Then the last child, little Freddie, I have a photo of him in shorts and a collar shirt with a small bow tie. I could just bite those cheeks. He went next up the hill in the dark. But he was my little genius and figured out what had happened. He ran to get help."

"Well, at least little Freddie made it," I said, and veered away from Mrs. Krull, right off the path and directly into the trees. At the moment, I didn't care where I was going. I stumbled in a rut between two trees, still light headed. The last thing I heard Mrs. Krull say as I groped blindly through the underbrush was, "He ran out onto the highway to flag down a car, and the driver didn't see him till it was too late."

I tramped unsteadily forward, kicking downed owl carcasses, like empty birthday piñatas, out of my way. Mrs. Krull's sad bullshit had sucked out their life. It struck me that the potential of her drivel was like a terrible superpower, and I had a brief vision of her walking through the sky on a blue day, dressed in white robes, with a halo, a six-foot uprooted sunflower chained to her ankle, gliding along behind her.

It was a fear-soaked hour or more, submerged in the dark, skinning my shins, taking branches to the face, before I returned to the patio. Sitting in the wrought-iron chair at the table, I popped the beer I'd been carrying and lit up a smoke. I noticed that the house was perfectly silent and dark.

"I missed the whole goddamn thing," I thought. "I never got to ask my question, Lynn has long been tongue-kissed by the smartest man in the world and seen God, and I'm a castaway in Owl Forest. What the fuck?"

After finishing the cigarette and half the beer, I got up and checked the kitchen door. To my surprise and elation, it was unlocked. I opened it and stepped into the silence of the dark house. Without even closing the door behind me, I was off on a beeline for the front door. Who knows how long it took to cross the kitchen, to reach the entrance to the living room, which, itself, was vast. Only when passing the occasional window did the moonlight allow me to see where I was going. Otherwise, I slammed against furniture and at one point might have tripped over a body.

My tendon was acting up badly, so I stopped after a long while by one of the windows and had another smoke. While I rested, I looked outside and saw that it was snowing. As soon as I saw the snow, I heard the wind howl. "Great," I said. I put the cigarette out on the windowsill and left it there. No more than a dozen limping steps later, I collided with the edge of the food table and got a thrill to know I was making progress. A little ways after that I saw small intermittent bursts of flame in the distance. That flame was my lighthouse. For some reason I believed it would bring me to the front door and my escape. So entranced was I with the rhythmic fire that grew ever more prominent with each painful step that I was almost upon the source of the phenomenon before I realized what was causing it. The scene suddenly materialized out of the dark, no more than six feet in front of me.

There was Jenny, completely naked, her sagging yet emaciated body perched in the throne of the smartest man in the world with her legs spread and hooked over its wooden arms. Kneeling in front of her was the fire-eater with his head between her legs, only this time it wasn't fire he was eating. I watched as Jenny glowed from inside like a jack-o'-lantern, saw the silhouettes of her ribs and spine and heart. Then she gave a slight moan, opened her mouth, and a burst of flame shot out. I took a step back and stared in amazement.

I was afraid they'd see me there, but I was also afraid to move. Finally—I don't know what possessed me, it was like some kind of momentary insanity—I yelled, "I see you." The fire-eater never even turned around but kept working like he was nonunion. Jenny lifted herself a little and turned to look at me. She reached up to her chin, and then grabbing it, literally pulled her face off like it was a rubber mask. The jaws of her skull head creaked open. There came a moan and then she shot a long burst of fire at me. I ran, but felt the sting of her flaming tongue on my left earlobe.

The next thing I knew, I was standing out on the front lawn. It was freezing and the snow was driving down. I passed the neon Mullions sign, no longer lit, on my way to the street. Heading in the direction Lynn and I had initially come, I shivered, huddled inside my suit jacket, the collar flipped up and doing nothing for me. I had no idea where I was or how to get home, and there was a considerable chance I might freeze to death.

In my desperation I was going to give my phone one more try, and when I looked down, I saw Lynn's shawl half covered in the drifting snow. I picked it up and put it to my face. On a sunny Halloween thirty-two years ago, we took a bottle of tequila and climbed a mountain. At the top there was a rundown shack. Inside there was a metal bed frame, a three-legged chair with a frayed wicker seat fallen in the corner, and a warped desk with a rash of pale fungus. Dead leaves and brittle news pages littered the floor. The door hung by one hinge; there was broken glass beneath the single window. In a drawer of the desk, Lynn found a mildewed dictionary and in it a letter from 1932. The envelope was marked RETURN TO SENDER. The closing read: *Love you forever.*

A car came slowly down the road toward me and when it got

close, its headlights flicked on and off. It drew up next to me, a late-model Mercedes. The window went down, a cloud of cigar smoke escaped, and I saw it was Dornsberry. "Get in," he said. "The owls are waking up." For just a second, I was going to tell him to fuck off, but the promise of owls, not to mention the bitter cold, humbled me. I hobbled around to the passenger side and got in.

"Are you going to town?" I asked him.

"Yeah, I'll drop you at your place."

The car was so warm and it felt great to get off my feet. "I ran into the owls earlier," I said.

Dornsberry's cigar had vanished. Both of his black-gloved hands were on the leather steering wheel. He seemed affable, like some whole different Dornsberry I'd never met. "I told Jenny," he said, "you gotta poison those fucking owls. What a liability. I told her, what eats owls? Get some of that. Like weasels or something. Maybe a wolf . . . whatever."

"They seem put off by Mrs. Krull," I said.

"Well, nobody said they were stupid," said Dornsberry. "They're just mean as hell. I was back in the forest tonight, scared out of my wits they'd catch me. I've been bitten by those things before. Luckily, for some reason, every one of the little bastards was knocked out. I stole two of their eggs." He reached into his pocket with his right hand and brought out a large brown egg. "Take this one," he said.

What the hell, I took it and put it in my pocket. "Thanks," I said.

"Each time it lays, every she-owl drops two eggs, no more no less. It is said that if you place one of these eggs in the hand of a sleeping woman, she will tell you only the truth. Have her hold the other, though, and she will tell only lies."

"Where'd you hear that?" I asked.

"The smartest man in the world told me," he said.

Just his name set me off. I had a thing or two to say to Dornsberry about the smartest man, but before I could launch into it, he said, "Here's your place."

I looked out the window and saw my house, a snowdrift going halfway up the front steps. The sight of it almost brought tears to my eyes. I opened the door and got out. "Thanks," I called back, and shut the door. I took a single step, then I heard the passenger window slide down. Turning to see what was up, I caught a glimpse of Dornsberry flipping me the bird. "You're such a pussy," he said, revved the engine, and tried to peel out in the snow. The car shot off down the street sideways on the ice, righted itself for a moment, and then crashed into the light pole on the corner.

The lights were out in our bedroom. Lynn was in bed asleep. She lay on her side, her hair not so long anymore, right arm sticking out from beneath the covers. With the greatest care I eased down on the edge of the mattress next to her. I sat for a time with my eyes closed and then carefully placed the owl egg in her right hand.

"Did you ask the smartest man in the world your question?" I whispered.

Perhaps half a minute passed before she murmured, "Yes."

"Did he answer it?" I asked.

"Yes," she finally said.

"Did he kiss you?"

"Yes."

"What was it like?"

"His tongue was like four hot dogs."

"Did you see God?"

"No, I saw you, stumbling through the dark forest, lost."

"What was your question?" I asked.

"If you still loved me."

"And what was his answer?"

"He said his answer had two parts. The first part was yes, and for the second part he got off his throne and kissed me."

I almost didn't ask it, but finally I said, "Are you in love with the smartest man in the world?"

"Yes," she said.

I took the egg out of her hand and got up. For a long time, I stood by the bedroom window, staring into the dark at the falling snow, listening to the screech of the wind. "After all these years," I said, and then spotted, out on the street in front of the house, a figure trudging by. It was too dark for me to make out the form, but when the egg shattered in my hand, I knew it must be Mrs. Krull. As the yolk dripped through my fingers, I vowed to become the smartest man in the world.

A Note About "86 Deathdick Road"

A lot of writers disparage suburbia as a bland, numbing wasteland, but oh the drama that lurks there, the surreal antics and machinations. This story was spurred by a New Year's Eve party I reluctantly agreed to attend once. After I arrived, I found out that there would be no alcohol served and that the order of the night was card games. There was a particularly horrid giant painting of the McMansion we were actually in, hanging over a gold couch covered in protective plastic. The only thing I knew about the people who owned the place was that the husband had recently been caught cheating on his wife of twenty-four years, and to make amends for his indiscretion he bought his family an in-ground swimming pool with a gigantic, twisting slide. Add to that germ of suburban fever an unaccountable interest of mine at the time in owls. I bought this CD of North American owl calls, put it on my portable player, and broadcast it out in the Pine Barrens. A lot of people warned me that the owls would attack me if I kept doing it, as they are very territorial. They were right, so I stopped even though I felt that I was on the verge of a real breakthrough in communicating with them. This story was published by editor Nick Gevers in the PS Publishing anthology *Book of Dreams*. I am proud to say that the wonderfully weird J. K. Potter cover art pertains to my story.

After Moreau

I, Hippopotamus Man, can say without question that Moreau was a total asshole. Wells at least got that part right, but the rest of the story he told all wrong. He makes it seem like the Doctor was all about trying to turn beasts into humans. The writer must have heard about it thirdhand from some guy who knew a guy who knew something about the guy who escaped the island by raft. In fact, we were people first, before we were kidnapped and brought to the island.

I was living in a little town, Daysue City, on the coast in California. Sleepy doesn't half describe it. I owned the local hardware store, had a wife and two kids. One night I took my dog for a walk down by the sea, and as we passed along the trail through the woods, I was jumped from behind and hit on the head. I woke in a cage in the hold of a ship.

People from all over the place wound up on the island. Dog Girl was originally from the Bronx, Monkey Man Number Two was from Miami, and they snatched Bird Boy, in broad daylight, from a public beach in North Carolina. We all went through Moreau's horrifying course of injections together. The stuff was an angry wasp in the vein, and bloated me with putrid gases, made my brain itch unbearably. Still, I can't say I suffered more than the others. Forget House of Pain, it was more like a city block. When you wake from a deep, feverish sleep and find your mouth has become a beak, your hand a talon, it's terrifying. A scream comes forth as a bleat, a roar, a chirp. You can't conceive of it because it's not make-believe.

Go ahead, pet my snout, but watch the tusks. No one wants the impossible. What human part of us remained didn't want it, either. It was a rough transition, coming to terms with the animal, but we helped each other. After we had time to settle into our hides, so to speak, there were some good times in the jungle. Moreau could only jab so many needles in your ass in a week, so the rest of the time we roamed the island. There was a lot of fucking too. I'll never forget the sight of Caribou Woman and Skunk Man going at it on the beach, beneath the bright island sun. The only way I can describe it is by using a quote I remember from my school days, from Coleridge about metaphor, "the reconciliation of opposites." I know, it means nothing to you.

We all talked a lot and for some reason continued to understand each other. Everybody was pretty reasonable about getting along, and some of the smarter ones like Fish Guy helped to develop a general philosophy for the community of survivors. "The Seven Precepts" are simple and make perfect sense. I'll list them, but before I do I want to point something out. Keep in mind what it states in the list below and then compare that to the dark, twisted version that appears in Laughton's film version of the Wells novel *Island of Lost Souls*. Monkey Man Number One and a couple of the others took the boat to Frisco, and by dark of night robbed a Macy's. One of the things they brought back was a projector and an eight-millimeter version of the flick. I believe it's Bela Lugosi who plays Speaker of the Law. I'll refrain from saying "hambone" for the sake of Pig Lady's feelings. That performance is an insult to the truth, but, on the other hand, Laughton, himself, was so much Moreau it startled us to see the film. Here are the real Seven Precepts, the list of how we live:

1. Trust Don't Trust
2. Sleep Don't Sleep
3. Breathe Don't Breathe
4. Laugh Don't Laugh
5. Weep Don't Weep
6. Eat Don't Eat
7. Fuck Whenever You Want

You see what I mean? Animal clarity, clean and sharp, like an owl's gaze. Anyway, here we are, after Moreau. We've got the island to ourselves. There's plenty to eat—all the animals that resided naturally and the exotic beasts Moreau brought in for the transmission of somatic essence—the raw ingredients to make us them. A good number of the latter escaped the fire, took to the jungle, and reproduced. There are herds of suburban house cats that have wiped out the natural ostrich population and herds of water oxen that aren't indigenous.

Actually, there's also a tiger that roams the lower slopes of the island's one mountain. Ocelot Boy thought he could communicate with the tiger. He tracked the cat to its lair in a cave in the side of the mountain, and sat outside the entrance exchanging growls and snarls with the beast until the sun went down. Then the tiger killed and ate him. The tiger roared that night and the sound of its voice echoed down the mountain slope. Panther Woman, who lay with me in my wallow, trembled and whispered that the tiger was laughing.

She also told me about how back in the days of the Doctor, when her tail and whiskers were still developing, she'd be brought naked to his kitchen and made to kneel and lap from a bowl of milk while Moreau, sitting in a chair with his pants around his ankles, boots still on, petted his knobby member. I asked Panther Woman why she thought he did it. She said, "He was so smart, he was stupid. I mean, what was he going for? People turning into animals partway? What kind of life goal is that? A big jerk-off." We laughed, lying there in the moonlight.

Where was I? I had to learn to love the water, but otherwise things weren't bad. I had friends to talk to, and we survived because we stuck together, we shared, we sacrificed for the common good. Do I have to explain? Of course I do, but I'm not going to. I can't remember where this was all headed. I had a point to make here. What I can tell you right now is that Rooster Man went down today. He came to see me in the big river. I was bobbing in the flow with my real hippo friends when I noticed Rooster calling me from the bank. He was flapping a wing and his comb was moving in the breeze. Right behind him, he obviously had no idea, was a gigantic alligator. I could have called a warning to him, but I knew it was too late. Instead I just waved good-bye. He squawked bloody murder, and I finally dove under when I heard the crunch of his beak.

Tomorrow I've got tea with the Boar family. I ran into old man Boar and he invited me and Panther Woman over to their cave. The Boars are a strange group. They all still wear human clothes—the ones that can do anyway. Old man Boar wears Moreau's white suit and his Panama hat. It doesn't seem to faze him in the least that there's a big shit stain on the back of the pants. I've shared the Doctor's old cigars with Boar. He blows smoke like the boat's funnel and talks a crazy politics not of this world. I just nod and say yes to him, because he puts honey in his tea. Panther and I crave honey.

The other day, when he offered the invitation, Boar told me under his breath that Giraffe Man was engaged in continuing experiments with Moreau's formulas and techniques. He said the situation was dire, like a coconut with legs. I had no idea what he meant. I asked around, and a couple of the beast people told me it was true. Giraffe couldn't leave well enough alone. He was injecting himself. Then a couple days after I confirmed old Boar's claim, I heard they found Giraffe Man, a bubbling brown mass of putrescence on the floor of what remained of the old lab.

We gathered at the site and Fish Guy shoveled up Giraffe's remains and buried them in the garden out back. Monkey Man Number Two played a requiem on the unburned half of the piano and Squirrel Girl, gray with age, read a poem that was a story of a tree that would grow in the spot Giraffe was buried and bear fruit that would allow us all to achieve complete animality. Everybody knew it would never happen, but we all wished it would.

When I loll in the big river, I think about the cosmos as if it's a big river of stars. I eat fish and leaves and roots. Weasel Woman says it's a healthy diet, and I guess it is. How would she know, though, really? As long as I stay with the herd of real hippos, I'm safe from the alligators. There have been close calls, believe me. When standing on land in the hot sun, sometimes I bleed from all my pores to cool my hide. Panther Woman has admitted this aspect of my nature disgusts her. To me she is beautiful in every way. The fur . . . you can't imagine. She's a hot furry number, and she's gotten over her fear of water. I'm telling you, we do it in the river, with the stars watching, and it's a smooth animal.

If you find this message in this bottle, don't come looking for us. It would be pointless. I can't even remember what possessed me to write in the first place. You should see how pathetic it is to write with a hippo paw. My reason for writing is probably the same unknown thing that made Moreau want to turn people into beasts. Straight-up human madness. No animal would do either.

Monkey Man Numbers One and Two are trying to talk some of the others into going back to civilization to stay. They approached me and I asked them, "Why would I want to live the rest of my life as a sideshow freak?"

Number Two said, "You know, eventually Panther Woman is going to turn on you. She'll eat your heart for breakfast."

"Tell me something I don't know," I said. Till then, it's roots and leaves, fucking in the wallow, and bobbing in the flow, dreaming of the cosmos. Infrequently, there's an uncertain memory of the family I left behind in the old life, but the river's current mercifully whisks that vague impression of pale faces to the sea.

That should have been the end of the message, but I forgot to tell you something. This is important. We ate Moreau. That's right. He screamed like the bird of paradise when we took him down. I don't eat meat, but even I had a small toe. Sweet flesh for a bitter man. Mouse Person insisted on eating the brain, and no one cared to fight him for it. The only thing is, he got haunted inside from it. When we listened in his big ears, we heard voices. He kept telling us he was the Devil. At first we laughed, but he kept it up too long. A couple of us got together one night and pushed him off the sea cliff. The next day and for months after, we searched the shore for his body, but never found it. Monkey Man Number One sniffs the air and swears the half-rodent is still alive on the island. We've found droppings.

A Note About "After Moreau"

Of all the film versions of the H. G. Wells novel *The Island of Dr. Moreau*, I've always been partial to the 1932 *Island of Lost Souls*, directed by Erle C. Kenton and starring the amazing Charles Laughton as the good doctor himself. The film has a great script, written by Philip Wylie, a well-known science fiction writer (whose 1930 novel, *Gladiator*, would become one of the main inspirations for the character of Superman), and Waldemar Young (grandson of Brigham Young), who wrote at least two brilliant scripts that I know of, *The Unknown* and *London After Midnight*, for Tod Browning of *Freaks* fame. Bela Lugosi shows up in *Island of Lost Souls* as Speaker of the Law, one of Moreau's genetic anomalies, but the real attraction in that flick is Laughton, who plays the doctor like a mix of W. C. Fields and Sydney Greenstreet at his most menacing. There's a scene where Moreau is explaining his work to the shipwrecked hero, and while speaking, lies slowly back onto a nearby hospital gurney, folds his hands, and crosses his legs. It's just so unexpected and yet so revealing of the character. I wrote my Moreau story as an homage to Laughton's portrayal. Of course, it veers sharply away from the Wells version, but that's what happens when you begin fiddling with the genetics of a fiction. Nick Mamatas, when he was fiction editor at *Clarkesworld*, pulled this one out of the slush pile and, with a few key edits, sent it slouching into print.

The Hag's Peak Affair

Don't ask me how I know this. If I told you, it would cost me my life. Let's just say I know certain people and they've told me certain things. These are guys who, for fun, hold their palms over an open flame until the skin blisters—Manchurian candidates with minds of their own. They've told so many lies in their lives that they've run out and can now tell only the truth.

In the hidden place where they keep John F. Kennedy's "missing" brain, an underground warren of a hundred miles of crisscrossing tunnels and cavernous storerooms, there exists an eight-foot Plexiglas tube filled with chemically treated water the color of piss. Floating in it midway between top and bottom is a gray, five-and-a-half-foot misshapen body. The figure appears to have human attributes, but the face is erupted into a moonscape of huge cysts, and there are smaller bumps and warts everywhere on the skin. The staring eyes are bright orange; the hands and feet webbed and clawed with points of bone, not nail. It's a female, with what appear to be human sex organs. The posture of the body is slightly bent and twisted at the hips. The left shoulder carries a huge upheaval of flesh. Her hair is sparse and green—long strands of gauzy seaweed. And then there are the fins on her wrists, by her ears, on her back like small wings, and a ridge of short spikes projecting from her vertebrae, gill slits on the neck just beneath the jawbone. A brass plaque affixed to the metal base of her container holds a twelve-digit number that's her official title, but one of the MPs who guards the tunnels, a man of a poetic frame of mind and plenty of time to daydream, calls her Sirena, and that's how she's generally referred to among those who patrol that subterranean hive of secrets.

The paperwork on this living curio, for the thing is not dead, but kept in a drug-induced coma, fills an entire wall of filing cabinets in the facility's vast document repository. The drawers are crammed with the results of a million tests, reams of learned commentary, and the testimony of those who captured the creature. Stacked atop as high as the rocky ceiling sits a paper trail of what was and should be done in the name of obliterating all knowledge of her. Besides the president and the joint chiefs, few are privy to this information. It would take an intelligent person reading for a solid decade to finally get somewhere near the heart of the gray enigma, but these certain people I know have skills that allow them to always strike first at the heart.

Sometime during the month of January 1975, while some of my friends' friends were being investigated due to the furor over Watergate, a small, clandestine band of hand-picked, highly trained government operatives was sent to a remote mountain location in northern New York state near the Canadian border. Atop that mountain, referred to as Hag's Peak in the official documents, there existed an abandoned development of houses that had originally been constructed a decade earlier as living quarters for the families of those workers who toiled at a highly classified research facility some fifty miles due south.

The place, known as Chanticleer, was like a suburban community from Long Island—half-acre yards with manicured front lawns and split-level houses, a school, a playground, a post office, a movie theater, a small village of stores—physically torn up by the roots and transported to a vast meadow bordered by woods on the upper southern face of a mountain. At the center there was a helicopter pad big enough to accommodate three birds at once, transportation for the scientists' commute to the lab four times a week. The entirety of Chanticleer was surrounded by a fifteen-foot brick wall with a band of electrified razor wire running along its top. It was said that to have been there on a normal day, though, after the helicopters had departed, was to walk the streets of some upper-middle-class American neighborhood, dogs barking, the sound of a lawn mower, kids playing.

The whole thing was a tidy little covert setup built and funded by money surreptitiously funneled out of the Social Security pension fund. The research scientists, working on a project that some said had to do with time travel and others have told me was definitely a particle-beam weapon, simply knew too much. As an alternative to shooting them at the end of every workday, Chanticleer was conceived of and built as a way to accommodate decent lives for them and their families as they devoted their years to furthering the deadly power of those who run those who run the government.

All well and good but for one tiny worm in the apple. In an effort to avoid any bill of sale and ensure the secret nature of the development, the land it was built on was purchased from a conglomerate friendly to those in power. You may have heard of it, National Product Inc. As it's said in the business world, "NPI grows the food you eat, owns the trucks that move it, makes the refrigerator you store it in, the stove you cook it on, the fork you eat it with, the plate you eat it from, and the porcelain bowl you crap it into." Unfortunately, they also ran Haulaway Technologies, the largest waste-disposal company in the free world, collecting, moving, and dumping the country's garbage. When I say garbage, think big. It not only whisked away potato peels and coffee grounds but also the festering sins of the Cold War.

From the mid to late fifties Haulaway hauled away hundreds of tons of nuclear waste and weapons-grade biological material. A lot of it was buried on the southern-facing slopes of Hag's Peak, especially beneath a certain meadow bordered by woods. Blue steel barrels, a containment solution for a Norman Rockwell past, could never be expected to hold for long the fierce demons of America's will to power. In mere years that glowing stuff left those barrels looking like lace and leeched into the soil. Haulaway executives were eventually informed of this. As a precaution they covered the meadow over with fresh dirt hauled in from a New Jersey landfill at the taxpayers' expense and moved on to besmirch some other pristine site. Time passed. No one cared. You've heard of Love Canal, a disaster that would make the headlines a few years later? Love Canal, my friend, was a valentine compared to Chanticleer.

So, on that cold night, in 1975, a fine snow falling across the mountainside, those operatives I mentioned earlier, dressed in Hazmat gear and brandishing Nod-X74s, short-barreled automatic weapons that fired a barrage of tranquilizer rounds, came to the wall that surrounded the top-secret community. There was no entrance, because when the place had closed down some years earlier any openings were bricked over. They blew the wall with plastic explosives.

The team had been briefed as to the fact that they might encounter a "hostile entity" but were given no indication as to what or who this entity might be. That information was, as the government official told them, strictly on a need-to-know basis. The operatives felt they needed to know, so before the mission, their leader contacted certain people he knew who knew certain things and was told that the brass didn't have a clue about the nature of the threat. What could be told was that at the end of the summer of '74, two local deer hunters working the southern slope of Hag's Peak were attacked and killed by what was generally believed by the public to be a bear. When the autopsy on their remains was completed, though, the coroner in Darton Mills, the largest small town close to the mountain, made a call to Washington, D.C., only hours before he disappeared from the face of the earth.

The Hazmat gear they wore was no doubt hot and prohibitive of vision and movement, but they'd been warned not to remove it. What they saw through night vision goggles behind their visors reinforced that warning. They'd memorized the layout of the streets and locations of each residential, municipal, and commercial building, but nothing had prepared them for the sight of the riotous growth of vegetation that appeared to flourish—massive twisting roots and limbs, tentacles of vines hung with enormous fruit like pale deformed pumpkins—in the freezing mountain temperatures. I was told, "It was like a Mayan ruin covered with growth only it was really a suburban neighborhood." Here's how another of my contacts had put it: "Did you ever see Walt Disney's *Sleeping Beauty*, where the wicked queen casts a spell and these thorny vines burst out in all directions to cover the palace in a web?"

With weapons slung over their backs and fifteen-inch survival knives in hand, they hacked their way through the tangle and found Freedom Street, the main thoroughfare, which was cracked and broken, a type of glowing flower sprouting in bunches from the fissures. Snow swirled around them as they advanced into the lonely heart of the place. The tranquilizer rounds tipped them to the fact that they were after some kind of animal. If the possible hostile had been known to be a human, they'd have definitely been outfitted to kill.

They turned onto Liberty Road, toward the school, making their way around and through a hedge of bramble to where the street was fairly clear. On one of the lawns there was a bicycle, laid down as if a kid had just dropped it. There was a lawn jockey, a ride-on mower, a covered swing, a tattered flag hanging outside a front door. At the school, they fanned out, each taking a hallway, and they passed room after room of empty desks, the vines having invaded from cracks in the floor and shattered windows. The blackboards were still filled with assignments and class notes. On one was written, in pink chalk, the phrase "Ontogeny recapitulates phylogeny." Books lay open, coats still hung in the closets, bag lunches with kids' names lined the shelves. Two operatives met at the gym and stared into a gigantic box of roots, a thicket that reached above the basketball rims. Strange, brightly colored mice with feathered wings moved amid the mesh of branches.

It's believed she struck from behind while they stared in wonder, and there are those who interpreted that as a sign of intelligence. Others disagreed, but there was no question that she was fierce. Those bone nails were ostensibly claws, and the wounds found on the operatives' bodies indicated she had great strength. A few minutes later, she killed another, ripping out his throat in one swipe, and attacked a fourth before the remaining two men could pump enough tranquilizer into her to put her down. From then on she would be imprisoned in sleep.

None of the government's top scientists knew what she was or where she'd come from. They brought in the alien specialists from Groom Lake because her gray coloring put some higher-up in mind of a pair of dead space beings the navy had pulled out of a craft that had crashed in the Indian Ocean off the coast of Madagascar. "You've got a different bag of lint here," said one of the specialists. "From the DNA evidence, this looks home-grown." Her DNA was, at base, human, but then outlandishly mutated. The reigning theory for a very long time was that some years after the community was evacuated a female vagrant had found a breach in the wall and entered Chanticleer. Recon teams that investigated after the creature's capture did note two breaches in the wall—the one blown by the operatives and another where a huge pine had fallen across it, obliterating a five-foot section. So this vagrant moved in and lived amid the rapidly changing environment, herself rapidly changing. It was thought that she no doubt lived during the early part of her stay on canned foods left behind, and then, when her claws came in, she hunted deer in the surrounding woods. They'd found a bone heap of animal remains just outside the wall where it had crumbled beneath the fallen tree.

If they could have nuked Chanticleer, they would have. Instead they decided to pump concrete over the closed wall and bury the place. Before that operation was to begin, though, they allowed a five-person team of scientists two weeks to study the new world that had sprung into being. Two weeks was barely enough time to scratch the surface, so the research party decided to spend the time taking as many samples as they could. Among the five who went into Chanticleer, one was a young botanist, Rabella Cayce. In the first few days of her stay within the walls, she took up the practice of climbing through the branches as a way to reach certain spots unattainable due to tangled barriers of roots. It was difficult going with the burden of the Hazmat suit, and she'd discovered a kind of large white squirrel that could be aggressive. More than once she had to use her Taser against them.

One of my contacts met Ms. Cayce a few years later when she was on the run from those who'd sent her into Chanticleer. He'd infiltrated a small group who knew her story and were trying to help her, but that's all I can say about how she'd come to him. The months of frantic escape, never staying in the same place two nights in a row, had left her drained, and when he told me about their meeting he said he could still recall the dark half circles beneath her vacant eyes. Her hair was long and frizzled and appeared as if it had begun to fall out. It was a shame, for, as he said, "I could tell she'd once been a good-looking woman." On a beautiful fall evening, they sat on the darkened porch of his log cabin retreat at the edge of Lake Salamander, and she told him her story.

On the third day that she was traversing the branch web that ensconced much of Chanticleer's neighborhood, she came upon a spot where beneath her she saw a backyard uncluttered with roots or vines. She hung down from the canopy above it and let herself drop onto a concrete patio next to an in-ground pool. The water in the pool had gone black and was covered by the odd, perfectly round yellow leaves of the mutated branches. Those leaves were disturbed by a constant bubbling at the center of the watery rectangle. There were lawn chairs and a redwood picnic table with benches; a frayed umbrella sticking through its center. Lying on the grass, which had taken on the consistency of fur, next to the barbecue, she discovered what looked like a book. She picked it up and saw that the cover of it had patches of mold and a rash of barnacles. The pages were rippled with water damage, but as she flipped through them, she noticed that they were handwritten instead of typeset. What she had in her possession was a diary, and that diary told the woeful tale of the demise of Chanticleer.

Over the remaining days of the two-week research stint, she'd read the thoughts and experiences of Henrietta Wilde, a wife of one of the researchers, a physicist, Dr. Mason Wilde, who'd been employed by the government to help engineer weapons of merciless destruction. Rabella never informed her superiors about the diary, although she was aware that her silence on the subject, if discovered, could mean her job. When she left Chanticleer, she snuck the book out in a sample case and eventually smuggled it away from the realm of government influence to her apartment in Washington, D.C. The reading of those pages, the plight of Henrietta Wilde, so affected her she felt it her mission to get word of the atrocity out to the public, to anyone who would listen. When she didn't show up for work one day, they went looking for her. As they trailed her back and forth across the United States, hints of the existence of the book surfaced.

The night after she stayed with my contact at the cabin on Salamander Lake, Rabella left before sunup in an old Honda Civic, whose license plate number he'd recorded. One of my contact's contacts paid handsomely for that information and any hints she might have dropped as to where she was going. Eventually, I read online that her headless remains were discovered in a dry streambed on the northern boundary of the Mojave Desert. I have it from reliable sources that the diary was never recovered. So, as was expected, she was silenced, but not before she told the story of Henrietta Wilde, the same one that was told to me.

Henrietta Wilde's title in the parlance of the late sixties would have been "housewife." She was twenty-six when she went to live at Chanticleer along with Mason, her husband, and their three-year-old son, Henry. It's not known what she initially thought of their move to the slope of Hag's Peak, for she didn't start recording her life until well into her second year there, but by the time the diary picks up, in her first entry, she admits to being "bored stiff" and "losing her mind to the monotony." Unlike most of the other wives in the neighborhood, she'd been to four years of liberal arts college and had a degree in literature. Upon graduation, she'd had ambitions to become a writer like the great Shirley Jackson, but after marriage and the birth of her son, she'd put those ideas to rest, convincing herself of their silliness.

The long hours of the afternoon, while Henry napped, a seeming eternity before the helicopter would return with Mason, as she wrote, "made my soul itch." She hated television, had already read all of the novels worth reading in Chanticleer's tiny library, and couldn't stand the company of the other wives, who spent an inordinate amount of time shopping in the small village for clothes and shoes and handbags with which to dress up and go nowhere. Their conversations were primarily about the plots of soap operas, the brilliance of their children, and how smart their husbands were. When drunk, they grew morose and talked about sex. To fight the long hours, she bought a blank diary one day. In her first entry, she wrote about the fact that inserted between two pages of the book was a mimeographed reminder that anything written by one of the citizens of Chanticleer during their stay would need to be destroyed upon leaving.

She'd loved her husband, but as the time went by and he became more deeply involved in the difficult work he was doing, he grew increasingly distant from her and their son. Henry was her one pleasure. In her fourth entry in the book, she wrote, "I feel like a prisoner here, but to see Henry's eyes filled with the wonder of the world is a secondhand freedom I'd die without." She spent the mornings and the time after naps with the child, pushing him in his stroller up and down the few streets of town, watching him at the playground, bobbing in the backyard pool, or reading to him, sitting on a blanket in the meadow out behind the post office where the cool mountain breezes swept down from the peak.

When Henry started kindergarten the days became even longer and lonelier. To stave off madness, she started an exercise regimen of sit-ups, push-ups, jogging around the perimeter of the circular wall, and swimming laps. Every weekday afternoon, she'd arrive at the school at least fifteen minutes early and pace back and forth until Henry came running out. She never told Mason but it was around this time that she took up smoking. She'd sit at the picnic table, go through half a pack of cigarettes, and fill the pages of her diary. Two pages of the book, written at this time, were taken up with a plan (including a map) for escape. She wrote nothing to make one believe that she was being ironic, but she must have known it was impossible.

In the middle of the following summer, two children from the neighborhood were diagnosed with leukemia. Henrietta reported that everyone used the same phrase in reference to the diagnosis—"a tragic coincidence." When two more little girls displayed symptoms of the same disease in late fall, she knew it was no coincidence. Although she'd not spent time building any friendships among the other women to this point, she began to approach them one by one and whisper her theory to them. "It's no fucking coincidence," she said and she was surprised to find that each of them agreed with her. The shopping trips to the little village gave way to meetings, under the guise of tea parties, in a different house two afternoons a week.

Of course, the sick children and their families could not leave Chanticleer. A field hospital was set up within the boundary of the wall and that's where they were treated. It was made evident to the fathers of those affected that they were required to continue working. The women, though, had formed a bond of solidarity and felt strength in their numbers. Henrietta wrote about the other women to say, "I underestimated them. Any one of them has as much if not more courage, cunning, and love for their children as me. When we drink now, we talk of escape." They approached the lieutenant colonel in charge of the community and demanded that tests be done to determine what was causing their children to become ill. He agreed to their demands but took no action. Then right around the time the first child died despite the doctors' treatments and their predictions (they'd never seen a form of the disease so virulent before), a rash of cases broke out, and not all were children this time.

Mason contracted something. The doctors weren't sure what it might be. He turned a shade of gray, and lost his nails and hair. Large lesions formed on his back and chest. When not caring for Henry, Henrietta spent all of her time at the field hospital. The women of the community whose families had not been affected stepped in to help her with child care. Mason died a month into his illness and was buried in a makeshift cemetery on that piece of meadow where she'd once read to Henry. And then Henry became sick, and before five months was up, he was buried alongside his father in the poisoned earth that had killed them.

The lieutenant colonel finally ordered a full evacuation of Chanticleer. Henrietta signed the sheet that assured she was accounted for in the helicopter, but at the last second ducked away. When her name was called before liftoff, one of the other women shouted, "Present," in her voice. She hid in the basement of her house and listened to the choppers carrying the survivors away. Only when the workers came two days later to brick up the opening to Chanticleer did she wake from her stupor. She spied on their progress from her attic window, watching carefully their every move. And then they left. The sun was setting, and the only sound was the mountain wind.

When the community was evacuated, everything was left behind. Only the citizens were taken out. Henrietta had no way of knowing what I know, that every last one of them was killed execution style, duct tape wrapped around the wrists and ankles, a kneeling position, one bullet to the base of the skull. The cover-up of that killing spree was funded by a federal sales tax put on alcohol. Instead, she lived on inside the walls of Chanticleer. She found generators and manuals about how to employ them. There were years of sustenance in the canned goods left behind, and a king's ransom in wine and bottled water. She scavenged the neighborhood, invading houses and stores.

As to what her solitary existence was like in the seasons that followed, you can use your imagination. In one particular entry in her diary she writes that if she were to ever try to sell her story to Hollywood, she'd pitch it as *"Robinson Crusoe* meets

'Rappaccini's Daughter.' " She survived on her imagination, her writing, and the ritual of exercise. As a way to fill her days, she began invading the homes of her neighbors and tried to read the nature of their families like an archeologist might, sifting through the artifacts left behind. She discovered hidden letters that told of secret affairs, and sinister photographs of wives in bondage, heartbreaking artwork of children, and then the mundane remains of fashions in the closet, curtains, the things that filled their refrigerators, that hung on the walls in their bedrooms. "I feel like a ghost sometimes," she wrote. "It's as if I, like Mason and Henry, died and am held here to bear witness to all that's been left behind." Sometimes her discoveries would fill her with a mild excitement, for instance, "Today, I came to the realization that Margi Nelson was a transvestite and that her husband was well aware of it. I sat in the shadows of their living room, staring out at the late-afternoon sky, and imagined for hours the story of their lives."

Three-quarters of the way through the diary, Henrietta made her first entry concerning changes at Chanticleer— "Almost overnight, great disruptions of the earth with thick roots poking through everywhere." Soon after, she noted that a fissure had formed in the bottom of the swimming pool. She feared that she'd lose the water, but didn't. Instead a glowing light shone through the crack and formed a cloud of phosphorescence down deep in the twelve-foot section. "When I swim through that bright plume, it feels like I'm out in the sun and its rays are leaching into me, burning away my misgivings." A month following, she commented on the ashy shade of her complexion.

As Henrietta continued to record the process of her metamorphosis and the mutation of the world around her, her writing slowly became more disorganized, her expressions more erratic. Her penmanship debilitated from a neat script to some private system of slash marks and poorly formed circles. Before her entries fell completely into the incomprehensible, she confessed to spending more and more time in the pool. "The crack in the bottom has opened up into a rock tunnel through which I can swim to the other pools in the neighborhood," she wrote. Of course, I have doubts about the actuality of the pool-tunnel system, but to whom would she be lying? I believe she was beginning to lose her human sense of reality at this point. The last thing she recorded that makes sense is a dream she had while floating in the light at the deep end. "The sky was blue. White clouds. Henry in my arms, giggling."

The day after Rabella Cayce and her four colleagues left Chanticleer, the community was covered over with a few million tons of concrete, like cake mix poured into a giant pan whose edge was the circular wall. A modern village of Pompeii, it waits for future generations to reveal its secrets. How little they will understand about the nature of their find. The strange life forms will be evident. The radiation and the viral strains should still be a nasty brew for thousands of years. They may understand the point of the community, and, in reviewing existing documents, who ordered it built, but what they'll miss, as we miss even now, is the reason for it.

Don't ask me how I know this, but under the influence of a long-distance mind-control expert, a psychic known in the black-ops community as Garland, a certain MP of a poetic frame of mind who guards a gray figure will, on an appointed day, at a given hour, draw his sidearm and shoot out the glass of Sirena's cylindrical tank, freeing her from the prison of sleep. He will then turn the gun on himself. She will awaken to roam the dim tunnels of the hive of secrets, free to hunt and feed, desecrating the most sacred heart of our nation. My contacts and I have estimated that she'll kill dozens before they stop her.

A Note About "The Hag's Peak Affair"

The initial spark of this idea came to me many, many years ago, during a long stint on the overnight shift at a central security station in a town in upstate New York. My job was to sit in front of a big board with audio speakers and lights, listening and watching for warnings of break-ins at homes and businesses around town. The place was located at the end of a hallway that ran the length of the back of a mostly boarded-up strip mall in a part of town that had fallen on hard times. The only two businesses still operating in the mall were a doughnut shop and an X-rated bookstore.

In my security station (more like just a concrete bunker), there was a video monitor that watched that hallway 24/7. The security company actually had a lot of high-end customers (well, as high-end as that town could muster), and night-security personnel had to be vigilant about the security of the central station as well as the properties of the clients around town in case bad guys stormed the station and took us out in order to run rampant, looting the town.

My boss really got into this scenario, and every night before he left and I started on my eight hours of staring at the board and snoozing, he'd recount how it would all go down. "They'll come in with guns blazing," he'd say. He was a kooky guy and had a lot of weird bullshit stories. One I remember was about some Czechoslovakian twin doctors who created a cure for cancer out of horse hooves, but were forced out of business by a nefarious conspiracy concocted by the AMA because doctors didn't really want to cure cancer.

In any event, the door of the central station was only stormed once, and that was by my boss's wife, whom he'd caught cheating on him with a guy who sold cheese to grocery stores. He had called me and told me not to let her in the station, even though she was actually part owner of the security company. That night she came by and pounded on the outer door and demanded through the intercom that I let her in. Of course, I let her in. What did I give a shit? I wasn't going to hassle his wife just like I wasn't going to throw myself into a hail of bullets for minimum wage.

Anyway, what's important here is that in that hallway I watched all night on the video camera, waiting for criminals to attack, the concrete floor was severely buckled in one spot. It had a huge fissure in it, and a side of the crack was raised about five inches over the other side of it. I'd see rats crawl out of that hole and scurry up and down the hallway. And, man, the stink in that grim corridor was like the Devil's farts—some kind of mutated cabbage miasma that on a bad night could make your eyes water.

One afternoon I was talking to my boss and this guy, Wes, the alarm technician, and I asked them what was going on in the hallway. The tech laughed and said, "That's the entrance to Hell." My boss told me that the strip mall we were in was built years ago over a landfill. The only problem was, they never put in any vents to leach off the methane gas, and now it was pushing its way up to the surface. The boss, who had a mad combover and always wore glasses with smoky lenses, like some kind of spy/used-car salesman, shook his head, and said, "If I lose the

business in my divorce settlement, I'm gonna go out in the hallway and light a cigarette and blow this whole fucking place to
kingdom come." Wes and I laughed, but the boss didn't. I didn't
stick around long after that.

I was only there long enough to contemplate the idea of
structures and complexes being built to cover over the sins of
the past. I thought of Love Canal. I wondered, how many places
must there be like this in the country that nobody remembers
or cares about yet? What kind of biological or nuclear detritus
of the Cold War must be lying dormant, waiting to rear its ugly
head and storm the metaphorical security door of our placid
lives? Those long nights in the central station, contemplating
the invisible, rising evil, gave rise themselves to a nascent story
concept I entertained my half-sleeping imagination with. I
thought of it as "Neptune's Daughter."

The Coral Heart

His sword's grip was polished blood coral, its branches perfect doubles for the aorta. They fed into a guard that was a thin silver crown, beyond which lay the blade (the heart), slightly curved, with the inscription of a spell in a language no one could read. He was a devotee of the art of the cut, and when he wielded this weapon, the blade exactly parallel to the direction of motion, the blood groove caught the breeze and whistled like a bird of night. He'd learned his art from a hermit in the mountains where he'd practiced on human cadavers.

That sword had a history before it fell to Ismet Toler. How it came to him, he swore he would never tell. Legend had it that the blade belonged first to the ancient hero who'd beheaded the Gorgon; a creature whose gaze turned men to smooth marble. After he'd slain her, he punctured her eyeballs with the tip of his blade and then bathed the cutting edge in their ichor. The character of the weapon seized the magic of the Gorgon's stare and, ever after, if a victim's flesh was sliced or punctured to the extent where blood was drawn, that unlucky soul would be turned instantly to coral.

The statuary of Toler's skill could be found throughout the

realm. Three hardened headless bodies lay atop the Lowbry Hill, and on the slopes three hardened heads. A woman crouching at the entrance to the Funeral Gardens. A score of soldiers at the center of the market at Camiar. A child missing an arm, twisting away with fear forever, resting perfectly on one heel, in the southeastern corner of the Summer Square. All deepest red and gleaming with reflection. There were those who believed that only insanity could account for the vast battlefields of coral warriors frozen in the kill, but none was brave enough to speak it.

The Valator of Camiar once said of the Coral Heart, "He serves the good because it is a minority, leaving the majority to slay in the name of Truth." The Valator is now, himself, red coral, his head cleaved like a roasted sausage. Toler dispatched evil with dedication and stunning haste. It was said that the fate of the sword was tied to that of the world. When enough of its victims had been turned to coral, their accumulated weight would affect the spin of the planet and it would fly out of orbit into darkness.

There are countless stories about the Coral Heart, and nearly all of them are the same story. Tales about a man who shares a name and a spirit with his weapon. They're always filled with fallen ranks of coral men. Some he kicks and shatters in the mêlée. There is always betrayal and treachery. A few of these stories involve the hermit master with whom he'd studied. Most all of them mention his servant, Garone, a tulpa or thought-form creation physically coalesced from his focused imagination. The descriptions of killing in these classical tales are painstaking and brutal, encrusted with predictable glory.

There are a handful of stories about the Coral Heart, though, that do not end on a battlefield. You don't hear them often.

Most find the exploits of the weapon more enchanting than those of the man. Your average citizen enjoys a tale of slaughter. You, though, if I'm not mistaken, understand as well the deadly nature of the human heart and would rather decipher the swordsman's dreams than the magic spell engraved upon his blade.

And so . . . in the last days of summer, in the Year of the Thistle, after transforming the army of the Igridots, upon the dunes of Weilawan, into a petrified forest, Ismet Toler wandered north in search of nothing more than a cold day. He rode upon Nod, his red steed of a rare archaic stock—toes instead of hooves and short, spiral horns, jutting out from either side of its forelock. Walking beside Toler, appearing and disappearing like the moon behind wind-driven clouds, was Garone. The servant, when visible, drifted along, hands clasped at his waist, slightly hunched, the hood of his brown robe always obscuring any definitive view of his face. You might catch a glimpse of one of his yellow eyes, but never both at once.

As they followed a trail that wound beneath giant trees, leaves falling everywhere, Toler pulled the reins on Nod and was still. "Was that a breeze, Garone?"

The tulpa disappeared but was as quickly back. "I believe so," he said in a whisper only his master could hear.

Another, more perceptible gust came down the trail and washed over them. Toler sighed as it passed. "I'm weary of turning men to coral," he said.

"I hadn't noticed," said Garone.

The Coral Heart smiled and nodded slightly.

"Up ahead in these yellow woods, we will find a palace and you will fall in love," said the servant.

"There are times I wish you wouldn't tell me what you know."

"There are times I wish I didn't know it. If you command me to reveal my face to you, I will disappear forever."

"No," said Toler, "not yet. That day will come, though. I promise you."

"Perhaps sooner rather than later, master."

"Perhaps not," said Toler and nudged his mount in the ribs. Again moving along the trail, the swordsman recalled the frozen expressions of his victims at Weilawan, each countenance set with the same look of terrible surprise.

In late afternoon, the travelers came to a fork in the trail, and Garone said, "We must take the right-hand path to reach that palace."

"What lies to the left?" asked Toler.

"Tribulation and certain death," said the servant.

"To the right," said the swordsman. "You may rest now, Garone."

Garone became a rippling flame, clear as water, and then disappeared.

As twilight set in, Toler caught sight of two towers silhouetted against the orange sky. He coaxed Nod into a gallop, hoping to arrive at the palace gates before nightfall. As he flew away from the forest and across barren fields, the cool of the coming night refreshing him, he thought, "I have never been in love." Every time he tried to picture the face of one of his amorous conquests what came before him instead were the faces of his victims.

He arrived just as the palace guards were about to lift the moat bridge. The four men saw him approaching and drew their weapons.

"An appeal for lodging for the night," called Toler from a safe distance.

"Who are you?" one of the men shouted.

"A traveler," said the swordsman.

"Your name, fool," said the same man.

"Ismet Toler."

There was a moment of silence, and then a different one of the guards said, in a far less demanding tone, "The Coral Heart?"

"Yes."

The guard who had spoken harshly fell to his knees and begged forgiveness. Two others sheathed their swords and came forward to help the gentleman from his horse. The fourth ran ahead into the palace, announcing to all he passed that the Coral Heart was at the gate.

Toler dismounted and one of the men took Nod's reigns. The swordsman approached the guard who knelt on the ground, and said, "I'll not be killing anyone tonight. I'm too weary. We'll see what tomorrow brings." The man rose up, and then the three guards, with Toler's help, turned the huge wooden wheel that lifted the moat bridge.

Inside, the guards dispersed and left Toler standing at the head of a hall with a vaulted ceiling, all fashioned from blue limestone. People came and went quietly, keeping their distance but stealing glances. Eventually, he was approached by a very old man, diminutive of stature, with the snout and mottled skin of a toad. When the little fellow spoke, he croaked, "A pleasure, sir," and offered his wet hand as a sign of welcome.

Toler took it with a shiver. "And you are?" he asked.

"Councilor Greppen. Follow me." The stranger led on down the vast hall, padding along at a weary pace on bare, flat feet. The slap of his soles echoed into the distance.

"May I ask what manner of creature you are?" said Toler.

"A man, of course," said the councilor. "And you?"

"A man."

"No, no, from what I hear you are Death's own Angel and will one day turn the world to coral."

"What kind of councilor can you be if you believe everything you hear?" said Toler.

Greppen puffed out his cheeks and laughed; a shrewd, wet sound. He shuffled toward the left and turned at another long hall, a line of magnificent fountains running down its center. "The Hall of Tears," he croaked, and they passed through glistening mist.

As Toler followed from hall to hall, he gradually adopted the old man's pace. The journey was long, but time suddenly had no bearing. The swordsman studied the people who passed, noticed the placement of the guard, marveled at the colors of the fish in the fountains, the birds that flew overhead, the distant glass ceiling through which the full moon stared in. As if suddenly awakened, he came to at the touch of the councilor's damp hand on his arm.

"We have arrived," said Greppen.

Toler looked around. He was on a balcony that jutted off the side of the palace. The stars were bright and there was a cold breeze, just the kind he'd wished for when heading north from Weilawan. He took a seat on a simple divan near the edge of the balcony, and listened as Greppen's footfalls grew faint. He closed his eyes and wondered if this was his lodging for the night. The seat was wonderfully comfortable and he leaned back into it.

A moment passed, perhaps an hour, he wasn't sure, before he opened his eyes. When he did, he was surprised to see something floating toward the balcony. It was no bird. He blinked and it became clear in the resplendent starlight. It was a woman, dressed in fine golden robes, seated in a wooden chair, like a throne, gliding toward him out of the night. When she reached the balcony and hovered above him, he stood to greet her.

"The Coral Heart," she said as her chair settled down across from the divan. "You may be seated."

Toler bowed slightly before sitting.

"I am Lady Maltomass," she said.

The swordsman was intoxicated by the sudden scent of lemon blossoms, and then by the Lady's eyes—large and luminous. No matter how he scrutinized her gaze, he could not discern their color. At the corners of her lips there was the very slightest smile. Her light brown hair was braided and strung with beads of jade. There was a thin jade collar around her neck, and from there it was a quick descent to the path between her breasts and the intricately brocaded golden gown.

"Ismet Toler," he finally said.

"I grant you permission to stay this night in the palace," she said.

"Thank you," he said. There was an awkward pause and then he asked, "Who makes your furniture?"

She laughed. "The chair, yes. My father was a great scholar. By way of his research, he discovered it beneath the ruins of an abbey at Cardeira-davu."

"I didn't think the religious dabbled in magic," said Toler.

"Who's to say it's not the work of God?"

The swordsman nodded. "And your councilor, Greppen? Another miracle?"

"Noble Greppen," said the Lady.

"Pardon my saying, Lady Maltomass, but he appears green about the gills."

"There's no magic in it," she said. "His is a race of people who grew out of the swamp. They have a different history than we do, but the same humanity."

"And what is your story?" said Toler. "Are you magic or miracle?"

She smiled and looked away from him. "I'll ask the questions," she said. "Is that the Coral Heart at your side?"

"Yes," he said and moved to draw the sword from its sheath.

"That won't be necessary," she said. "I see the coral from here."

"Most people prefer not to see the blade," he said.

"And pardon my asking, Ismet Toler, but how many have you slain with it?"

"Enough," he said.

"Is that a declaration of remorse?"

"Remorse was something I felt for the first thousand."

"You're a droll swordsman."

"Is that a compliment?" he asked.

"No," said Lady Maltomass. "I hear you have a tulpa."

"Yes, my man, Garone."

To Toler's left, there was a disturbance in the air, which became a pillar of smoke that swirled and coalesced into the hooded servant.

"Garone, I present to you the Lady Maltomass," said Toler, and swept his arm in her direction. The tulpa bowed and then disappeared.

"Very interesting," she said.

"Not a flying chair, but I try," he said.

"Well, I also have a tulpa," said the Lady.

"No," said Toler.

"Mamresh," she said, and in an instant, there appeared, just to the right of the flying chair, the presence of a woman.

She was naked and powerfully built. "A warrior," thought the swordsman. His only other impression before she disappeared was of the deep red color of her voluminous hair.

"You surprise me," he said to the Lady.

"If you'll stay tomorrow," she said, "I'll show you something I think you'll be interested in. Meet me among the willows in the garden after noon."

"I'm already there," he said.

She smiled as the chair rose slowly above the balcony. It turned in midair and then floated out past the railing. "Good night, Ismet Toler," she called over her shoulder.

As the chair disappeared into the dark, Greppen approached. He led the swordsman to a spacious room near the balcony. The councilor said nothing but lit a number of candles and then called good night as he pushed the door closed behind him.

Toler undressed, weary from travel and the aftereffects of the drug that was Lady Maltomass. He lay down with a sigh, and then summoned his servant. The tulpa appeared at the foot of the bed.

"Garone, while the palace is sleeping, I want you to search around and see what you can discover about the Lady. A mysterious woman. I want to know everything about her. Take caution, though, she also has a tulpa." Then he wrapped his right hand around the sheath of the Coral Heart, clasped the grip with his left, and fell asleep to dream of kissing Lady Maltomass beneath the willows.

Toler arrived early to the gardens the following day. The entrance led through a long grape arbor thick with vines and dangling fruit. This opened into an enormous area sectioned into symmetrical plots of ground, and in each, stretching off into the distance, beds of colorful flowers and pungent herbs.

Their aromas mixed in the atmosphere and the scent confused him for a brief time. Everywhere around him were bees and butterflies and members of Greppen's strange race, weeding, watering, fertilizing. The swordsman asked one where the willows were, and the toad man pointed down a narrow path into the far distance.

It was past noon when he arrived amid the stand of willows next to a pond with a fountain at its center. He discovered an ancient stone bench, partially green with mold, and sat upon it, peering through the mesh of whiplike branches at sunlight glistening on the water. There was a cool breeze and orange birds darted about, quietly chirping.

"Garone," said Toler, and his servant appeared before him. "What have you to report about the lady?"

"I paced through every inch of the palace, down all its ostentatious halls, and found not a scrap of a secret about her. In the middle of the night, I found her personal chambers, but could not enter. I couldn't pass through the walls nor even get close to them."

"Is there a spell around her?" asked the swordsman.

"Not a spell, it's her tulpa, Mamresh. She's too powerful for me. She's blocking me with her invisible will from approaching the Lady's rooms. I summoned all my strength and exerted myself and she merely laughed at me."

Toler was about to speak, but just then heard his name being called from deeper in amid the willows. Garone disappeared and the swordsman rose and set off in the direction of the voice. Brushing the tentacles of the trees aside, he pushed his way forward until coming upon a small clearing. At its center sat Lady Maltomass in her flying chair. Facing her was another of the ancient stone benches.

"I heard someone speaking off in the distance, and knew it must be you," she said. He walked over and sat down across from her.

"I hope you slept well," said the Lady.

"Indeed," said Toler. "I dreamt of you."

"In your dream, did I tell you I don't like foolishness?"

"Perhaps," he said, "but the only part of it I witnessed was when we kissed."

She shook her head. "Here's what I wanted to show you," she said, lifting a small book that appeared to be covered with a square of Greppen's flesh.

"Is the cover made of toad?" he asked, leaning forward to get a better look at it.

"Not precisely," she said, "but it's not the cover I wanted to show you." She opened the book to a page inside, and then turned the volume around and handed it to him. "What do you see there?" She pointed at the left-hand page.

There was a design that was immediately familiar to him. He sat back away from her and drew his sword. Bringing the blade level with his eyes, he studied the design of the inscribed spell. He then looked back to the book. Three times he went from blade to book and back before she finally said, "I'll wager they are identical."

"How did you come upon this?" asked Toler, returning his sword to its sheath. "The blade has never left my side since it came to me."

"No, but the weapon is old, and it has passed through many men's hands. In fact, there was a people who had possession of it, two centuries past, who deemed it too dangerous to be at large in the world. They didn't destroy it but studied it. One of the things they were interested in was the spell. For all of their effort, though, they were only able to decipher two words of it. There might be as many as ten words in that madly looping script. My father, digging in the peat bogs north of the Gentious quarry, hauled two clay tablets out of a quivering hole in the ground. Those heavy ancient pages contained reference to the sword, to its legend, and the design of the blade's script. Also included was the translation of the two words."

"What were they?" he asked, wrapping his fingers again around the grip of the weapon.

"My father worked with what was given on the tablet and deciphered three more of the spell's words."

"What were they?"

"The words he was certain of were—Thanry, Meltmoss, Stilthery, Quasum, and Pik."

"All common herbs," said Toler.

She nodded. "He believed that all the words constituted a kind of medicine that, if prepared and inserted into one of your victim's coral mouths, would reverse the sword's power and return them to flesh. The blade's damage could, of course, have been a death blow, in which case there would be no chance of returning them to life, but those who succumbed to only a nick, a scratch, a cut, would again be flesh and bone and draw breath."

"I've often wondered about the inscription," he said. "Your father was a wise man."

"I'm giving you the book," she said. "When I heard you'd turned up at the gate, I remembered my father telling me about his discoveries. The book should belong to the man who carries the weapon. I have no use for it."

"Why would the blade hold an antidote to the sword's effects, and yet be written in a language no one can understand?" asked Toler.

"That fact suggests a dozen possible motives, but I suppose the real one will remain a mystery." She held the book out toward him. As he leaned forward to take it from her, she also leaned forward, and as his fingers closed on the book, her lips met his. She kissed him eagerly, her mouth open. They parted and he moved closer to the edge of the stone bench. He put his hands on her shoulders and gently drew her toward him.

"Wait, is that Greppen, spying?" she said, bringing her arms up between them. Toler drew his sword as he stood and spun around, brandishing it in a defensive maneuver. He saw no sign of Greppen, heard no movement among the willow branches. What he heard instead was the laughter of Lady Maltomass. When he turned back to her, she was gone. He looked up to see the chair rising into the blue sky. As she floated away toward the tree line, he yelled, "When will I see you next?"

"Soon," she called back.

Two days passed without word from her, and in that time, all Toler could think of was their last meeting. He tried to stay busy within the walls of the palace, and the beauty of the place kept his attention for half a day, but ultimately, in its ease and refinement, palace life seemed hollow to one who'd spent most of his life in combat.

On the evening of the second day, after dinner, he summoned Councilor Greppen, who was to see to his every need. They met in Toler's room, and the toad man brought a bottle of brandy and two glasses. As he poured for himself and the Coral Heart, he said, "I can smell your frustration, Ismet Toler."

"You can, can you, Prince of Toads? Tell her I want to see her."

"She'll summon you when she's ready."

"She is in every way a perfect woman," said Toler, sipping his brandy.

"Perfection is in the eye of the beholder," said Greppen. "If you were to see my wife, considered quite a beauty among our people, you might not agree."

"I'm sure she's lovely," said the swordsman, "but I feel if I don't soon have a tryst with Lady Maltomass, I'm going to go mad and turn the world to coral."

Greppen laughed. "The beast with two backs? Your people are comical in their lust."

"I suppose," said Toler. "How do you do it? With a thought?" He sipped at the brandy.

"Very nearly," said Greppen, lifting the bottle to refill his companion's glass.

"Here's a question for you, Councilor," said Toler. "Does she ever leave the chair?"

"Only to go to bed," he said. "I would think of all people, you might understand best. She shares her spirit with it as you do with the Coral Heart. She knows what the world looks like from above the clouds. She can fly."

Toler finished his second drink, and told Greppen he was turning in. On the way out the door, the councilor called back, "Patience." Once in bed, again Toler summoned Garone and sent him forth to discover any secrets he might. The swordsman then grasped the sheath and the grip of his sword and fell into a troubled sleep.

He tossed and turned, his desire for the lady working its way into his dreams. Deep in the night, her face rose above the horizon, bigger than the moon. He looked into her eyes to see if he could tell their color, but in them he saw instead the figures of

Garone and Mamresh on the stone bench, beneath the willows, in the moonlight. His tulpa's robe was pulled up to his waist, and Mamresh sat upon his lap, facing away, her legs on either side of his. She was panting and moving quickly to and fro, and he was grunting. Then Garone tilted his head back and the hood began to slip off.

Toler woke suddenly to avoid seeing his servant's face. He was drenched in sweat and breathing heavily. "I've got to get away from here," he said. Still, he stayed on, three more days. On the evening of the third day, he gave orders for the grooms to ready Nod for travel early in the morning. Before turning in, he went to the balcony and sat, staring out at the stars. "Garone, you were right," he said aloud. "I've fallen in love, but tribulation and certain death might have been preferable." He dozed off.

A few minutes later, he awoke to the sound of Greppen's footfalls receding into the distance. He sat up, and as he did, he discovered a pale yellow envelope in his lap. *For the Coral Heart* was inscribed across the front. The back was affixed with wax, bearing what he assumed was the official seal of the House of Maltomass, ornate lettering surrounding the image of an owl with a snake writhing in its beak. He tore it open and read, *Come now to my chambers. Your Lady.*

He sprang up off the divan and summoned Garone to lead him. They moved quickly through the halls, the tulpa skimming along above the blue marble floors like a ghost. In the Hall of Tears, they came upon a staircase and climbed up four flights. At the top of those steps was a sitting room, at the back of which was a large wooden door, opened only a sliver. Toler instructed Garone to stand guard and to alert him if anyone approached. He carefully opened the door and entered into a dark room that led into a hall, at the end of which he saw a light. He put his left hand around the grip of the sword and proceeded.

Before reaching the lighted chamber, he smelled the vague scent of orange oil and cinnamon. As he stepped out of the darkness of the hall, the first thing that caught his attention was Lady Maltomass, sitting up, supported by large silk pillows, in her canopied bed. The coverlet was drawn up to her stomach and above it she was naked. The sight of her breasts halted his advance.

"Come to practice your swordsmanship?" she said.

He swallowed hard and tried to say, "At your service."

She laughed at his consternation. "Come closer," she said, her voice softer now, "and dispense with those clothes."

He undressed before her, quickly removing every article of clothing. When he stood naked before her, though, he still had on his belt and the sheathed sword.

"One sword is useful here, the other not," she said.

"I never take it off," he said.

"Hurry now. Put it right here on my night table."

He reluctantly removed the sword. Then he sat on the edge of the bed and put his arms around her. They kissed more passionately than they had in the clearing. He ran his fingers through her hair as she clasped her hands behind his back and kissed his chest. He moved his hands down to her breasts and she reached for his prick. When their ardor was well inflamed, she pulled away from him, and then slowly leaning forward, whispered in his ear, "Do you want me?"

"Yes," he said.

"Then, come in," she said and, grabbing the corner of the blanket, threw it back for him.

For a moment, Ismet Toler wore the same look of terrible surprise that was fixed forever on the faces of his victims, for Lady Maltomass was, from the waist down, blood coral. He glimpsed the frozen crease between her legs and cried out.

Garone appeared suddenly at his side, shouting, "Treachery!" Toler turned toward his servant just as Mamresh, bearing a smile, appeared and pulled back the hood of his tulpa's robe. The swordsman glimpsed his own face, with yellow eyes, in the instant before the thought form went out like a candle. He buckled inside from the sudden loss of Garone. Then, from out of the dark, he was punched in the face.

Toler came to on the floor, gasping as if he'd been underwater. Greppen was there, helping him off the floor. Once Toler had regained his footing and clarity, he turned back to the bed.

"Imagine," said Lady Maltomass, "your organ of desire transformed into a fossil."

Toler was speechless.

"Some years ago, my father took me to the market at Camiar. He'd been working on the translation of the spell upon your sword, and he'd heard that you frequented a seller there who dispensed drams of liquor. He wanted to present you with what he'd discovered from the ancients about the sword's script. Just as we arrived at the market, a fight broke out between five swordsmen and yourself. You defeated them, but in the mêlée you struck a young woman with an errant thrust and she was turned to coral."

"Impossible," he shouted.

"You're an arrogant fool, Ismet Toler. The young woman was me. My father brought me back here a statue, and prepared the five herbs from his research into an elixir. He poured it down my hard throat, and because it was made of only half the ingredients of the cure, only half of me returned."

Greppen tapped Toler upon the hip and, when the swords-man looked down, handed him the Coral Heart.

"Now you face my tulpa," said the Lady.

Toler heard Mamresh approaching and drew the sword, drop-ping the sheath upon the bed. He ducked and sidled across the floor, the weapon constantly moving. He turned suddenly and was struck twice in the face and once in the chest. He stumbled but didn't go down. She moved on him again, but this time, he saw her vague outline and sliced at her torso. The blade passed right through her and she kicked him in the balls. He doubled over and went down again.

"Get up, snake," called Lady Maltomass from the bed.

"Please rise, Ismet Toler," said Greppen, now standing before him.

He lifted himself off the floor and resumed a defensive crouch. He kept the blade in motion, but his hands were shak-ing. Mamresh attacked. Her hard knuckles seemed to be ev-erywhere at once. No matter how many times Toler swung the Coral Heart, it made no difference.

After another pass, Mamresh had him staggered and reeling from side to side. Blood was running from his nose and mouth.

"I've just given her leave to beat you to death," said Lady Maltomass.

The vague outline of a muscled arm swept out of the air, and Toler slid beneath it, turned, and made the most exquisite cut to the ghostly figure's spine. The blade didn't even slow in its arc.

She closed his left eye and splintered his shin with a kick. Toler was on the verge of panic when he saw Greppen standing in the corner, tiny fists raised in the air, urging Mamresh to the kill. The tulpa came from the left this time. The swordsman had learned the sound of her breathing. Before she could strike, he tucked his head in and rolled into the corner where Greppen stood. He could hear her right behind him.

He reached out with his free hand and grabbed the toad man by the ankle. Then, as Toler rose, he lifted the blade and, with unerring precision, gave a deft slice to the councilor's neck. He turned quickly, and Greppen's blood sprayed forth in a great geyser. It washed over Mamresh, and she became visible to him as she threw a punch at his left eye. He moved gracefully to the side, tossing Greppen's now coral body at her. It passed through her face, briefly blocking her view of him. Toler calmly sought a spot where the blood revealed his assassin and then lunged, sending the blade there.

Mamresh gasped, and her visible face contorted in terror as she crackled into blood coral. He turned back to the bed, and the Lady was still. He now could ascertain the color of her eyes, and they were a deep red. He'd made her mind coral in the act of defeating her tulpa. He dropped the sword and lay down beside her. Pulling her to him, he tried to kiss her, but her teeth were shut and a slow stream of drool issued from the corner of her mouth.

Toler discovered Nod gutted and decapitated in a heap upon the stable floor. After that, he spared no one, but worked his way down every hall and through the gardens, killing everything that moved. It was after midnight when he left the palace in the flying chair and disappeared into the western mountains.

People wondered what had happened to the Coral Heart. Some said he'd died of frostbite, some, of fever. Others believed he'd finally been careless and turned himself into a statue. Seven long years passed and the violence of the world had been diminished by half. Then, in the winter of the Year of Ice, a post rider galloped into Camiar and told the people that he'd seen a half-dozen bandits turned to coral on the road from Totenhas.

A Note About "The Coral Heart"

I got the idea for this story from reading a book about the sixteenth-century Mannerist artist Giuseppe Arcimboldo. You may know him from his portraits of people composed from different types of fruit or sea creatures or books. As if those paintings aren't remarkable enough, he also worked in other forms—sculpture, jewelry, and the design of elaborate stage sets. One object of his creation was a sword with a handle made of red coral, the coral appearing like the major arteries of the heart. From the image of that decorative weapon (it could not be used in battle as the handle was too fragile) my story grew. The phenomenon of the "tulpa" or "thought form" is supposedly a real entity, which I first came across when reading about Alexandra David-Neel, a Belgian explorer and spiritualist who, in 1924, traveled through Tibet when nonnatives were forbidden there. She reports having conjured a tulpa in the form and character of Friar Tuck, whom she eventually had to kill due to the fact that it had taken on a life of its own.

The Double of My Double Is Not My Double

I saw my double at the mall a couple of weeks ago. I was sitting on a bench outside a clothing store. Lynn was inside, checking out the sales. My mind was pretty empty as I watched the intermittent trickle of shoppers on their way to something else. Out of the corner of my eye, I noticed a person sit down next to me. I turned and saw who it was and laughed. "Hey," I said. "How's business?"

He was dressed in a rumpled suit and tie and he looked tired. Sighing to catch his breath, he sat back. There was a weak smile on his face. "Double drill," he said.

"Knowing me, I wouldn't think there'd be that much to it," I told him.

His eyes half-closed and he shook his head.

"You must be at it all day," I said.

"And into the night," he said. "On top of all of it, I've had to get a part-time job."

"You're moonlighting as my double?"

"I'm dipping things in chocolate at that old-fashioned candy store on Stokes Road. Four hours a day for folding cash. Remember a couple of meetings back after we started talking, I told you

I was living in that giant house out by the wild-animal rescue, the last cul-de-sac before the road turns to dirt? The mortgage on that place is crushing."

"I thought you were living with like four or five other doubles, splitting the cost," I said.

"Yeah, but my double salary isn't cutting it. Dipping things in chocolate, though, pays extraordinarily well. I make a hundred dollars every four-hour session."

"That's pretty good. What do you dip?"

He leaned forward and took out a pack of cigarettes. He offered me one, but I'd quit, and he looked slightly wounded by my refusal. When he sparked his big chrome lighter, I noticed the pale hue of his complexion, the beads of sweat, the slight shaking of his hands. There was a pervasive aroma of alcohol.

He took a drag and, leaning forward, elbows on his knees, said, "You name it, I'll dip it. It started with fruit, and by the time they brought in the first steak, I knew it was gonna get out of hand. Finally, the old Swedish guy who runs the place took off his shoe and handed it to me. A chocolate loafer. After I fished it out and it dried, he and his wife laughed their asses off."

"You don't look well," I told him. "You've put on weight and you're pale. You look like the Pillsbury dough boy on a bender." The right arm of his glasses was repaired with Scotch tape.

"Well," he said. "This is what I've come to talk to you about."

He was a wreck. I looked away. Nobody wants to see themselves tear up, watch their own bottom lip quiver.

"It seems I have a double," he said, his voice cracking slightly.

A moment passed before I could process the news. "You're a double and yet you have a double? How's that work?"

"It's rare," he said, "but it happens. You know, as your double, I don't bother you that often. I've not brought you any ill luck like in the legends. I'm just around and you see me maybe once or twice a year, we have a friendly chat, and I go on my way. The kind of double I have, though, is not benign, as I am to you; it's an evil emanation."

"Is your double also my double?" I asked.

"Not precisely. He's not got our good looks. For the most part he exists as a cloud, a drifting smog. But he can take physical form for short periods of a few hours. A shape-shifter. Insidious. He's always hovering, repeating what I say in a high-pitched voice, appearing to my friends and fucking them over, making them think it's me. When I complain to him, he laughs and pinches my second chin. All night, he whispers paradoxical dreams into my ear, their riddles frustrations dipped in chocolate. He's my double, but your psyche used me to birth him."

"You're losing me," I said. "Are you saying I'm responsible?"

"Well, it's your orbit that I'm trapped in. Everything issues from you. He's been haunting me for the past six months. Can you think of some bleak or grim thought you might have had back half a year that could have sown the seed?"

"Grim thoughts?" I said. "I have a couple dozen a day."

"He's trying to supplant me as your double. If he takes my position, your ass'll be in a sling. He'll grind you down to powder."

"What are we gonna do?" I asked.

"He goes by the name Fantasma-gris."

"Spanish?"

"Yeah, it means Gray Ghost."

"I don't even know Spanish," I said. "I did a couple years of it in high school. I can say meatball, count to ten, that's it."

"Somehow something about Fantasma-gris dribbled out of your mind. Just sit tight till I figure out a plan," he said, resting his hand lightly on my forearm. He stood quickly. "Then I'll be back in touch."

"A plan for what?"

"To kill him." He spun away then and lumbered off down the center of the mall. I watched him go and realized he was limping. I was wondering what was with his suit and tie. I hadn't worn one in three years.

"Are you ready?" asked Lynn. She was standing before me, holding a big bag from the store she'd been in. I got up and put my arm around her shoulders as we headed off.

She said, "Let's go get dinner somewhere."

I agreed. We left the mall and went out into the parking lot. As we drove to the restaurant Lynn had decided on, I was preoccupied, thinking about Fantasma-gris. I wanted to tell her about it, but she'd made it clear years earlier that she didn't want to hear any double talk. When I'd finally cornered my double downtown one day and spoken to him for the first time, I told Lynn about it.

"What do you mean, 'a double'?" she'd said.

"A doppelgänger. My twin. It's metaphysical, you know, like a spirit. I've been seeing him around for about a year now, and today, I went up to him and told him I knew what he was."

She smiled and shook her head as I spoke, but at one point she stopped and squinted and said, "Are you serious?"

I nodded.

"Do you understand what you're saying?" she'd asked.

"Yeah."

"You better get to a shrink. Don't think I'm heading toward retirement with a kook." She'd walked over to where I sat and leaned down to put her arms around me. "You gotta get your shit together," she said.

Lynn made me an appointment and I went to see this woman, Dr. Ivy, who asked me about the double. I told her everything I knew. Her office smelled of patchouli and there was low, moaning music piped in from somewhere. She was a very short, fairly good-looking woman with long dark hair and a faint scar on her right cheek. For some reason, I pictured her cutting herself on her own plum-painted thumbnail. Every time I spoke, she nodded and jotted things down on a pad. I was transfixed by the sight of an ivy tattoo on the wrist of her writing hand, and at the end of the session, she wrote me a scrip for some head pills.

I bought them and read the warnings. In print so tiny I had to use a magnifying glass to read, it said my throat could close up, I might get amnesia, bleed from my asshole, lose my hearing, develop a strange taste of rotten eggs in my mouth, or be drawn to reckless gambling. I took them for two days and felt like a walking sandbag. On the third morning, I flushed them down the bowl. I'd learned my lesson. I never went back to see Dr. Ivy, but then I never mentioned my double to Lynn again.

At the restaurant, I ordered ravioli and Lynn got a salad. We both had wine, me red, her white. The place was dark but our table had a red candle. We talked about the kids and then we talked about the cars. She told me what was going on at her job. We bitched about politics for ten minutes. All along, though, I wanted to tell her what the double had told me in the mall, but I knew I shouldn't. Instead, I said to her, "I was thinking about Aruba today. That was a great vacation."

She took my cue and started reminiscing about the blue water, the sun, the balcony in our room that opened onto a courtyard filled by the branches of an enormous tree with orange flowers and crawling with iguanas the size of house cats. I reminded her of our jeep journey to the desert side of the island and the stacked stone prayers that littered the shore. It was a great trip, and I took real pleasure in recalling it with her, but yes, I had an ulterior motive.

It was on that vacation that I first saw my double. While she spun out her descriptions of the Butterfly Pavilion, an attraction we'd visited, or the night we ate at a restaurant on the edge of a dock, ocean at our backs, party lights, a guy with a beat-up acoustic guitar playing "Sleepwalk," I was, in that memory of Aruba, elsewhere, standing at midnight, after she'd fallen asleep, smoking a joint on the open second-floor landing of our building.

Beneath me was a lighted trail that cut through the tall bamboo. I was bone weary, and my eyes were half closed. We'd gone kayaking that day. I wondered how the kids were getting along without us but my thoughts were distracted by the strong breeze whipping the bamboo tops. I was just about to flick the roach away and ascend the concrete steps to my left when I saw someone pass by on the path.

The fellow was about six foot, a little stooped, thick in the chest and well overweight. He leaned into the wind, holding a floppy white beach hat to his head with his left hand. With the next gust, his yellow Hawaiian shirt opened, the tails blowing behind him to reveal his gut. He turned his head suddenly and looked up at me for a moment before disappearing into the bamboo. The glasses, the big head, his dull look seemed familiar. I tried to place where I might have seen him before, but I was too tired.

The next day, we took a jeep over to the barren side of the island and visited an abandoned gold mine. There was a three-story busted and rusted concrete and tin structure built into the side of an enormous sand dune. The place was spooky inside and Lynn and I held hands as we went from room to room. There was nothing really to see but rotted furniture and rusted metal bed frames in a maze of rooms that led on to other tunnels and rooms. I started to feel claustrophobic, and said I'd had enough. She agreed.

As we made our way toward where we remembered the exit being, another party of sightseers passed by in a hallway to our left. An older gentleman with a cane and a white-haired woman following him. She nodded to us and smiled. Then a second later, the guy from the night path went by, whistling, the sound of his tune echoing through the rooms and back into the heart of the sand dune. I saw him for only an instant, but knew it was him and knew I recognized him from somewhere.

At least three more times, I caught sight of him in Aruba, and then in the last few days we were there, he seemed to have vanished. The next time I saw him was on the plane going home. Lynn and I had taken our seats, and he passed down the aisle toward the back. His presence surprised me. I sat up, and as he went by, he looked down, straight into my eyes. It wasn't until after takeoff that I realized he was me.

I was petrified the whole flight home, thinking *doppelgänger.* Trapped with one in midair, no less. In Poe, in Hoffmann, in Stevenson, the double was always grim business. I didn't even want to consider the dark foreboding of legends and folklore. But, for all my perspiration, we landed safely and that was that. I saw him briefly at the baggage terminal, walking away, carrying a battered blue suitcase. A few months went by before I caught sight of him in town one snowy afternoon.

"I love it when we can get away and have adventures," said

Lynn, almost in a whisper. She lifted her wineglass and motioned for a toast.

"Me too," I said. The glasses clinked. After that I put the double out of my mind, and by the time we went to bed, I'd convinced myself it was all nonsense.

Two days later, I went out to the garage to put a couple of old pizza boxes in the recycle container. I put the boxes in the container and let the lid slam down. As I turned, he struck the chrome lighter and lit a cigarette. I did a little jump and grunted. He'd never been anywhere near my house before. Although my heart pounded, I felt immediately indignant.

"I'll only be a minute," he said, sensing my anger. "I have a plan to get rid of Fantasma-gris."

I took a deep breath and calmed down. "You know," I said, "I don't know . . ."

"Listen, if he gets through me, you're next. Believe me, you're through if he takes me out."

"Okay," I said. "Okay."

"Someday this week, it's gonna go down, so be ready. And I'm warning you, this is gonna be viscerally brutal. Savage. I don't want you to think this is in any way some kind of psycho breakdown bullshit, you know, all a fancy. There's gonna be blood involved."

He spoke in a harsh tone, and as he went on, I inched back away from him. He looked worse than he had at the mall. I realized he must be sleeping in that suit.

"Whatever," I said, and brushed past him into the house, locking the door to the garage behind me. Lynn was in the kitchen, and I went up there to be close to her. She seemed to me to have powers greater than the double's. I really wanted to tell her, but I didn't.

"Were you calling me?" she asked. She stood at the stove, stirring chili. "I thought I heard a voice from the garage."

"I was singing," I said and put my arms around her. Right then is when I wished I hadn't flushed the pills. Reckless gambling seemed preferable.

The next day, while Lynn was at work, I made an emergency appointment with Dr. Ivy. I knew it was grasping at straws, but I thought if all else failed she'd write me another scrip to cancel the double. For the first five minutes of the session, she gave me shit about stiffing my second appointment and not calling. I just grinned and said sorry when she was through. Finally, she picked up her pad and pen, the music came on as if by magic, and she said, "So, last we spoke, you told me of your double."

"He's back," I said.

"Tell me," she said and leaned forward, her pen at the ready.

"I just want to make one thing clear at the start," I said. "The double of my double is not my double." She nodded as if she understood, and I let it all out for her—the meeting in the mall, the invasion of my garage, and Fantasma-gris. It took me the whole hour to tell her. When I was finished, there was only one minute left of the session for her to speak.

"I'll write you," she said. "What did you do with the last prescription?"

"I threw it in the toilet."

She stared hard at me and tapped her pen on her prescription pad. I noticed that the tattoo around her wrist wasn't ivy at all but actually barbed wire. "Here's something different," she said. "There'll be a slight sense of euphoria, but it should allow you to get through your normal day and also eradicate your double problem."

"Sounds awesome," I said and meant it.

"A slight sense of euphoria" was a bit of an understatement. The next day, after Lynn left for work, I took one of the pills and settled down to a doubleless eight hours. A half hour later, sitting at my computer, Dr. Ivy's cure kicked in, and the world appeared literally brighter. Things looked crisp. I breathed more deeply and sat up straight. I was hyperaware. Looking at the story I'd been writing, I couldn't get to the plot because the shapes of the letters were too distracting. A few minutes passed and then I was floating on a pink cloud, everything recalibrating to a slower focus. I felt so good, I actually laughed.

The drug made me brave, and instead of getting back to work, I dove deep into a rational analysis of my double, determined to figure it all out as much as I could. Staring out the window at the trees and the white house across the street, I plumbed and divided, spinning theories to rival relativity. I kept returning to one question, though. Why Aruba? To answer it might be to solve the puzzle. I got an urge to write up what I remembered of the vacation, to make an official dossier about it. I opened a new screen and wrote as fast as I could, rarely stopping to correct errors.

An hour into it, my ardor for Aruba dried up and I found myself fluffing off, surfing the Web with the word "doppelgänger" in the Google search box. I stumbled upon a site that had a news story about scientists who were able to induce in their subjects the experience of having a double by electrically stimulating a region of the brain known as the left temporoparietal junction. The subjects reported a "shadowy person standing behind them."

I thought back to the night I'd first seen him, scurrying down the bamboo trail. That day Lynn and I had gone ocean kayaking. The plastic board you were supposed to float on didn't look anything like any kayak I'd ever seen. I couldn't keep from falling off it. I'd teeter for a few minutes and then over I'd go. Repeatedly getting back up on the thing in deep water exhausted me in no time, and I was just barely able to dog-paddle to a broken-down dock I used to get back on dry land. I wondered if somewhere in the mêlée, I'd maybe hit my head and the double was born of a concussion.

I couldn't recall a bump, but I was sure I'd solved the puzzle of Aruba. The revelation gave me a sense of accomplishment and confidence until five minutes later when, looking out the window, I saw a car just like mine pull up out in front of my house. The door opened and my double got out. He walked around the car, dressed in that rank suit, heading for our front door. The sight of him made my heart race. "Something's wrong here," I said aloud. There was a knocking at the front door. Shadow, the dog, went nuts, barking like the vicious killer he wasn't. I got up from my chair, feeling slightly dizzy, slightly doomed, and went to put a shirt on. Once I was up, I hurried, not wanting the neighbors to see me in his condition.

I pushed Shadow away and opened the door. "You shouldn't be here," I said.

"But I am."

"I took these pills that are supposed to cancel you."

"Fuck those pills," he said. "What do you think? I'm playing games?" He stepped toward the door as if to enter, and I shut it quickly. He got his forearm on it before I could lock him out and he pushed his way in, sending me stumbling backward a few steps.

"I want you out of here," I said.

"Calm down," he said and closed the door behind him.

I backed away into the kitchen, looking right and left for a pair of scissors or a knife lying on the counter. He followed.

"We've got a job to do," he said. "Fantasma-gris is coalescing like a motherfucker."

"I'm not killing anyone or anything," I said, and noticed he wouldn't look me in the eye.

"I've got him tied up in the trunk of your car. We'll off him and then drive out to the Pine Barrens and sink his body in some remote pond. I have two twenty-pound dumbbells. Nobody has to know." He pushed back the bottom of his suit jacket and grabbed a pistol he'd had in the waist of his pants.

The instant I saw the gun, I was useless with fear.

"Let's go," he said and waved the gun at me.

I went to the living room and stepped into my shoes, grabbed my sweatshirt. We left through the front door. The double drove. I sat still, breathing deeply, in the passenger seat. As he pulled away from the curb, I heard a banging and muffled screams issuing from the trunk.

"If you want to get rid of him," I said, "why don't you just get rid of him yourself? Leave me out of it."

"Step up to the plate and quit your whining," he said. Then he turned and yelled over his shoulder, "Shut the fuck up," to Fantasma-gris, who was making a racket.

We drove south toward the Barrens on the long road that led past the animal rescue and eventually turned to dirt. Just before the asphalt gave out, he made a left and drove slowly down a short block of enormous old houses with porches and gabled roofs. We came to a driveway through the trees that opened into a cul-de-sac. At the turn farthest in sat a huge wreck of a house, brown paint peeling, cedar boards fallen from the walls, the supports of the porch railing busted out.

"My place," he said, turning off the car. He pointed to it with the gun.

"Nice," I said.

"For the money, it's not so great."

I noticed that two of the second-floor windows were broken and there were bricks missing from the chimney.

"Okay, let's get this asshole out and kill him. I figure we can do the job in my room and then take him out to the woods after nightfall."

We got out of the car. It was cold, headed toward evening, and the breeze was reminiscent of the one in Aruba when I'd seen him on the bamboo trail. My mind was knotted with plots to escape.

"Aren't there other people in your house?" I asked. "They'll hear us shoot him."

"Just doubles. They don't give a shit. They've got their own losers to contend with." He went to the trunk and I followed him. Holding the gun at the ready, he put the car key in the lock and turned it. The trunk slowly opened upward, and I peered inside to catch a glimpse of Fantasma-gris.

I don't know what I expected, some kind of smoke goblin maybe, but what I saw was like a white marble or limestone statue of a guy in a fetal position. "What the hell?" I said.

"He's hardened," said my double. "I dipped him in white chocolate. That's how I caught him. He was at my job this morning, busting my balls, and I finally snapped. I grabbed him quick and threw him into the vat. By the time he crawled out,

I'd gotten my gun from my jacket on the back of the dipping-room door."

"This is crazy," I said.

"You're telling me. Grab his ankles, we'll take him up to the house."

Fantasma-gris was a lot lighter than he looked. He was no-where near as big as us, and I can't say his face, a mask of white chocolate, looked anything like me. I had a passing inclination I'd seen it before, though. His lips still moved and mumbled threats. He cursed and called us names. At first it freaked me out, but by the time we reached the steps of my double's place, I found him annoying. On the way in the front door, I acciden-tally slammed his left foot on the door jamb and half his shoe with half a foot cracked off. He howled like a wounded animal within his sweet shell. A quick look told me he was hollow.

The old house was falling apart, water stains on the ceilings and molding coming loose. There were cracks in the lathing of the walls. The floor of the foyer was bare, worn wood. We care-fully set Fantasma-gris down so we could take a breather. The double waved me over to him. I approached and he put his arm lightly around my shoulder, the gun to my stomach.

"I have to go straighten up my room before you're allowed in," he whispered, his breath on fire with booze. He was sweat-ing and ripe with the scent of body funk dipped in chocolate. "If you do anything foolish, I'll hunt you down and kill you and take over your life. You understand?"

My mouth was so dry. I nodded.

"Now, go sit in the parlor with May till I come back." He pointed to an entrance off to the left of the foyer. I took a step toward it and saw a near-empty room filled with twilight, dust bunnies slowly rolling across a splintered floor, bare walls, a dusty chandelier. In the corner by a cold fireplace, a tilting couch on three legs with torn and sweat-stained floral upholstery. At the upright end sat a woman reading a book. She looked over as I entered. Out in the foyer, Fantasma-gris repeatedly screamed, "Fuck."

The minute I saw her face, I knew I knew May from the neighborhood. Lynn was actually pretty good friends with her. "You're May's double?" I asked.

She nodded and smiled. May was our age, a big-boned woman with a ruddy face. She was the swimming instructor at the local Girl Scout camp in the summer. Lived around the corner from us, next to the lake.

"You look just like her," I said.

"Well, that's the idea," she said.

"Do you know me?"

She nodded but said nothing.

"How is May?" I asked and sat carefully on the broken end of the couch.

"She's all right. She had a hysterectomy last fall and I think she's starting to slow down a little. Overall, though, she gets along."

"You live here with my double?"

"Yeah, me and a few others."

"What's he like? You can be honest."

"No disrespect, but he's a total dick. I think he's crazy."

I heard someone descending the steps at the back of the house. "Listen, do me a favor," I said. "Get word to my wife that I'm here and to come get me. You know her, right?"

"If I get a chance," she said. "I'm due downtown in a couple of minutes. May's in the grocery store, and I'm scheduled to appear in the frozen food aisle. If I get a chance I'll have her call Lynn."

I gave her a silent thumbs-up and then my double was at the entrance.

Before we lifted Fantasma-gris, my double broke off his double's pinkie finger and stuck it in his mouth like a cigarette. "Got a light?" he said. Screams of agony issued from the chocolate.

His room was on the second floor and I was out of breath by the time we arrived. We set the double up in a chair. The position he'd come from in the trunk was perfect for sitting, although he was somewhat slouched forward. I was afraid if he fell, he'd shatter all over the floor.

"How come the Fantasma smog didn't leak out when I knocked his toes off? The fucking thing's hollow," I said.

"The chocolate is his prison."

I took a seat on the edge of his bed and my double settled down at a little table by the window. Our prisoner faced me, but my double stared out the window. "As soon as it's nightfall," he said, "we go to town on him."

"Why nightfall?" I asked.

"Cause that's the way you kill him. In the dark."

While I considered whether to bolt for the door or not, I looked at Fantasma-gris's face. The white mask was off-putting. It had very prominent cheeks, eggshell smooth, that I recalled having seen before in a book, on a Noh mask from the fifteenth century.

Out the window, through the trees, there was still the sight of a thin red line at the horizon with night layered on top. Fantasma-gris was whispering to me, trying to communicate something, but I couldn't make it out. He seemed to be losing power.

"Okay, now," said the double. He lifted the gun and cocked the trigger. "Let's have some fun." He pointed it at me.

I put my hands up and turned my head.

"Get up."

I stood, trembling.

"Go over and eat his face."

"I'm not hungry," I said.

"Get the fuck over there," he said and fired the gun into the ceiling.

I jumped and was next to Fantasma-gris in an instant.

"Bite his nose off to spite his face."

I leaned over and opened my mouth, but the prospect of sinking my teeth into a white chocolate nose made me sick. So very faintly, I heard, "Help me, help me . . ." I gagged and then turned away.

"I said eat his damn face," said the double and lunged from his chair toward me. I reached down, grabbed Fantasma-gris's right arm at the wrist with both hands and pulled it off. The double meant to pistol-whip me, but I brought the chocolate arm around like a baseball bat and hit him in the side of the head. White shards exploded everywhere and my double went over like a ton of bricks. The gun flew out of his hand. My instinct was to run, but I remembered all along that I'd have to get the keys from him.

I leaped on him and fished the keys out of his left pocket where I'd seen him stow them earlier. Just as I got up and made to split, he grabbed me by the ankle and tripped me. I went over and smashed into our prisoner, who toppled to the floor with me on top of him and was crushed to smithereens. The leg of the chair rammed into my stomach and knocked the wind out of me. I couldn't move.

As he predicted, there was blood. It trickled out of the corner of my double's mouth. He fetched the gun and aimed it at me. "I'm through with you," he said.

The door opened then and Lynn walked in. "What the hell's going on here?" she said, standing with her hands on her hips. The double immediately lowered the gun and gazed at the floor.

I finally caught my breath and said, "You see, my double. I told you."

"Give me the gun," she said and walked straight over to the double and took it out of his hand. "You two are ridiculous."

The double said, "My double is pretending to be me and tried to kill me. He busted my head with a chocolate arm."

"No," I said, "I'm the real one."

Lynn backed up three steps, raised the pistol like they do in cop shows and pulled the trigger once. I squinted with the din of the shot, and when I looked, my double had a neat round hole in his forehead. His eyes were crossed and smoke issued from the corners of his mouth. He teetered for a heartbeat and then fell, face forward, on the floor. The body twitched and convulsed.

From out in the hallway, I heard May's voice ask, "Is everything all right in there?"

"Swell," called Lynn, and then stepped around behind the double, took aim with the gun again, and put two more slugs in the back of his head. She dropped the gun on top of him and said, "Let's get out of here." She helped me up and we held hands, as we had in the gold mine. Passing May on the stairs, Lynn called a thank-you over her shoulder.

We got into my car and I breathed a sigh of relief. The double was gone for good. "How'd you know which of us was the real one?" I asked as I hurriedly pulled away from the curb.

"It didn't matter," she said. "Whichever one of you was in that fetid fucking suit wasn't coming back to the house."

"What if you chose wrong?" I asked.

"Come on," she said. "I know you." Then she disappeared.

Later that evening, I made coffee and Lynn and I sat on our respective ends of the couch in the living room. "You'll never guess who I met today." I said.

She took a sip of coffee. "Who?"

"Your double," I said.

She was about to raise the cup again but froze. A smile broke out on her face.

"You need a trip to Dr. Ivy," I said.

She shook her head. "I know, what a hypocrite, but I didn't see my double before you told me about yours."

"Why didn't you let me know?"

"It didn't matter as much if I had one, I just didn't want *you* to go crazy."

"So you're as crazy as I am," I said.

"In my own way."

"But your double was actually helpful. How come yours is cool and mine was an asshole?"

"Think about it," she said.

I did and while I did she took a folded napkin out of the pocket of her sweatpants. She held it up in the palm of one hand and opened it with the other. Between her thumb and index finger, she lifted up a white chocolate ear and let the napkin flutter down. She broke off a piece and handed it to me. We had it with our coffee while she told me that it was in the chapel with the image of Copernicus on the ceiling, in that ancient castle in Krakow, where we'd been told we could experience "The Ninth Chakra of the World," that she'd first seen herself.

A Note About "The Double of My Double Is Not My Double"

Doubles (doppelgängers) abound in *Crackpot Palace*—some more obvious than others. I've long been interested in the phenomenon in literature and film and have somewhere among my things a sheet of paper on which for years I kept a list of stories, novels, and movies in which I encountered the Double theme. Some sharp editor will someday take this theme up for a story anthology and create a very interesting book of fiction. The doppelgänger seems to go beyond the bounds of imagination, though. In my story offered here in the collection, the scientific study that the protagonist mentions stumbling upon online is actually real—the fact that the electrical stimulation of a region of the brain known as the left temporoparietal junction caused subjects to report a "shadowy person standing behind them." To offer more evidence that the double phenomenon might be more than mere fiction, one can also consider the testimony of Sir Ernest Shackleton's experience with the Third Man syndrome. He writes about it in his book *South*. He was on a mountain-climbing expedition on St. George's Island, beyond the tip of South America, in severe polar conditions. His party, comprised of himself and two other men, was under great stress, carrying on through stark glacial conditions for a thirty-six-hour stretch. He and the others reported feeling the definite presence of a fourth person in their party. Other Antarctic explorers and mountain climbers have also admitted to the phenomenon, as well as those involved in storms at sea and shipwrecked castaways. Scientists believe that the syndrome is related to great physical and mental stress and may be the impetus for the concept of the guardian angel. T. S. Eliot was influenced by having read Shackleton's firsthand account of the experience and included these lines in his poem *The Waste Land:*

> *Who is the third who walks always beside you?*
> *When I count, there are only you and I together*
> *But when I look ahead up the white road*
> *There is always another one walking beside you*
> *Gliding wrapt in a brown mantle, hooded*
> *I do not know whether a man or a woman*
> *- But who is that on the other side of you?*

I often wonder if other fiction writers sometimes experience the sensation of being at least two people—the one who lives life outwardly, moving amid the populace, talking, laughing, gossiping, eating meals, and participating in history, and the one who writes the stories. They often seem like two different people to me. The one smarter and more capable about everyday life but not really knowing how to write stories, and the story writer, who feels lost in the everyday world, intuitive and adept when it comes to characters and plots and the flow of language. Crackpot, I know.

Daltharee

Y ou've heard of bottled cities, no doubt—society writ minuscule and delicate beyond reason: toothpick-spired towns, streets no thicker than thread, pinprick faces of the citizenry peering from office windows smaller than sequins. Hustle, politics, fervor, struggle, capitulation, wrapped in a crystal firmament, stoppered at the top to keep reality both in and out. Those microscopic lives, striking glass at the edge of things, believed themselves gigantic, their dilemmas universal.

Our research suggested that Daltharee had many multistoried buildings carved right into its hillsides. Surrounding the city there was a forest with lakes and streams, and all of it was contained within a dome, like a dinner beneath the lid of a serving dish. When the inhabitants of Daltharee looked up, they were prepared to not see the heavens. They knew that the light above, their Day, was generated by a machine, which they oiled and cared for. The stars that shone every sixteen hours when Day left darkness behind were simple bulbs regularly changed by a man in a hot-air balloon.

They were convinced that the domed city floated upon an iceberg, which it actually did. There was one door in the wall of the dome at the end of a certain path through the forest. When opened, it led out onto the ice. The surface of the iceberg extended the margin of one of their miles all around the enclosure. Blinding snows fell, winds constantly roared in a perpetual blizzard. Their belief was that Daltharee drifted upon the oceans of an otherwise frozen world. They prayed for the end of eternal winter so they might reclaim the continents.

And all of this: their delusions, the city, the dome, the iceberg, the two quarts of water it floated upon, were contained within an old glass gallon milk bottle, plugged at the top with a tattered handkerchief and painted dark blue. When I'd put my ear to the glass, I'd hear, like the ocean in a seashell, fierce gales blowing.

Daltharee was not the product of a shrinking ray, as many of these pint-size metropolises are. And please, there was no magic involved. In fact, once past the early stages of its birth it was more organically grown than shaped by artifice. Often, in the origin stories of these diminutive places, there's a deranged scientist lurking in the wings. Here too we have the notorious Mando Paige, the inventor of submicroscopic differentiated cell division and growth. What I'm referring to was Paige's technique for producing superminiature human cells. From the instant of their atomic origin, these parcels of life were beset by enzymatic reaction and electric stunting the way tree roots are tortured over time to create a bonsai. Paige shaped human life in the form of tiny individuals. They landscaped and built the city, laid roads, and lurched in a sleep-walking stupor induced by their creator.

Once the city in the dome was completed, Paige introduced more of the crumb-size citizenry through the door that opened onto the iceberg. Just before closing that door, he set off a device that played an A flat for approximately ten seconds, a preordained spur to consciousness, which brought them all awake to their lives in Daltharee. Seeding the water in the gallon bottle with crystal ions, he soon after introduced a chemical mixture that formed a slick, unmelting icelike platform beneath the floating dome. He then introduced into the atmosphere fenathol nitrate, silver iodite, and anamidian betheldine to initiate the frigid wind and falling snow. When all was well within the dome, when the iceberg had sufficiently grown, when winter ruled, he plugged the gallon bottle with an old handkerchief. That closed system of winter, with just the slightest amount of air allowed in through the cloth, was sustainable forever, feeding wind to snow and snow to cold to claustrophobia and back again in an infinite loop. The Dalthareens made up the story about a frozen world to satisfy the unknown. Paige manufactured three more of these cities, each wholly different from the others, before laws were passed about the imprisonment of humanity, no matter how minute or unaware. He was eventually, himself, imprisoned for his crimes.

We searched for a method to study life inside the dome but were afraid to disturb its delicate nature, unsure whether simply removing the handkerchief would upset a brittle balance between inner and outer universes. It was suggested that a very long, exceedingly thin probe that had the ability to twist and turn by computational command could be shimmied in between the edge of the bottle opening and the cloth of the handkerchief. This probe, like the ones physicians used in the twentieth and twenty-first centuries to read the hieroglyphics of the bowel, would be fitted out with both a camera and a microphone. The device was adequate for those cities that didn't have the extra added boundary of a dome, but even in them, how incongruous, a giant metal snake just out of the blue, slithering through one's reality. The inhabitants of these enclosed worlds were exceedingly small but not stupid.

In the end it was my invention that won the day—a voice-activated transmitter the size of two atoms was introduced into the bottle. We had to wait for it to work its way from the blizzard atmosphere, through the dome's air filtration system, and into the city. Then we had to wait for it to come in contact with a voice. At any point a thousand things could have gone wrong, but one day, six months later—who knows how many years that would be in Dalthareen time—the machine transmitted and my receiver picked up conversations from the domed city. Here's an early one we managed to record that had some interesting elements:

"I'm not doing that now. Please, give me some room . . ." she said.

There is a long pause filled with the faint sound of a utensil clinking on a plate.

"I was out in the forest the other day," he said.

"Why?" she asked.

"I'm not sure," he told her.

"What do you do out there?" she asked.

"I'm in this club," he said. "We got together to try to find the door in the wall of the dome."

"How did that go?" she asked.

"We knew it was there and we found it," he said. "Just like in the old stories . . ."

"Blizzard?"

"You can't believe it," he said.

"Did you go out in it?"

"Yes, and when I stepped back into the dome, I could feel a piece of the storm stuck inside me."

"What's that supposed to mean?" she said.

"I don't know."

"How did it get inside you?" she asked.

"Through my ears," he said.

"Does it hurt?"

"I was different when I came back in."

"Stronger?"

"No, more something else."

"Can you say?"

"I've had dreams."

"So what," she said. "I had a dream the other night that I was out on the Grand Conciliation Balcony, dressed for the odd jibbery, when all of a sudden a little twisher rumbles up and whispers to me the words 'Elemental Potency.' What do you think it means? I can't get the phrase out of my head."

"It's nonsense," he said.

"Why aren't *your* dreams nonsense?"

"They are," he said. "The other night I had this dream about a theory. I can't remember if I saw it in the pages of a dream magazine or someone spoke it or it just jumped into my sleeping head. I've never dreamt about a theory before. Have you?"

"No," she said.

"It was about living in the dome. The theory was that since the dome is closed, things that happen in the dome only affect other things in the dome. Because the size of Daltharee is, as we believe, so minuscule compared to the rest of the larger world, the repercussions of the acts you engage in in the dome will have a higher possibility of intersecting each other. If you think of something you do throughout the day as an act, each act begins a chain reaction of mitigating energy in all directions. The will of your own energy, dispersed through myriad acts within only a morning, will beam, refract, and reflect off the beams of others' acts and the walls of the closed system, barreling into each other and causing sparks at those locations where your essence meets itself. In those instances, at those specific locations, your will is greater than the will of the dome. What I was then told was that a person could learn a way to act at a given hour—a quick series of six moves that send out so many ultimately crisscrossing intentions of will that it creates a power mesh capable in its transformative strength of bending reality to whim."

"You're crazy," she said.

There is a slight pause here, the sound of wind blowing in the trees.

"Hey, whatever happened to your aunt?" he asked.

"They got it out of her."

"Amazing," he said. "Close call . . ."

"She always seemed fine too," she said. "But swallowing a knitting needle? That's not right."

"She doesn't even knit, does she?"

"No," she said.

"Good thing she didn't have to pass it," he said. "Think about the intersecting beams of will resulting from that act."

She laughed. "I heard the last pigeon died yesterday."

"Yeah?"

"They found it in the park, on the lawn amid the Moth trees."

"In all honesty, I did that," he said. "You know, not directly, but just by the acts I went through yesterday morning. I got out of bed, had breakfast, got dressed, you know . . . like that. I was certain that by midday that bird would be dead."

"Why'd you kill it?" she asked.

There's a pause in the conversation here, filled up by the sound of machinery in the distance, just beneath that of the wind in the trees.

"Having felt what I felt outside the dome, I considered it a mercy," he said.

"Interesting . . ." she said. "I've gotta get going. It looks like rain."

"Will you call me?" he asked.

"Eventually, of course," she said.

"I know," he said. "I know."

Funny thing about Paige, he found religion in the later years of his life. After serving out his sentence, he renounced his crackpot science and retreated to a one-room apartment in an old boardinghouse on the edge of the great desert. He courted an elderly woman there, a Mrs. Trucy. I thought he'd been long gone when we finally contacted him. After a solid fifteen years of recording conversations, it became evident that the domed city was failing—the economy, the natural habitat were both in disarray. A strange illness had sprung up amid the population, an unrelenting, fatal insomnia that took a dozen of them to Death each week. Nine months without a single wink of sleep. The conversations we recorded then were full of anguish and hallucination.

Basically, we asked Paige what he might do to save his own created world. He came to work for us and studied the problem full time. He was old then, wrinkles and flyaway hair in strange, ever-shifting formations atop his scalp, eyeglasses with one ear loop. Every time he'd make a mistake on a calculation or a technique, he'd swallow a thumbtack. When I asked if the practice helped him concentrate, he told me, "No."

Eventually, on a Saturday morning when no one was at the lab but himself and an uninterested security guard, he broke into the vault that held the shrinking ray. He started the device up, aimed it at the glass milk bottle containing Daltharee, and then sat on top of the bottle, wearing a parachute. The ray discharged, shrinking him. He fell in among the gigantic folds of the handkerchief. Apparently he managed to work his way down past the end of the material and leap into the blizzard, out over the dome of the city. No one was there to see him slowly descend, dangerously buffeted by the insane winds. No one noticed him slip through the door in the dome.

Conversations eventually came back to us containing his name. Apparently he'd told them the true nature of the dome and the bottle it resided inside. And then after some more time passed, there came word that he was creating another domed city inside a gallon milk bottle from the city of Daltharee. Where would it end? we wondered, but it was not a thought we enjoyed pursuing as it ran in a loop, recrossing itself, reiterating its original energy in ever diminishing reproductions of ourselves. Perhaps it was the thought of it that made my assistant accidentally drop the milk bottle one afternoon. It exploded into a million dark blue shards, dirt and dome and tiny trees spread across the floor. We considered studying its remains, but instead, with a shiver, I swept it into a pile and then into the furnace.

A year later, Mrs. Trucy came looking for Mando. She insisted upon knowing what had become of him. We told her that the law did not require us to tell her, and then she pulled a marriage certificate out of her purse. I was there with the Research

General at the time, and I saw him go pale as a ghost upon seeing that paper. He told her Mando had died in an experiment of his own devising. The wrinkles of her gray face twisted, and sitting beneath her pure silver hair, her head looked like a metal screw. Three tears squeezed out from the corners of her eyes. If Mando died performing an experiment, we could not be held responsible. We would, though, have to produce the body for her as proof that he'd perished. The Research General told her we were conducting a complete investigation of the tragedy and would contact her in six weeks with the results and the physical proof—in other words, Mando's corpse.

My having shoveled Daltharee into the trash without searching for survivors or mounting even a cursory rescue effort was cause for imprisonment. My superior, the Research General, having had my callous act take place on his watch, was also liable. After three nerve-racking days, I conceived of a way for us to save ourselves. In fact it was so simple it astounded me that neither one of us, scientific minds though we be, had leaped to the concept earlier. Using Mando's own process for creating diminutive humanity, we took his DNA from our genetic files, put it through a chemical bath to begin the growth process, and then tortured the cells into tininess. We had to use radical enzymes to speed the process up given we had only six weeks. By the end of week five we had a living, breathing Mando Paige, trapped under a drinking glass in our office. He was dressed in a little orange jumpsuit, wore black boots, and was in the prime of his youth. We studied his attempts to escape his prison with a jeweler's loupe inserted into each eye. We thought we could rely on the air simply running out in the glass and him suffocating.

Days passed and Paige hung on. Each day I'd spy on his

meager existence and wonder what he must be thinking. When the time came and he wasn't dead, I killed him with a cigarette. I brought the glass to the very edge of the table, bent a plastic drinking straw that I shoved the longer end of up into the glass, and then caught it fairly tightly against the table edge. As for the part that stuck out, I lit a cigarette, inhaled deeply, and then blew the smoke up into the glass. I gave him five lungfuls. The oxygen displacement was too much, of course.

Mrs. Trucy accepted our story and the magnified view of her lover's diminutive body. We told her how he bravely took the shrinking ray for the sake of science. She remarked that he looked younger than when he was full size and alive, and the Research General told her, "As you shrink, wrinkles have a tendency to evaporate." We went to the funeral out in the desert near her home. It was a blazingly hot day. She'd had his remains placed into a thimble with some tape across the top, and this she buried in the red sand.

Later, as the sun set, the Research General and I ate dinner at a ramshackle restaurant along a dusty road right outside of Mateos. He had the pig knuckle with sauerkraut and I had the chicken croquettes with orange gravy that tasted brown.

"I'm so relieved that asshole's finally dead," whispered the Research General.

"There's dead and there's dead," I told him.

"Let's not make this complicated," he said. "I know he's out there in some smaller version of reality, he could be filling all available space with smaller and smaller reproductions of himself, choking the ass of the universe with pages and pages of Mando Paige. I don't give a fuck as long as he's not here."

"He is here," I said, and then they brought the martinis and the conversation evaporated into reminiscence.

That night as I stood out beneath the desert sky having a smoke, I had a sense that the cumulative beams generated by the repercussions of my actions over time, harboring my inherent will, had reached some far-flung boundary and were about to turn back on me. In my uncomfortable bed at the Hacienda Motel, I tossed and turned, drifting in and out of sleep. It was then that I had a vision of the shrinking ray, its sparkling blue emission bouncing off a mirror set at an angle. The beam then travels a short distance to another mirror with which it collides and reflects. The second mirror is positioned so that it sends the ray back at its own original source. The beam strikes and mixes with itself only a few inches past the nozzle of the machine's barrel. And then I see it in my mind—when a shrinking ray is trained upon itself, its diminutive-making properties are canceled twice, and as it is a fact that when two negatives are multiplied they make a positive, this process makes things bigger. As soon as the concept was upon me, I was filled with excitement and couldn't wait to get back to the lab the next day to work out the math and realize an experiment.

It was fifteen years later, the Research General had long been fired, when Mando Paige stepped out of the spot where the shrinking ray's beam crossed itself. He was blue and yellow and red and his hair was curly. I stood within feet of him and he smiled at me. I, of course, couldn't let him go—not due to any law but my own urge to finish the job I'd started at the outset. As he stepped back toward the ray, I turned it off, and he was trapped, for the moment, in our moment. I called for my assistants to surround him, and I sent one to my office for the revolver I kept in my bottom drawer. He told me that one speck of his saliva contained four million Daltharees. "When I fart," he said, "I set forth armadas." I shot him and the four assistants and then automatically acid-washed the lab to destroy the Dalthareen plague and evidence of murder. No one suspected a thing.

I found a few cities sprouting beneath my fingernails last week. There were already rows of domes growing behind my ears. My blood no doubt is the manufacture of cities, flowing silver through my veins. Crowds behind my eyes, commerce in my joints. Each idea I have is a domed city that grows and opens like a flower. I want to tell you about cities and cities and cities named Daltharee.

A Note About "Daltharee"

This story originally appeared in *The Del Rey Book of Science Fiction and Fantasy,* edited by Ellen Datlow, and got some good reviews as well as coverage in the *Los Angeles Times*. It would be almost impossible to be my age and, in writing a bottled-city story, not have been influenced by Kandor, the capital city of the planet Krypton, which was shrunken and bottled by Superman's nemesis, Brainiac. The most interesting thing to me about "Daltharee" is that it just barely misses adding up and making sense. This was intentional on my part; I was interested for a while in stories that are made to be consciously misshapen or broken in some way. No one ever complained about the fact that the shrinking of the city, Daltharee, and the smaller and smaller reproductions of it really don't account for its proliferation and/or its infecting of the scientist/protagonist, Mando Paige. The story seems like it ought to make sense, and in a way, that seems to have been enough for readers.

Ganesha

On a floating platform adrift in the placid Sea of Eternity, Ganesha sat on his golden throne beneath a canopy of eight cobras. The eyes in his elephant head gazed out past the moon; his big ears rippled in the breeze. Each of his four human hands was occupied, so his trunk curled up to scratch his cheek, the itch a manifestation of evil in the million-and-second reality. In one hand he held the pointed shard of his broken tusk, using it to write on parchment held by the second hand. In his third hand was a lotus flower, and his fourth hand was turned palm out to show a red tattoo of a cross with bent arms, meaning "be well." He wore baggy silk pants the color of the sun, but no shirt to cover his chest and bulging gut. His necklace was a live snake, as was his belt. At his feet sat Kroncha, the rat, nibbling a stolen modak sweet.

In the west, something fell out of the sky, sparking against the night. Ganesha watched its descent and, when it collided with the sea, a great sizzle and a burst of light becoming dark again, he marked the spot by pointing his trunk. He stood and stretched. "A journey," he said to Kroncha. The rat followed and they went to the edge of the floating platform, where a boat had appeared, an open craft lined with comfortable pillows. In a blink, they were aboard. Ganesha rested his weighty head back, one hand holding a parasol to block the moonlight, and crossed his legs. They remembered only after they had pushed off to bring the modak sweets, and so the sweets appeared. The wind picked up and gently powered the boat to sea.

After a brief eternity, they reached the spot where the object had fallen.

"There it is," said Kroncha, who was sitting atop the parasol. As Ganesha rose, the rat scurried down his back.

The boat maneuvered next to the floating debris. Ganesha leaned over and picked something out of the water. "Look at this," he said and held up a prayer. It wriggled in his hands for a moment before he popped it in his mouth and ate it.

"Where to this time?" said Kroncha, leaning his elbow against the bowl of sweets, shaking his head.

"My favorite, New Jersey," said Ganesha, and his laughter, the sound of om, gave birth to realities.

They took the Turnpike south from the Holland Tunnel, Ganesha perfectly balanced on Kroncha's small back. The rat did seventy-five and complained bitterly of tailgating. At the traffic tie-up, they leaped in graceful arcs from the roof of one car to the next, landing in perfect silence and rhythm. Back on the road, Ganesha eventually gave instructions to take the number 6 exit south. Kroncha complied with relief.

In the next instant, it was the following afternoon, and Kroncha carried Ganesha across a vast, sunburned field toward a thicket of trees next to a lake. In among the trees, there were picnic tables, and sitting at one of them, the only person in the entire park, was a dark-haired teenage girl smoking a cigarette. She wore cutoff jeans and a red T-shirt, sneakers without socks. When she saw the elephant-headed god approaching, she laughed out loud, and said, "I thought you might show up this time. I burned five cones of incense."

"A tasty morsel," said Ganesha as he dismounted from the rat with a little hop. His stomach and chest jiggled. The girl stood and walked toward him. When she came within reach, he lifted his trunk and wrapped it around her shoulders. She closed her eyes and patted it softly twice. "Florence," he whispered in an ancient voice.

"I changed my name," she said, turning and heading back toward the table.

Ganesha laughed. "Changed your name?" he said and followed her. "To what, Mithraditliaminak?"

She took a seat on one side of the bench, and he shimmied as much of his rear end as he could onto the opposite side, lifting hers a couple of inches off the ground. The wooden planks beneath them quietly complained as the two leaned back against the edge of the table.

"Call me Chloe," she said.

"Very well," said Ganesha.

"Florence is a crappy name," she said, "like an old woman with a girdle and a hairnet."

"You have wisdom," said Ganesha, and allowed the bowl of sweets to appear on the table between them.

"Chloe's much more . . . I don't know . . . I love these things," she said, lifting one of the golden rice balls. "How many calories are they, though?"

"Each one's a universe," he said, lifting a modak with the end of his trunk and bringing it to his mouth.

"I'll just have a half," she said.

"She'll just have a half," said Kroncha, who sat at their feet.

"If you bite it, you'll be compelled to finish it," said Ganesha.

Her lips were parting and the sweet was just under her nose. Its aroma went to her eyes and she saw a beautiful garden alive with butterflies and turquoise birds, but even there she heard his warning.

"No," she said and put the sweet back into the bowl.

"Aha!" he said, and picked up the abandoned modak. He stood up suddenly, her end of the bench falling three inches, and he waddled a few feet away from the picnic table. Standing in a small clearing amid the thicket, his elephant head trumpeted, his human legs danced, and his four arms spun. As his clarion note echoed out through the trees and across the field and lake in all directions, he gave a little kick, and threw the modak into the sky.

Her gaze followed its trajectory, first golden against the blue day and then, all of a sudden, a ball of fire streaking away through the night. The eyeblink replacement of sun with moon nearly made her lose her balance. Still, she managed to watch until the sweet became a star among the million other stars. When Ganesha, glowing slightly in the dark, turned to face her, she clapped for him. He bowed.

Once they were situated back on the bench, the girl lit a cigarette. Ganesha gently waved her smoke away with his ears, and curled his trunk over his left shoulder. Kroncha climbed on the bench between them, curled up, and went to sleep.

She leaned forward, her elbows on her knees, and turned her head to look at him. "It's night now?" she asked.

He nodded, pointing to the moon and stars with three of his hands.

"What happened to the day?" she asked.

"You'll get it back later," he said.

"Got my report card today," she said and took a drag.

"A triumph, no doubt," he said.

"When my father saw it, he checked my pulse. My mother was in tears. I can't help it, though, their frustration is comical to me. Like a report card. What does it really mean?"

"An excellent question," said Ganesha.

"Should I care?"

"Do you feel as if you should?"

"No," she said, and flicked the glowing butt away onto the dirt.

"You've outwitted that conundrum then," he said.

She leaned over slightly and began petting the sleeping Kroncha.

"When I saw you in the time of the red leaves, you told me you were in love," said Ganesha.

She smiled. "An elephant never forgets," she said. "I hate that part."

"The young gentleman with the tattoo of Porky Pig on his calf?"

She nodded and smiled, "You know Porky Pig?" she said.

Ganesha waved with all four hands. "That's all, folks."

"Simon," she said. "He was okay for a while. We used to bike out to the forest, and he helped me build a little shrine to you out of cinder blocks from the abandoned sand factory. I brought out your picture, and we'd go there at night, drink beer and light incense. He was really cute, but under the cute there was too much stupid. He was always either grabbing my tits or punching me in the shoulder. He laughed like a clown. After I dumped him, I rode out to the forest, to the shrine, one day and found that he'd wrecked it, tore your picture to scraps and kicked over the thing we'd built, which, now that I think about it, looked a lot like a barbecue pit. Then he told everyone I was weird."

"Aren't you?" asked Ganesha.

"I guess I am," she said. "Poe's my favorite writer, and I like to be alone a lot. I like the sound of the wind in the trees out by the abandoned factory. I like it when my parents are asleep at night and aren't worrying about me. I can feel their worry in my back. I have a lot of daydreams—being in a war, being married, making animated movies about a porcupine named Florence, running away, getting really good at poetry, having sex, getting really smart and telling people what to do, getting a car and driving all over."

"Sounds like you'll need to get busy," said Ganesha.

"Tell me about it," she said. "My specialty is napping."

"A noble pursuit," he said.

"The other day," she said, "when I took a walk in the afternoon, I went all the way out to the factory. I sat on that big rock next to it and watched the leaves blowing in the wind. In a certain configuration of sky and leaves, I saw this really detailed image of a mermaid. It was like she was there flying through the air."

He closed his eyes and tried to picture it.

"A rabbit hopped out from behind a tree then, and I looked away for a second. When I looked back to the leaves, she was gone. No matter how I squinted or moved my head, I couldn't find her there anymore."

"Nevermore," whispered Kroncha from sleep.

"I thought it might have been a sign from you."

"No," said Ganesha, "that was yours."

"I've wanted to write a poem about it," she said. "I can feel it inside me, there's energy there to do it, but when I sit down and concentrate—no words. All that happens is I start thinking about other stuff. I'm afraid I'll look away from her one day, and she'll be gone, as well, from my memory."

"Well," he said, sitting forward, "am I the destroyer of obstacles or am I not?" As he spoke, the color drained from him and he became a gleaming white. Out of thin air appeared four more arms to make eight, and in his various hands he held a noose, a goad, a green parrot, a sprig of the kalpavriksha tree, a prayer vessel, a sword, and a pomegranate. His eighth hand, empty, he turned palm up as if offering something invisible to her.

"You are definitely the Lakshmi Ganapati," she said, laughing.

The seven items suddenly disappeared from his hands, but he remained the color of the moon. "Show me the things you think about instead of the mermaid," he said.

"How?"

"Just think about them," he said. "Close your eyes."

She did, but after quite a while, she said, "I can't even picture . . . Oh, wait. Here's something." Her eyes squinted more tightly closed. She felt the image in her thoughts gather itself into a bubble and exit her head. It tickled the lobe of her left ear like a secret kiss as it bobbed away on the breeze. She opened her eyes to see it. There it floated, five feet from them, a clear bubble with a scene inside.

"Who's that?" asked Ganesha.

"My mother," she said.

"She's preparing something."

"Meat loaf."

"Do you like it?" he asked.

"Gross," she said.

"Not exactly a modak," he said. "Let's see more."

She closed her eyes and thought, and eventually the bubbles came in clusters, exiting from both ears. Each held a tiny scene from her life. They bobbed in midair and sailed on the breeze, glowing pale blue. Some had risen to the tallest branches of the trees and some lit snaking paths through the thicket toward the lake or field.

"There goes Simon," she said, as the last few bubbles exited her right ear.

"Call them back," said Ganesha.

"How?"

"Whistle," he said.

She did, and no sooner had she made a sound than all of the glowing bubbles halted in their leisurely flights and slowly reversed course. She whistled again, and they came faster and faster, flying from all directions, each emitting a musical note that made their return a song that filled the surrounding thicket. Their speed became dizzying, and then, at once, they all collided, exploding in a wave of blue that swamped the picnic table. The blue blindness quickly evaporated to reveal a man-shaped creature composed of the bubbles. Now, instead of scenes, each globe held an eye at its center. The thing danced wildly before Chloe and Ganesha, sticking out its long, undulating tongue of eyes.

She reared back against the table. "What is it?"

"A demon. We must destroy it," said Ganesha, and leaped off the bench. The ground vibrated with his landing, and this startled the demon, which turned and fled, its form wavering, turning momentarily to pure static like the picture on the old television in her parents' den.

"Kroncha, to the hunt," said Ganesha, his color changing

again, blue and red swirling through moon-white and mixing.

The rat rubbed its eyes, stood up, and jumped down to the ground. As Ganesha squatted upon Kroncha's back, the rat asked, "A demon?"

Ganesha now brandished the point of his broken tusk as a weapon. "Correct," he said. Kroncha inched forward, building speed.

Chloe was stunned by what she'd seen. She wanted to follow but was unable to move.

"I suspected as much from the moment she refused the modak," said the rat.

Ganesha nodded and they were off.

It wasn't until god and vehicle were just a faint smudge of brightness weaving away through the trees that Chloe overcame the static in her head and woke from amazement. The thought that called her back was that the demon could easily return and she would have to battle it alone. She tasted adrenaline as she bolted from the bench. Across the clearing and into the trees she sprinted, afraid to call out for what might be watching.

At one point, early on, she thought she would catch them, but Kroncha moved deceptively fast and suddenly the path had disappeared. The ground was uneven and riddled with protruding roots. She hurried as best she could, still driven by fear. "Where's my day?" she whispered. The night was getting cold. She passed through a forest she'd not known existed, waiting for the demon to pounce at any moment and thankful for the moonlight.

The trees eventually gave way to a sandy mountain path littered with boulders. She knew there were no mountains within a hundred miles of where she lived. "I'm in a dream within a dream," she thought, and climbed up onto a flat rock to rest. Her legs hurt and she realized she was exhausted. She lay back and looked for her star, but it was lost among the others.

"If I fall asleep here and then wake, I'll wake from this dream and be back at the picnic table in late afternoon," she thought. She closed her eyes and listened to the breeze.

She knew she'd slept but it seemed only for the briefest moment, and when she opened her eyes she groaned to see more night. There was soft sand beneath her, not rock, and it came to her that she was in a new place. Remembering the threat of the demon, she stood quickly and turned in a circle, her hands in fists. The moonlight showed, a few yards away, a mountain wall with a cave opening. Within the cave, she perceived a flickering light.

"It's in there," she thought, and at that instant, Ganesha's broken tusk appeared in her left hand. "We must destroy it," she remembered him saying and realized that she'd never retrieve her day unless she confronted the demon. An image came to her mind of her mother making meat loaf and it weighed her down, slowed her, as she moved toward the opening in the mountain. She fought against it as if against a strong, silent wind. And then a cascade of other memories beset her—Simon, her father, her condescending English teacher, a group of kids snickering as she passed, her image in the bedroom mirror . . . Still she struggled, managing to inch along, drawing closer to the light within. At the entrance, she hesitated, unable to move forward, and then holding the tusk in front of her, point out, she swung her arm, slicing a huge gash in the malevolent resistance. There was a bang, the myriad bubble eyes that composed her demon exploding, and its power over her bled away quickly into the night.

The cave's interior was like a rock cathedral, the ceiling vaulting into the shadows above. Instead of the demon there was a shining blue woman holding a lotus flower, floating six feet off the ground. She wore a jade-green gown and a helmet made of gold. The blue vision smiled down upon Chloe, and the girl felt a beautiful warmth run through her, putting her at ease and filling her with energy.

"I am the shakti," said the blue woman.

"The power?" asked Chloe.

The woman nodded. She motioned for the girl to sit at the table between them where lay a blank sheet of paper. Chloe sat on the stone bench and turned the tusk around in her hand, from a weapon to a pen. The shakti gave her light, and she wrote, the tusk moving like an implement made of water over the page, birthing words almost before she thought them.

A Week of Faces in the Trees

I saw her there
with flowing hair
green against the blue
A woman in a tree
a woman of the sea
and then I thought of you
Her tail of leaves
swam through the breeze
she nodded into light
Her eyes were figs
her fingers twigs
outstretched as if in flight
Then I thought of you and me

alone together by the sea,
beneath the sun some time ago
We found blue glass there
amid the clumps of mermaid hair
and I quoted Edgar Allan Poe
"Everything we see and seem
is but a dream within a dream."
You smiled and shook your head
When summers into winters passed
through every different color glass
I learned the lie in what I'd said
The woman in the tree is gone
Out beyond the blue beyond
I turn away and slowly walk
Wondering tomorrow what I'll see
who the blowing leaves will be
what I'll have to say to me when we talk

Back in the late afternoon, at the picnic table in the thicket by the lake, Florence folded the piece of paper that held her poem and slipped it into her back pocket. Then she capped her pen and climbed up on top of the table to sit with legs crossed, staring out at the sun's last reflection on the lake. She had a smoke and watched the world turn to twilight, the stars slowly appear. Among them, she was surprised to be able to identify her own, and she reached up into the sky for it. It burned in her hand at first with a cold fire, but as she drew it toward her mouth, it became the sweet modak.

"A universe," said Kroncha, sitting at the foot of Ganesha's throne on the floating platform in the Sea of Eternity. "She'll have no room for meat loaf tonight."

Ganesha nodded and his stomach jiggled when he laughed, the echo of his mirth pervading a million realities, crumbling a million obstacles to dust.

A Note About "Ganesha"

I'd been researching the figure of Ganesha for a while, thinking about writing a story about him but never really feeling like I'd gotten to the bottom of things. While I was looking into this stuff, I had a student in my writing class, an older guy. He was a retired doctor who'd been born and raised in India. He was a good guy, had a great sense of humor. We used to talk after class a lot. One day I asked him about Ganesha. He knew a lot about the god and pointed out certain authentic texts on the Internet about him. He also had some cool ideas about Ganesha's significance in the modern world and his relationship to the phenomenon of computing due to the fact that he was able to take down the Mahabharata from Vyasa without pause and with full understanding. At the end of the semester, after the last class, I asked him what he thought about my writing the story. He didn't say anything for a while, but eventually he said, "If you write it with an open heart, Ganesha will accept it." In the moment, I thought, "Solid," but on the drive home that day a question slowly dawned on me, specifically, "What the hell did he mean by 'an open heart'?" I never saw the doctor again, but I thought about his statement for a long time before I could write the story. It is undoubtedly the story of a cultural appropriation. What happens when we adopt aspects of other cultures and incorporate them into our lives in a way perhaps not fitting their original intended meaning or use? Is this always negative or, if one goes about it with an open heart, are there worthwhile things to be learned? This story appeared in the anthology *The Beastly Bride: Tales of the Animal People,* the last in a series of four YA books (*The Green Man, The Faerie Reel, Coyote Road*) edited by Ellen Datlow and Terri Windling and illustrated by Charles Vess. I loved working on the stories for them.

Every Richie There Is

Richie's left arm doesn't work; neither does his face. The arm hangs limp, like the catch of the day, but the face, like a maniac appliance, clicks through far too many major emotions in the course of a minute. You see every Richie there is in the time it takes for him to proudly reel off the first and last names of all of the executives he has met while working for the last thirteen years in the print shop at Mrs. Paul's fish stick factory. It's like a Richie train passing before your eyes and your first reaction is to want to run home and sharpen a screwdriver.

He rents the downstairs of one side of a duplex next door, and our places are separated by only a narrow concrete driveway that we share. The house he lives in, like some ancient druid earth mound, is a magnet for tragedy. There was a woman who used to live upstairs who tried to commit suicide after she jilted her boyfriend and he succeeded in killing himself. After he was gone, I heard her sing love songs at the top of her voice along with the stereo. Then she took some pills and broke all the plates. There was a young pregnant mother with bad teeth and three kids who was addicted to alcohol and smack and who, after she fled in the middle of the night, was being hunted by the FBI. One night, after she had the baby, she asked me to go to the bar and buy her a twelve-pack of beer. Thinking of the child, I refused and gave her all my cigarettes instead. There was a stoned-out Laurel and Hardy couple who sold satellite dishes. During the day they were filled with hippie sincerity but they duked it out every Saturday night. And there is the woman who lives above him now, Patty Playpal, whose boyfriend socked her in the face because he couldn't stand her incessant, coke-fueled blather for another second. Richie, fifty-four, with a ball-peen-to-the-forehead personality, must have felt this place drawing him across time and space the way a trout feels the persistent tug of the hook.

Suzie is his only companion. She's dark and noble and has a wide ass. Her collar is black, studded with chrome points, and her favorite thing, next to Richie, is a rubber cheeseburger. He comes home from lunch every day to walk her and at night he takes her to the park. When he's not yelling at her to stay out of the road, he slips her button-size pizza snacks. He does all of the talking and she does most of the barking. You can see he's a lonely guy. In fact, he exudes loneliness like a gray perfume from his Sears work pants and stretched out T-shirts, from the hair that peeks out of his ears, and his laugh that is like the cry of someone falling from a skyscraper. Whenever he sees my wife or me outside, he's immediately there with some dry-ass conversation about home heating bills or methods for flea eradication. He must watch us all the time. When we take the kids and dog to the park, we are there no more than ten minutes before Richie shows up, wondering why he saw me out of work on the previous Wednesday at two thirty in the afternoon. I tell him I was watching the kids, and this brings on his raucous Saint Vitus dance of mirth as if he were a child on the verge of wetting his pants. We keep the boys at a distance for fear that someday he will explode or catch on fire.

Over the past year, I have been caught in many a discussion with Richie. They are one-way affairs, since he is the expert and you are in need of his knowledge. Most of these lost moments are spent on how he was able to save money. He shops at three different grocery stories—one for meat, one for treats, one for paper products. I tilt my head to the side and nod as if he is relaying the recipe for eternal youth, but all the time I'm waiting for him to take a breath so I can cut in and say my good-byes. While I wait, I'm picturing him—evangelical late-night television, blue clouds of generic cigarette smoke, and half a bottle of store-brand diet orange. Richie likes his treats. "You know, your Yodels, some fudge swirl ice cream, pretzel rods," he says. His kid brother "blew his brains out with a shotgun." This story is always punctuated by a long, sophisticated exhalation of cigarette smoke. His ex, Barbara was "the finest gal in the world." "Never loved her, never really loved her," he repeats like a Greek chorus. The woman who lives above him tells me that when he knows she is home he jerks off and moans loud enough to rattle her bathroom fixtures. Once a month, he tells me either a racist story or one in which a guy has an incredibly big dick.

I often wonder why I feel obligated to talk to him. A lot of times when I know he is outside in his front yard, I stay in or go out the back door. I have a wife and two kids and a demanding job, so why do I have to care about Richie? Pity is a dead little animal in your heart. I've really wanted to tell him, "Look, Richie, you're a big loser. You're a boor, a moron, and a pervert." But now Richie has cancer, and he is half the Richie he used to be. Sorrow is bad enough, but sick sorrow—get me a cross and a wooden stake. His kidney has been removed and three inches of his left thigh bone have been eaten away. He needs crutches to get around and spends all his time sitting on his couch, watching the women's workout shows and listening to, as he puts it, "the light classics." When my wife or I leave the house, he cannot come out any longer, but I know he is in there, watching. At night I hear Suzie, jingling her collar in the tiny backyard, and the sound of Richie blubbering travels through the wall of his house and up the canyon of the driveway into my attic office window. These same sobs I heard once before, long ago, from a child lost at the World's Fair. The first night I heard Richie, a bat crawled through the hole in our bedroom ceiling and flew low and silent, circling in the dark.

The doctors have rigged Richie with a shoulder holster device that slowly emits an experimental drug into his system. If it is supposed to make him appear yet more grim and withered, melt his face to a Kleenex-thin skin that fits his skull like a driving glove, it's working. He labors feverishly at a little table, figuring and refiguring his bills with pencil and paper, and reading, as if studying for a final exam, every scrap of information from the insurance company.

When he calls, I never recognize his voice. "Who is it?" I ask, and he says, "It's Bitchy Richie," shrill and defensive, almost daring me to despise him. In recent calls he has told me about his past addiction to methamphetamine, his two marriages, his grown sons who tell him he was a failure as a father. When I can't listen to any more of it, I ask, "How's the leg?" My wife says he is confessing his life to me over the phone. Carrying Richie's sins must change me in some way, because every night my three-year-old comes to sleep in our bed with us. I wake in the middle of the night and he is patting my shoulder. The only time I do not have Richie somewhere in my head is when I'm killing bats with my son's toy broom. They come every night now, and I can't afford to fix the roof.

One night I wake to the whisper flap of leather wings and have a premonition that Richie will die during a blizzard. After a couple of days Patty Playpal upstairs will take the coke spoon out of her nose long enough to smell something bad and finally notice Suzie howling above the drone of her own monologue. She will find the remains of Richie hunched over his table, about to make the final calculation. I don't think I will be moved to go to the funeral, definitely not to the wake. I can always say the kids have colds. After that, I will be expecting his ghost for a few months. Not horrifying—perhaps just a glimpse of Richie at midnight, in the park, calling for Suzie, who has remained behind. Then, when that's over, I'll think of him from time to time, probably in summer, because he used to let me borrow his electric lawn mower. My memory will grasp the whole sad Richie saga for an instant, and I will get up off the stoop and go in for supper. Maybe that night, when the kids are sleeping, I'll say to my wife, "Remember Richie?" She'll shiver a little and shake her head, and then the two of us will bust out laughing.

It's so hard to do good in this world, so hard to love and keep oneself aloft. Every day I pray that Richie will go away to the hospital so that I can forget about him and pretend that life is more than just an experimental drug. He doesn't call anymore and his crying has grown weaker. I paid the guy who lives behind me to climb on the roof and patch the place where the bats were crawling in. The rain still leaks through, but we catch it in buckets and flush it down the toilet. My sons grow bigger every day, and I watch vigilantly so that I can snatch away their loneliness before they notice it. I am constantly telling my wife how beautiful she is. I listen to her carefully, trying to find the person she was before we met fourteen years ago. All the dreams I have now are of some northern land with massive hills and overcast sky. I am there alone on business and can only speak to my family by phone. Each night it becomes more and more difficult to remember the name of my hometown, my number, my reason for being where I am. The people on the street are few, and when I ask them where the bus station is they snicker and give me bad directions. When awake, I'm keenly attuned to coincidence, searching wood grain and clouds for faces, trying with all my heart to rediscover my place in the story.

A Note About "Every Richie There Is"

This story, which first appeared in the literary journal *Puerto Del Sol* in 1993, is basically true. For those who have read my previous collection, *The Drowned Life*, the final story in that book, "The Golden Dragon," takes place right around the same time, when we were living in the same duplex, and involves one of the same characters. If the mood ever strikes me, I have at least one more story to write about that time, and it is about the house that the character Richie inhabits in this tale. That story is a ghost story, as, in a way, both "Every Richie" and "The Golden Dragon" are.

The Dream of Reason

The renowned luminist, Amanitas Perul, who lived a secretive life in his private observatory, Dark See, atop a hill outside the university town of Veldanch, was said by some to be so dedicated an observer of the natural world as to achieve a kind of scientific sainthood. By others he was reviled as the vainest of men, who spent hours before the mirror contemplating his own chalk-powdered visage and wore his thigh-length hair in a vertical architecture of complex knots and ringlets like an ingenious city of a thought. The enigmatic Perul had two theories—one, that distant stars were made of diamond and, two, that matter was merely light slowed down. One night when he was in his observatory, preparing to climb a ladder to the eyepiece of the world's largest telescope, his two theories happened to collide in his mind, and from the resultant slow explosion, like a flower opening, the notion of an amazing experiment revealed itself to him. He went immediately to his desk and wrote out the equations for the highly influential research that would eventually become known as the *Dream of Reason*.

Perul had already done experiments on the deceleration of light and found that heavy gases, like carkonium and tersus margolium, kept at low temperatures actually impeded a sun-beam's progress to the point where his precision gear-work sensors were able to record its speed. The leap of imagination that led to the famous experiment was his consideration that if he used starlight instead of sunlight, the beam in question would have had to lose more of its speed, having traveled eons farther through the frigid gas of space. Perul believed that the stars were diamonds and reflected back the light of our sun, so that the journey out to the star, the speed-diminishing act of rebound, and then the lengthy trip back would greatly impede light's velocity. He dared to wonder, if he managed to slow a beam of starlight sufficiently to where it fell into matter, would it produce diamond dust since the last thing it had touched was a star?

Once Perul's concept became known, the University of Veldanch was eager to fund his efforts. At the late age of forty, he dove headlong into the problem of overcoming the speed of light. For four years, Perul ran experiment after experiment with different gases, using ice by the cartload to try to lower their temperatures, and little by little the beams of light slowed, like clockwork running down. In the late summer of the fourth year of the *Dream of Reason*, he reduced the speed of a beam of starlight so much that its course could be charted with the naked eye. And then in autumn, he had a breakthrough with a rare gas siphoned from the dung of cattle and named by those farmers who gathered it Lud Fog. He reported that he'd slowed light to the walking speed of a very old woman.

At this point Perul acknowledged that the gases had done their job, but for the last step in the experiment, he'd have to devise some manner in which he could slow light into matter. He conceived of a great stadium with glass tubes, holding, within, specially curved mirrors so that the beam could circle the thousands of concentric rings. As the freshly slowed light, having traveled the great distance of space and passed through the chilled Lud Fog, made continuous loops around the glass tube tracks, eventually, it might meet its end and fall out of thin air as diamond dust. The one problem with this solution, as Perul saw it, was that the stadium that held the glass tubes would necessarily have to cover an area the size of the continent of Ishvu.

Perul's research came to a halt, his thinking stymied by an inability to conceive of a practical physical manifestation for a light trap (as he referred to the theoretical device in his notes) that would be compact enough to actually construct and also be large enough to hold the voluminous concentric rings of a track he had already proven mathematically would be necessary to effectively allow a star beam's life to run down into matter. The problem was a paradox, and in his imagination it took the form of the Senplesian mythological figure of the two-headed monster, the Frakkas. In the ancient story, when the hero Marianna wields her sword and cuts off one head of the accursed beast, she then must deal with the other, but while she is in the act of severing the second head, the first grows back. One who does not know the myth might think an easy solution would be to sever them both with one blow, but the Frakkas has a serpent's body, long and wriggling, with a head at either end, making a single-stroke solution impossible. It must not have been much solace to Perul that in the myth, the beautiful warrior goddess Marianna is always battling the Frakkas, cutting off one head and then the other to protect mankind from the creature's potential chaos.

It was reported, years later, by Perul's servant, the reliable

Elihu Arbiton, that the scientist fell into a deep depression over the problem. He spent many more hours than usual staring into the mirror. At times he'd pound his temples with closed fists as if hoping to dislodge a frozen thought. Perul could be found roaming the halls of the observatory at night with a lit candle, going room to room. When Arbiton inquired what his master was searching for, Perul, obviously sleepwalking with eyes closed, would murmur that he'd heard a ghost calling to him in whispers the secret solution to the light trap. "I can only hear part of what she's saying," said Perul. "She's here and I must find her." When Arbiton noticed that Perul had shaved off his eyebrows and on his powdered visage wore a black-penciled version instead over only his left eye, an arch more like an arrowhead pointing up, he realized that his master was on the verge of a nervous breakdown. A group of influential scientists from the university got together and convinced the great luminist that a vacation was needed.

For the first time, Amanitas Perul was seen in different spots around the continent. Descriptions of his unmistakable appearance mark these reports as more than likely reliable. A café operator in the town of Libledoth on the southern coast of Ufdicht told a historian, "Yes, the man with the ridiculous hairdo, like a doll's house on his head, came every day in the late afternoon, to sit on the sidewalk, stare at the setting sun, and drink bottle after bottle of Rose Ear Sweet. When the sky would darken and the stars would appear, he'd leave immediately, but if it was overcast he'd stay till we were forced to kick him out. I asked him once why when the stars began to shine, he'd scurry away. He grabbed me by the shirt collar, pulled my face close to his, and said, 'Because they mock me.'" Perul was spotted at the great dam at Indel Laven, tearing up pages of paper filled with numbers and tossing the scraps into the frothy roar of runoff thundering beneath him. From many corners came news that he'd fallen, as he'd hoped light would into matter, into the use of winterspice and had a special pipe he smoked it from—a single mouthpiece but two bowls on wriggling stems jutting away from each other at an angle, both carved in the likeness of a Frakkas head.

More than a year after he'd left his observatory to travel the continent, he wound up one morning in Cravey-by-the-Sea, stumbling along the shore of the Inland Ocean high on winterspice and watching the comforting show of turquoise waves rolling and breaking against the pink sand. The day was fair, and beautifully blue. The sun was bright. Exhausted, he sat down on the sand. At this point, as he wrote later in his autobiography, he'd not thought of the problem of the light trap in months. All of his concerns about the experiment had lain down and dozed off for the longest time. A sense of calm came over him, and he considered all he'd been through, all the stupidity of his travels and the extent to which his own mind had tortured him over his inability to find the answers he'd been looking for. He reviewed his thoughts—the complexly conspiratorial nature of his fears, the impossibly infinite tangle of scheming and knotted self-admonishment. It struck him, like lightning out of the blue, that the only possible light trap both compact enough and vast enough to manage the last step in the deceleration of a star beam was, of course, the human mind.

"Think of the world, a globe spinning in space, and then think of the sun and the dark distances to the stars. Think of it all at once, all of it, and you can without any trouble," wrote the luminist upon his return home to Dark See. Elihu Arbiton was given a sheaf of pages that held a special diet to have the kitchen help prepare and also orders to awaken his master every day at precisely sunrise. Perul gave himself two weeks of true rest in order to regain his strength for the last part of the experiment. Every morning he strolled the grounds at daybreak, swam laps in the pool, breakfasted on peeled sections of chali fruit and a bowl of unflayed dost bran, meditated in the study with the windows covered and but one lit candle to focus his mind upon. In the afternoons, he did light calculations and read the philosophy of Herden Bylat—*The Crucial Degree of Probable Hope*. At night, he eschewed the mirror, and went to sleep to ethereal hymns played by a cellist sitting just down the hall from his room.

On the day Perul was to begin again on his signature work, he summoned Elihu Arbiton to him and ordered him to go down to the city of Veldanch and find someone who would be willing to act as a subject in the experiment. "Let them name their price," Perul said, "for there is danger in this, and they must understand that an autopsy will be undertaken upon their remains when they eventually pass away." He handed over to Arbiton a set of contracts for the chosen individual to sign. The servant nodded and left with the contracts rolled up beneath his arm. He traveled on horse with another horse in tow and was in the town before the workday had begun. Although the money was a great temptation to those he approached, Arbiton had difficulty performing his assignment. As he discovered, the bishop of Veldanch had taken umbrage at the fact that Perul had named his observatory Dark See, a luminist's joke, pointing to the fact that the master of the estate spent all his nightly hours staring into the pitch of space to study light. When Bishop Gazbrak had reprimanded Perul about the estate's name, reminding him that a see can only be the domain of a bishop, the scientist had reportedly laughed in his face. Afterward, Gazbrak warned his congregations to steer clear of Perul or risk losing their souls.

With the day sliding into late afternoon and still no one contracted to act as subject in his master's experiment, Arbiton headed into the last quadrant of town that he had not yet covered. There, amid the crumbling buildings and unpaved streets, he came upon the Debtor's Prison, an institution he'd all but forgotten existed. He breathed a sigh of relief at the sight of the wretched place. And so it was that from the bowels of that dark hellhole, Perul's servant brought forth a young woman, Enche Jenawa—a still healthy specimen, who had not yet lost to poverty her looks or the glint of intelligence in her eyes. The warden suggested her, thinking kindly of the girl and believing it a crime perpetrated by the kingdom that Enche should serve a sentence for her dead father's financial excesses. When Arbiton put the deal before her, all the young woman asked was if she'd again be able to see the sunlight, and when Arbiton nodded, she signed. He then paid off the girl's debt and gave the warden a little something for his troubles. As he led the girl out of the prison of shadows, into the late-afternoon sun, she covered her eyes against the brightness.

It was well after dark by the time Arbiton and Enche reached Dark See. Perul was waiting in the observatory for their arrival, curious to see who his future subject might be. So much hinged on this aspect of the experiment that his nerves had gotten the better of him and he'd retrieved his old winterspice pipe and calmed himself with a double dose of the drug. Now many histories of these events tell a Romantic tale and would have it that Perul was smitten with Enche Jenawa from the moment he laid eyes upon her and vice versa, but reality as reported by Arbiton and recorded by Perul himself will just not bear the weight of this fiction. Enche was brought before her new employer. She curtsied as was the practice, and Perul nodded and, leaning close to her, said only one word, "Circles." Then he asked Arbiton to take the girl to the kitchen, feed her, and then show her to her room.

When Arbiton pushed back the door of her room in order for her to enter, Enche smiled, for the room was beautifully appointed and done up in a most remarkable manner. The walls were papered with a pattern of small red circles on a yellow background, and the window over the circular bed was round as a ship's porthole. The light fixtures were globes, the rugs were round, and even the pillows, the tables, the chairs were round. "This is lovely," she said, unable to believe that no more than hours earlier she was lying in the dark, in a stall covered with straw, a chain around her left ankle, starving. She'd only been at the prison for a week, but it had been an absolute certainty to her that she would be raped before long by the giant prison guard with one eye who served rotten gruel twice a day. Having left that behind, she was now only taxed by Arbiton's suggestion, "Amanitas Perul requests that you think of circles as often as possible." She laughed outright and nodded. "I'll think of circles all night. In fact I'll dream of circles if need be," she said. "Very good," said Arbiton, and left her to herself.

The next morning after breakfast, Enche's tutor arrived. She was introduced to him, a tall, thin gentleman with a long smooth face and eyeglasses, dressed in lavender jacket and trousers. She could not tell if he was old or young, but the gleam from his completely bald head slightly disturbed her still sensitive vision. "Mr. Garreau," he said to her and smiled, and she answered with her name. Arbiton showed them to another room done up all in circles. There was a chair for her to sit in, facing a desk behind which he sat, a chalkboard behind him. And her lessons began with him leading her in an hour-long chanting of the word "circle." This was followed by a fifteen-minute break, and then another hour of the same word, accompanied by circling of the head and rolling of the eyes. Before lunch there were two more hours in which she was instructed to trace circles in the air with her index finger. Mr. Garreau encouraged her and also scolded when her circles wavered into ovals or worse. After the midday meal, and a brief respite out upon the grounds of the estate where Enche and Mr. Garreau walked in large circles, they returned to their workroom where she drew circles on the chalkboard and was then lectured by her tutor about the philosophy of circles. "Truth lies at the end of a circle," he told her. She nodded and he was obviously pleased.

Every night, just before she turned in, Enche was ushered to Perul's study, where he loaded the two-headed pipe with winterspice and encouraged her to smoke with him. During these sessions, he did not converse with her, but occasionally merely intoned the word "circles," and she repeated. With the drug in her system, when she finally lay down to sleep at night, she did dream of circles, wild imaginings of mouths pronouncing the letter O, and eyeballs loose and rolling, and hoops of fire and ice, and frantic races run in a ring between herself and a doughnut with legs. Arbiton reports that the young woman rather enjoyed her lessons, and told him on one occasion that thinking of all of those circles was a pleasant thing, so much more comforting than her thoughts in her previous life, which were all frayed ends and ragged paths that went nowhere.

One day, after lunch, she was not instructed to go back to the workroom with Garreau, but was led by Perul himself, to a closet in his own private bedchamber where hung two racks of women's clothes—dresses both formal and casual. She was allowed to choose whatever fashions she wanted and told that from that point onward they belonged to her. At night, as always, the smoke and Perul's simple, monotonous suggestion of "circles."

While Enche's mind was being transformed into the great stadium of circular paths for the light to travel, Perul was hard at work in the observatory, fitting together rods of glass tubing, painted black on the outside, to lead from the telescope's eyepiece to the gas chambers where chilled Lud Fog would wait. From the chambers, it would then travel to a small room where, through a single tube, the ray of starlight would proceed to its intended trap. The luminist had spent many hours scanning the night sky for just the right star whose refracted light he'd use in the experiment. Eventually the perfect choice came to him, not through direct observation but from one of his star charts. By accident one night, while looking for information on another heavenly body, he saw an entry for Mariannus, a specimen of particular brightness available for viewing from late summer through all of autumn. There was a mythological story attached to it. Apparently, it shone in the sky as a signal to humanity that the warrior goddess Marianna was still bravely battling the Frakkas. "Of course," Perul wrote after noting his discovery and final choice.

Two months of adjusting the artifacts for the experiment and lessons on the circle passed, but little is known of the daily particulars of Dark See during this preparatory span. One of the only pieces of evidence that remains is a single scrap of a page of a letter written by Enche to her sister. This was only discovered last year in one of Elihu Arbiton's old books now in the Veldanch archives. Some think it a forgery, but the content makes me trust in its veracity. I reproduce it for you here: . . . *circles and circles and circles, my head is spinning, my heart is spinning. I dream tornadoes and speak loops. Thoughts race around inside my head like Hoffmann hounds at the old racetrack at Temkin. I'm in love with Mr. Garreau, my tutor. He's a shiny-headed, hapless sot, but that is precisely what attracts me to him. Every day he brings me gifts, large, small, circles. Before long, I hope to give him my circle. The servant seems jealous, the master, unconscious . . .*

On the night of the first freeze, Perul went to Enche's room and shared with her two bowls of winterspice as he had every night of her stay. That night, though, instead of simply exhaling a cloud as she'd been wont to do, she blew smoke rings. This was the sign the luminist had been waiting for. He recorded the event in a joyous entry, and at the end of it, he wrote, "We shall begin." The next day, Arbiton was ordered to go to Veldanch and purchase ten wagonloads of ice to be delivered the following evening. Enche was relieved of her lessons for the day, and she chose to take a picnic lunch into the woods accompanied by Mr. Garreau. Perul was busy from dawn to dusk, rechecking his calculations and going over every connection of the glass tubing. He consulted the almanac to make sure the skies the following night would be clear, and found they would be. It is said by some that that evening, after Enche did not arrive on time for dinner, Perul went out to look for her, and found her and Mr. Garreau together, locked in an embrace and kissing. When they noticed that Perul was watching, they stepped quickly apart. "We're practicing circling the tongues," Garreau called to his employer. Supposedly, Perul called back, "Circles," and returned to the observatory.

The experiment was begun. In a small room just off the observatory, Enche lay on her stomach, on a tall flat bed, her neck tilted so that her chin rested on the surface of the platform. She directly faced the end of a short, clear tube, its opening positioned directly at her left eye. Circling her head was a strap that held a device whose two thin claw ends were inserted beneath her eyelid. This "eye stay," as it was called, once a tool of the torturer who wanted to deny a victim's need for sleep, disabled the blinking response of the eye. Arbiton stood on one side of Enche and Perul on the other. "Good luck, sir," said the servant, and his employer answered, "If we're lucky, luck will have nothing to do with it." Checking his pocket watch again and noting that the moment had come when the star had risen to its calculated position, he pulled a cord that was attached through a hole in the wall to the shutter on the eyepiece of the great telescope.

Arbiton put the intervening time between the pull of the cord and the appearance of the ray of light at five minutes. Perul stated four and three-quarters minutes, precisely as he'd predicted. It came, like a bright thread, slowly inching its way through the center of the clear tube aimed at Enche's eye. It literally punctured the lens, like a needle going through flesh— a pliant shudder at the iris and then a hair-thin trickle of blood. The instant it entered, the girl screamed as if she were on fire. Her body quickly began shuddering and Arbiton reached for her. Perul interceded, saying, "Two more seconds," and Arbiton later attested they were the longest two seconds of his life. Finally, when the necessary time had passed, Perul himself swept her off the table and carried her to her room. She was unconscious and already burning with a fever. All the rest of that night the luminist and his servant sat by her bedside, brought cool compresses for her head, and forced sips of water into her. Arbiton states that at one point he'd thought she was going to die and was severely shaken, and it was precisely at that point that Perul said to him, "There is starlight in her head."

Enche awoke before dawn and complained of sparks behind her eyes and a terrible headache, and then fell back into a fitful sleep. When she awoke again the following afternoon, she didn't exhibit any signs of pain, but she wore an odd, dull affect. "Circles," Perul repeated to her for an hour, but Arbiton, having seen enough, overstepped his bounds and demanded that his employer leave her alone. And this is precisely where Arbiton left the history of the experiment. Perul fired him on the spot. With no emotion and few words: "You are dismissed." Arbiton states that he "stood stunned for a moment," but when Perul again started intoning the word "circle," he knew his time at Dark See was over. He left the room, packed his things, and at twilight descended the hill carrying his bag.

From this point forward, we must rely on Perul's notes for what is known to be true. He records that Enche never achieved a consciousness more than a general stupor. She could be led around, and fed, and would speak occasionally, but it was never as if she had fully wakened from sleep. "I'm racing," she'd suddenly yell. "My soul is dizzy," she'd whimper. When he'd put his hands to her head, he stated that he could feel it hum with the energy of the stars. On the second night after the experiment, when Enche had been put to bed, he wrote, "Her condition could continue in this manner for a lifetime, and one thing I foolishly overlooked is how much younger she is than myself. I could very well pass on before seeing the results of this experiment. Steps must be taken, and I see a way to gain fast results and perhaps help the poor girl's condition in the process." Following these words was a detailed plan for a person-size canister in which Enche could fit, submerged in Lud Fog.

At this point all manner of speculation might enter the story of the *Dream of Reason*, but there is little reliable information. After the plans for the larger Lud Fog chamber, there comes only one more word from Perul—"Monstrous"—scrawled across an otherwise blank page of his journal. The next authenticated piece of evidence of what transpired comes from Issac Hadista, a hunter, who, when interviewed years after the experiment had become famous, told that he'd been hired by Perul to hunt a strange and dangerous figure that haunted the woods behind the observatory. "The man's hair had fallen," said Hadista, "like a ship going under. And he told me the thing I hunted looked like a young woman but was really a demon loosed on the world because of a failed experiment he'd conducted. He begged me not to shoot her in the head, saying it would release her ancient spirit into the atmosphere and would infect me and overtake my soul. 'Through the heart,' he told me. 'It's the only way.'"

Hadista set off through falling snow, in amidst the barren white trees of the wood. With the snow on the ground it was easy to track her. She lurched out of the shadows at twilight, bouncing from tree trunk to tree trunk, moaning loudly. According to Hadista, her flesh was a pale green (some attribute this to her having spent considerable time in the Lud Fog). She sensed the hunter's presence and came down a snow-covered trail toward him, one hand out in front, calling, "Help me." "I was not fooled by the demon's scheming," Hadista stated. "I lifted my rifle and shot her through the heart, and then a second time before she fell dead." On his way back to the observatory, carrying her body as he'd been instructed, he recounted, "It was pitch black, and all I had to light my way were the stars."

When Perul performed the autopsy upon the brain of Enche Jenawa, what he found astounded him. The diamond dust he'd expected was absent, but what was there changed, in a moment, his entire conception of the nature of stars and the formation of the universe. What he found there, at the core of the young girl's gray matter, was, instead, *nothing*. "Nothing," Perul wrote in his results. "I should have known, but there it is." And from the experiment later named the *Dream of Reason*, humanity came to learn that the stars were made of nothing—hard, shiny, chips of nothing. Cosmologists understood now that at the dawn of everything there was nothing, and when the universe burst to life, the nothing was shattered and thrown out into the darkness of space to make way for the sun and the Earth. Science had prevailed, and Perul was lauded with honorariums and testimonials at the University of Veldanch.

After this experiment to end all experiments, Perul retired from research and returned to the town of Libledoth where every night he frequented the café and drank to excess bottles of Rose Ear Sweet. His use of the winterspice increased as well, and in only a few years his appearance grew haggard, his hair now a frizzled storm cloud over his shoulders. He turned to mysticism in his later years and claimed that he could contact the spirit world. In messages from the other side that he would record during long bouts of automatic writing, the spirits told him that the stars were giant balls of flaming gas, like the sun. These and other delusions began to crowd out his reason. He ended his days in Debtor's Prison, completely insane, mumbling to himself and endlessly turning tight pirouettes.

A Note About "The Dream of Reason"

I remember when my novel *The Physiognomy* came out, a number of reviewers said that it had an anti-science message. What foolishness. I'm most definitely pro-science, but I am also most definitely anti bad science or quackery. I'm afraid there's a difference. Would it have been better if I'd written admiringly about the crackpot philosophy and practices of physiognomy? This story, "The Dream of Reason," is also a look at the scientific method gone awry with the exception of perhaps one aspect, which I wasn't even aware of when writing it. In the story, Perul believes that stars are made of diamond and their twinkling is merely caused by the reflection of the sun. As it turns out, this bit of fictional whim-wham has a sort of truth to it. The story was written in 2008. In 2011, astronomers discovered a heavenly body about four thousand light years from Earth, an eighth of the way to the center of the Milky Way, most likely the remnant of a once massive star. It has lost its outer layers to the effects of the pulsar it circles and is now a planet made almost entirely of diamond. Who knows what other future half-truths lie dormant within the pages of this story?

The War Between Heaven and Hell Wallpaper

Just before I dozed off to sleep last night, I had a vision. I saw, with my eyes closed, a room that was wallpapered with the most amazing scenery of a battle between angels and demons. It was brilliantly colorful and so amazingly detailed. I can still see the deep red of the evil horde, their barbed tails and bat wings—classic Madison Avenue horned demons, but playing for keeps, slaying angels with their tridents. The angels wore billowing white robes and, of course, had feathered wings in contrast to the slick bat-like ones of the enemy. Halos, gleaming swords, harps to call the troops to charge, they poured out of the clouds, riding beams of light toward Earth, where the demons crawled out of cracks in the ground, smoking volcano craters, and holes in giant trees. The middle part of the wall, from just above knee height to the top of the rib cage, was taken up by the actual battle. The upper part held scenes in Heaven as the troops made ready to descend and the dead and wounded were brought in. The lower part of the wall was the stalactite-riddled caverns of burning Hell, showing the incredible numbers of Satan's minions. If you've ever seen the *Where's Waldo?* books—it looked like one of those, or at least every inch was as crowded with as many characters, painted in the style and color of Matthias Grünewald. One thing to keep in mind—I knew this was a war *between* Heaven and Hell, not the war *in* Heaven in which Lucifer and his posse were evicted.

The sight of this wallpaper jazzed me back to consciousness, and I said to Lynn, who was dozing off herself, "I just saw War Between Heaven and Hell wallpaper." She was silent for a while, but I knew from her breathing she wasn't asleep. "What do you think of that?" I said. She laughed. "I have to get up early tomorrow," she said. A few moments later I was describing it to her. When I was done, I said to her, "What do you think that means?" "You've got a screw loose," she said. "It was so colorful and intricate," I told her. "Great," she said, and a few seconds later, she was lightly snoring.

I lay awake for a while and contemplated the War Between Heaven and Hell wallpaper. In my imagination a woman got this wallpaper installed in a room in her house. Eventually she noticed that the scenes changed each day while she was at work. On the days when she had a bad day at the office, Satan's troops had gained the advantage, and the days when things went well for her, Heaven took the lead. Months went by and Heaven really started to kick ass, pushing the demons back into Hell and then invading the smoky underworld in order to finish them off. The last battalion of winged demons had pulled back into the frozen parts at the center of Hell where they'd amassed their infernal artillery and battle beasts, falling into a siege amid the ice mountains. The angels surrounded the last bole of Hell and used longbows and spears.

For the woman to take all of this in each night, she had to get down on the floor and move a desk out of the way to see the spot where the final battle was taking place. Just as it looked like the demons were going to be obliterated, she started to feel bad for them. She felt an uneasiness with the lack of balance represented by the wallpaper's scenario. Since the wallpaper scenes had something to do with what happened to her through the day, she decided to try to turn the tide of the battle by performing acts of evil, things that would reflect badly upon her and ensure she would have a bad day. She put her plan into practice, and the demons began to rally. A call came through on her cell phone, and Satan engaged her as an agent in the War Between Heaven and Hell. That's when I fell asleep.

I woke up this morning from a dream of a kind of monastery in a snowy wood. I think a monastery is a place where monks live, but this place had Catholic priests living in it. Lynn and I came to it after slogging through swamps and through a snow-covered forest. We were totally lost. The place was built from the most marvelous-smelling rosewood, and it seemed to have been carved from enormous blocks of it rather than put together with nails and screws. The trees came right up to the sides of the walls, as if the monastery had been there for a very long time and they had grown up next to where it was built. There were a number of larger buildings linked to each other by screened hallways. Some of these buildings were more than one story and were decorated with gargoyles of demons and angels.

We were met by a priest out in the yard behind the open gates at sundown. We were weary and hungry. He told us to hurry if we wanted to eat. We followed him through the winding, dark hallways of the place. The shadows were kept at bay only by lit candles. We were led to a small kitchen and given a piece of stale bread and a bowl of onion soup. The priest introduced himself as Father Heems. He was a very downtrodden-looking fellow, his face filled with worry lines, and his hands shaking slightly. He told us the place was haunted by the Holy Ghost, and that the spirit was angry. Just the night before we arrived it had strangled the caretaker, whose body he pointed out to us lying next to the stove wrapped in black plastic and tied at the feet and head. "You've got to keep moving. You can't sleep till dawn. If you doze off, the ghost will strangle you through your dreams. A breeze will pass over you and you will feel it tightening its fingers around your throat."

We got up from the table and started walking. "That's it," cried Heems, "keep moving." Three other priests, two very old ones and a slow heavy one, and Lynn and I, along with Heems, moved through the corridors of the place—up stairs, down stairs, through catacombs, along balconies. When we passed through the dungeon, there was a cell with straw on the floor and about a dozen young children milling around behind the bars. The heavy priest told us that the children were safe from the ghost at night behind the bars. I asked, "Why don't we go in there too?" And Heems yelled, "Pipe down and keep moving." Every time I'd begin to feel tired and slow down I'd hear the wind blow outside and feel a breeze creeping down the hallway.

Somewhere in the middle of the night, Father Heems called out to one of the other old priests as we made our way along, "Where is Father Shaw?" This almost made me stop in my tracks, because Father Shaw was the head priest at the church I went to as a kid. He was stern to the verge of cruelty and looked like an emaciated Samuel Beckett. We all hated him. Even the parents hated him. When we kids went to the church for any kind of instruction, like before First Communion or for Confirmation training, he'd appear and spew rants about how we were a bunch of little sinners and he wished we could feel Christ's pain from the crucifixion. Anytime I ever went to Confession and that little door in the dark confessional would slam back and I'd see his profile through the grating, I'd nearly crap my pants. The prayers he'd give you to say for even some minor infraction of disobedience would be an onerous weight.

Soon after the mention of Father Shaw, daylight came and we could finally stop walking. In some kind of weird chain of events and reasoning, Heems made me the new caretaker for the time Lynn and I would stay there, which if I had my preference was not going to be very long. First, though, we had to figure out where we were. Once the other priests left us alone for a few minutes, Lynn asked me, "What's with the kids in the dungeon?" "That's not cool," I said. But then Heems was back with a canvas bag for me with a shoulder strap on it and a long stick with a nail poking out the end. I got the idea that I was meant to police the grounds. So I started around the outside of the building, poking candy wrappers (there were a lot of candy wrappers for some reason). When I made my way around half the building, I came to a little alcove, and lying in the middle of it on the snow was Father Shaw—dead. He was leaking from somewhere onto the snow, and the snow had turned the color of Mountain Dew. His flesh was rotted and yellow. The second I saw him I started breathing through my mouth to avoid smelling him. I thought, "Do I have to clean this shit up all by myself?" Time skipped here, and I was tying a string around the plastic that covered his legs. I woke up.

While eating breakfast, I realized why Father Shaw had appeared in this dream. I'd mentioned him to Lynn not two days earlier. We were at a wedding in South Jersey, staying in a place called the Seaview in Absecon. It's a really old hotel and golf resort. That's where the wedding reception was being held. Lynn had stayed there once for a conference she was participating in, and she told me that the hallways of the place reminded her of the hotel in *The Shining*.

After the reception was over, we went and got our room, hung out for a while, and then headed downstairs to the bar to have a drink. On the way, we passed a room, like a study, with wooden paneling and stuffed chairs and glassed bookcases and with a plaque over the door on the outside that read SHAW. I immediately thought of Father Shaw and told Lynn about him. The memory of his face prompted me to recall that my father was in the hospital to have a cyst removed once when we were kids, and when he returned from his stay, I'd overheard him say to my mother that Shaw had been in there at the same time, dying of cancer. "All of his great solace in God went right out the window," my father said. "Shaw wailed just as loud as the rest of the sinners." At the moment he said this, he was eating a cracker with a sardine on it. He gulped down the cracker in one bite, licked his forefinger, his thumb, and then smiled, giving the advantage to either Heaven or Hell. I'm still not sure which.

A Note About "The War Between Heaven and Hell Wallpaper"

Everything that happens in this story, the dreams, the thoughts, the dialogue, the places and people, is all true. The series of events, because they happened so closely together and seemed centered around the theme of religion, made them cohere for me as a story, albeit one with a kind of strange structure. That odd structure, though, and the real-life events that read like fiction, were perfect for a new anthology I'd heard of, *Interfictions 2*, to be published by Small Beer Press. The editors were Delia

Sherman and Chris Barzak. As a little something unusual, I thought that for the after note for this story, I'd attach another little story, also influenced by my experience with religion.

The House in the Woods in the Snow

Our Lady of Lourdes was the church my mother took my brother and sister and me to when I was young, I'm talking around five or six years old. In the woods to the left of the church parking lot, there was a little ancient red house—squat, falling apart, with a tar paper roof and a single window.

One Sunday, after the ten-stone tedium of a mass, the hair-raising scent of incense, the Latin droning of Father Toomey, the shifting eyes of the statues, my aunt Gertie singing like a cat with its tail caught in a closing door, the chest thumping, the tinkling bells, I was just giving a sigh of relief that it was again, finally over, when my mother informed Jim, my older brother, and me (my sister was just a baby) that we had to start Sunday school that day. Tears came to my eyes. We stepped outside the church into the dark day, snow falling fast all around us, and she pointed to that creepy little red house barely visible in the woods. I said nothing, but Jim's response was, "What . . . more?"

We were herded across the parking lot, through a couple of snowdrifts and in among the trees. There was a nun waiting for us at the door, wearing a sour expression, as if she were sniffing something less than the Holy Ghost. "Bring them in," she instructed my mother. We entered, along with a bunch of other scared kids, and were ordered to sit on the long benches that lined the walls. Then my mother left, and the nun went and sat behind a desk at the front of the room. This was Sunday school, and if church was a boring creep show, this little enterprise upped the weird quotient for me by about 150 percent.

Religion was mysterious to me, and I was put off by church because it had too much to do with pictures and statues and stories about pain and suffering. I wanted to go home and put on my Davy Crockett coonskin cap and grab a stick that looked like a gun and run through the backyards and woods of the neighborhood, having adventures, or get my old man to read the Sunday funnies to me in his hundred voices.

The nun yelled at a few kids for whispering and banged a long ruler on the desk. She introduced herself as Sister Stephen, which threw us for a loop. Then she asked us this question, "What do you think happens to your pets when they die?" "More death," I thought. "Here we go." A kid raised his hand and said his pet dog had died and that his mother told him that it went to Heaven.

"Wrong," said Sister Stephen, put out by his ignorance. "They can't go to Heaven, because they don't have a soul."

Kids stared and nodded.

As it turned out, the dead pets went to neither Heaven nor Hell, but to Limbo. This was a new one on us—Limbo. My first thought was of my parents' drunken weekend barbecues; a long bamboo stick that came in a rolled-up rug, Harry Belafonte singing on the record player out the back window, and Mr. Farley bending backward beneath the stick till he fell on his ass. But I was immediately brought to attention again when Sister said, "Dead pets and dead babies who haven't been baptized, that's who goes to Limbo."

I wondered if dead babies had no souls. And then my imagination kicked in and I envisioned Limbo—a quiet, idyllic place populated by nothing but pets and babies. It seemed like a good place to go. Obviously much better than Hell, what with its eternal fires, serpents, and bat-winged, pitch-fork-wielding demons. Eternal suffering—sort of like church, but only longer and a lot hotter. Actually, Limbo even seemed better than Heaven, the rewards of which—clouds, harp music, and angels—after a long life of always doing the right thing seemed pretty underwhelming. What would you do for the rest of eternity after you learned to play the harp really good?

I imagined a land of babies, but babies who could talk and walk around, run, drive cars even, play Davy Crockett, read the Sunday funnies to each other, wear top hats and dress in tuxedos if they wanted. And with them would be pets. I loved pets.

I'd had a little orange bird my parents had bought me, which I kept in a cage in the living room by the front window. It sang every morning and at night. I'd called it Q and sometimes I'd let it out and it would fly around and then go back to its cage. One day, for a drunken barbecue, my mother made forty deviled eggs, and the smell of those eggs killed the bird. The smell almost killed us too. Q hung upside down from his stick perch. We buried him in the backyard and I made a cross out of twigs to mark the grave. It took me almost a whole week and a half to forget about him. But now I saw him again while sitting in that old wooden house, the snow covering the world outside the window—his orange, puff-ball self, flitting around in the land of Limbo, landing gently on the heads of gentle babies, making them laugh.

Sunday school carried on, yelling, ruler banging, kids with more wrong answers, and then it was over, and I knew that God could, if he wanted, be merciful. We went to the little red house for about a year or so, until my mother was too hungover for church on Sundays. Then Jim was assigned the task of taking me to church, and we'd walk all the way up Higbee Lane and cross the death-defying Sunrise Highway, and go farther and farther to Our Lady of Lourdes.

We took that trek exactly three times, and on the fourth Sunday, as we passed a side street on our way up Pine Avenue, Jim said, "We're going this way today." I was stumped, because the way he was pointing was in the other direction from the church. I nervously followed him. We ended up at the deli, where he bought a quart of chocolate milk and a package of chocolate chip cookies. When we left the deli, he directed me to a spot behind the stores where no one ever went. We sat on empty milk crates and he divvied up the cookies. We passed the chocolate milk back and forth. At one point he took one of the cookies and held it up like the priest did with the host and mumbled some mumbo jumbo and we laughed like hell.

And then, not so long ago, I read that the Vatican, as if on a whim, abolished Limbo. Q and the other pets and the dead babies, where did they all go? The Lord giveth and the Lord taketh away.

Relic

Out at the end of the world on a long spit of land like a finger poking into oblivion, nestled in a valley among the dunes, sat the Church of Saint Ifritia, constructed from twisted driftwood and the battered hulls of ships. There was one tall, arched window composed of the round bottoms of blue bottles. The sun shone through it, submerging altar and pews. There was room for twenty inside, but the most ever gathered for a sermon was eleven. Atop its crooked steeple jutted a spiral tusk some creature had abandoned on the beach.

The church's walls had a thousand holes and so every morning Father Walter said his prayers while shoveling sand from the sanctuary. He referred to himself as "Father" but he wasn't a priest. He used the title because it was what he remembered the holy men were called in the town he came from. Wanderers to the end of the world sometimes inquired of him as to the church's denomination. He was confused by this question. "A basic church, you know," he'd say. "I talk God and salvation with anyone interested." Usually the pilgrims would turn away, but occasionally one stayed on and listened.

Being that the Church of Saint Ifritia could have as few as

three visitors a month, Father Walter didn't feel inclined to give a sermon once a week. "My flock would be only the sand fleas," he said to Sister North. "Then preach to the fleas," she replied. "Four sermons a year is plenty," he said. "One for each season. Nobody should need more than four sermons a year." They were a labor for him to write, and he considered the task as a kind of penance. Why he gave sermons, he wasn't sure. Their purpose was elusive, and yet he knew it was something the holy men did. His earliest ones were about the waves, the dunes, the sky, the wind, and when he ran out of natural phenomena to serve as topics, he moved inward and began mining memory for something to write.

Father Walter lived behind the whalebone altar in a small room with a bed, a chair, a desk, and a stove. Sister North, who attended a summer sermon one year, the subject of which was "The Wind," and stayed on to serve Saint Ifritia, lived in her own small shack behind the church. She kept it tidy, decorated with shells and strung with tattered fishing nets, a space no bigger than Father Walter's quarters. In the warm months, she kept a garden in the sand, dedicated to her saint. Although he never remembered having invited her to stay on, Father Walter proclaimed her flowers and tomatoes miracles, a cornucopia from dry sand and salt air, and recorded them in the official church record.

Sister North was a short, brown woman with long dark hair streaked with gray, and an expression of determination. Her irises were almost yellow, catlike, in her wide face. On her first night amid the dunes, she shared Father Walter's bed. He came to realize that she would share it again as long as there was no mention of it during the light of day. Once a season, she'd travel ten miles inland on foot to the towns and give word that a sermon was planned for the following Monday. The towns she visited scared her, and only occasionally would she meet a pilgrim who'd take note of her message.

In addition to the church and Sister North's shack, there were two other structures in the sand dune valley. One was an out-house built of red ship's wood with a tarpaulin flap for a door and a toilet seat made of abalone. The other was a shrine that housed the holy relic of Saint Ifritia. The latter building was woven from reeds by Sister North and her sisters. She'd sent a letter and they'd come, three of them. They were all short and brown with long dark hair streaked with gray. None had yellow eyes, though. They harvested reeds from the sunken meadow, an overgrown square mile set below sea level among the dunes two miles east of the church. They sang while they wove the strands into walls and window holes and a roof. Father Walter watched the whole thing from a distance. He felt he should have some opinion about it, but couldn't muster one. When the shrine began to take form, he knew it was a good thing.

Before Sister North's sisters left to return to their lives, Father Walter planned a dedication for the relic's new home. He brought the holy item to the service wrapped in a dirty old towel, the way he'd kept it for the past thirty years. Its unveiling brought sighs from the sisters, although at first they were unsure what they were looking at. A dark lumpen object, its skin like that of an overripe banana. There were toes and even orange, shattered toe-nails. It was assumed a blade had severed it just above the ankle, and the wound had, by miracle or fire, been cauterized. "Time's leather" was the phrase Father Walter bestowed upon the state of its preservation. It smelled of wild violets.

There was no golden reliquary to house it; he simply placed it in the bare niche built into the altar, toes jutting slightly beyond the edge of their new den. He turned and explained to the assembled, "You must not touch it with your hands, but fold them in front of you, lean forward, and kiss the toes. In this manner, the power of the saint will be yours for a short time and you'll be protected and made lucky."

Each of them present, the father, Sister North and her sisters, and a young man and woman on their honeymoon who wandered into the churchyard just before the ceremony got under way, stepped up with folded hands and kissed the foot. Then they sat and Father Walter paced back and forth whispering to himself as was his ritual prior to delivering a sermon. He'd written a new one for the event, a fifth sermon for the year. Sister North was pleased with his industry and had visited his bed the night he'd completed it. He stopped pacing eventually and pointed at the ancient foot. The wind moaned outside. Sand sifted through the reeds.

Father Walter's Sermon

When I was a young man, I was made a soldier. It wasn't my choosing. I don't know. They put a gun to my head. We marched through the mud into a rainy country. I was young and I saw people die all around me. Some were only wounded but drowned in the muddy puddles. It rained past forty days and forty nights and the earth had had its fill. Rivers flooded their banks and the water spilled in torrents from the bleak mountains. I killed a few close up with a bayonet and I felt their life rush out. Some I shot at a distance and watched them suddenly drop like children at a game. In two months' time I was a savage.

We had a commanding officer who'd become fond of killing. He could easily have stayed behind the lines and directed the attack, but, with saber drawn, he'd lead every charge and shoot and hack to pieces more of the enemy than the next five men. Once I fought near him in a hand-to-hand mêlée against a band of enemy scouts. The noises he made while doing his work were ungodly. Strange animal cries. He scared me. And I was not alone. This Colonel Hempfil took no prisoners and would dispatch civilians as well as members of his own squad on the merest whim. I swear I thought I'd somehow gone to hell. The sun never shone.

And then one night we sat in ambush in the trees on either side of a dirt road. The rain, of course, was coming down hard and it was cold, moving into autumn. The night was an eternity, I thought. I nodded off and then there came some action. The colonel kicked me where I sat and pointed at the road. I looked and could barely make out a hay cart creaking slowly by. The colonel kicked me again and indicated with hand signals that I was to go and check out the wagon.

My heart dropped. I started instantly crying, but so as not to let the colonel see me sobbing, I ran to it. There could easily have been enemy soldiers beneath the hay with guns at the ready. I ran onto the road in front of the wagon and raised my weapon. "Halt," I said. The tall man holding the reins pulled up and brought the horses to a stop. I told him to get down from his seat. As he climbed onto the road, I asked him, "What are you carrying?" "Hay," he replied, and then the colonel and the rest of our men stormed the wagon. Hempfil gave orders to clear the hay. Beneath it was discovered the driver's wife and two daughters. Orders were given to line them all up. As the driver was being escorted away by two soldiers, he turned to me and said, "I have something to trade for our freedom. Something valuable."

The colonel was organizing a firing squad when I went up to him and told him what the driver had said to me. He thanked me for the information, and then ordered that the tall man be brought to him. I stood close to hear what he could possibly have to offer for the lives of his family. The man leaned over Hempfil and whispered something I could not make out. The colonel then ordered him, "Go get it."

The driver brought back something wrapped in a dirty towel. He unwrapped the bundle and, whisking away the cloth, held a form the size of a small rabbit up to the colonel. "Bring a light," cried Hempfil. "I can't see a damn thing." A soldier lit a lantern and brought it. I leaned in close to see what was revealed. It was an old foot, wrinkled like a purse and dark with age. The sight of the toenails gave me a shiver.

"This is what you will trade for your life and the lives of your family? This ancient bowel movement of a foot? Shall I give you change?" said the colonel, and that's when I knew all of them would die. The driver spoke quickly. "It is the foot of a saint," he said. "It has power. Miracles."

"What saint?" asked the colonel.

"Saint Ifritia."

"That's a new one," said Hempfil and laughed. "Bring me the chaplain," he called over his shoulder.

The chaplain stepped up. "Have you ever heard of Saint Ifritia?" asked the colonel.

"She's not a real saint," said the priest. "She is only referred to as a saint in parts of the holy writing that have been forbidden."

Hempfil turned and gave orders for the driver's wife and daughters to be shot. When the volley sounded, the driver dropped to his knees and hugged the desiccated foot to him as if for comfort. I saw the woman and girls, in their pale dresses, fall at the side of the road. The colonel turned to me and told me to give him my rifle. I did. He took his pistol from its holster at his side and handed it to me. "Take the prisoner off into the woods where it's darker, give him a ten-yard head start, and then kill him. If he can elude you for fifteen minutes, let him go with his life."

"Yes, sir," I said, but I had no desire to kill the driver. I led him at gunpoint up the small embankment and into the woods. We walked slowly forward into darkness. He whispered to me so rapidly, "Soldier, I still hold the sacred foot of Ifritia. Let me trade you it for my life. Miracles." As he continued to pester me with his promises of blessings and wonders, the thought of killing him began to appeal to me. I don't know what it was that came over me. It came from deep within, but in an instant his death had become for me a foregone conclusion. After walking for ten minutes, I told him to stop. He did. I said nothing for a while, and the silence prompted him to say, "I get ten yards, do I not?"

"Yes," I said.

With his first step, I lifted the pistol and shot him in the back of the head. He was dead before he hit the ground, although his body shook twice as I reached down to turn him over. His face was blown out the front, a dark smoking hole above a toothful grimace. I took the foot, felt its slick hide in my grasp, and wrapped it in the dirty towel. Shoving it into my jacket, I buttoned up against the rain and set off deeper into the woods. I fled like a frightened deer through the night, and all around me was the aroma of wild violets.

It's a long story, but I escaped the war, the foot of Saint Ifritia producing subtle miracles at every turn and once making me invisible as I passed through an occupied town. I left the country of rain, pursued by the ghost of the wagon driver. Every other minute, behind my eyes, the driver's wife and daughters fell in *their pale dresses by the side of the road in the rain and nearly every night he would appear from my meager campfire, rise up in smoke and take form. "Why?" he always asked. "Why?"*

I found that laughter dispersed him more quickly. One night I told the spirit I had plans the next day to travel west. But in the morning, I packed my things up quickly and headed due south, toward the end of the world. I tricked him. Eventually, the ghost found me here, and I see him every great while, pacing along the tops of the dunes that surround the valley. He can't descend to haunt me, for the church I built protects me and the power of Saint Ifritia keeps him at bay. Every time I see him his image is dimmer, and before long he will become salt in the wind.

The impromptu congregation was speechless. Father Walter slowly became aware of it as he stood, swaying slightly to and fro. "The Lord works in mysterious ways," he said, a phrase he'd actually heard from Colonel Hempfil. There was a pause after his delivery of it during which he waved his hands back and forth in the air like a magician, distracting an audience. Eventually, two of the sisters nodded and the honeymoon couple shrugged and applauded the sermon.

Father Walter took this as a cue to move on, and he left the altar of the shrine and ran back to the church to fetch a case of whiskey that the Lord had recently delivered onto the beach after a terrific thunderstorm. The young couple produced a hash pipe and a tarry ball of the drug that bore a striking resemblance to the last knuckle of the middle toe of Saint Ifritia's foot.

Late that night, high as the tern flies, the young man and woman left and headed out toward the end of the world, and Sister North's sisters loaded into their wagon and left for their respective homes. Father Walter sat on the sand near the bell in the churchyard, a bottle to his lips, staring up at the stars. Sister North stood over him, the hem of her habit, as she called the simple gray shift she wore every day, flapped in the wind.

"None would stay the night after your story of murder," she said to him. "They drank your whiskey, but they wouldn't close their eyes and sleep here with you drunk."

"Foolishness," he said. "There's plenty still left for all. Loaves and fishes of whiskey. And what do you mean by murder?"

"The driver in your sermon. You could have let him live."

He laughed. "I did. In real life, I let him go. A sermon is something different, though."

"You mean you lied?"

"If I shot him, I thought it would make a better story."

"But where's the Lord's place in a story of cold-blooded murder?"

"That's for him to decide."

Sister North took to her shack for a week, and he rarely saw her. Only in the morning and late in the afternoon would he catch sight of her entering and leaving the shrine. She mumbled madly as she walked, eyes down. She moved her hands as if explaining to someone. Father Walter feared the ghost of the driver had somehow slipped into the churchyard and she was conversing with it. "Because I lied?" he wondered.

During the time of Sister North's retreat to her shack, a visitor came one afternoon. Out of a fierce sandstorm, materializing in the churchyard like a ghost herself, stepped a young woman wearing a hat with flowers and carrying a traveling bag. Father Walter caught sight of her through blue glass. He went to the church's high doors, opened one slightly to keep the sand out, and called to her to enter. She came to him, holding the hat down with one hand and lugging the heavy bag with the other. "Smartly dressed" was the term the father vaguely remembered from his life inland. She wore a white shirt buttoned at the collar with a dark string tie. Her black skirt and jacket matched, and she somehow made her way through the sand without much trouble in a pair of high heels.

Father Walter slammed shut the church door once she was inside. For a moment he and his guest stood still and listened to the wind, beneath it, the distant rhythm of the surf. The church was damp and cold. He told the young lady to accompany him to his room, where he could make a fire in the stove. She followed him behind the altar, and as he broke sticks of driftwood, she removed her hat and took a seat at his desk.

"My name is Mina GilCragson," she said.

"Father Walter," he replied over his shoulder.

"I've come from the Theological University to see your church. I'm a student. I'm writing a thesis on Saint Ifritia."

"Who told you about us?" he asked, lighting the kindling.

"A colleague who'd been to the end of the world and back. He told me last month, 'You know, there's a church down south that bears your saint's name.' And so I was resolved to see it."

Father Walter turned to face her. "Can you tell me what you know of the saint? I am the father here, but I know so little, though the holy Ifritia saved my life."

The young woman asked for something to drink. Since the rainwater barrel had been tainted by the blowing sand that day, he poured her a glass of whiskey and one for himself. After serving his guest, he sat on the floor, his legs crossed. She dashed her drink off quickly, as he remembered was the fashion in the big cities. Wiping her lips with the back of her hand, she said, "What do you know of her so far?"

"Little," he said and listened, pleased to be, for once, on the other end of a sermon.

Mina GilCragson's Sermon

She was born in a village in the rainy country eighty-some-odd years ago. Her father was a powerful man, and he oversaw the collective commerce of their village, Dubron, which devoted itself to raising Plum fish for the tables of the wealthy. The village was surrounded by fifty ponds, each stocked with a slightly different variety of the beautiful fan-tailed species. It's a violet fish. Tender and sweet when broiled.

Ifritia, called "If" by her family, wanted for nothing. She was the plum of her father's eye, her wishes taking precedence over those of her mother and siblings. He even placed her desires above the good of the village. When she was sixteen, she asked that she be given her own pond and be allowed to raise one single fish in it that would be her pet. No matter the cost of clearing the pond, one of the largest, she was granted her wish. To be sure, there was much grumbling among the other villagers and even among If's siblings and mother, but none was voiced in the presence of her father. He was a proud and vindictive man, and it didn't pay to cross him.

She was given a hatchling from the strongest stock to raise. From early on, she fed the fish by hand. When she approached the pond, the creature would surface and swim to where she leaned above the water. Fish, to the people of Dubron, were no more than swimming money, so when Ifritia bequeathed a name on her sole charge, it was a scandal. Unheard of. Beyond the limit. A name denotes individuality, personality, something dangerously more than swimming money. A brave few balked in public, but If's father made their lives unhappy and they fell back to silence.

Lord Jon, the Plum fish, with enough room to spread out in his own pond and fed nothing but table scraps, potatoes and red meat, grew to inordinate dimensions. As the creature swelled in size, its sidereal fish face fleshed out, pressing the eyes forward, redefining the snout as a nose, and puffing the cheeks. It was said Jon's face was the portrait of a wealthy landowner, and that his smile, now wide where it once was pinched, showed rows of sharp white teeth. A fish with a human face was believed by all but the girl and her father to be a sign of evil. But she never stopped feeding it and it never stopped growing until it became the size of a bull hog. Ifritia would talk to the creature, tell it her deepest secrets. If she told something good, it would break out into its huge, biting smile, something sad and it would shut its mouth and tears would fill its saucer-wide eyes.

And then, out of the blue, for no known reason, the fish became angry with her. When she came to the edge of the pond, after it took the food from her hand, it splashed her and made horrid grunting noises. The fish doctor was called for and his diagnosis was quickly rendered. The Plum fish was not supposed to grow to Lord Jon's outsize dimensions; the excess of flesh and the effects of the red meat had made the creature insane. "My dear," said the doctor in his kindest voice, "you've squandered your time creating a large purple madness and that is the long and short of it." The girl's father was about to take exception with the doctor and box his ears, but in that instant she saw the selfish error of her ways.

After convincing her father of the immorality of what they'd done, she walked the village and apologized to each person privately, from the old matrons to the smallest babies. Then she took a rifle from the wall of her father's hunting room and went to the pond. On her way there, a crowd gathered behind her. Her change was as out of the blue as Lord Jon's, and they were curious about her and happy that she was on the way to becoming a good person. She took up a position at the edge of the water, and whistled to the giant Plum fish to come for a feeding. The crowd hung back, fearful of the thing's human countenance. All watched its fin, like a purple fan, disappear beneath the water.

Ifritia pushed the bolt of the rifle forward and then sighted the weapon upon a spot where Jon usually surfaced. Everyone waited. The fish didn't come up. A flock of geese flew overhead and it started to rain. Attention wandered, and just when the crowd began murmuring, the water beneath where Ifritia leaned over the pond exploded and the fish came up a blur of violet, launching itself to the height of the girl. Using its tail, it slapped her mightily across the face. Ifritia went over backward and her feet flew out from under her. In his descent, Jon turned in midair, opened his wide mouth, and bit through her leg. The bone shattered, the flesh tore, blood burst forth, and he was gone, out of sight, to the bottom of the big pond with her foot.

She survived the grim amputation. While she lay in the hospital, her father had the pond drained. Eventually, the enormous fish was stranded in only inches of water. Ifritia's father descended a long ladder to the pond bed and sloshed halfway across it to reach Lord Jon. The creature flapped and wheezed. Her father took out a pistol and shot the fat, odious face between the eyes. He reported to others later that the fish began to cry when it saw the gun.

The immense Plum fish was gutted and Ifritia's foot was found in its third stomach. Her father forbade anyone to tell her that her foot had been rescued from the fish. She never knew that it stood in a glass case in the cedar attic atop her family home. As the days *wore on and her affliction made her more holy every minute, the foot simmered in Time, turning dark and dry. She learned to walk with a crutch, and became pious to a degree that put off the village. They whispered that she was a spy for God. Dressing in pure white, she appeared around every corner with strict moral advice. They believed her to be insane and knew her to be death to any good time.*

Mina held her glass out to Father Walter. He slowly rose, grabbed the bottle, and filled it. He poured himself another and sat again.

"Did she make a miracle at all?" he asked.

"A few," said Mina and dashed off her drink.

"Can you tell me one?"

"At a big wedding feast, she turned everybody's wine to water. She flew once, and she set fire to a tree with her thoughts."

"Amazing," said Father Walter. He stood and put his drink on the desk. "Come with me," he said. "There's something I think you'll want to see." She rose and followed him out the back door of the church. The sand was blowing hard, and he had to raise his arm in front of his eyes as he leaned into the wind. He looked back and Mina GilCragson was right behind him, holding her hat on with one hand. He led her to the shrine.

Inside, he moved toward the altar, pointing. "There it is. Saint Ifritia's foot," he said.

"What are you talking about?" said Mina, stepping up beside him.

"Right there," he said and pointed again.

She looked and an instant later went weak. Father Walter caught her by the arm. She shook her head and took a deep breath. "I can't believe it," she said.

"I know," he said. "But there it is. You mustn't touch it with your hands. You must only kiss the toes. I'll stand outside. You can have a few minutes alone with it."

"Thank you so much," she said, tears in her eyes.

He went outside. Leaning against the buffeting wind, he pushed aside the bamboo curtain that protected the shrine's one window. Through the sliver of space, he watched Mina approach the altar. Her hands were folded piously in front of her as he'd instructed. He realized that if she'd not worn the heels, she'd never have been able to reach the foot with her lips. As it was she had to go up on her toes. Her head bobbed forward to the relic, but it wasn't a quick kiss she gave. Her head moved slightly forward and back, and Father Walter pictured her tongue passionately laving the rotten toes. It both gave him a thrill and made him queasy. He had a premonition that he'd be drinking hard into the night.

After the longest time, Mina suddenly turned away from the foot. Father Walter let the bamboo curtain slide back into place and waited to greet her. She exited the shrine, and he said, "How was that? Did you feel the spirit?" but she never slowed to answer. Walking right past him, she headed toward the outhouse. The sand blew fiercely but she didn't bother to hold her hat and it flew from her head. Mina walked as if in a trance. Father Walter was surprised when she didn't go to the outhouse, but passed it, and headed up out of the valley into the dunes. On the beach, the wind would have been ten times worse. As she ascended, he called to her to come back.

She passed over the rim, out of sight, and he was reluctant to follow her, knowing the ghost of the driver might be lurking in the blinding sandstorm. He turned back toward the church, his mind a knot of thoughts. Was she having a holy experience? Had he offended her? Was she poisoned by the old foot? He stopped to fetch her hat, which had blown up against the side of the outhouse.

That night his premonition came true, and the whiskey flowed. He opened Mina GilCragson's traveling bag and went through her things. By candlelight, whiskey in one hand, he inspected each of her articles of clothing. When holding them up, he recognized the faint scent of wild violets. He wondered if she was a saint. While searching for evidence in the aroma of a pair of her underpants, Sister North appeared out of the shadows.

"What are you up to?" she asked.

"Sniffing out a holy bouquet. I believe our visitor today may have been a saint."

"She was nothing of the sort," said Sister North, who stepped forward and backhanded Father Walter hard across the face. His whiskey glass flew from his grasp and he dropped the underpants. Consciousness blinked off momentarily and then back on. He stared at her angry, yellow eyes as she reached out, grabbed his shirt, and pulled him to his feet. "Come with me," she said.

Outside, the sandstorm had abated and the night was clear and cool and still. Not letting go, she pulled Father Walter toward the shrine. He stumbled once and almost fell and for his trouble, she kicked him in the rear end. Candlelight shone out from the shrine's one window, its bamboo curtain now rolled up. Sister North marched the father up to the altar and said to him, "Look at that."

"Look at what?" he said, stunned by drink and surprise.

"What else?" she asked.

And upon noticing, he became instantly sober, for the big toe of the holy foot was missing. "My god," he said, moving closer to it. Where the toe had been was a knuckle stump of sheared gristle. "I thought she was sucking on it, but in fact she was chewing off the toe," he said, turning to face Sister North.

"You thought she was sucking on it . . ." she said. "Since when is sucking the holy toes allowed?"

"She was a scholar of Saint Ifritia. I never suspected she was a thief."

Sister North took a seat and gave herself up to tears. He sat down beside her and put his arm around her shoulders. They stayed in the shrine until the candles melted down and the dawn brought birdcalls. Then they went to his bed. Before she fell asleep, the sister said to him, "It happened because you lied."

He thought about it. "Nahh," he said. "It was bound to happen someday." He slept and dreamt of the driver's wife and daughters. When he woke, Sister North was gone.

Sister North's Sermon

Father—

By the time you find this, I'll already be four miles inland, heading for the city. I mean to bring back the stolen toe and make amends to Saint Ifritia. She's angry that we let this happen. You, of course, bear most of the responsibility, but I too own a piece of guilt. It may take me a time to hunt down Mina GilCragson. I'll try the university first, but if she's not a scholar, I fear she might be a trader on the black market, trafficking in religious relics. If that's the case the toe could at this moment be packed on the back

of a mule, climbing the northern road into the mountains and on through the clouds to the very beginning of the world. If so, I will follow it. If I fail, I won't be back. One thing I've seen in my sleep is that at the exact halfway point of my journey, a man will visit the church and bring you news of me. If he tells you I am dead, then burn my shack and all my things and scatter my ashes over the sea, but if the last he's seen of me I'm alive, then that means I will return. That, I'm sure of. Wake up and guard the foot with your very life. If I return after years with a toe and there is no foot, I'll strangle you in your sleep. Think of me in bed and in the morning when you shovel sand pray for me. There are four bottles of whiskey under the mattress in my shack. You can have three of them. I spent a week of solitude contemplating your sermon and realized that you didn't lie. That you actually killed the driver of the hay wagon. Which is worse? May the sweet saint have mercy on you.
*   —Sister*

Two days later, Father Walter realized he'd taken Sister North for granted, and she was right, he had killed the driver just as he'd described in his sermon. Without her there, in her shack, in the shrine, in his bed, the loneliness crept into the sand dune valley and he couldn't shake it. Time became a sermon, preaching itself. The sand and sun and sand and wind and sand and every now and then a visitor, whose presence seemed to last forever until vanishing into sand, a pilgrim with whom to fill the long hours, chatting.

Every one of the strangers, maybe four a year and one year only two, was asked if they brought word from Sister North. He served them whiskey and let them preach their sermons before blessing them on their journeys to the end of the world. Sometimes an old man, moving slowly, bent, mumbling, sometimes a young woman, once a child on the run. None of them had word from her. In between these occasional visits from strangers lay long stretches of days and seasons, full of silence and wind and shifting sand. To pass the long nights, he took to counting the stars.

One evening, he went to her shack to fetch the second bottle of her whiskey and fell asleep on her bed. In the morning there was a visitor in the church when he went in to shovel. A young man sat in the first pew. He wore a bow tie and white shirt, and even though it was in the heart of the summer season, a jacket as well. His hair was perfectly combed. Father Walter showed him behind the altar and they sat sipping whiskey well into the afternoon as the young man spoke his sermon. The father had heard it all before, but one thing caught his interest. In the midst of a tale of sorrows, the boy spoke about a place he'd visited in the north where one of the attractions was a fish with a human face.

Father Walter halted the sermon and asked, "Lord Jon?"

"The same," said the young man. "An enormous Plum fish."

"I'd heard he'd been killed, shot by the father of the girl whose leg he'd severed."

"Nonsense. There are so many fanciful stories told of this remarkable fish. What is true, something I witnessed, the scientists are training Lord Jon to speak. I tipped my hat to him at the Aquarium and he said, in a voice as clear as day, 'How do you do?'"

"You've never heard of a connection between Saint Ifritia and the fish?" asked Father Walter.

The young man took a sip, cocked his head, and thought. "Well, if I may speak frankly . . ."

"You must, we're in a church," said the father.

"What I remember of Saint Ifritia from Monday Afternoon Club is that she was a prostitute who was impregnated by the Lord. As her time came to give birth, her foot darkened and fell off just above the ankle and the child came out through her leg, the head appearing where the foot had been. The miracle was recorded by Charles the Bald. The boy grew up to be some war hero, a colonel in the war for the country of rain."

The young man left as the sun was going down and the sky was red. Father Walter had enjoyed talking to him, learning of the exploits of the real Lord Jon, but some hint of fear in the young man's expression said the poor fellow was headed all the way to the end, and then one more step into oblivion. That night the father sat in the churchyard near the bell and didn't drink, but pictured Sister North, struggling upward through the clouds to the beginning of the world. He wished they were in his bed, listening to the wind and the cries of the beach owl. He'd tell her the young man's version of the life of Saint Ifritia. They'd talk about it till dawn.

For the longest time, Father Walter gave up writing sermons. With the way everything had transpired, the theft of the toe, the absence of Sister North, he felt it would be better for the world if he held his tongue and simply listened. Then deep in one autumn season when snow had already fallen, he decided to leave the sand dune valley and go to see the ocean. He feared the ghost of the driver every step beyond the rim but slowly continued forward. Eventually he made his way over the dunes to the beach and sat at the water's edge. Watching the waves roll in, he gave himself up to his plans to finally set forth in search of Sister North. He thought for a long time until his attention was diverted by a fish brought before him in the surf. He looked up, startled by it. When he saw its violet color, he knew immediately what it was.

The fish opened its mouth and spoke. "A message from my liege, Lord Jon. He's told me to tell you he'd overheard a wonderful conversation with your Sister North at the Aquarium restaurant one evening a few years ago, and she wanted to relay the message to you that you should write a new sermon for her."

Father Walter was stunned at first by the talking fish, but after hearing what it had to say, he laughed. "Very well," he said and lifted the fish and helped it back into the waves. When he turned to head toward the church, the driver stood before him, a vague phantom, bowing slightly and proffering with both hands a ghostly foot. "Miracles . . ." said a voice in the wind. The father was determined to walk right through the spirit if need be. He set off at a quick pace toward the sand dune valley. Just as he thought he would collide with the ethereal driver, the fellow turned and walked, only a few feet ahead of him, just as they had walked through the dark forest in rain country. In the wind, the holy man heard the words, "I get ten yards, do I not?" repeated again and again, and he knew that if he'd had the pistol in his hand, he'd have fired it again and again.

With a sudden shiver, he finally passed through the halted ghost of the driver and descended the tall dune toward the church. The words in the wind grew fainter. By the time he reached the church door and looked back the driver was nowhere to be seen along the rim of the valley. He went immediately to his room, took off his coat, poured a glass of whiskey, and sat at his desk. Lifting his pen, he scratched across the top of a sheet of paper the title, "Every Grain of Sand, a Minute."

When he finished writing the sermon it was late in the night, and well in his cups, he decided on the spot to deliver it. Stumbling and mumbling, he went around the church and lit candles, fired up the pots of wisteria incense. As he moved through the shadows, the thought came to him that with the harsh cold of recent days, even the sand fleas, fast asleep in hibernation, would not be listening. He gathered up the pages of the sermon and went to the altar. He cleared his throat, adjusted the height of the pages to catch the candlelight, and began.

"Every grain of sand a minute," he said in a weary voice. With that phrase out, there immediately came a rapping at the church door. He looked up and froze. His first thought was of the driver. The rapping came again and he yelled out, "Who's there?"

"A traveler with news from Sister North," called a male voice. Father Walter left the altar and ran down the aisle to the door. He pushed it open and said, "Come in, come in." A tall man stepped out of the darkness and into the church's glow. Seeing the stranger's height, he remembered the driver's, and took a sudden step backward. It wasn't the ghost, though, it was a real man with thick sideburns, a serious gaze, a top hat. He carried a small black bag. "Thank you," he said and removed his overcoat and gloves, handing them to Father Walter. "I was lost among the dunes and then I saw a faint light issuing up from what appeared in the dark to be a small crater. I thought a falling star had struck the earth."

"It's just the church of Saint Ifritia," said the father. "You have news of Sister North?"

"Yes, Father, I have a confession to make."

Father Walter led the pilgrim to the front pew and motioned for the gentleman to sit while he took a seat on the steps of the altar. "Okay," he said, "out with it."

"My name is Ironton," said the gentleman, removing his hat and setting it and his black bag on the seat next to him. "I'm a traveling businessman," he said. "My work takes me everywhere in the world."

"What is your business?" asked the father.

"Trade," said Ironton. "And that's what I was engaged in at Hotel Lacrimose, up in the north country. I was telling an associate at breakfast one morning that I had plans to travel next to the end of the world. The waitress, who'd just then brought our coffee, introduced herself and begged me, since I was traveling to the end of the world, to bring you a message."

"Sister North is a waitress?"

"She'd sadly run out of funds, but intended to continue on to the beginning of the world once she'd saved enough money. In any event, I was busy at the moment, having to run off to close a deal, and I couldn't hear her out. I could, though, sense her desperation, and so I suggested we meet that night for dinner at the Aquarium.

"We met in that fantastic dining hall, surrounded by hundred-foot-high glass tanks populated by fierce leviathans and brightly colored swarms of lesser fish. There was a waterfall at one end of the enormous room and a man-made river that ran nearly its entire length with a small wooden bridge arching up over the flow in one spot to offer egress to either side of the dining area. We dined on fez-menuth flambé and consumed any number of bottles of sparkling lilac water. She told me her tale, your tale, about the sacred foot in your possession.

"Allow me to correct for you your impressions of Saint Ifritia. This may be difficult, but being a rationalist, I'm afraid I can only offer you what I perceive to be the facts. This Saint Ifritia, whose foot you apparently have, was more a folk hero than a religious saint. To be frank, she went to the grave with both feet. She never lost a foot by any means. She was considered miraculous for no better reason or no lesser than because she was known to frequently practice small acts of human kindness for friends and often strangers. Her life was quiet, small, but I suppose, no less heroic in a sense. Her neighbors missed her when she passed on and took to referring to her as Saint Ifritia. It caught on and legends attached themselves to her memory like bright streamers on a humble hay wagon."

"The foot is nothing?" asked Father Walter.

"It's an old rotten foot," said Ironton.

"What did Sister North say to your news?"

Ironton looked down and clasped his hands in his lap. "This is where I must offer my confession," he said.

"You didn't tell her, did you?"

"The story of her search for the missing toe was so pathetic, I didn't have the heart to tell her the facts. And yet, still, I was going to. But just as I was about to speak, beside our table, from out of the man-made river, their surfaced an enormous purple fish with a human face. It bobbed on the surface, remaining stationary in the flow, and its large eyes filled with tears. Its gaze pierced my flesh and burrowed into my heart to turn off my ability to tell Sister North her arduous search had been pointless."

Father Walter shook his head in disgust. "What is it she wanted you to tell me?"

"She wants you to write a sermon for her," said Ironton.

"Yes," said the father, "the news preceded you. I finished it this evening just before your arrival."

"Well," said the businessman, "I do promise, should I see her on my return trip, I will tell her the truth, and give her train fare home."

For the remaining hours of the night, Father Walter and his visitor sat in the church and drank whiskey. In their far-flung conversation, Ironton admitted to being a great collector of curios and oddities. In the morning, when the businessman was taking his leave, the father wrapped up the foot of Saint Ifritia in its original soiled towel and bestowed it upon his guest. "For your collection," he said. "Miracles."

They laughed and Ironton received the gift warmly. Then, touching his index finger and thumb to the brim of his hat, he bowed slightly, and disappeared up over the rim of the dune.

More time passed. Every grain of sand, a minute. Days, weeks, seasons. Eventually, one night, Father Walter woke from troubling dreams to find Sister North in bed beside him. At first, he thought he was still dreaming. She was smiling, though, and her cat eyes caught what little light pervaded his room and glowed softly. "Is it you?" he asked.

"Almost," she said, "but I've left parts of me between here and the beginning of the world."

"A toe?"

Sister North's Sermon

No, only pieces of my spirit, torn out by pity, shame, guilt, and fear. I tracked Mina GilCragson. She's no scholar, but an agent from a ring of female thieves who specialize in religious relics. The toe was sent along the secret Contraband Road, north to the beginning of the world. I traveled that road, packing a pistol and cutlass. And I let the life out of certain men and women who thought they had some claim on me. I slept at the side of the road in the rain and snow. I climbed the rugged path into the cloud country.

In the thin atmosphere of the Haunted Mountains, I'd run

out of food and was starving. Unfortunately for him, an old man, heading north, leading a donkey with a heavy load, was the first to pass my ambush. I told him I wanted something to eat, but he went for his throwing dagger, and I was forced to shoot him in the face. I freed the donkey of its burden and went through the old man's wares. I found food, some smoked meat, leg bones of cattle, and pickled Plum fish. While I ate I inspected the rest of the goods, and among them I discovered a small silver box. I held it up, pressed a hidden latch on the bottom, and the top flipped back. A mechanical plinking music, the harmony of Duesgruel's Last Movement, played, and I beheld the severed toe.

I had it in my possession and I felt the spirit move through me. All I wanted was to get back to the church. Taking as much of the booty from the donkey's pack as I could carry, I traveled to the closest city. There I sold my twice-stolen treasures and was paid well for them. I bought new clothes and took a room in a fine place, the Hotel Lacrimose.

I spent a few days and nights at the amazing hotel, trying to relax before beginning the long journey home. One afternoon while sitting on the main veranda, watching the clouds twirl, contemplating the glory of Saint Ifritia, I made the acquaintance of an interesting gentleman. Mr. Ironton was his name and he had an incredible memory for historical facts and interesting opinions on the news of the day. Having traveled for years among paupers and thieves, I was unused to speaking with someone as intelligent as Ironton. We had a delightful conversation. Somewhere in his talk, he mentioned that he was traveling to the end of the world. At our parting, he requested that I join him for dinner at the Aquarium that evening.

That night at dinner, I told Ironton our story. I showed him the toe in its small silver case. He lifted the thing to his nose and announced that he smelled wild violets. But then he put the toe on the table between us and said, "This Saint Ifritia you speak of. It has recently been discovered by the Holy of the Holy See that she is in fact a demon, not a saint. She's a powerful demon. I propose you allow me to dispose of that toe for you. Every minute you have it with you you're in terrible danger." He nodded after speaking.

I told him, "No, thank you. I'll take my chances with it."

"You're a brave woman, Ms. North," he said. "Now what was the message you had for your Father Walter?"

As I told him that I wanted you to know I was on my way and to write a sermon for me, an enormous violet fish with a human face rose out of the water of the decorative river next to our table that ran through the restaurant. It startled me. Its face was repulsive. I recalled your telling me something about a giant Plum fish, Lord Jon, and I spoke the name aloud. "At your service," the fish said and then dove into the flow. When I managed to overcome my shock at the fish's voice, I looked back to the table and discovered both Ironton and the toe had vanished.

I had it and I lost it. I felt the grace of Saint Ifritia for a brief few days at the Hotel Lacrimose and then it was stolen away. I've wondered all along my journey home if that's the best life offers.

Sister North yawned and turned on her side. "And what of the foot? Is it safe?" she asked.

He put his arm around her. "No," he said. "Some seasons back I was robbed at gunpoint. A whole troop of bandits on horses. They took everything. I begged them to leave the foot. I explained it was a holy relic, but they laughed and told me they would cook it and eat it on the beach that night. It's gone."

"I'm so tired," she said. "I could sleep forever."

Father Walter drew close to her, closed his eyes, and listened to the sand sifting in through the walls.

A Note About "Relic"

Although this story may, like the previous one, seem to have something to do with religion, it's really more a story about faith. It appeared in *The Thackery T. Lambshead Cabinet of Curiosities: Exhibits, Oddities, Images, and Stories from Top Authors and Artists*, edited by Jeff and Ann VanderMeer. What's nice about writing fiction for the VanderMeers is that it goes without saying that the weird, the idiosyncratic, is always warmly welcome. In this particular instance, Jeff told me not to worry about the length of the story but to "go long" if I liked, and I did. "Relic" was inspired by my reading of the book *Rag and Bone: A Journey Among the World's Holy Dead* by Peter Manseau, a fascinating study that details the myths, legends, and crazy true-life stories behind the remains of saints and the sacred from many religions. Besides Manseau's work, I have to admit, I also lifted the idea of a scene from Richard Bausch's great World War II novel, *Peace*, a book I highly recommend. "Relic" is one of two or maybe more stories in my collection that deals with an errant foot, but then *Crackpot Palace* has many secret passageways that connect its rooms, so that two tales told in different styles and seeming to have different concerns might actually be secretly linked through image or idea.

Glass Eels

Between a spreading magnolia and a forest of cattails that ran all the way to the estuary stood Marty's dilapidated studio. The walls were damp, and low-tide stink mixed with turpentine and oils. It was late on a Saturday night in early March. They drank beer and passed a joint. Len spoke of insomnia, a recent murder out on Money Island, and a buck he'd seen with pitch-black antlers. Marty told about a huge snake on the outside of the studio window and then showed Len his most recent paintings—local landscapes and a series of figures called *Haunted High School.*

"That chick looks dead," said Len, pointing at a canvas with a pale girl in a cheerleading outfit, smoking a cigarette. In the background loomed an abandoned factory, busted glass and crumbling brick. A smokestack.

"She's haunted," said Marty. "I gotta sell a couple of these in the next gallery show in Milville on Third Friday. I need enough to fix the roof. We're fuckin' broke."

"I heard there was a guy in a van buying glass eels before daybreak in the parking lot behind the burned-out diner on Jones Island Road," said Len.

"The state banned it back in the nineties, didn't they?" Marty asked.

"Yeah, *they* banned it," Len said and laughed. "I heard one kilogram is going for a thousand dollars. That's two pounds of eel for a grand."

"How many eels is that?"

"You gotta remember," said Len, "they're only two inches long, see-through thin. So you have to do a fair amount of dipping to bring up two pounds, but not enough to call it work."

"Are you saying we should do this?"

"Well, we should do it just once. Think of your roof."

Marty nodded.

"Shit, I could use the money for my prescriptions," said Len.

"How much can you make in a night?"

"Most guys do about a kilogram and a half to two. Some do a little better. But there are times when a person'll bring in twenty or even more."

"How?"

"They know a spot no one else knows, a certain creek, or gut, or spillway, where saltwater and freshwater come together and the glass eels swarm. And I was thinking today, after I heard that they were going for a grand, that there was a place my father would take me fishing for eels at the end of July. We'd barbecue them."

"How long ago?"

"Thirty years."

"You think we could find it?"

"Nothing changes around here," Len said. "Myrtle's Gut. Down the end of your own block out here. At the marina, we get in a canoe and paddle a little ways and there's a big island of reeds. It's pretty sturdy to walk on, but the water is everywhere and if you take a wrong step in the dark you could fall in up to your neck. There used to be a trail through the reeds into the middle of the island. Sort of at the center is a spot where this creek comes up from underground and winds its way for three turns, once around a myrtle bush, on its way out to the Delaware."

"That ain't real," Marty said.

"Yeah," said Len, "that's what it is. A freshwater creek that runs out to the reed island beneath the floor of the bay and then surfaces."

"And the eels that go there swim underground up into the freshwater streams?"

"Eels will do anything they have to do to get where they're going. On their way back out to sea to spawn, if a creek dries up, they'll wriggle right across the land. Years ago on a full-moon night in August you could club eels passing through. It was an event. The guy who owned the best meadow for it had a stand nearby that sold corn dogs and lemonade. Everybody clubbed a couple. There were guys there who'd take your eels and smoke them for you for a half dollar."

"Sounds like *Lord of the Flies*."

"The underground protects them on the way out, so why not on the way in?"

"How do you see them at night when they're so small?"

"They're like tiny ghosts, especially in the moonlight."

"So we go out there in a canoe?"

"We'll need a couple of coolers and some nets, a couple of flashlights."

"I can't run, man. If we get caught, there's no way I can run."

"Forget it, no one's gonna see us. Nobody gives a shit. The last time I saw a cop down here was about a year and a half ago when Mr. Clab's coffin went on a voyage. Remember, they found it on the beach next to the marina?"

"The cop said there was an underground stream beneath the cemetery that washed the box out to the bay."

"You see," said Len, "there's your proof of what I'm saying."

Len and Marty sat on the damp ground beside the spreading myrtle bush at the second bend in the gut. There was a breeze. Between them lay a pair of lit flashlights like a cold camp-fire. They were dressed warmly, with hats, gloves, and scarves. Beside them were coolers and nets. Len took out a joint and said, "We gotta wait for the moon."

"Why?"

"The tide. The moon's gonna rise in about five minutes, nearly full, and in a half hour it'll be a good way up the sky and big as a dinner plate. The eels will come in with the tide."

"It's dark as shit out here," said Marty.

"Nice stars, though," said Len. He passed the joint.

Marty took a hit and said, "The other night, after you left, it started raining hard. I went up to bed. When I got under the covers, Claire's back was to me. I knew she was awake. I told her what you said about the eels, and I told her if something happened where I got caught she would have to bail me out. A few seconds passed and, without turning around, she asked, 'How much can you make?' 'Maybe a couple of thousand,' I told her. The rain dripped in. She said, 'Do it.' "

Len laughed. "That's what I call a working marriage." He leaned forward and took the joint from Marty's hand.

"Do you think Matisse ever did this?" asked Marty.

"I don't think Matisse was ever a substitute teacher."

"The other day they sent me to teach English in a separate

school for all the truants and delinquents. They call it the Hawthorne Academy. Jesus, it's the worst. Fights, a couple an hour. Crazy motherfucker kids. They're being warehoused by the state until they reach the legal age and can be released into society."

"Haunted High School," said Len. He pointed into the sky. "Here comes the moon."

"Nice," said Marty.

They sat quietly for a long while, listening to the flow of the gut and the wind moving over the marshland. Len lit a cigarette and said, "I saw a guy in town this afternoon. I think I remember him from 'Nam."

"Oh, lordy, no Vietnam stories. Show some mercy."

"I'll just tell you the short version," said Len.

"Never short enough. When do the eels show up?"

"Listen, I saw this guy, Vietcong. We never learned what his real name was but everybody on both sides called him Uncle Fun. I was shown black-and-white photos of him. We were sent into the tunnels with an express mission to execute this guy. The tunnels were mind blowing, mazes of warrens; three, four floors; couches; kids; booby traps. He was a fucking entertainer, like a nightclub act, only he played the Vietcong tunnel systems instead of Vegas. He told jokes and sang songs. For some reason they wanted us to cancel his contract ASAP."

"You're a one-man blizzard of bullshit," said Marty.

"Fuck you. Intel said that at the end of every performance he laughed like Woody Woodpecker."

"What was he doing downtown this afternoon, trying out new material in the parking lot of City Liquors? You been taking your pills?"

"Shit, they're here," said Len. "Grab a net."

The moon shone down on the bend in the gut and the water bubbled and glowed with the reflection of thousands of glass eels. Len and Marty scooped up dripping nets of them like shovelfuls of silver.

"Do we need to put water in the coolers to keep them alive?" asked Marty.

"Are you kidding? They're tough as hell. They'll keep for hours just like they are."

"The black eyes creep me."

"A glass eel the size of a person would be the Holy Ghost."

Marty drove his old Impala. Len was in the passenger seat. The nets were in the back, the coolers in the trunk. They headed north, away from the marina, past Marty's house, and turned at the cemetery onto a road that went over a wooden bridge. It led to a narrow lane lined with oak and pine. The deer looked up, their eyes glowing in the headlights.

"You know that giant tree up at the end of the road here, where you make the turn? The one with the neon-orange pentagram on it? Star with a circle around it. What's that all about?" asked Marty.

"That's Wiccan, I think. Nature witches, they've been here for a long, long time. They mark the important crossroads."

"Witches?"

"I've run into a few. You hear stories about spells and shit, but I never witnessed any of that. They just seem like sketchy hippies."

"Me and Claire call it the Devil Tree. Which way am I going there?"

"You want to make a left. Then, in a quarter of a mile, make a right. I hope the buyer's there again."

"How much do you think we've got?"

"I'd say about eight grand. Maybe more."

"Jeez."

"These eels have never been successfully bred in captivity," said Len. "When it comes to eels you can only take."

"You trying to make me feel guilty?"

"Yeah, but fuck it, we need the cash. The parking lot of the old diner is up here on the right, just past these cattails."

Behind the burned-out shell of Jaqui's All Night Diner, in a parking lot long gone to weeds, Len and Marty stood before the open back doors of a large van. Inside was a lantern that gave a dim light. Behind the lantern, a teenage girl sitting on a crate aimed a shotgun at them.

"We'll see what you have," said a heavyset man to their right. He wore a tweed suit jacket and had a pistol tucked into the waist of his jeans. Before him on a makeshift wooden platform was a large antique balance scale, one end a fine net, the other a flat plate holding four-kilogram cylinders of lead.

"Snorri," called the buyer, and a huge guy with a crew cut, wearing a shoulder holster, appeared from around the side of the van.

"Pour these gentlemen's eels, I have to weigh them," said the buyer. Snorri lifted the first cooler and carefully poured out the eels into the net of the scale. The weighing took a while. Every time the scale moved it creaked. The wind blew strong and whipped the reeds that surrounded the parking lot. The girl with the shotgun yawned and checked for messages on her phone.

"That's the last of them," said the buyer, clapping his hands. "One more calculation, though. I subtract for the water the eels have on them. I only pay for eels, not water." He laid three small white gull feathers on the flat plate of the scale and leaned over to read the difference. "You have a little more than nine kilograms here. I can give you eight thousand."

"I heard it was a thousand a kilogram," said Len.

"One hears what one wants," said the buyer.

"I know from a reliable source that last night you were paying a grand."

"Supply and demand," said the buyer.

"Explain it," said Len.

"Eight grand or I can have Snorri explain it to you in no uncertain terms."

The girl in the van laughed.

"We'll take the eight grand," said Marty. "Chill out," he said to Len. "We're talking eight grand for an hour and a half of fishing."

"Okay," said Len.

Snorri stepped back, taking the gun from its holster. The buyer leaned into the van and stuffed eight stacks of banded hundreds into a yellow plastic grocery bag. He handed the bag to Marty. "Check it," he said.

Marty held the bag open and counted the stacks in a whisper. He reached in and felt the money. He lifted the bag and smelled it. "Thanks," he said.

"An hour and a half," said the buyer. "That's very fast for what you brought in."

"We don't mess around," said Len.

"Where were you?"

"Over west," said Len, "in the woods by the bay south of Greenwich."

"Can you be more specific?"

"Have Snorri explain it to you," said Len and laughed on his way back to the Impala.

They got in the car. Marty backed out past the remains of the diner and onto the road. "Why'd you have to be such an asshole with the guy? I thought they were gonna shoot us in the back with every step I took."

"They're not gonna shoot us. Think about it, they need us. If we're getting a bit less than a grand for a kilogram, think what the buyer is making per kilogram from aquafarms in Asia."

"Too many guns for me."

"Quit your cryin', we've got four grand apiece. You can get your roof fixed and I can medicate. Harmony will reign."

"I'm happy for the four grand," said Marty. "In your honor, I'm gonna paint a series, maybe eight canvases, each a scene from the career of Uncle Fun."

"Put him in a tux and make him look like a North Vietnamese Bobby Darin."

"Hey, there's somebody behind us."

Len looked over his shoulder. "We'll know soon enough if it's a cop. When you get to the Devil Tree, keep going, don't make the turn. Head down the road a ways and then turn back by the old glass factory. We can lose him in the dunes."

"Could just be somebody out driving."

"I kind of doubt it," said Len. "We've got eight thousand dollars in cash here and it's three in the morning on one of the loneliest roads in the world. When you get to the tree, hit the gas. We'll see if he keeps up."

"I can't drive fast at night. I can't see dick."

"You gotta lose this fucker now."

The Impala suddenly accelerated. Len whooped and called, "Faster." Marty was hunched up over the steering wheel, peering into the dark.

"They're definitely on our asses," said Len. "Turn in at the glass factory."

"I don't know where the turn is. You're gonna have to warn me."

"Okay, okay, okay . . . Now!"

Marty cut the wheel. The back tires skidded sideways and the car did a one-eighty. He put it in reverse, turned around, and they were headed into the maze of sand dunes.

"Go to the right," said Len. "That's where it gets crazy."

"You know your way through here?"

"Nobody knows their way through here. I used to play here as a kid and I'd get lost and turned around all the time."

"How's that gonna help us?"

"Make a left after this next dune. Twenty minutes of driving around in this bullshit in the dark and that guy's gonna forget all about us and go home. Just keep dodging him for a while and then I'll get us back to the road."

"That plan sucks."

"That's its strength."

"Oh, shit," said Marty. "I'm past empty."

"You're kidding," said Len and leaned over to look at the dashboard. "Oh, man."

"I forgot to gas up."

"That's just fuckin' dandy."

"It's running on fumes, should I try to make it back to the road?"

"No, go deeper in. We'll hide somewhere with the lights out. Make as many crazy turns as you can."

"I don't like it."

"When the car craps out, shut up. We're gonna run silent, run deep."

The Impala died in a cul-de-sac bounded by three enormous sand dunes.

"Kill the lights," said Len. "Crack a window so we can hear better and then turn everything off. That guy's probably home having a beer right now, cursing us 'cause we gave him the slip."

Len unzipped his jacket and reached down the front of his shirt. He cocked back his chin and pulled out a large scabbard and knife on a leather strap around his neck. Taking the strap off, he removed the knife, ten inches, with a hunting blade and grip guard, and stowed it up his jacket sleeve, hilt first.

"What's that for?"

"Whatever," said Len. Then he whispered, "I remember, once we had Uncle Fun surrounded and he managed to give us the slip . . ."

"Run silent," said Marty.

They sat quietly in the dark. Off to the east an owl called.

Len and Marty stood ten yards in front of the Impala. Three guys in black hoodies and ski masks surrounded them. The one in front of them held a .22 pistol with a homemade silencer on it. Marty shivered and clutched the yellow grocery bag. The moon was gone from the sky. Dark clouds raced and it smelled like rain.

"What you two have to learn is that if you harvest glass down here, you need to pay us fifteen percent of your take," said the guy with the gun.

"Are you ladies pro-eel or something?" asked Len. "I mean

the outfits. You look like eels. It's the first thing I thought when I saw you."

"Nobody's pro-eel, asshole. We're pro-cash. We poach the poachers. Like the food chain."

"That silencer have a wipe?" asked Len.

"What difference does it make? I could shoot you with a cannon out here and nobody'd know."

"Listen, I was born down here," said Len. "I have as much right to these eels as you do."

"Wait, man, listen," said Marty. "It's just like a tax. Everything has a tax on it. So we pay for eight grand, twelve hundred or something. Let it go and let's get out of here."

"I'm not paying anything," said Len. "He can suck my glass eel."

"That's it for you," said the guy in the mask, and he raised the gun.

Len ducked as the shot sounded, the gruff sudden cough of an old man. When he sprang up, he had the knife in his hand. In one swift motion he slashed the blade across the wrist of the masked man's gun hand. The sharp metal bit in deep and severed the tendon. The gun dropped. The guy screamed. Marty, pissing his pants, turned and ran.

Len took a backhanded swipe and the blade tore open the throat beneath the ski mask. Blood poured and the scream turned to a gurgle. Len pivoted to follow Marty and was hit in the left side of the head with a baseball bat. He staggered sideways a few steps before his feet went out from under him. The masked guy with the bat took off after Marty while his remaining partner stood over Len and drew a .22 with a silencer from the pocket of his hoodie. Len's jaw was busted and jutting to the side. He blinked and grunted. The cough of the gun sounded twice.

Marty worked like crazy to climb the dune but he got nowhere. Finally, he turned and lay back against the slope. He held the bag of money out toward the two masked men who stood only a few yards below him. One held a flashlight trained on the painter. The other held the pistol.

"I just wanted to fix my fuckin' roof. Take the money."

"We're gonna throw your bodies in an eel pond," said the guy with the flashlight. "In August when the old ones head to the Sargasso to spawn, you'll go with them." He laughed, high pitched and insane.

Marty quit weeping. "Uncle Fun?" he asked. "Is it you?"

"This loser's lost his mind," said the gunman to his partner. "I'll give you Uncle Fun," he said to Marty and pulled the trigger three times.

A Note About "Glass Eels"

Joyce Carol Oates, editor of the anthology *New Jersey Noir*, where this piece originally appeared, told me that upon first reading my story she thought the phenomenon of glass eels was completely fabricated, making the story surreal. So much of Jersey is like that, from the statehouse to the Barrens. I have to thank Kevin, Hiroko, and Chieko Quigley for turning me on to the history of the glass eel trade in South Jersey, which was altogether real. I do want to say one thing about the character of Len, which might add some insight to his nature. "Do the math" is what I'll tell you concerning him. It was a great pleasure to get a chance to write a story for Joyce Carol Oates, whose stories have entranced me for years and whose book *Wild Nights!* is my idea of a perfect collection. A tip of the hat in thanks to Johnny Temple, publisher of Akashic Books, for allowing me to use "Glass Eels" in my collection long before it should have become eligible. If you're a noir fan, check out Akashic's exemplary series of anthologies organized by locale, from Brooklyn to Haiti.

The Wish Head

Stan Lowell was awake at 6:10 on that Saturday morning near the end of September when the phone rang. He'd been up half the night, sitting at his desk, nursing the phantom pain in his ivory foot. Lately, he'd gotten into the habit of taking morphine pills. When he'd started in midsummer, one would do the trick, but he'd graduated to three as the cooler weather came on. Dr. de Vries never would have approved. Luckily, the amputation site flared up only once a week, no more, no less. Always sometime after midnight. Which midnight it would be, though, was ever the question. The drug never eased the infernal ache, somehow separate from his body but no less agonizing. He sat through each episode in a stupor, listening to the ticking of the grandfather clock and the wind in the oak outside the study window.

On the third ring of the phone, he looked up and realized the pain had fled, as it usually did, at the first sign of daylight. Only on overcast mornings did it linger past breakfast. Stan scrabbled out of the chair, shook his head, and rubbed his face. He hobbled across the study and lifted the receiver.

"Lowell," he said.

"Coroner," said a quiet voice on the other end of the line.

"Detective Groot?" said Stan.

"Death never sleeps."

"Where?"

"You know where Hek's Creek runs along the west side of the Polson place?"

"The fishing spot," said Stan.

"Yeah," said Groot. "Bring the camera. I'm heading back out there now."

"I'll meet you there."

Stan dressed in the only suit he had, a brown one, which he kept cleaned and pressed for official county business. He had a hat that matched it pretty well, which he hardly ever wore, and a mustard-colored tie held in place by a gold clip in the shape of a honeybee. Last, he put on the circular glasses, which did nothing for his vision but did, as his late, former boss Dr. de Vries had predicted, in conjunction with the suit, convince the citizens of Midian County of Stan's "relative intelligence." By the time he slipped sock and shoe over the ivory foot, which had the scrimshawed image of a devil beneath the heel, his left calf muscle had unclenched and the stiffness had worked itself out. He grabbed his bag and the camera and, no longer hobbling, but moving almost gracefully, left his house. Out on the porch, he felt the cold and stared out at the giant white clouds above the yellowing treetops. For a moment, he forgot where he was going.

He drove through the center of Midian proper. In addition to it, there were two other towns, Hekston and Verruk, that comprised the county and thus his jurisdiction. Situated along the Susquehanna River, north of Chenango, it was the smallest county in the state of New York, and existed only due to the factories of Madrigal's Loom, "manufacturers of fine woven products," and some ingenious gerrymandering on the part of politicians. Each of the three towns had a main street, a factory, and a few neighborhoods. Midian, slightly larger than its brethren, had the hospital, a movie theater, and the county library. Factory towns nestled amid farmland and sugar maple forest.

Leaving town, Stan passed the first of Madrigal's redbrick monstrosities, its smokestack jutting into the blue sky. He thought of the three factories as hives, one in each town, abuzz with electric weaving. De Vries had told him that old man Madrigal had been the father of Midian County. "At times the place bears a striking resemblance to the jackass," he'd said. Whatever shortcomings William Madrigal might have had, though, it was clear enough to all that without his commerce, the twentieth century would never have taken hold in that locale. Thanks to Madrigal's tenacity, the modern age had sunk its roots and slowly spread like the forest. Now, even in the midst of the Depression of the 1930s, Madrigal's sons kept it all going through a combination of cuts in workforce, hours, and wages. In addition to their sheer determination, they counted on those roots to keep the whole enterprise from sliding away down the river.

With the banks of the Susquehanna in view, Stan took a left and headed up a steep road canopied by orange leaves. Halfway to the top of the hill, the pavement ended and the road turned to dirt track. Off to his right, through breaks in the trees, he caught glimpses of the sparkling flow. At the top of the hill, a meadow was fenced by a stone wall, which, he'd once been told, dated back to the 1700s. He spotted Groot's black Model B and a Midian squad car pulled over to the side of the track. He parked behind them and grabbed his bag, strapped the camera around his neck.

The meadow grass was loaded with dew and a light haze drifted just above the ground, although the sky was clear and bright. He noticed red leaves on the stand of trees that hid the creek, and realized winter was closer than he'd thought. Up ahead, a short, bald man, stocky, in a long black coat, the hem of which trailed in the wet grass, took four steps into the meadow, stopped, flashed a silver lighter and lit a cigarette. His face was as wide as Edward G. Robinson's, his lips turned down at the corners.

"Morning," said Groot as Stan approached.

"What have we got, Detective?"

"A floater," he said and took a drag. "But, ah . . ." Groot looked off to the west. "There's something different about this one."

"What?"

"You've got to see it for yourself," he said and turned back, smiling.

As always, Stan was disconcerted by the dark round birthmark at the center of the detective's forehead, often mistaking it for a fly. Whenever Stan glanced at it, he had the sense Groot was watching him.

They walked in among the trees and due north to the creek.

"The waterline's way up since the flood in July," said Groot. "Two kids came fishing this morning early and found the body. They ran back to town and their parents took them to the station. Loaf is watching it so it doesn't head downstream any farther. We left it in the water for you."

"Officer Lougher?" said Stan. "Midian's finest?"

Groot smiled, shrugged, and flicked his smoke away onto the fallen leaves. The water came into sight and Stan was surprised to see how much it had risen. They stepped into a clearing along the bank and Officer Lougher turned and tipped his cap to Stan.

"You'll want to be seeing this," said the cop and waved for the coroner to step closer to where the willows hung over a natural pool. It was a legendary fishing spot, a centuries-old depression where the water was trapped and turned slowly before rejoining the swifts of Hek's Creek.

As Stan drew near, he saw something pale, slowly turning in the calm green eddy. The surface was littered with willow leaves, here and there a yellow one from a maple, and amid this debris of autumn floated a young woman, faceup, naked, her long black hair fanned about her head. Her arms lolled peacefully at her sides; her legs were slightly open, dandelion seed in the black tangle of pubic hair; her breasts peaked above the waterline. Stan noticed no obvious signs of corruption in the flesh, but the open eyes still glistened, the startled gaze of the recently drowned.

Groot sidled up next to the coroner. "Every time I look at her I think she's alive," he said quietly.

"She's not," said Stan.

"It's the smile," said Lougher. "What's she smiling about?"

"*Risus sardonicus*," said the coroner. "A spasm of the facial muscles after death. But this isn't the usual grin. The eyebrows aren't lifted, the mouth isn't open, her teeth aren't showing. Instead, she looks like she's lost in a fond memory."

"I thought she was mocking me," said the cop.

"She's got a secret," said Groot.

"She's certainly got something," said Stan. He raised the camera and unlocked the bellows. "I'll get a couple of shots of her in the water and a couple on the bank here when we pull her out."

"I looked around a few hundred yards along the creek in either direction. Didn't see anything. She probably washed down from Hekston. The creek's deep enough since the flood," said Groot as Stan snapped away.

Stan lowered the camera. "She'd have been in the water for quite a while," he said. "I'm surprised she looks as good as she does. No noticeable bloating. What time did the kids find her?"

"About five thirty," said Lougher.

"Okay, Loaf, let's get her out of there," said Stan.

The officer leaned over and lifted an eight-foot wooden pole with pulleys and, running its length, a stiff cord with a small noose at the end. "I haven't fished here since I was a kid," said Lougher as he dangled the noose out above the young woman's left foot.

"Be gentle," warned Stan and handed them each a pair of gloves.

"Like a mother," said the officer as he reeled the body in.

Groot joined them and they hoisted the dead girl onto the bank. They moved her with such ease it was as if she were simply sleeping. Her skin was as cold as ice and yet firm to the touch. She exuded an aroma of flowers.

"Roses," said Groot.

"Wisteria," said Lougher, who then sniffed again and changed his verdict to "Lilac."

Stan stared at her expression. Her face was undeniably beautiful but the smile now appeared more wistful than serene. A hint of loss had at some point crept into it. He set the camera down and got on his knees next to her. Moving her head carefully from side to side and lifting her shoulders, he looked for the pooling of blood—lividity—caused by the posture of a corpse in the water. There were no signs in the usual spots for a drowning victim. This meant the young woman had floated, flat on her back, most of the way from wherever she'd come, and yet rigor mortis hadn't seemed to set in yet.

"Pretty recent?" asked Groot, lighting another cigarette.

"I can't tell," said Stan. "Could be. No wrinkling, no foaming, no trace of insects. When you guys get her to the hospital, I'll take a look at her and see. Most unusual, though," he said, lifting the camera. He backed away and snapped a string of pictures.

Groot walked him halfway across the meadow.

"I'm going to the diner for breakfast," said Stan. "I'll be over to the hospital in about an hour or so."

The detective nodded. "The body'll be there. I'll come for the lowdown when I get off this afternoon."

"By the way," said Stan before turning toward his car, "how's your wife doing? Last I saw you, she wasn't well."

"Oh, yeah, it was just the flu. She told me the other day that she's ready for me to retire," he said, his fat face slowly forming a grin.

"What'd you tell her?"

"I laughed," he said and laughed without making a sound.

Stan limped over the uneven ground back to his Chrysler. On his way to town, he recalled the summer's flood—sudden, massive, and devastating. People had lost houses, cars, pets. He'd seen more than a couple of floaters, as Groot called them, that week in July, but none of them looked like this girl. As he drove along, he played Best Guess. Someone up in Hekston would ID her from the photos. The loom there had been hit the hardest with layoffs, and since the flood a bad spirit pervaded the place. Murder, suicide, an ill-fated accident, none of them would surprise him in the least. As he pulled to the curb outside the diner, he dismissed the foul-play theory as preposterous. De Vries had always told him never to trust a best guess.

Stan sat in his usual seat at a table by the window that looked out on the corner of Ninevah and Oak. Bissie Clayton brought him his free coffee.

When Lowell had returned from Europe, the only one of twelve young men from the county to make it home alive, it was late winter, 1919. He was on crutches, still weak from the effects of the mustard gas, and the father he'd meant to please by enlisting in the Marines was dead. Junietta Poole, the girl he'd been going with, had run off to New York City with his cousin. His mother was losing her mind, and his older brother and sister had fled to Binghamton and Syracuse respectively. He couldn't find work; who wanted an amputee? One day during that dark time, as he was passing the diner, Bissie came out onto the sidewalk and called to him.

"You're the boy from the war," she said. "Lowell."

Stan stopped and nodded.

"Whenever you want, come and see me for coffee and a meal. Don't be shy," she said.

He thanked her, but it was weeks before he took her up on it. He waited till he was desperate for a decent meal. Bissie was as good as her word. Before he left Clayton's that day, she slid a piece of paper along the counter to him. On it was a name and address. "Go see this fella. He wants to talk to you about a job," she said. Even after he started working for de Vries, and was able to pay for his meals at the diner, Bissie never charged him for coffee. The doctor liked to recount a story about Bissie from when she was much younger and a stranger had tried to rob the cash register when her back was turned. "She beat him into the emergency ward at Midian General with a skillet," he'd said. "Two more whacks and I'd have been doing an autopsy on him."

"Lowell," she said. "You're here early for Saturday." She took a seat across from him and set the pot down on the table. There was a jar between them holding dried chrysanthemums. A fly, like Groot's birthmark, bothered the window glass. Bissie filled the seat and then some, her forearms like James Braddock's, her sparse white hair trapped in a spiral by bobby pins. On the days she made soup, she wore a hairnet.

"There was a body up in the creek," he said. "Not for general knowledge, you understand. Off the record."

"I already heard," she said. "A girl?"

Stan nodded.

"I heard she looked like an angel."

"Not knowing what an angel looks like, it would be difficult for me to corroborate that," he said and sipped his coffee.

Bissie laughed. "You're a wiseass," she said.

"Actually, there was something . . . *interesting* about her."

She stood and smoothed her apron. "You should be that interested in the live ones," she said, and walked back toward the counter where two out-of-towners in hunting gear waited for her. "The usual?" she called back over her shoulder.

"Yeah," said Stan.

The plate of creamed chipped beef came, a steaming cloud of froth on toast. He ate it three times a week and knew it would eventually kill him, but Bissie made it even better than they had in the service. He washed it down with the coffee, which, though free, wasn't good but was hot, and tried to determine from memory how old the young woman in the pool had been. He surmised late twenties, but she could have been younger. With that smile, the bright eyes, her beauty, he could, at the very edges of his imagination, picture her walking, laughing, sleeping. Then something strange occurred that had never happened before, her name came to him out of the blue—*Alina.*

The coroner's official offices were next to the morgue, in the basement of Midian General Hospital. One of the rooms, which was no bigger than a large closet, held a desk with a lamp, a chair, and two filing cabinets. Three times larger was the autopsy room with a table and counters and as many of the latest tools, testing equipment, and paraphernalia as de Vries had been able to wheedle out of the county, state, and federal governments. He'd done pretty well by the office until the Depression hit, had even gotten Stan a salary as his assistant although the workload for the entire county was light. Keeping up with the advancements in forensics went right out the window, though, once the "dirty thirties" rolled in. When the county threatened to eliminate the assistant position, de Vries retired and handed the reins over to Stan. Not long after, he died.

A portrait of the old man hung above the coroner's desk. It was Stan's habit, before every autopsy, to sit for a minute with his mentor. Occasionally, de Vries's voice would sound in his head, usually no more than a line or two and always something he'd actually said when he was living.

"What of Alina?" Stan thought as he studied the portrait— the pointed white beard and thick eyebrows, the shelf of a forehead, and a smile like the doctor was chewing a cricket with his right molar.

"Don't name the dead," Stan heard the doctor say. "They have their own names. They're not pets."

He found her laid on her back on the table in the autopsy

room. At first glance, the body looked as fresh as when they'd pulled it from the creek. On the counter lay a note penciled in Groot's terrible handwriting: *right buttock*. As Stan pulled on gloves and set out his instruments, he noticed the faint scent of flowers. Then he turned to her and saw her smile. It appeared not to have physically changed one iota but now it conveyed something wholly different, a deep sense of irony he'd not detected before. He was certain that if she could, she'd be shaking her head in disapproval. Loaf had said he thought she was mocking him, and now Stan understood why.

He began by rolling her onto her left side, per Groot's note. What he found on the right buttock was a surprise—a mark of raised skin as if she'd been branded by a hot iron. The scar was old, no more than four inches around, some sort of symbol he couldn't quite make out. It appeared to be an oval, filled with crosshatching, and there were five small projections; four round, one pointed. Holding her in place, he moved his position from nearer her head to down by her legs and from that new perspective the wound became clear. It was a crude rendering of a turtle. He rolled her completely onto her front and then fetched his pencil and pad. As he sketched the figure, he had the faintest inkling that he'd seen it somewhere before.

He undertook a gross examination of the corpse, checking for bruising, cuts, or scrapes. As he worked methodically through his autopsy checklist, it slowly dawned on him that the preservation of Alina's corpse was something quite remarkable. He'd read about other such cases. Religious history was littered with them. Incorruptible flesh, the scent of flowers. De Vries had shared his opinion on the matter. "Most of them are fakes," he'd said. "And the ones that are real have been preserved intentionally by people or by the environment in which the cadaver was laid to rest. There's nothing holy about it. They're desiccated turds. End of story."

Considering the tenor of the times, a miracle didn't sound as bad to Stan as it had to the doctor. Still, he wondered, if it *was* a bona fide miracle, what would it change? He couldn't think of a single thing and continued with the examination. He checked the girl's airway, which was clear; looked for insects or larvae but found none, which could obviously be due to the fact that she'd been in the water; collected a few willow leaves from her long hair; and drew some blood. Taking the vials to the work counter, he prepared three slides and used the rest to set up chemical tests for poisoning.

Eye to the microscope, he looked for a number of things, but he was most interested to see if perhaps the blood held any freshwater organisms. He'd learned of the technique from de Vries, who'd said he'd heard of it from others, although it was not yet a widely known or approved test. "If the victim drowns," he'd said, "their attempts to breathe, their gasping, will draw the water deeply into their lungs, all the way to the capillaries, where blood and oxygen meet and are exchanged. It's possible that microscopic organisms from the river will have time to travel to distant locations in the body's bloodstream before death steps in."

"Steps in," thought Stan, and it struck him as to how often the doctor had ascribed human qualities to the final process. He adjusted the focus and peered into Alina's blood. He pored over the slides for three-quarters of an hour, but they revealed nothing. The tests for toxins revealed nothing. Not only was he sure she'd not drowned, but it seemed that she'd never actually died. Instead, she was just dead.

He considered cutting her open, but of late there were rumblings from the state about his lack of credentials as a forensic medical examiner. He wasn't a doctor, and therefore not a medical examiner; nor did he have any official forensics education. What he did have was more than a decade working as an apprentice to de Vries, who had been a doctor and, although he had no special degree confirming it, had been considered a forensics expert.

After retirement, de Vries had pulled strings with the governor's office to have Stan appointed to the county coroner's position, which gave him the legal right to investigate a death in any manner he saw fit, whether he was a doctor or not. Stan knew his tenure was out of the ordinary, and at times he felt pangs of guilt about it, but he was also certain he'd gotten a better education at de Vries's side than he might have at a university. The days when de Vries's name carried weight in the county or at the statehouse, though, were swiftly receding into the past. Dr. Rashner, the state medical examiner, would have to come over from Albany to take a look at Alina. Given the layoffs at the capital and the turgid manner in which things moved through the bureaucracy now, it could take a while. He didn't like to think of the young woman stuck in a cold drawer in the basement of Midian General, but he also felt some relief at being able to foist the determination of cause of death off on Rashner. "It can be *his* miracle," thought Stan. "I'll be happy just to keep my job."

While he was writing up his report at the counter in the autopsy room, he stopped, stuck on precisely the words he might use to describe her appearance. He needed to dispense with "remarkable" or "unusual" and instead stick to cold, clinical, physical descriptions. He turned and looked at Alina. Her body lay as he'd left it on completion of his examination, her head cocked to one side. She was staring at him. Her smile was the expression of an old friend, as if he'd made a foolish joke that was funnier for the inevitability of his foolishness than for the joke itself. He got off his stool, approached the table, and studied her pale lips. Her face was like a fine marble sculpture, and the moment he had that thought, he remembered de Vries teaching him how to make a death mask.

The doctor had been a man primarily of the nineteenth century, but when he passed into the modernity of the twentieth, he smuggled, like plundered artifacts, old secrets and forgotten techniques. Before photography was widely available, when an unidentified corpse was discovered, the coroner or examiner would use plaster to capture the exact features of a victim in a mask to be used for possible identification after burial. The corpse that de Vries had used to demonstrate the craft belonged to Leon, the erstwhile hospital janitor, who'd been found dead in his apartment from a self-inflicted gunshot wound to the heart. "We will memorialize Leon Chechik," said the doctor, who'd been the dead man's chess opponent for twenty years.

Today, Stan worked quickly, as de Vries always had. "If there's anything worth doing, it's worth doing fast," the old man liked to say. The recipe for the plaster, the steps of the procedure all came back to Stan in a rush. He worked as methodically as the grandfather clock, mixing the plaster, cutting strips of gauze. After covering her face entirely with Vaseline, he began to apply wet strips of bandage. He started beneath her chin and worked his way up, pressing the slippery cloth firmly to the contours of her jaw. As the plaster spread above the lips, he thought of her sinking into white water. Within an hour of starting, he reached her scalp. While the bandage covering dried, he called the hospital cafeteria and requested they send him two eggs.

The next stage of the procedure was to cast a finer plaster mask from the bandage mold. The trick, as de Vries had told him, was to achieve just the right consistency of plaster. You wanted it to adhere to the inside of the crude mask without dripping or sloughing off. Stan remembered the doctor adding two eggs to the final mixture and referring to it as the "batter." This was to be applied to the bandage mask with a tongue depressor, "Like you're frosting a cake, but on the inside," de Vries had said.

Stan felt a sense of relief as he gently pried the cast off Alina's face, but her smile, when it came into view, revealed her displeasure. "My apologies," he said, but her expression scorned him as he applied Vaseline to the inside of the mask. Once the eggs were delivered and the batter was mixed, he turned away from her and went to work. "You want a mask, not a bust," de Vries had said. "Keep the internal layer thin." Stan followed every instruction and the end result was remarkable. He'd not only reproduced her looks, but even the smile was intact. Although whatever she'd actually felt was beyond him, at least in plaster she finally seemed at peace.

By the time Detective Groot arrived, the corpse had been assigned to a drawer in the icebox, and Stan sat, jacket off, sleeves rolled up, in his small office, smoking a cigarette. He lifted his leg and pushed an empty seat toward the detective, standing in the doorway. Groot took off his coat and shoulder holster, draped them over the back of the chair, and sat down with arms folded.

"Good day?" asked Stan.

"Just some broke people fighting with each other. Everybody's getting ground down. More of the same."

"I'm not surprised."

"How's the Mona Lisa?" Groot asked.

Stan shook his head, and said, "It beats me. I don't know what killed her. I'm pretty sure she didn't drown. Another cardiopulmonary arrest, if you catch my drift."

"What'd she have in her stomach?" asked Groot.

"I didn't open her up. It's a bad time politically for me to be playing doctor. I'm gonna call in Rashner and let him take a look."

"Understood," said Groot. "But it'd be good to have something to go on. They're gonna give me maybe two days to try to figure this out, and after that she goes into the lost and found with the rest of the unknowns and we let the devil figure it out."

"I know," said Stan. "There's really nothing. I took her prints, so you can check those, for what they're worth. The turtle on her rear end looked to be done with a thin, heated piece of metal. That could be significant if you can find who made the brand or who did the branding."

"Jesus," said Groot. "A turtle on your ass. What does it mean? All I can think of is how the turtle beat the rabbit."

"That's a tortoise and a hare."

"Same bunk," said Groot. "Slow and steady wins the race."

"I took some more shots here you can use to look for an ID," said Stan.

"I'll ask in town tomorrow morning and then go up to Hekston and see what I can find."

"You'll find something."

"I was thinking about her all day," said Groot. "I think she has to be a suicide."

"Why?" said Stan.

The detective shook his head. "I don't know. I guess I just can't think of anything else."

"I came up with a name for her over my creamed chipped beef this morning," said Stan. "Alina."

"Whoa," said Groot in a near whisper. "Alina . . ."

Stan laughed, but something in the way the detective winced made him decide not to reveal the death mask.

The detective stood and slowly slipped on his holster and jacket. "I'll let you know what I find."

"Good enough," said Stan.

Groot saluted and left, whistling "Moon Glow" on his way down the hall.

Stan pulled into the driveway at dusk, exhausted from the exertions of the day and all the previous night. He gathered his bag, the camera, and a green cardboard box and headed for the porch. When he reached the front door, he found it unlocked. He entered the living room. There was a small blond woman wearing a sizable pair of glasses, sitting on the couch. On the low table in front of her was an ashtray, a pack of Camels, an open bottle of Old Overholt, and two tumblers, one a quarter full. Soft music came from the cabinet radio standing next to the staircase.

"You started the party without me?" said Stan.

"I had a realization today," she said to him, leaving her shoes on the floor and curling her legs up under her flowered skirt. "Come here and I'll describe it to you." She patted the empty seat next to her on the sofa.

"Oh yeah?" he said. He walked into the dining room and left his things on the table, draped his jacket over the back of a chair. "A realization, no less."

He sat down and put his arm around her. She sipped her drink. "A lot of people come to the library during the day who are out of work," she said. "They have no place else to go, nothing to do. They come and, even if they haven't read anything since grade school, they start reading again."

"Well, that's good," said Stan.

"Sure," she said, and shrugged Stan's arm off to lean forward. She poured him a drink and handed it to him. She lit a cigarette, took a drag, and gave that to him. "But I noticed today that the people who don't have anything to do but read, read differently than the ones who are still working."

"How?" asked Stan, giving her back the cigarette.

"With a kind of desperation," she said.

"You mean, like it's a chore?"

"Worse than a chore," she said. "I thought up a phrase for it this afternoon: infernal labor."

"Why?"

"I don't know what it boils down to in the end," she said. "I have to think about it some more. I heard you were up by the creek this morning."

"News travels in Midian," he said.

"A young woman?" she asked.

He nodded. "I can't figure out what killed her. It's the damnedest thing. She's preserved somehow. Like a saint."

"Intriguing," she said.

"Intriguing but frustrating." He stood up, went to the dining room, and returned with the green cardboard box. He set it on the table before her and sat down again. "Cynthia," he said. "You may find this strange."

"Stranger than you?" she said.

He reached forward and lifted the lid off the box.

"What is it?" she asked, peering inside. A moment later, she said, "Oh, that is disturbing."

"It's a death mask," he said. "The young woman."

She took it in her two hands, and brought it up to stare at it face-to-face.

"Smell it," he said.

She wrinkled her nose and looked at him.

"Do it," he said and nodded.

She brought the thin plaster visage closer. "Like a garden," she said and smiled.

"And the smile?" asked Stan.

Cynthia took a long look, holding the face at arm's length. "Not *always* nice," she said. She put the mask back in the box.

"I haven't seen that smile yet," he said.

"What ones have you seen?" she asked.

He took up his drink and listened to the music.

Later, just after midnight, Stan had a dream about the war, the shrapnel in his foot, the mustard gas poisoning of the wound, the amputation, the pain, and he woke to it, grunting.

"What is it?" said Cynthia.

Stan rolled to a sitting position at the edge of the bed. "It's the goddamn foot," he said. "Two nights in a row."

"Is there something you can take for it?" she asked.

"I'll get it," he said. "Just go back to sleep." He lifted himself onto his good foot and then slowly brought the ivory one to the floor. Ever so gently, he applied pressure until it could bear his weight without making him scream. He hobbled to the door-way, grabbed his robe, and went for his bag. "Two nights in a row," he said and downed three pills at once with a shot of Old Overholt. Then he picked up the mask and the cigarettes. In his study, he listened to the wind and the clock. The ghostly ache was far worse than usual. Cynthia had asked him earlier why he'd made the mask, and he hadn't been able to answer. Now, groggy and high, he found all kinds of answers.

At dawn Cynthia helped Stan from his study to the bed. He lay his head on the pillows, and she spread the blanket over him. He could barely keep his eyes open to say good-bye. She was already wearing her coat and hat before he managed to get the word out. She kissed him and, as always when she stayed overnight, left early, not wanting to be seen by the neighbors as she made her way up the street.

Flat on his back, staring at the ceiling like a body in the pool at Hek's Creek, Stan remembered the last time he'd asked her to marry him. A month earlier, in the library, just after closing. He was helping her in the stacks. She was squatting down, arranging a bottom row while he reshelved books from a cart next to him. He said simply, "Will you marry me?" It was his second try in as many years.

She laughed and stood up. "You're sweet," she said. She drew closer to him and put her arms around his waist. He kissed her. She hugged him and stepped away, bringing her hands up in front of her. "No," she said.

"A peculiar woman" was how de Vries had described her. Stan's relationship with the librarian had begun in the last year of the doctor's life. The old man had ticked off the reasons for his negative assessment—her clock garden, her voluminous reading, her insistence on being heard. "A good heart, but peculiar," he'd said. "And not all that good-looking."

As for her part, Cynthia said of de Vries, "He has a brilliant mind and a ponderous ego."

At the time, Stan had pretended not to understand either of

them, but now he wondered as he drifted into a swiftly moving dream of the summer flood.

Five hours later, the phone rang and its persistence pulled him from the depths. As he lifted the receiver next to the bed, he checked the alarm clock. It was 11:15 A.M.

Bleary, rubbing his eyes, he propped himself on his elbow and said, "Lowell."

"Coroner," said Groot.

"Yes, Detective," said Stan.

"I'm in a pay phone at the Rexall in Hekston."

Stan was about to ask why, but the events of the previous day came back to him. "Did you find something?" he asked.

"Are you busy today?" asked Groot.

"What have you got?"

"I want you to come up here and identify a body."

"A dead one?"

"Not exactly. Meet me at the Windemere bar down by the river, next to the factory. Veersland Street."

"It'll take me about an hour to get there."

"Twelve thirty. I'll be way in the back in a booth," said Groot and hung up.

Stan replaced the receiver and fell back into the bed and the lingering scent of Cynthia's perfume. Now that he was fully awake, he discovered he was nauseated from the whiskey and pills. He lay still for five minutes but eventually rolled out of bed and stumbled to the bathroom. Twenty minutes later, he'd puked, showered, and shaved. Staring into the mirror, he rinsed the razor and took in his weary eyes and pale complexion. The ghost of a pain was making him old.

* * *

He dressed in the brown suit, the mustard tie, the gold bee clip, gathered his bag and the camera, and stepped out the front door into a brisk, blustery day. He got in the old Chrysler and headed north, out of town. Soon the blocks of houses became pasture. The cows gave way to fields of dry cornstalks, which gave way to nothing but deep woods on either side of the cracked highway. Leaves tumbled and blew and the brooding clouds moved swiftly, suddenly revealing beams of sunlight and just as quickly swallowing them.

The journey to Hekston may have been beautiful, especially that time of year, but the town itself held a bad old memory that never faded, no matter how many years had passed or how many times Stan visited there on business. It had happened sometime after he'd started with de Vries, in the winter of '21. The road was dirt back then. The doctor was summoned by the police about a murder, the victim of which they'd just discovered. At that time, Stan worked in the doctor's office and only assisted him in the autopsy room. This time, de Vries had said, "I want you to come along." Stan was excited at the prospect. The murderer was still at large.

The victim, Mrs. Obalan, a large, middle-aged woman, bloated, with skin the palest green, lay in a blood-drenched sheer nightgown on her dining room table. Her throat was slit and a chunk of flesh had been torn from her upper arm, another from her left cheek. De Vries hadn't been in the room a minute before he pointed to the brutal wounds and said, "Teeth marks." Sullivan, Hekston's chief of police, a big, dull-looking man with a neck beard, leaned closer to see what the doctor was indicating. He nodded. "Are ya saying he ate her?" De Vries pointed to a pool of vomit on the floor. "I'm afraid it was a repast too rich," said the coroner with a smile. Stan could hardly bear the sight of the woman's remains, but when the mess on the floor was pointed out, he got dizzy. He'd seen men slaughtered by the dozen in France and nearly died himself, but this was something else entirely. He backed away into the living room of the apartment and just made it to the couch before passing out.

Later, while the doctor was filling out paperwork in Sullivan's office and Stan was sipping a cup of black coffee that the chief had promised, "always helps when you're caught between a shit and a sweat," one of the Hekston cops came in and said, "We got a report Obalan is holed up in that old carriage house behind the church." The chief took his feet off the desk and grabbed his hat. Standing, he said, "You want to come along, Doc?" De Vries said, "Of course." He and Stan rode in the back of the chief's car. The officer who'd brought the news sat up front in the passenger seat.

Night was falling fast and it had begun to lightly snow when they pulled up in front of the church. There was a patrol car there and a cop standing by the corner of the building. Sullivan got out of the car holding a flashlight. He drew his gun and motioned for de Vries and Stan to follow at a distance. As they came up to the corner of the church, the cop who'd been standing lookout turned and put his finger to his lips. He pointed toward the carriage house, and whispered, "In there. I seen him moving around before it started to get dark."

Sullivan and his men trotted across the open field. They held up outside the broken door and the flashlight beam came on. As the police entered the dilapidated building, de Vries grabbed Stan's arm and pulled him out of the sheltering shadows of the church. He fell once as they crossed the field, but the doctor helped him up and supported him the rest of the way. By the time the coroner and his apprentice reached the carriage house the police had already passed through two rooms. In the third, an empty garage, Sullivan and his men stood just inside the doorway. The chief pointed the flashlight into a corner of the darkness. There sat a heavyset man in his late forties, balding, with a gray mustache, his back against the wall. He wore a white, sleeveless undershirt, the front covered in dried blood, which was also smeared across his lips and cheeks.

He stared, glassy-eyed, into the beam of light, and said, "She made me sick."

Sullivan aimed and fired. Stan didn't have a chance to look away. The bullet struck Obalan in the right temple, slamming his head back into the wall. His body twitched twice but remained seated. The wound smoked for a moment, appearing in the glow of the flashlight like a spirit leaving the body. There was hardly any blood.

After the echo of the gunshot died away, de Vries said, "Innocent until proven guilty, I assume."

The chief shrugged and said, "A clear-cut case of resisting arrest."

Nothing nearly as harrowing would happen on the job again. In the years that followed, Stan learned that the position of coroner was a relatively quiet one, lonely afternoons spent discovering and recording the secrets of those in whom life had lost interest. Still, the memory of that day in Hekston, with its pathetic horror and de Vries turning a blind eye to Obalan's summary execution, never diminished.

Stan pulled into town and headed down toward the river. Bad memory notwithstanding, Hekston didn't look that much different from Midian. People were on the street, going about their business, steam billowed from the factory. He passed the grade school and saw a gang of kids gathered in a ring, playing at some game. A flag flew outside the municipal building.

He found the Windemere, a sagging wooden establishment with a wraparound porch, on the bank of the Susquehanna. Its sky-blue paint was chipping and its windowpanes were smeared. Stan figured it had obviously been a house at one time prior to the turn of the century. As he climbed the steps to the front door, he checked his watch to make sure he wasn't late.

Inside, it was dark, and it took a moment for his vision to adjust. He stood in the entrance and watched the forms of three old men on stools cohere out of the shadows. The light behind the bar was dim. A white-haired woman in a plaid flannel shirt, sleeves rolled up, waved Stan over and said, "What'll you have?"

"I'm just here to meet someone," he said.

"A stout fella?"

Stan nodded. "That could be him."

"Go on," she said and nodded toward the dark back of the place.

He stepped around some tables and peered down a long row of booths. Way at the end, just barely visible, a leg jutted into the aisle. As he approached that table, he heard Groot's voice.

"You're punctual," he said.

"The job drives you to it," said Stan as he took a seat on the bench across from the detective. "Who are we hiding from?"

Groot said, "I gave Loaf a few pictures of the girl to pass around Midian and I came up here at daybreak. I showed the girl's picture everywhere. No one knows her. Never seen her. I drove over to where Hek's Creek comes off the Susquehanna and it's moving pretty fast. By then it was around ten thirty. I decided to stop and get some lunch, so I came in here for a sip. While the woman up there was drawing my beer, I showed her the photo. I asked her,

'Do you recognize this person?' She said, 'No.' But when I went to sit down, she told me, 'Wait, let me see that again.' She looks at it, smiles, and says, 'Yeah, I've seen her.' "

"Where?" asked Stan.

Groot took out his cigarettes and put one in his mouth. He flipped the lighter open and sparked it. Instead of lighting the butt, though, he held the flame aloft, toward the wall. "Right here," he said.

The flame illuminated a small painting Stan hadn't previously noticed. He stood and leaned in close to the picture, careful not to let Groot set his tie on fire. It was a portrait of a young woman with long black hair, wearing a white gown. She stood on an oddly shaped boulder that had a profile like a face, an outcropping of a nose. She and her perch glowed, as if standing in moonlight, against a black background darker than her hair and sparsely dotted with stars. The lighter went out, but a moment later Groot managed to revive the flame. "The smile, Coroner," he said.

No matter how many times Stan looked away and then back at the painted face, he saw his Alina, exactly as she'd looked on the autopsy table. "It's her," he said.

Groot closed the lighter and slipped it back in his coat pocket. "You know why no one knows her?" asked Groot.

Stan sat and shook his head.

"I found a date in the bottom-right-hand corner. 1896."

"She looks the same after almost forty years?"

Groot took a sip of his beer. "The whole thing's cocked up," he said.

"Does the bartender know who did the painting?"

"She said it's always been here, as long as she can remember. This place was a bar for quite a while before Prohibition, and even in the dry years it masqueraded as a restaurant with a speakeasy in the basement. What I need to find out is who lived here when it was a residence, but that might be hard to come by."

"You've got to find some old-timers," said Stan.

Groot nodded.

The detective took the painting off the wall and carried it in two hands to the bar. Stan followed him. "I got to confiscate this as evidence," he said to the bartender.

"No one's gonna miss it," she said. "I'm probably the only one who knows it's there."

"I'll return it to you when the investigation is complete," said Groot. "Do you know anybody in town who might be familiar with local history, going back a ways?"

The bartender grabbed a coaster and a pencil. As she wrote, she said, "Try this guy. Joe Venner. He's old as dirt, but he's got a good memory. Still comes in here on the days he can get his body out of bed. I'll call him and tell him you're coming over. He'll be glad for the company." She handed the cardboard circle to the detective. He shifted the painting under one arm, said, "Thanks," and looked at the address.

Out in the parking lot, Groot said to Stan, "Did I hear her describe me as 'stout'?"

"Yeah. 'Stout fella,'" said Stan.

Groot spat. "You want to go talk to this guy?"

"The old man?"

"We'll show him the painting."

They took Groot's Model B. Ten minutes later, they were in a furnished room over a delicatessen, sitting at a table with the venerable Joe Venner, an obviously shrunken man, curled like an autumn leaf. He wore a moth-eaten cardigan over a flannel shirt and sipped at a pint of Overholt. Stan noticed that the man's glasses were even thicker in the frame and lenses than Cynthia's. The space was cramped beneath slanted ceilings of exposed wood. There was one small window at knee height that lit a patch of floor. The old man had a bed, a desk, a bookcase, and a trunk used as a dresser. There was a single bare bulb suspended from a cord overhead.

"What do you want to know?" asked Venner.

"Can you tell us who this is?" said Groot, holding up the painting. "The picture is dated 1896." Setting it down in front of Venner, he said, "What about the girl? Do you remember her?"

The old man winced, tilted his glasses an inch downward, and stared at the portrait of the woman on the rock. He touched a trembling finger to his lips and then shook it at the painting. "I don't know who she is," he said.

"Do you know any local artist who might have painted it?" asked Groot.

"I don't know shit about art," said Venner. "I worked every day of my life till I couldn't work anymore, first in the fields, then in the loom. The novels I read have pictures on the covers. That's what I know about art."

"Okay," said the detective. "Thanks for your time." He reached forward to lift the painting off the table.

"Not so fast," said the old man, putting a hand on Groot's right forearm. "The big rock in the picture is a real place. I remember it from when I was a kid." Venner went silent for a time, dredging his memory.

Stan asked, "Do you remember where?"

The old man nodded. "It's in the woods halfway between here and Verruk. Nobody lives out that way, so the rock's probably still there. Some people called it the Wish Head and some called it the Witch Head, depending on what side of the Susquehanna you lived on. I went there a couple of times with my parents. We walked for miles over fields and through the woods to get to it. People came from all around to climb up on the head. There was a place for your first foot in the groove of stone that was the chin of the face. There was a place to hold on in the right eye, and the nose was like a platform. You were supposed to get up there on top, and this part I can't remember for sure. But it was either that you made a wish, or you prayed to God, something along those lines."

"If you wished up there, it came true?" asked Groot.

Venner laughed and sipped at his bottle. He nodded. "I suppose that was the idea. People said it was 'ground magic,' like it comes up out of the earth through the head."

"Do you remember what you wished for?" asked Stan.

"Only the one of them. I must have been ten or eleven."

"Did it come true?" asked Groot.

"Hell no, I wished I'd never get old," said Venner.

Stan let out a laugh.

"I whispered my wish to my father that night before going to bed. I didn't understand then why *he* laughed," said the old man.

"There's young and then there's young," said Groot. "You're young in the head, Mr. Venner."

"A very sharp recall," said Stan.

"You two don't know yet," he said. "When you get old, you think more about the past than about what you did five minutes ago. Time changes."

"We're gonna go out to the Wish Head, can you draw us a map?"

It was midafternoon, the temperature had dropped and the sky had grown darker. A strong wind blew leaves across the field in the woods. Positioned in the very center of the open expanse in the trees, as if consciously placed there, was a flat-topped granite behemoth that really did have the contours of a human head. It took no stretch of the imagination to see that, nor to read the expression it wore, one of subtle contempt. Groot stood face-to-face with the boulder, jotting notes in a pad.

"What are you writing?" asked Stan. "It's a boulder."

"My impressions," said the detective.

"What have you got so far?"

"Big gray rock," said Groot.

"Do you feel any ground magic?" asked Stan.

The detective cocked his head as if listening for it. Stan looked back from the center of the field at the woods. A gust of wind brought the first drops of rain.

"Maybe," said Groot.

"I know what you mean," said Stan. "I've seen enough. Let's get out of here."

"Hold on a minute," said Groot. "We're not done yet."

"I was afraid you'd say that," said Stan.

"I'm too old and too fat. By the time I made it up there, I'd have to wish for my last breath."

"You're talking to a man with a fake foot."

"Think about how wonderful it is up there."

"I'm afraid of heights."

"You can make a wish," said the detective.

"Oh, shit," said Stan and took off his jacket and necktie and handed them to Groot. As he approached the stone face, he tried to remember what Venner had said about climbing it. He immediately found the groove in the lips of the old frowning face and secured his good foot. He hoisted himself up against the rock and was able to grab the depression in the eyehole. From there it was a mad scrabble upward.

"Very athletic," called Groot when Stan reached the nose.

Working to catch his breath, Stan said, "If I get struck by lightning, tell Cynthia I love her."

"Will do," said the detective.

Stan turned toward the forehead. "This is crazy," he said, and then went into a crouch. A second later, he sprang upward against the hard rock and grabbed for the edge of the boulder's flat top. He managed to get a handhold, and then swung his leg up over the ledge. From there, he used his arms to pull himself forward onto the crown of the head.

Groot applauded.

Stan stood up and, a little dizzy from the height, stepped away from the edge. He gazed out across the field and felt the wind and a light rain on his face. "Make a wish," he heard from below.

"If it comes true, you might not be there when I come down," Stan called back. He looked up into the dark sky. "A wish," he whispered, and thought about what he wanted. The first idea he came to was to pray for Cynthia to marry him. But just as quickly came the thought, "What if it came true?" That's when he hit upon something more practical. He closed his eyes, raised his hands out at his sides, and made his plea to the powers of the earth that the ghost pain in his foot be exorcized and leave him forever. Doubt ruled his mind, but somewhere in one of its hidden corners existed the anticipation that he'd feel something, a twitch of electricity in his joints, a fluttering of the heart. What he felt, after giving it two solid minutes, was nothing. He opened his eyes and realized the rain was falling steadily now.

"How goes it?" called the detective.

"Less than magical," said Stan, who lowered himself to his knees and crawled back to the edge.

"Watch your step," said Groot as Stan dangled off the nose, trying to achieve a foothold in the lips.

"There," said Stan, finally anchoring himself in the groove. As he let his weight down, his dress shoe slipped on the wet rock and he fell backward onto the ground.

"What did you wish for?" asked Groot, helping him up.

Stan stood, his white shirt and trousers marked with dirt, and arched his back. "I'll tell you if it comes true," he said.

The detective handed him his jacket and tie. "Did anything happen up there?"

"Yeah, I banged my knees a dozen times and got cuts all over my hands."

"But ground magic?" said Groot as he took out his notebook.

By the time they made it back through the woods, and to the car, darkness had fallen and the rain had become a downpour. On the return to Hekston, the radio played quietly, and the wipers beat beneath the music. The detective drove slowly through the storm. "Deer all over the road this time of year," he said.

"I know," said Stan. "Take your time."

"We did a lot today," said Groot. "But really, at the end of it all, I've got nothing but a big rock."

"You've got the painting," said Stan.

"That has to be a coincidence."

"The fact that it's the spitting image of a young woman in the icebox in the basement of Midian General or that *you* found it?"

"I don't like it," said the detective. "Any of it."

From that point on, with the exception of Groot singing along to the radio—"Heaven, I'm in heaven"—they drove the rest of the distance to Hekston in silence.

There were quite a few cars in the parking lot, and the Windemere glowed from within. Groot pulled up behind Stan's car. The rain had slowed to a drizzle.

"Okay, Coroner," he said. "That's enough for one day."

"That's plenty for me," said Stan.

He opened the door, and before he could say good night, the detective said, "Wait, I want you to take the painting."

"Why?"

Groot reached into the backseat, grabbed the picture by the frame, and lifted it into the front. "Go ahead. Take it over to the hospital tomorrow and take a look at it with her there. I want to make sure what we're seeing is what we're seeing."

Stan touched the painting and for an instant felt the loneliness of the dark back booth where they'd found it. He got out of the car. "Driving home from Hekston with this thing in the backseat. Jeez, I'd rather climb the rock again," he said.

"That's what I was thinking," said the detective and hit the gas. The sudden velocity slammed the door shut, and the car traveled a graceful arc through the parking lot, spitting gravel in its wake.

The moment Groot was gone, Stan felt Hekston's dark spirit closing in. He clasped the painting hard under his right arm and made for his car. As he walked, memories of the Obalan case came back in brief flashes. Before getting in, he stowed the picture in the trunk to avoid any possibility of it appearing in his rearview mirror during the trip. Pulling out of the parking lot, he headed up the street toward the highway turnoff, his mind buzzing like one of Madrigal's mills, weaving strands of the Wish Head, Alina, Joe Venner, the painting, scenes from that long-ago night with de Vries into a snarled and snarling tapestry. It was hard to concentrate, and he traveled slowly until he reached the town limits. The rain began to fall in earnest, and he flicked on the wipers. Once he was over the town line, his thoughts calmed a little and he picked up speed.

There was no moon and the long stretch of highway through the woods was pitch black. Stan hadn't seen another set of headlights for miles. He thought about his wish made standing atop the boulder. He remembered the rain on his face and the rush of the wind. The scene was vivid in his mind when a six-point buck stepped, seemingly from out of nowhere, into the beams of the headlights. He was stunned. The creature was fewer than twenty yards away and was staring directly at the oncoming car. The light gleamed in its enormous eyes. Stan jammed the brake pedal with his ivory foot before his good one was even off the gas and cut the wheel to the right with both hands. The car went into a skid, the back end hurtling toward the animal. He braced for impact, but it never came. Instead, the car snaked off onto the shoulder of the highway, over a small rise and down into a hollow ringed by oaks where it rolled to a smooth stop. The branches overhead blocked the rain. With the exception of Stan's heavy breathing, it was perfectly silent and perfectly dark.

He sat forward and turned the key. The car gave him more silence for his effort. He tried a dozen times, whispering strings of curses. Deciphering what might be wrong was out of the question. He was no mechanic. The thought of being out on the highway in the dark, rain drenching him, trying to flag somebody down, made him weary beyond reckoning. He slowly reached for the door handle, but before his fingers touched the metal, he felt the invisible worm begin to gnaw at the heel of his missing foot. The second he noticed it, the pain started to spread, and he pictured the scrimshaw devil dancing.

"Not again," he said aloud and pulled himself up to a kneel-

ing position on the front seat. The pain moved to where the arch
of the foot should have been as he leaned over the seat into the
back and rummaged through his bag. He felt the small bottle of
pills and pulled them out. Removing the cork stopper, he carefully poured the bottle's contents into his hand. Then he turned
and sat back in the driver's spot. He reached into his pocket for
his lighter. Like the glow from Groot's lighter in the back booth
at the Windemere, Stan's flame revealed something startling.
There were only four pills in his palm. All he had with him. He
popped them in his mouth and swallowed them dry.

There followed a long dark period of intense agony, which set
him sweating and groaning, but soon enough he forgot about
how long a time it had been. His eyes adjusted to the night and
he could now make out the dials on the dashboard, the empty
pill bottle on the seat, and beyond the windshield, the silhouette shapes of tree trunks. The drug, of course, had nothing to
do with the pain, but it did distract him with slippery thoughts
and bouts of twisting memory.

Often, when in the throes of this pain, he thought about the
ivory foot, saw its off-yellow sheen and its delicate sculpture—
the cuticles, each articulated toe. He'd never experienced a
twinge of discomfort from what wasn't there until he was fitted
for the prosthesis. He recalled de Vries revealing why he'd ordered that the foot be made from ivory. "I once knew an old
man," said the doctor. "He had been a sailor. He had an ivory
hand, which had been made for him in Java by a native crafts-
man. The fingers were frozen in the act of taking something,
but at the same time you swore the pale thing moved of its own
accord. The old man told me that unlike modern metal pros-
thetics, ivory holds on to the life of the limb."

"And what's so good about that?" Stan said aloud and came

suddenly back to the fact that he was stuck in the woods in a dead car miles from Midian.

He rolled down the window, took out his cigarettes, and lit one. "It holds on to the life of the limb," he said and shook his head. "More like its death." His hands trembled from the pain he'd again become aware of. His only escape was into memory, and he began to let his thoughts slip away to the first phantom attack, two weeks after the foot had been fitted, but something he saw through the smoke drew him out of his reverie. He tossed the cigarette and waved his hand to clear the air. Through the windshield, he recognized the dim image of a pair of eyes staring in at him. He felt a jolt of panic in his chest, and then a second pair of eyes slowly divulged themselves. Stan looked out the side windows, and more were there as well. The deer crowded around his car, staring in. He wondered how long they'd been there watching him writhe and complain.

"What do you want?" he yelled and they bolted, vanishing into the night. He rolled up the window and locked the doors.

Stan slept and woke later to the dark. The first thing he realized, after recalling he was stranded, was that the pain was gone. He couldn't believe it, and concentrated hard to try to feel its bite. Not sunrise yet and the ivory foot felt fine and he'd actually dozed off. He rubbed his face with both hands, smoothed his hair back, and took a few deep breaths. No longer groggy but still somewhat giddy from the pills, he leaned forward and turned the key.

The sudden sound of the engine coming to life momentarily frightened him. Then he let out a laugh. He put the car in reverse and eased down on the gas pedal. The Chrysler responded, backing slowly up out of the ring of trees. At the top of the rise, he cut the wheel to the left, hoping to bring the front around so he wouldn't have to back down onto the highway. When the car was perpendicular to the incline, he felt the pull of gravity and feared the vehicle might tumble on its side, so he shifted quickly and spun the wheel in the opposite direction. Gliding down across the shoulder and out onto the road, he beeped the horn. The highway was empty and there were no deer along the tree line. Off to the east, the sky had begun to lighten.

When he got into Midian around nine, he needed sleep, but there was something he wanted to tell Cynthia. He drove over to the library, at the edge of town, forgetting halfway there why he wasn't heading for bed.

The Midian County Library had been a gift to the community from William Madrigal. In the late '20s he'd had an abandoned estate completely refurbished, from the marble floors to the gold-leaf constellations painted on the dark blue ceilings. Handcrafted bookshelves lined the three stories, the mansion's rooms turned into library sections. What had been the nursery now contained the library's entire holdings on philosophy. The kitchen held crime and adventure. The master bedroom, history. Madrigal hadn't skimped in his endowment, and the place continued to have a healthy budget even through the lean years.

In the center of that rectangular mansion was a courtyard, sixty feet square, open to the sky. In the confines of that space, Cynthia had planted her clock garden—a circular bed, divided by white stones into twelve equal wedges, the points meeting at the center. Within each bed was planted a different type of flower chosen for the time of day it either opened or closed. Some were wild, like the hawksbeard and foxglove, and some were planted each year from seed, like the zinnias. As the flowers opened and closed around the circle, they told the time of day. Goat's beard opened first, then chicory, and later, around six, the dandelions. At the halfway point of daylight hours, the clue to the time was in a blossom's closing.

On the south side of the garden, facing it, was a curved stone bench. Stan sat next to Cynthia, holding her hand, his eyes half closed. It was cold in the courtyard and the garden was devastated. Curled brown maple leaves had blown over the walls and were trapped amid the drooping stalks. Colored petals were scattered on the dirt. A handful of black-eyed Susans held on, wilted at the edges, as did most of the wedge of chrysanthemums. Time had run out for everything else, though, including Stan, who lifted his legs and curled up on the stone.

He tried to tell her about his day with Groot and the near accident, but his mind kept veering off the highway toward sleep. "There was a painting," he told her, "and this big rock, and we talked to an old man." His strings of phrases ended in sighs.

"You're exhausted," she said.

"Thank you," he whispered, blinking like a tired child.

"I've got to get back to work," said Cynthia. "What did you want?"

"The pain in my foot, I know it's gone. I made a wish." He folded his arms and laid the side of his face against the cold stone. "Do me a favor and look up the Wish Head or Witch Head in local history. It's out on the way to Verruk," he told her.

"What is it?"

"A giant rock in a field."

"Okay," she said. She got up and patted him on the shoulder. Turning, she headed through the remains of the garden toward the courtyard door. She looked back at him once more before entering the building. Stan lay on the stone bench, eyes closed, and dozed in the early morning sun.

* * *

That afternoon, in the empty autopsy room in the basement of Midian General, Groot sat on a high stool, his heels hooked on the bottom rung, and Stan leaned against the lab counter, telling the detective about his ordeal in the woods.

Groot laughed. "Well, in about two hours, I'm officially done with this case," he said. "They're making me move on to something new. Your Alina is bound for the Heartbreak file."

"Rashner's sending his guys this evening to pick her up and take her to Albany so he can do an autopsy. When you leave, I have to bag her for them."

"I hope she at least perplexes the asshole."

"That would be sweet of her," said Stan.

"Go get the painting," said Groot. "Before she's gone I want to match the painting and the body."

Stan went into his office and returned with the canvas they'd picked up in Hekston. He led the way into the morgue and Groot followed.

"The quietest spot in town," said the detective as Stan leaned over and opened the door to the bottom slab in the refrigerated unit.

"Alina," he said as she rolled forth. When she was completely in view, Stan stood straight, and he and Groot were quiet for a moment, contemplating her expression.

"She looks pissed off," said the detective.

"I'd say pensive," said Stan. He held the painting at arm's length. "What do you think?"

Their glances moved from the painted figure to the body and back.

"The eyes are definitely a match," said Groot. "And the mouth is very close."

"I think it looks just like her," said Stan.

"As close as you can get with a painting."

"What does it mean, though?"

"I don't know," said Groot. "One thing I did happen upon, though, this morning at the diner. These two guys from the factory were having coffee and talking about hunting and such in the area when they were kids. I lost track of what they were saying for a while, and then one says, 'Some of these turtles around here live over a hundred and fifty years.'"

"You think the brand on her rear end has something to do with that?" asked Stan.

"Who the hell knows," said Groot. "Close her up. I've had enough."

As the drawer holding the body rolled back into darkness, Stan said, "You want the painting?"

Groot hesitated, then grinned until he caught the coroner glancing away from his birthmark. "I gotta take it back to Hekston next time I go up that way."

"Will you dig around any more for this case?" Stan asked, heading for his office. Groot followed.

The detective shook his head. "This shit doesn't make sense to me. I'd rather forget it. I'm retiring anyway."

Stan laughed. "Been talking with your wife some more?"

"Oh, yeah," said Groot and took a seat near the office door. Stan rested the painting against the wall as he sat down at his desk. He swiveled the chair around to face his associate.

"What are you going to do when you retire?"

"My wife wants to move to the ocean. Which one she means or whether she means it, I'm not sure."

"You'll miss Midian," said Stan.

"I don't think so," said Groot. "This case gave me the jitters."

He obviously had more to say but hesitated, closed his eyes momentarily and shook his head. "I wasn't gonna tell you this, but on my way back from Hekston last night, I passed this woman, standing on the side of the road. In the middle of nowhere out there in the woods. Not a stitch of clothes on her. Long hair."

"Alina?" asked Stan.

"It happened so fast, I never got a good look at her, but it was enough of a look to know I didn't want to go back for another. I never slowed down. Somewhere between there and home, I decided to retire."

"Are you sure you saw something?"

"No," said Groot and stood up. "I'm not, really."

Stan leaned back, grabbed the painting, and handed it to him. They shook hands. "Here's to the devil taking off till the end of the year."

"Good luck, Detective."

"Coroner," said Groot, tipped his hat, and stepped into the hallway.

That night, Stan lay next to Cynthia in his darkened bedroom. He had his arm around her. Her glasses lay on the nightstand, her head rested on his chest.

"The Wish Head," she said. "I found two brief articles about it. It was either erected or discovered by a group called the Schildpad in the late 1620s. They were a pagan group made up of Dutch trappers and traders who lived by their wits in the woods. They believed there was some kind of magical energy in the earth, you could draw its power into you by standing atop the Wish Head."

"The old man, Venner, said the same thing about the rock," said Stan.

"There was a brief piece about a witch, Griet Vadar, associated with the Schildpad, who lived in the 1800s. She was captured by settlers in the area, tried, weighted with stones, and thrown in the Hekston River. That's pretty much all there was."

"The *Schildpad*?" said Stan. "Never heard of them."

"Sort of like a homespun religion, created out of the life they lived in the wilderness. *Schildpad* is Dutch for turtle," she said. "They were turtle lovers." She laughed and lifted herself up to see if he was smiling. "Sounds crazy," she said.

They rested back on the pillows. It seemed only a minute or two before he felt, in her heartbeat, her breathing, that she was asleep. He thought he'd have no problem following, but something wasn't right. He knew it wasn't the fact that they'd had to close the case on Alina. That was a turn of events both he and Groot favored. The mystery of what had happened needed to be laid to rest in one of the dark drawers in the basement of the hospital and locked up for good. He recalled de Vries explaining to him once, "There's going to be times when you have to admit you're stumped." But he was already there, more than willing to move on. Then he thought of the word "stumped" and realized what it was that kept him awake.

Ever since his encounter with the deer the previous night, all through the long drive that followed, sleeping on the cold stone bench before the clock garden, meeting with Groot, bagging Alina for Rashner's flunkies, and making it through the rest of his day—all those hours and he'd not felt the slightest twinge of pain from his foot. Where there was no pain, there was nothing. The ivory piece no longer felt like an extension of himself, but just some cold block of something swinging off his ankle. It wasn't so much painless as it was lifeless now.

"The granting of my wish?" he wondered and pictured himself standing upon the stone head in the field. "Cured by earth magic." He rolled out of bed, careful not to wake Cynthia, and limped to where his robe hung. He put it on and left the bedroom. On his way down the hall to his study, he whispered, "Or cursed by Griet Vadar?"

Sitting in the same comfortable chair he had occupied during his bouts with the phantom limb, he poured a tall whiskey from the decanter on his desk. He sipped and listened to the wind in the trees outside the window and to the beat of the grandfather clock. It became clear to him that the emptiness was seeping out of the ivory appendage and invading the rest of his body. He drank faster, thinking that might stave it off. "Calm down," he whispered to himself. "A dead woman is not stealing your soul." He poured another drink, downed a quarter of it, and had a creeping inclination to add a couple of morphine pills to the mix. "Not smart," he thought. "I'm getting all worked up just so I can have an excuse to take the drug." To distract himself, he got up and walked across the room to fetch the mask, which lay atop a pile of books on a shelf. Returning to his chair, he held it in front of his face so that he was eye to eyehole with it.

The white visage was smiling, almost broadly. Her always closed lips appeared just on the verge of opening. If he hadn't been holding it, he'd have sworn the facial muscles moved, but what muscles?—it was plaster. She was beautiful, no doubt. He stared for a long time, the grandfather clock chiming the hour at some point. De Vries appeared in his memory, standing over the corpse of a cherubic-faced child he'd just finished sewing up. "Remember," the old man had said, "death is our business, but we should never become friends with it. It's single-minded and exquisitely shrewd."

Stan poured some more whiskey into the glass on his desk.

His entire body felt numb, his mind dull. "What do I want?" he wondered. He closed his eyes and swayed, sitting forward in the chair. The wind blew outside, and the tall clock chimed again. He fell back, the mask hanging from a finger hooked through its right eyehole. His eyes were closed, he was breathing deeply, but in the next instant, he sprang up and hurled the mask. The white face shattered against the glass clock face and littered the floor. Crossing the office, he opened his bag and retrieved his pills. Returning to the chair, he placed them within easy reach on the desk. He freshened his drink and waited.

The pain started so subtly, like an eye opening, and that was all for a while. When he felt the first twinge of real discomfort, he took two pills and washed them down with a long swallow. Then there it was, the pain as he'd missed it, moaning like a ghost. He winced, he groaned, and his mind swirled with dark thoughts. At one point, he had a premonition that Groot would never see retirement. He saw the dogged detective clutch his chest and fall over into the field before the Wish Head. Then the birthmark lifted off, and flew, buzzing through the coroner's skull.

Stan was awake when the phone rang at 6:06 the next morning. He pulled himself out of the chair and answered it. "Midian coroner," he said.

"Stanley, is that you?" The voice was angry. "What the hell do you think you're doing?"

"Dr. Rashner, did you get the body?" Stan asked.

"Are we playing games? Are you mocking me?"

"I don't know what you mean," said Stan.

"I read your report. Incorruptible flesh, a victim who has

died but exhibits no signs of death. Then I open the body bag, and what do I find?"

"The woman?"

"A bag of rotten leaves dug up from the creek bed. Have you lost your mind?" yelled Rashner.

There was silence, and then the medical examiner said, "I want an explanation."

Stan looked up, noticed the first light coming through the window, and realized the pain had once again vanished. He lifted his left leg a few times to feel the life in it. Rashner was still talking, but Stan hung up, his attention drawn to something on the floor. Alina's mouth had separated from the mask and lay unbroken. He walked over to the smile, hesitated for a moment, and then picked up the piece of plaster. Brushing it lightly with his thumb, as if *it* had kissed him, he slipped it into the pocket of his robe.

Weiroot

Weiroot, you madman, what do you think you're doing, sitting in the chill of the night, winking at the winking stars? Are you sending them a message? Come visit me? And what if they were to? What if in say a year or two a star fell, swept down out of the dark, trailing green fire, and smashed with an explosion of sparks and black diamond debris into the dunes surrounding your wooden plank palace? What would you do then? Oh sure, you'd call for your four marble men without faces, those savage quadruplets whose stone sculpted arms move with supple grace. "If they get obstreperous, let them have it," you'd whisper and the four white dolts would nod and flex.

But then, imagine your surprise when the rock from space breaks open and out crawls a little fat baby, purple as a plum, with a ridge of webbed spikes like a lady's open fan running from the crown of its head back to the base of the skull, orange eyes, and a little O of a mouth. You know you'd gasp and wave your arms in the air . . . well, at least you'd wear a look of consternation and shake your head, and who wouldn't? But then, even the four stone flunkies would make amazed faceless expressions when the little fellow from beyond the moon would say, "Feed me, Weiroot," in a psychic voice that sounded between the ears. That would snarl your line of thought. So, I can see it now, you'd scoop that star baby up in your robed arms and shuffle with your lame stride back into that cockeyed palace.

Then what? A cold leg of mutton? A rasher of game hens from the forest beyond the dunes? Octopus and eel heads you purchased that morning from Yakus, the Bold but Battered? And the miracle is, the babe devours all of it. That's right, that cute little mouth holds rows of needle teeth, and he's got an appetite. He takes off one of the stone goon's index fingers in the feeding. Then surprise and a portion of horror when the mewling fright drops a neat little pile of space scat onto the clean-swept floor of the dining room. You'd be screaming orders like a second lieutenant in the pontiff's royal guard, "Drop the rose petals!" "Man the shovel!" "Haste and earnest effort in the name of all that's holy!"

And after the tumult and chaos of the exigencies of biologic existence, then the quiet time, holding the snoozing fin head cradled in your arms, rocking in the rocker next to your telescope out on the open-air observatory while the wind transforms the face of the dunes to a whole new physiognomy, the ocean laps the shore in the distance to the south, and the night birds sing in the forest to the north. In that peaceful time, that's when the deal will be sealed and you'll promise your life in protection and care for the helpless fellow. Because, Weiroot, even though your face is a rippling moonscape of healed wounds, your posture is worse than that of your listing home, and you're feared by those who don't know you as a strange and cantankerous entity outside of society, the Man Who Escaped Hell, you are no more nor less than any man—a hungry heart and a wavering will.

That's right, don't deny it. You're thinking, "Here's my family. Here's my opportunity to care and have someone return the emotion." I see right through your schemes. Your thoughts are utterly transparent to me. And oh, what great pleasure you will derive from naming the wee beast, like it's a puppy, like it's your own invention. You'll try Hartvill, Tharnweb, Wenslav to see how they roll off the tongue, every now and then checking the child's countenance to see if the word fits the face like a tailored mask. But all along, all along, you know you're slowly but resolutely spiraling in a decreasing orbit toward Weiroot Junior or Weiroot II, and the excitement of that has your big toe itching in your eel-skin ankle boot. When you're just about to grasp for one of these narcissistic monikers, something grabs you instead, some dim glimmer of reason, and you veer off and christen the child Oondeshai, which was the name of an island in Hell. Then a kiss to that purple brow and you lean back in your rocker and rock beneath the stars from whence he came, closing your eyes and falling into a dream of the future. Beautiful.

Or so you think, but wait, Weiroot. Just a second. Dreams are dreams and the future is like a hall of mirrors reflecting the past and offering up wavering illusions until everything shatters and you're cut to ribbons by shards of reality. Allow me to suggest where all this is leading. Little Oondeshai will be both a pleasure and a trial for some time, and, though difficult at first, you'll learn to give of yourself, to feed, comfort, and care for your charge. Your stone men will be put through their paces as they've never been, even in the ancient time when they were created to serve and protect a princess who knew no restraint in her demands, long before you found them in the cave in the sea cliff and brought them to life with an inadvertent sneeze.

There will rise up a hurricane of activity in the wooden

palace, all centered on the child, and every action will embrace him as its eye. This won't necessarily be bad, for it will take you away from your melancholic study, it will resurrect you from your pointless pondering of the stars. I don't deny there will be long walks among the dunes in which you will tell the boy stories, half true, half the product of your own skittering imagination, like the one about the man who teaches the monkey to be a man while the monkey teaches the man to be a monkey and they switch places only to discover deep philosophical truths they'd never before conceived of until the man puts the monkey in a cage and the monkey escapes and kills the man and then is shot by the man's wife, who loved the monkey turned man more than the man turned monkey. Yes, you'll fill the child's head with that kind of simplistic claptrap to make him a dreamer, and he'll show no revulsion when he runs his fingertips over your scarred, tree-bark face.

Together you'll fly dragon kites, running over the dunes, in the slanting light of cool evenings. You'll fish for Tillibar skeeners off the ocean cliffs with a long rope, a hook to snag Leviathan, and the stone quadruplets heaving and ho-ing, hoisting the wriggling silver behemoths of the deep high up the cliffside in the full moonlight. You'll teach him something like right from wrong, and punish him by confining him to his room. He'll stamp and howl like a fox in a leg trap and pass through the walls a hundred times, for this will be one of his special powers, and you'll patiently catch him and put him back and tell him NO! He'll, of course, say, "I hate you, Weiroot, you turd." You'll know he doesn't mean it, but still, these words will prick your heart like a thistle in the thumb. Later, there'll be the reconciliation and you'll give him an orange sugar god on a stick for apologizing.

Time will change you both like the wind changes the dunes. Both of you will grow, he physically, you inwardly, expanding to care for two. His purple complexion will lighten to a pale violet. His fin will recede to become a mere ridge of lumps. He'll lose the webbing on his fingers and toes, the split in his tongue will meld to a single point. He'll grow taller than you, and his alien abilities will manifest themselves—his ability to detect a lie, to see in the dark, to speak to the dead and know the secret thoughts of the marble quadruplets. All of this will have a profound effect on you.

Just to know that your stone servants have had inner lives all along and dreams and anguish will weigh upon your conscience, and you'll finally be forced to give them their freedom and bid them well in the world. They'll leave you one day at the end of summer when the leaves in the forest have begun to change and each will choose a direction of the compass and strike out on his own. You'll extend them each the favor of a pouch of coins, a knife, and a painted expression you or Oondeshai will draw upon their blank faces with the indelible ink of the red octopus. A smile for one, a frown for another, a quizzical look for his brother, and the last will be marked to show compassion. Then they'll be gone and it will be you and Oondeshai.

And he'll ask you about your past, and there will be no way to lie to him. So you'll have to say, "I'm the man who escaped from Hell." But this answer will only give birth to a hundred more questions and you'll walk with him on a bright morning over the dunes to the edge of the ocean and there you'll sit as the waves lap your feet and you'll tell him everything. "I, Weiroot, committed an unpardonable sin," you'll say. "Why?" he'll ask. And you'll begin, stuttering at first, and then your confession will flow like blood.

A Note About "Weiroot"

Longtime readers of my stories might recognize the character of Weiroot from an earlier piece titled "The Boatman's Holiday." This is the second entry in what I hope to be a series of stories in different styles, some with Weiroot as the protagonist, some with him as a tangential figure. I figure I'll do one every five or so years. I was lucky enough to have this story accepted for publication in my favorite incarnation of the magazine *Weird Tales*—the one with the cutting-edge fiction, eye-popping covers, and great nonfiction, edited by Ann VanderMeer and Stephen Segal.

Dr. Lash Remembers

I was working fifteen-hour days, traversing the city on house calls, looking in on my patients who'd contracted a particularly virulent new disease. Fevers, sweats, vomiting, liquid excrement. Along with these symptoms, the telltale signature—a slow trickle of what looked like green ink issuing from the left inner ear. It blotted pillows with strange, haphazard designs in which I momentarily saw a spider, a submarine, a pistol, a face staring back. I was helpless against this scourge. The best I could do was to see to the comfort of my charges and give instructions to their loved ones to keep them well hydrated. To a few who suffered most egregiously, I administered a shot of Margold, which wrapped them in an inchoate stupor. Perhaps it wasn't sound medicine, but it was something to do. Done more for my well-being than theirs.

In the middle of one of these harrowing days, a young man arrived at my office carrying an envelope for me. I'd been just about to set off to the Air Ferry for another round of patient visits in all quarters of the city, but after giving the lad a tip and sending him on his way, I sat down to a cup of cold tea and opened the card. It was from Millicent Garana, a longtime friend and colleague I'd not seen in months. The circumstances of our last meeting had not been professional. Instead, I'd taken her to the Hot Air Opera and we marveled at the steam-inspired metallic characters gliding through the drama, their voices like so many teakettles at the boil.

It was with that glittering, frenetic memory still twirling through my head that I read these words: *Dr. Lash, please come to my office this afternoon. When you have finished reading this, destroy it. Tell no one. Dr. Garana.* My image of Millicent, after the opera—her green eyes and beautiful dark complexion, sipping Oyster Rime and Kandush at the outdoor café of the old city—disintegrated.

Apparently it was to be all business. I needed to show I was up to the task. I pulled myself together, tidied up my mustache, and chose my best walking stick. There was a certain lightness to my step that had been absent in the preceding days of the new disease. Now as I walked, I wondered why I hadn't asked Millicent out on another nocturnal jaunt when last we parted. In my imagination, I remedied that oversight on this outing.

Only in the middle of the elevator ride to the Air Ferry platform, jammed in with fifty people, did I register a sinister thread in what she'd written. Destroy the message? Tell no one? These two phrases scurried around my mind as we boarded and later, drifting above the skyscrapers.

We were in her office, me sitting like a patient in front of her desk. I tried not to notice how happy I was to see her. She didn't return my smile. Instead, she said, "Have you had a lot of cases of this new fever?"

"Every day," I said. "It's brutal."

"I'm going to tell you some things that I'm not supposed to," she said. "You must tell no one."

I nodded.

"We know what this new disease is," she said. "You remember, I'm on the consulting board to the Republic's Health Policy Quotidian. The disease is airborne. It's caused by a spore, like an infinitesimal seedpod. Somehow, from somewhere, these spores have recently blown into the Republic. Left on their own, the things are harmless. We wouldn't have known they were there at all if the disease hadn't prompted us to look."

"Spores," I said, picturing tiny green burr balls raining down upon the city.

She nodded. "Put them under pressure and extreme heat, though, like the conditions found in steam engines, and they crack open and release their seed. It's these seeds, no bigger than atoms, that cause the disease. The mist that falls from the Air Ferry or is expelled by a steam carriage, the perspiration of ten thousand turbines, the music of the calliope in the park—all teeming with seed. It's in the steam. Once the disease takes hold in a few individuals, it becomes completely communicable."

I sat quietly for a moment, remembering from when I was a boy the earliest flights of Captain Madrigal's Air Ferry. As it flew above our street, I'd run in its shadow, through the mist of its precipitation, waving to those waving on board. Then I came to and said, "The Republic will obviously have to desist from using steam energy for the period of time necessary to quarantine, contain, and destroy the disease."

"Lash, you know that's not going to happen."

"What then?" I asked.

"There is no other answer. The Republic is willing to let the disease run its course, willing to sacrifice a few thousand citizens in order to not miss a day of commerce. That's bad enough, but there's more. We've determined that there's a sixty percent survival rate among those who contract it."

"Good odds," I said.

"Yes, but if you survive the fever stage something far more insidious happens."

"Does it have to do with that green discharge?" I asked.

"Yes," she said. "Come, I'll show you." She stood up and led me through a door into one of the examination rooms. An attractive young woman sat on a chair by the window. She stood to greet us and shake hands. I introduced myself and learned her name was Harrin. There was small talk exchanged about the weather and the coming holiday. Millicent asked her how she was feeling and she responded that she felt quite well. She looked healthy enough to me.

"And where did you get that ring?" my colleague asked of the young woman.

Harrin held up her hand to show off the red jewel on her middle finger.

"This ring . . ." she said and stared at it a moment. "Not but two days ago, a very odd fellow appeared at my door, bearing a small package. Upon greeting him, my heart jumped because he had a horn, like a small twisted deer antler, protruding from his left temple. The gnarled tip of it arced back toward the center of his head. He spoke my name in some foreign accent, his voice like the grumblings of a dog. I nodded. He handed me the package, turned, and paced silently into the shadows. Inside the outer wrapping there was a box, and in that box was this ring with a note. It simply read—*For you,* and was signed *The Prisoner Queen.*"

Millicent interrupted Harrin's tale and excused us. She took me by the arm and led me back into her office. She told her patient she would return in a moment and then shut the door. In a whisper, she said, "The green liquid initiating from the ear is the boundary between imagination and memory. The disease melts it, and even though you survive the fevers you can no longer distinguish between what has happened and what you have dreamed has happened or could have happened or should have. The Republic is going insane."

I was speechless. She led me to the opposite door and out into the corridor. Before I left, she kissed me. In light of what I'd been told, the touch of her lips barely startled me. It took me the rest of the day to recover from that meeting. I canceled all of my appointments, locked myself in my office with a bottle of Fresnac, and tried to digest that feast of secrets.

I never really got beyond my first question: Why had Millicent told me? An act of love? A professional duty? Perhaps the Republic actually wanted me to know this information, since I am a physician, but they couldn't officially announce it.

My first reaction was to flee the city, escape to where the cloud carriages rarely ventured, where the simply mechanical was still in full gear. But there were the patients, and I was a doctor. So I stayed in the city, ostensibly achieving nothing of medical value. Like my administration of the Margold, my decision to remain was more for me than any patient.

The plague spread and imagination bled into memory, which bled into imagination—hallucinations on the street, citizens locked in furious argument with themselves all over town, and the tales people told in response to the simplest questions were complex knots of wish fulfillment and nightmare. Then the Air Ferry driver remembered that to fly the giant vessel he was to ignore the list of posted protocols and flip buttons and depress levers at a whim. When the graceful, looming behemoth crashed in a fiery explosion into the city's well-to-do section, wiping out a full third of the Republic's politicos, not to mention a few hundred other citizens, I knew the end had come.

Many of those who had not yet lost their reason fled into the country and from what I'd heard formed small enclaves that kept all strangers at bay. For my part, I stayed with the sinking ship of state. Still tracking down and doing nothing for those few patients suffering from the onset symptoms of the disease.

Scores of workers remembered that their daily job was something other than what it had been in reality and set forth each day to meddle, renowned experts in delusion. Steam carriages crashed, a dozen a day, into storefronts, pedestrians, each other. A fellow, believing himself one of the gleaming characters at the Hot Air Opera, rushed up onstage and was cut to ribbons by the twirling metal edges of his new brethren. There was an accident in one of the factories on the eastern edge of town—an explosion—and then thick black smoke billowed out of its three stacks, blanketing the city in twilight at midday. The police, not quite knowing what to do, and some in their number as deranged as the deranged citizenry, resorted to violence. Shootings had drastically risen.

The gas of the streetlamps ran low and the city at night was profoundly black with a rare oasis of flickering light. I was scurrying along through the shadows back to my office from a critical case of fever—an old man on the verge of death who elicited a shot of Margold from me. As I'd administered it, his wife went on about a vacation they'd recently taken on a floating island powered by steam. I'd inquired if she'd had the fever and she stopped in her tale for a moment to nod.

I shivered again, thinking of her, and at that moment rounded a corner and nearly walked into Millicent. She seemed to have just been standing there, staring. The instant I realized it was her, a warmth spread quickly through me. It was I this time who initiated the kiss. She said my name and put her arms around me. This was why I'd stayed in the city.

"What are you doing out here?" I asked her.

"They're after me, Lash," she said. "Everybody even remotely involved with the government is being hunted down. There's something in the collective imagination of those struck by the disease that makes them remember that the Republic is responsible for their low wages and grinding lives."

"How many are after you?" I asked and looked quickly over my shoulder.

"All of them," she said, covering her face with her hand. "I can tell you've not yet succumbed to the plague because you are not now wrapping your fingers around my throat. They caught the Quotidian of Health Care today and hanged him on the spot. I witnessed it as I fled."

"Come with me. You can hide at my place," I said. I walked with my arm around her and could feel her trembling.

At my quarters, I bled the radiators and made us tea. We sat at the table in my parlor. "We're going to have to get out of the city," I said. "In a little while, we'll go out on the street and steal a steam carriage. Escape to the country. I'm sure they need doctors out among the sane."

"I'll go with you," she said and covered my hand, resting on the table with her own.

"There's no reason left here," I said.

"I meant to remember to tell you this," she said, taking a sip of tea. "About a week ago, I was summoned out one night on official business of the Republic. My superior sent me word that I was to go to a certain address and treat, using all my skill and by any means necessary, the woman of the house. The note led me to believe that this individual's well-being was of the utmost importance to the Republic."

"The president's wife?" I asked.

"No, the address was down on the waterfront. A bad area and yet they offered me no escort. I was wary of everything that moved and made a noise. Situated in the middle of a street of grimy drinking establishments and houses of prostitution, I found the place. The structure had at one time been a bank. You could tell by the marble columns out front. There were cracks in its dome and weeds poked through everywhere, but there was a light on inside.

"I knocked on the door and it was answered by a young man in a security uniform, cap, badge, pistol at his side. I gave my name and my business. He showed me inside, and pointed down a hallway whose floor, ceiling, and walls were carpeted— a tunnel through a mandala design of flowers on a red background. Dizzy from it, I stepped into a large room where I saw a woman sitting on a divan. She wore a low-cut blue gown and had a tortoiseshell cigarette holder. Her hair was dark and abundant but disheveled. I introduced myself, and she told me to take a seat in a chair near her. I did. She chewed the tip of tortoiseshell for a brief period, and then said, 'Let me introduce myself. I'm the Prisoner Queen.'"

My heart dropped at her words. I wanted to look in Millicent's eyes to see if I could discern whether she'd contracted the plague in recent days and survived to now be mad, but I didn't have the courage.

Although I tried to disguise my reaction, she must have felt me tremble slightly, because she immediately said, "Lash, believe me, I know how odd this sounds. I fully expected you not to believe me, but this really happened." Only then did I look into her face, and she smiled.

"I believe you," I said, "go on. I want to hear the rest."

"What it came to," said Millicent, "was she'd summoned me, not for any illness but to tell me what was about to happen."

"Why you?" I asked.

"She said she admired earnest people. The Prisoner Queen told me that what we have been considering the most terrible part of the disease, the blending of memory and the imagination, is a good thing. 'A force of nature,' was how she put it. There's disorganization and mayhem now, but apparently the new reality will take hold and the process will be repeated over centuries."

"Interesting," I said and slowly slid my hand out from under hers. "You know," I said, rising, "I have to get a newspaper and read up on what's been happening. Make yourself comfortable, I'll be right back." She nodded and took another sip of tea, appearing relaxed for the first time since I'd run into her.

I put on my hat and coat and left the apartment. Out on the street, I ran to the east, down two blocks and a turn south, where earlier that day I'd seen an abandoned steam carriage that had been piloted into a lamppost. I remembered noticing that there really hadn't been too much damage done to the vehicle.

The carriage was still there where I'd seen it, and I immediately set to starting it, lighting the pilot, pumping the lever next to the driver's seat, igniting the gas to heat the tank of water. All of the gauges read near full, and when the thing actually started up after a fit of coughing that sounded like the bronchitis of the aged, I laughed even though my heart was broken.

I stopped for nothing but kept my foot on the pedal until

I'd passed out beyond the city limits. The top was down and I could see the stars and the silhouettes of trees on either side of the road. In struggling to banish the image of Millicent from my mind, I hadn't at first noticed a cloud of steam issuing from under the hood. I realized the carriage's collision with the lamp must have cracked the tank or loosened a valve. I drove on, the steam wafting back over the windshield, enveloping my view.

The constant misty shower made me hot. I began to sweat, but I didn't want to stop, knowing I might not get the carriage moving again. Some miles later, I began to get dizzy, and images flashed through my thoughts like lightning—a stone castle, an island, a garden of poisonous flowers spewing seed. "I've got to get out of the steam," I said aloud to try to revive myself.

"The steam's not going anywhere," said the Prisoner Queen from the passenger seat. Her voluminous hair was neatly put up in an ornate headdress and her gown was decorated with gold thread. "Steam's the new dream," she said. "Right now I'm inventing a steam-powered space submarine to travel to the stars, a radiator brain whose exhaust is laughing gas, a steam pig that feeds a family of four for two weeks." She slipped a hand behind my head, and after taking a toke from the tip of the tortoise shell, she leaned over, put her mouth to mine, and showed me the new reality.

A Note About "Dr. Lash Remembers"

I wrote this story for Jeff and Ann VanderMeer's *Steampunk II: Steampunk Reloaded* anthology for Tachyon. Whenever I write a steampunk story, some reviewer, even if they like the story, inevitably mentions that it's *not really* steampunk. Normal steampunk to me seems like a pretty musty genre. When I think of it, the image of a room crammed with old furniture comes to mind. Most stories in this subgenre focus on the anachronistic/futuristic technology. My steampunk stories *are* steampunk, whether the reviewers know it or not, it's just that I'm focusing on the steam, not the junk that it animates. Steam is the new dream, baby. Actually, the Prisoner Queen appeared in a sequence of three dreams I had over a period of as many nights, and she definitely endorses the steam angle.

Daddy Longlegs of the Evening

It was said that when he was a small child, asleep in his bed one end-of-summer night, a spider crawled into his ear, traversed a maze of canals, eating slowly through membrane and organ, to discover the cavern of the skull. Then that spider burrowed in a spiral pattern through the electric gray cake of the brain, to the very center of it all, where it hollowed out a large nest for itself and reattached neural pathways with the thread of its web. It played the boy like a zither, plucking the silver strings of its own design, creating a music that directed both will and desire.

Before the invasion of his cranium, the child was said to have been quite a little cherub—big green eyes and a wave of golden hair, rosy cheeks, an infectious laugh. His parents couldn't help showing him off at every opportunity and regaling passersby with a litany of his startling attributes, not the least of which was the ability to recite verbatim the bedtime stories read to him each night. Many a neighbor had been subjected to an oration of the entirety of "The Three Rum Runtkins."

A change inside wrought a change outside, though, and, over the course of a few months, the boy's eyes bulged and drained of all color, to become million-faceted buds of gleaming onyx. His legs and arms grew long and willowy, but his body stayed short with a small but pronounced potbelly, like an Adam's apple in the otherwise slender throat that was his form. Although a fine down of thistle grew in patches across his back, arms, and thighs, he went bald, losing even brows and lashes. His flesh turned a pale gray, hinting at violet; his incisors grew to curving points and needed to be clipped and filed back like fingernails.

Horrified at the earliest of these changes, the boy's parents had taken him, first, to the doctor's, but when the medicine he was given did nothing but make him vomit and the symptoms became more bizarre, they took him to the clinic. The doctors there subjected him to a head scan. Photos from the process showed the intruder in negative, a tiny eight-legged phantom perched at the center of a dark, intricate web. It was determined that were they to remove the arachnid the boy could very possibly die. The creature had, for all intent and purpose, become his brain. The parents, confessing they feared for their lives, pleaded with the physicians to operate, but the ethical code forbade it and the family was sent home.

Not long after the trip to the clinic, the boy's mother opened his bedroom door one morning and beheld him suspended in the eye of a silver web that filled the room from floor to ceiling. She meant to scream but the beautiful gleaming symmetry of what he'd made stunned her. She watched as he turned slowly round to face away, and then from a neat hole cut in the back of his trousers that she'd never noticed before came a sudden blast of webbing that smacked her in the face and covered half her body. The door slammed shut as she reeled backward, and this time she *did* scream, tearing madly at the shroud whose sticky threads seemed spun from marshmallow.

Unable to bear the boy's presence any longer, his parents took him for a hike out into the forest. "I know a place where there are flies as big as poodles," his father said and the boy drooled. They took him deep into the trees, marking the trail as they went, and somewhere miles in, next to a lake, they bedded down on pine needles. While he slept, they quietly rose, tiptoed away, and then once out of earshot, ran for their lives. They never saw the boy again. Although no one in town could blame them, including the constable, and they faced no charges for their actions, the memory of their fear burrowed in a spiral pattern to the center of their minds and played them like zithers for the rest of their days.

Fifteen years later and a hundred miles from where he'd been born, the boy appeared one evening at the height of summer, not a man but something else. A woman living in an apartment of an otherwise empty building on the east side of the city of Grindly woke suddenly and looked up.

"There was enough moonlight to see him clearly," she said. "He hung above me, upside down, his hands and knees on the ceiling. He wore a jacket with short tails, and the long legs of his satin trousers were striped blue and red. I don't know how that hat—a stovepipe style—stayed on, as it had no chin strap. His feet were in slippers. The moment I saw him, he looked directly into my eyes. It didn't matter that he wore round, rose-colored glasses. Those evil blackberries that lurked behind still dazzled me. I screamed, he shrieked, and then he scuttled across the ceiling and out the open window. I heard him on the roof and then everything was silent." The woman told her friends and her friends told their friends, and word that something bizarre had come to Grindly spread like disease.

The *Gazette* put out a double edition, a whole four pages,

its entirety devoted to speculation concerning "Daddy Long-legs of the Evening," a moniker invented by the editor-in-chief. The name stuck, and over the course of a few more days was shortened by the populace, first to *Daddy Longlegs* and then to simply *Daddy*. "Watch out for Daddy," neighbors said as a salutation when they parted. Before people bedded down at night they practiced a ritual of checking closets and basements, the dark corners of attics and under beds, latching all windows and gathering crude weapons on their nightstands—a mallet, a wrench, a carving knife, a club.

After a few more sightings that he had scrupulously ar-ranged, allowing himself to be spotted crawling to the top of and then into a silent mill's crumbling smokestack, or travers-ing the soot-ridden mosaic of God's face on the inner dome of the railway station as the midnight train passed through, he was in their hearts and minds, and what was even more im-portant to him, their dreams. Of course, he meant to drain the citizenry of Grindly of their bodily fluids, but first, to enhance nourishment, it needed to be filtered, flavored, by nightmare.

When there wasn't a soul within the confines of the city wall who did not, in their dreams, flee, slow, heavy, and naked before him, or writhe in the coil of their blankets, mistaken in sleep for his web, he struck. It was deepest night when he entered the home of the haberdasher, Fremin, through the unlocked coal chute. The hinges on the iron door creaked a warning, but that noise merely became part of the dreams of the sleeping hus-band and wife as the triumphant laughter of Daddy Longlegs. They never woke when he bit them at the base of the skull. They never cried out as their fear-laden essence left them.

"Like old, worn luggage," the newspaper said, describing the condition of the corpses discovered two days later. When the medics tried to move the haberdasher's body to a stretcher, it split with a whisper like a dry husk and out of it poured thousands of tiny spiders. Police Inspector Kaufmann, the medics, the Fremins' neighbors who were present, all ran out of the building, and the inspector gave orders for the place to be torched at once. As the fire raged, the crowd that had gathered belabored the inspector, Grindly's sole lawman, with inquiries as to what he was prepared to do.

What Kaufmann was prepared to do was run, take the next train out of town for some shining new place free of rot and nightmares. The only thing preventing him was the fact that the train rarely stopped, but sped right through as if there really was no platform or station or city. "If I wait for that," he thought, "we might all be dead by the time it arrives." He turned to the citizens and said, "I'm going to hunt Daddy down and put a bullet in him." Only the inspector knew that it would necessarily have to be "*a* bullet," as he had only one left. Government supplies from the capital had dried up over a year earlier.

That night, Kaufmann slept slumped over his desk, pistol in hand, and dreamt of a time before the politicians in the capital had succumbed to a disease of avarice and sapped all of Grindly's resources for themselves. Once it had been known far and wide as "The Nexus of Manufacture," a gleaming machine of commerce where traffic filled the streets, faces filled the windows, nobody ate cabbage who didn't want to, and the inspector had a police force, enough bullets, and a paycheck. Again, in his sleep, he watched the city slowly rot from the inside out, and eventually stood on the platform at the station waving forlornly as even the petty criminals left town.

While Kaufmann dozed, Daddy was busy, slipping silently through the shadows. He could smell the terror of the populace, a sweet flower scent that drove his hunger. The music played on the strands of web behind his eyes directed his purpose, negating distraction, as he shuffled up a wall, found an unlocked window, and let the breeze in.

His first victim of that night was the pale and beautiful actress Monique LeDar, who still performed, nightly, one-woman shows of the classics, although the stage was lit by candles and squirrels scampered amid the rafters. She awoke in the midst of Daddy's feeding, and he saw her seeing herself in the myriad reflections of his eyes. He stopped, tipped his hat, and continued. She put her wrist to her forehead and perished.

The *Gazette* had the story in its late-morning edition the next day—"Daddy's Dozen," read the headline. At the end of the lead article that gave a list of the drained and the grisly condition in which each was found, there was printed a formal plea from Inspector Kaufmann for volunteers to help track the killer. That evening, he stood on the sidewalk in front of the Hall of Justice, a mausoleum of an old marble structure, dark and empty inside save for his office. The last set of batteries in the flashlight had died, so, instead, he held, like a torch, out in front of him, a small candelabra with three burning tapers. He'd been waiting for over an hour for the mob of volunteers to form in order to begin the hunt, but as it was, he stood alone. Taking the gun from his shoulder holster, he was about to strike out on his own when an old woman in a kerchief and a long camel hair winter coat hobbled slowly up to him.

"Can I help you, ma'am?" asked the inspector.

"I volunteer," she said.

He laughed. "This is dangerous work, my dear. We're after a cold-blooded killer."

The old woman opened her pocketbook and took out a black-jack. She waggled the tube of stitched leather with lead in the tip at Kaufmann's face.

"That's an illegal weapon," he said.

"Arrest me," she said and spat on the sidewalk.

The avenues and side streets of Grindly were empty. Even the drunks stayed home in fear of being drunk themselves. It was slow going and just as lonely for Kaufmann with Mrs. Frey in tow. He'd barely gotten the woman's name out of her. She followed five steps behind, not so much his posse as a haunting spirit. He respected her courage, her sense of civic duty, but found her quiet wheezing and the rhythmic squish of her galoshes incredibly annoying, and wondered how long it would be before he used his last bullet on either her or himself.

It was dinnertime in the city that never woke, the scent of boiled cabbage, the skittering of rats along the gutters. Occasionally, there was a lighted window and the distant, muffled sound of a radio or a child's glee or an argument, but for the most part Kaufmann and his deputy passed down empty streets of boarded storefronts and burned-out brownstones where the echo of the wind sounded like laughter in the shadows.

It was dinnertime for Daddy as well, and he moved along the rooftops, keenly aware of the warm spots in the cold buildings beneath, heat signatures of those who might find themselves on his menu. He was hunting for the essence of the young. His last kill of the previous night had been Tharshmon the watchmaker, a man made old by lack of work and self-respect. No one any longer cared to know the time in Grindly. It was better left unmentioned when the future arrived. As dozens of pocket watches chimed in Tharshmon's studio at three A.M., Daddy had interceded without a struggle. The bereft watchmaker's fluid was overripe, though, insipidly sweet and watery. It gave no energy but bruised the will and loosened the bowels.

Daddy skittered down the side of a four-story apartment building. At the lighted window on the third floor, he settled upon the fire escape. With his face to the glass, he saw two young children dressed in their pajamas, playing in a bedroom. He tried the window, but it was locked. He tapped at the glass with one long nail. Their big pink faces drew close to see him, and even before they undid the latch, his system was creating the chemical needed to digest their juices. He had learned it wasn't helpful to let them see him drool.

At the same moment, three blocks away, Inspector Kaufmann was passing the Water Works. He turned and peered back up the sidewalk to see Mrs. Frey's bent form inching along through the weak glow of the block's one working streetlight. He set the candelabra on the ground, holstered his gun, and took out his last cigarette. He'd traded a pair of official police handcuffs, with key, for the pack it came from. Leaning down, he lit it on the flame of the center candle. He was cold and tired, and every scrap of newspaper that rolled in the wind or bat that darted out of a blasted window momentarily paralyzed him with fear. He took a drag and heard Mrs. Frey's galoshes drawing closer.

The old woman had nearly caught up and there was still a good half of a cigarette left when he heard a desperate scream come from off to his right. "Shit," he said, flicked the unfinished butt into the gutter, drew his pistol, and ran across the street. There he entered an alley, and ran through the dark, avoiding piles of broken furniture and old garbage. The alley gave way to another street and then another alley, and when he was almost winded, there was again a shrill scream and he saw a woman at an open window three stories up. "My babies," she wailed. Kaufmann scanned the sides of the buildings for Daddy. He heard something move amid the trash, and caught a darker spot in the darkness out of the corner of his eye. As he lifted the gun, something wet and sticky smacked him in the face. He fired blindly.

By the time Kaufmann had wiped the web from his eyes, Daddy was gone, the distraught mother above had spotted the inspector and was yelling for his assistance, and behind him, Mrs. Frey, pocketbook on her wrist, the candelabra in her right hand, the blackjack in her left, shuffled inexorably closer. The inspector dropped the gun and ran away.

Daddy sat atop the smokestack of the abandoned Harris Electric Loom Mill, nursing the wound to his leg where the bullet had grazed his calf. The spider in his head unhooked the strings that sent pain, and then nestled back into the center of things, half high from the effects of the rich essence of youth. His imagination took off and he plucked the silver strands, composing as he played, spinning a web of an idea. "Herd them," Daddy said in a voice that cracked and clicked. The spare scattered pattern of the lights of Grindly required design.

Exhausted from running, Inspector Kaufmann leaned against the coral facade at the entrance to Grindly Station. His own thoughts were as scattered as Daddy's were inspired. Against what would have normally been his better judgment, he chose to believe that for some reason the train would, that night, stop at the platform and take him aboard. He hurried on so as not to miss it. His quick footsteps echoed across the wide rotunda and he passed through another set of doors into the dome that held the station platform. He was surprised to find himself the only passenger.

Kaufmann cupped his hand behind his ear and cocked his head toward the track in order to check for vibrations of the coming train. He thought he felt the merest rumble deep in his chest. After listening for a long time, all he really heard was the sound of water dripping. It interfered with the anticipation of escape. Then he realized it wasn't water dripping, but more a tapping. It stopped and then started again. He looked up at the inner dome and froze.

In an eyeblink, Daddy leaped down on a forty-foot thread of web and stood before Kaufmann. Mandibles clicked together and Daddy did a bad job of hiding the drool. From some forgotten byway of his brain, the inspector's years of experience on the streets of Grindly engaged. He made a fist and swung with everything he had. The punch hit the mark, cracking the left lens of Daddy's rose-colored glasses and sending him stumbling backward a few feet. The inspector didn't know whether to flee or continue to attack, and in the empty moment of his indecision, he definitely heard the train coming.

He made a move toward Daddy with fists in the air, but his nemesis twirled with insect precision and speed and clipped Kaufmann under the chin with a foot that struck like the tip of a bullwhip. The inspector was almost brought to his knees by the blow, but instead of going down he righted himself and backed off. Blood trickled from the side of his mouth. The train was louder now, and a faint light could be seen filling the tunnel. He looked down and saw that the backs of his heels were off the edge of the platform. He put his fists up and kept them moving.

When Daddy took one long-legged step to the left, Kaufmann saw salvation. The roar of the approaching train filled the tunnel and set the entire platform vibrating so that it was impossible to hear the squish of Mrs. Frey's galoshes. She inched up upon

Daddy from behind, the candelabra glimmering, the blackjack waggling in her grip. Kaufmann threw a flurry of jabs to distract the arachnid, and the old woman lifted the leather club as high as she could. The locomotive entered the station but didn't slow.

In the reflection of rushing windows, Daddy detected treachery. He spun in a blur, his mandibles severing Mrs. Frey's neck with a swift clip, like cutting a rose. From the hole in his trousers, he shot a blast of web at Kaufmann. It happened so quickly that the inspector could only stand motionless as the strand of sticky thread wrapped twice around his neck. The web's long tail was pulled in by the rush of the passing train and affixed itself to the handle on the back door of the caboose. Kaufmann was jerked off the platform by the neck, and flew behind the train. The last thing he saw in Grindly was the mosaic face of God. Mrs. Frey's head hit the platform then and spat.

The next evening, in an abandoned warehouse by the docks, Daddy stood in total darkness, emitting high-pitched squeals that called all the natural spiders of Grindly to him. When he felt their delicate heaving presence surrounding him, he clicked and *blzz*'d out his plan. He gave instruction on rethreading the human brain. He spoke of the ear and the path to take, warning of cul-de-sacs. "A quarter pound of fly meat for every human restrung," he promised. Spirits were high, but, later, when they returned to him for payment, he gleefully crushed them beneath his slippers.

By the time he got done with Grindly, the city shone and ran like one of Tharshmon's pocket watches. Everything moved as if to music. It became for Daddy a web of human thread. "Purpose without a point," he often reminded his human electorate, and they tacitly nodded. He continued to feed at night, roaming the rooftops and alleyways, leaving old luggage indiscriminately in his wake. People showed him smiles during the day, but, still, no one wanted to meet him in the dark. The reconfiguration of their brain patterns didn't eliminate terror, only their ability to react to it. "Fear and Industry" was Daddy's motto and it took him far.

After the train was again making scheduled stops at the station, Daddy boarded with a ticket to the capital one evening. He never returned to Grindly, but instead bit into the larger politics of the Realm and kept eating in a spiral pattern until he reached the center of everything. There, he made himself a nest.

A Note About "Daddy Longlegs of the Evening"

I stole the title for this story from the title of the Salvador Dalí painting, *Daddy Longlegs of the Evening—Hope!* I'd gone to a Dalí retrospective some years ago at the Philadelphia Museum of Art. It was a great show. They really had the goods, and it was all topped off in a dark last room by Dalí's hologram of Alice Cooper. Dalí's *Daddy* painting is one of those melt jobs, with weird figures draped on tree branches and ants crawling all over. A cool painting. But in the same show there was a drawing he had done, which I'm afraid I've never been able to find again in order to corroborate the title, of a guy with long, long legs, running. He's wearing a tall hat and maybe a scarf. Unless I'm just making this up in my mind, I think the figure was also wearing circular glasses. Seeing this image and thinking about the title of the painting gave rise to the idea of my Daddy—a boy transformed into a spidery monster. Once the image of my character came to mind, it morphed in my imagination into a figure from the old Fleischer brothers cartoons (Betty Boop, Coco the Clown, etc.) where the entire world could, at the drop of a dime, come to anthropomorphic life. One of the best compliments I've gotten as a fiction writer came from reading this story for the MFA students at the Stone Coast Writing program in Maine. Jim Kelly told me that one of his students, after hearing the reading, asked him—"Is he allowed to do that?"

Permissions

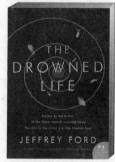
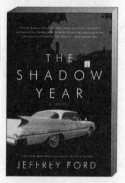
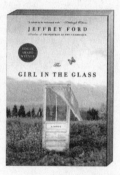
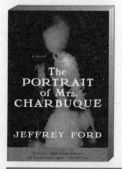